WE ARE NOT
AT WAR WITH SWEDEN!

Ray Stock

DEDICATION

This story is dedicated to my friend, Larry Leff, who recently passed away after a courageous struggle with Parkinson's. I miss you, Larry.

Cover illustration by Jim Morrissey

Acknowledgments:

First off, you need to know that dozens of literary agents declined interest in my description of this book. I'm told this is par for the course. So, I don't have to mention how grateful I am to any of them. I do wish there was one who took the risk and whom I could now shower with praise and gratitude. Yes, I do hope many of them will regret taking a pass on WE ARE NOT AT WAR WITH SWEDEN!

Regarding friends and family and inspirations: My mother is 103 years old as this is being printed. If she had read my manuscript a couple years ago, I doubt whether she would still be alive. We often differed in our tastes in literature.

My son-in-law, Greg Cotten with an e, an exceptional writer in his own right, offered insightful advice on strategy and structure and reaction to certain funny bits that helped confirm I was not in over my head. Most of the time.

My daughter, Sarah, was ever the encourager: "You can do this, Dad. Even if you can't read very well to your grandchildren, they think you're very funny."

Vonnie Wheeler, a thoughtful and brilliant friend, was the first to read an early manuscript "I really think you've got something here, Ray. Maybe it's what we all need right now." Way over the top, but thank you, Vonnie.

Caroline Turner, friend, national consultant, and author of "Difference Works", carefully screened the manuscript for ambiguity, poor taste, or anything highly questionable. Eventually she gave it her blessing. Bless you, Caroline.

My esteemed friend from Ford Kansas, Rundell Brown, scribbled, "I hope you have a good lawyer!" when he finished an early manuscript. Well, I've lawyered up.

Christina Jasso Haecock advised on the correct use of outrageous insults in Spanish. For example: *Tu madre se pone botas militarias.* (Your mother wears army boots).

Finally, my close friend, Michele Slentz, poured through this manuscript with several fine-toothed combs, catching errors and confusions and kindly drawing smiley faces next to passages that made her laugh.

Thank you all.

PART I

You can live your life in the safety and predictability of a parking lot.

More interesting things seem to happen in the No Parking Zone.

Jacob Finnegan

Saturday, April 1, 2017 Denver Colorado

"You want to run that by me again, Jake? I'm starting to wonder about you."

I expected as much, my idea seemed outrageous to me as well. We'd been friends for twenty-three years. Our careers were behind us; we really didn't have to prove anything to anyone. But I'd had an itch nagging at me for some time now.

"Hey, we're not dead yet, Edgar. And I'm sure not interested in talking about getting old or dying. That will come when it comes. We've still got pretty decent brains, don't we?"

"I can't remember the last time I checked. Maybe Christmas?"

"And the idea of sitting around every day soaking up the news, and bitching about what's going on in the world? Christ, it's depressing."

"True. I think it's contributing to various kinds of inflammation in my body." Edgar put down his coffee cup, spread his hands on the table and stared at me.   "But   why   a radio station?"

"Maybe it's been a dream of mine that I've ignored till now. What I really want is for us to have a radio show, a talk show, but don't we have to have a station first?"

"You and me? A radio show? And you're serious? Is it because we have faces for radio?

"And voices! Yours especially. A barbershop baritone. You'll be our Josh Groban. Me? Not so much. But maybe I'll be the straight man. Ask you a lot of questions. Read the weather report. Announce the time of day. Read the Breaking News."

"Breaking News? I thought you were fed up with the news?"

"Absolutely. But, we'll have our own take on breaking news. Like, *This just in: THE UNITED STATES IS NOT AT WAR WITH SWEDEN! I repeat: THE UNITED STATES IS NOT AT WAR WITH SWEDEN!*"

"You're talking about making up shit, aren't you?"

"Yes and no. Did you know that for several centuries, back in the days before ABBA, Sweden ruled over all of Russia? Absolutely true! No one messes with the Swedes."

"You mean those nice blonde folks that make all the cute straw Christmas tree ornaments?"

"Yes, those very people that are the Vikings, with all their War Gods like Odin and Thor and Baldur.

"Still, Jake?"

"Why not? That news statement is true. Truer than much of the hyped crap dished out on the news. The news diet that keeps everyone scared about everything. We can take the road unraveled. Maybe it'll cure your inflammation, your hemorrhoids, my cynical irritability."

"I thought you had the hemorrhoids, Jake? And I was irritable."

"Can't pick and chose like that, Edgar. Special gifts can't be swapped out.

Following several indulgent evenings at the Czech Bar on Broadway, going over and over this audacious notion, you could say we eventually talked ourselves into it, even after the reckless enthusiasm of the new idea was exposed and enough time passed for it to take on a bad smell. We eventually concluded that "makin' stuff up" was the stuff we were meant to do. It would take a while and much experimentation before we recorded our suspiciously termed "pilot show". Here's a taste of our early attempts to script a segment.

ME: Well, good morning out there, listeners. You've tuned, somehow, to the Radio Guys Morning Hour. I'm Jake, and the personality sitting across from me is my longtime friend, Edgar. So, if you're a first time listener, we say, Good to have you with us. We hope the feeling will be mutual. So, Edgar, tell our listeners what we've got for them this morning.

EDGAR: Right, Jake. We've got some righteous stuff including questions for our listeners, suggestions for our guests, and the only 100 percent true breaking news you'll find in all of broadcast.

ME: That's a bold claim, Edgar. I hope our listeners are braced for it. Any guests lined up?

EDGAR: Of course. This morning we have Miss Dorothy Presley, lead interior designer for Designing for Confined Spaces, right here in Denver. Currently she's choosing colors for the new wing of the county jail that's under construction.

ME: Impressive. Heady stuff. What else?

EDGAR: In place of a canceled interview with Newt Gingrich, we have Norv Egqvist, assistant coach of the Denver

East Girls High School Hockey Team. He has a new book out called, "Girls Can Be More Than Goalies". You know that's true, Jake, you've got a daughter who played hockey, right?

ME: True, Edgar. You think it's a broad enough topic for our audience? You know the complaints we sometimes hear.

EDGAR: I thought you didn't want Gingrich because he was too political and one-sided. In fact, when I suggested Norv Egkvist, you said great, it's time for our audience to learn about young women in hockey.

ME: I said we were going to be different from other talk shows and news shows. Not the partisan stuff, or the non-partisan stuff.

EDGAR: So let's go with Norv, I'll have Rex get him on the phone. (Rex is our man Friday, in this case Monday, and we'll hire him away from our competitors as soon as we locate him).

ME: So now it's time for our New Product of the Day, brought to you by **Skin Wipes**, *aloe-soaked lambskin hankies for every nook and cranny of your naked bodies. And what is the New Product today, Edgar?*

EDGAR: Sure, Jake. Today's new product comes right from the Wall Street Journal. It's brand new and it's called: The Hillary App. Imagine that.

ME: Hard to imagine, Edgar. Tell our listeners more.

EDGAR: Well, it says right here in the press release: The Hillary App: How to manage your e-mail and Facebook account to protect yourself against fraudulent accusations and give you plausible and implausible deniability about anything and everything. What's your take on the Hillary App, Jake?

ME: Hmmm. Doesn't it sound like a day late and a dollar short? For Hillary, Edgar?

EDGAR: Good point, Jake. Something like slamming the barn door after the horse escapes, right?

ME: Eloquent, Edgar, thank you. Well that's our new

*product for the day, folks. Brought to you at this time every broadcast, by **Skin Wipes**, scented for every sensation on any location of your naked bodies. Have at them with no fear of rashes or other allergic reactions. Although if you notice an increase in blood pressure or a decrease in appetite, there is a measurable hike in the possibilities of total paralysis or even death. Don't worry, it's all in the small print. What's next, Edgar?*

EDGAR: Unfortunately, Jake, Rex just handed me this note that he's been unable to contact, Norv Egqvist, assistant girls hockey coach at Denver East, so we have to move right into the part of our show where we ask the questions to our listeners.

ME: So, how does that work, exactly?

*EDGAR: Pretty easy, actually. We pose the questions to our listeners. Three questions. And our listeners don't have to go through all the hassle of calling in, then waiting on hold while Rex answers all the other callers. That's always a **bleeping** royal pain. They simply mail their answers to our station's postal box.*

*ME: By the way, for you first time listeners, that **bleep** was for the F-Bomb that Edgar let slip.*

*EDGAR: Sorry about that. My wife always nags at me to clean up my **bleeping** language. Can I say Shit, Jake?*

ME: Anytime, anyplace, Edgar. They even say that on Oprah now, I've heard.

*EDGAR: Well, that's a **bleeping** relief! Oh, shit, I'm sorry.*

*ME: (Interrupting) OK, Edgar. So here are the three questions selected for our listeners. The first question: **Who makes money off of Daylight's Saving Time?***

EDGAR: Yes! I've always wanted to know that. I'll bet there are quite a few people.

*ME: And the second question: **Are there any long-term negatives about getting tattoos?** That's a good one, eh, Edgar?*

EDGAR: I'll say. And you're the perfect test case for that question, Jake.

ME: I suppose you're referring to what happened at the New Year's Eve Party in the new Ink Studio on South Broadway. The guy crawling with Tats and offering freebies to the five guests whose names were drawn from the sterling punch bowl.

EDGAR: You were one of the lucky ones, Jake.

ME: And I asked him for a **Heart** *with* **I Love You Mom** *on my back. And he burned in* **My Plumber's,** *centered right at belt level on my backside. And you saw it all happening and didn't stop it, Edgar.*

EDGAR: Actually I was watching the blond tattooer, (is that a word?) tattoo This Bud's For You, on the breast of that Channel Ten weather lady. What lovely knocker's, Jake. Hard not to watch.

ME: (Struggling to get back on track.) Okay, Edgar, we've got a show to do here. So here's question number three: **Should women be allowed to drive automobiles?**

EDGAR: Sweet Jesus, Jake! I thought you were kidding around with that one last night. You scratched it off, remember?

ME: Oh no! Where is that other question? (Shuffling through the papers in front of me). Edgar, I think Rex has another BREAKING NEWS item. Why don't you take it while I find that third question.

EDGAR: Got your back, Jake. Good luck on your recovery. All right, listeners. Here's something that will surprise you: **BREAKING NEWS: THE NATIONAL AUDUBON SOCIETY NOW ADMITS TO THE EXISTANCE OF TREE GULLS.** *Yes, you heard it here first. Tree gulls! I've never seen one. But, maybe that's because I wasn't looking for them. Major stuff, Jake.*

ME: Thank you for the Breaking News alert. And now, listeners, for the third question to our audience: **Are women with pets happier than women with husbands?** *Hey, That's kind of similar to what Gloria Steinem wrote: "Want to feel alone? Get married."*

EDGAR: That's the spirit, Jake. Say, Rex has just given me another note. It seems several listeners have already called in asking, "What are the answers?" For the three questions, I presume.

ME: I mean Geez, Rex, those were three simple questions. Can't they think for themselves? Don't answer the calls unless they've got the answers.

EDGAR: Well, good listeners, Rex is signaling we're about out of time today. Thank you for joining us. Check in the newspaper, or ask Siri, or Cleo, or your favorite barista when our next broadcast of The Radio Guys will be brought to you by **Adam & Eve Environmentally Conscious Mattress Repairs**. *Meanwhile, so long, friends. All is well in the Mile High City. Be kind to each other.*

Monday, April 17, 2017

So now you have a very rough glimpse of where we're headed. I hope you'll continue to follow us on this journey. Even if it's just to keep up with the real Breaking News.

As you might expect, we had a ton of work to do before we were ready to launch an actual radio show. Or trashed the idea and licked our wounds. In either case, I figured we'd need three months, minimum. So, how would we find Rex? Pure logic. We wrote an ad and posted it in the paper and various social network sites. It read as follows:

Trolling for Rex. We're looking for a Gal Friday named Rex to help start up our radio talk show. At this point there is no starting pay. True nonprofit. When we become famous, things could change. We'd like a very smart person, who is flexible and imaginative and named Rex. Don't know how many hours a week yet. Phone number (Ours). Leave a message.

As it turned out, no Rex's. Closest thing was Roxanne. We later found out she caught the ad because she has a dachshund named Rex. So Roxy is our gal Friday. She's 38, has her own IT business, The Web Mistress, creating websites and managing social media for clients. And, she wears jeans very nicely. Welcome aboard, Roxy. We had no idea how lucky we were to find Roxy, a spitfire, and an idea person in one. One other thing about Roxy that would quickly make her invaluable, worth far more than the nothing we were paying her: She'd been a producer for two years at her university radio station a while back.

We popped for three months rent in a one-room downstairs office that was usually vacant on Gaylord. The kind of place that seems to be available when election time rolls around and candidates are looking for very cheap space to set up local operations. In this case, I recall that for four months it was neighborhood headquarters for Hillary.

I hoped three months would be what it would take to get us underway, to see if we had something to offer. I also hoped there would be very little juju left from the Hillary Campaign. I had volunteered there for four months, going door to door. **Moving Forward Together,** her lawn sign, rang out like a battle cry for a Meditation Workshop. A real yawner compared to Donald's **Let's Make America Great Again!** Evidently quite a few folks agreed.

Edgar and I worked about three hours a day at the beginning. Then we increased our time as we more clearly identified our needs. Roxy, whenever she could, which was considerable. In the one block retail area where we headquartered, there were five bars. We rotated, hoping to find potential listeners for when we became airworthy. We printed business cards to distribute. In addition to our names and phone numbers: *"Top Secret Project In Utero. Stay tuned."* It usually provoked questions, which we liked. And for which we made up answers. And in response, often shaking heads and suspicious, squinty eyes.

Thursday, April 20, 2017

Other considerations quickly emerged: The name of the show? When? How long? How often? Where would we broadcast from? How much would it all cost? What help did we need for content? How would we get the word out? All things that seemed natural and necessary. And, since we didn't know any better, all things we could explore without limits or preconceptions.

The content or format, as Edgar defined it, was pretty much "Making Up Stuff." For a talk show, I couldn't come up with an exact model to follow. Which was a good thing. So, a good deal of the time we knocked out short ideas for scripts. Neither of us could talk articulately for an hour or even five minutes without some sort of written guidelines.

We considered hiring some comedy writers to help with content. But soon we discovered that almost all working comedy writers were already employed to write content for our elected politicians in our nation's capitol. Few of whom, it seemed, could see the humor in their own behaviors. They were too self-absorbed to realize they were often the real jokes.

Roxy was our sounding board. She knew smart and she knew funny. Soon she also became a contributor.

Monday, May 1, 2017

Decisions made so far: We would broadcast once a week. The show might be called: The Radio Guys Talk. Or, Talk is Cheap. Or, Let's Talk. Or, something we hadn't thought of yet. Roxy suggested: Be Careful Who You Listen To. Oh, I almost forgot. What about: All Things Codswallop? For the time being we hung with The Radio Guys Talk.

Other than the show itself, the biggest decision would be where we would broadcast from. There was the possibility of recording the show after hours in any number of places around the city. Or, Roxy informed us, there was a dying AM station license for sale that we might consider. Price unknown at this time, but she'd make some phone calls.

We wanted something more novel than being isolated in a traditional radio studio. More fun for us. Maybe a live audience. That is if we could ever get people to be an audience. We took the risk to ask for help. If you have the gall, better call Saul.

In this case Saul was a six-foot-six, one hundred and forty-five pound dapper dude, seventy-some years of age, who knew everything and everyone who was anyone in the city of Denver. He walked the city, knife-blade thin, straight-backed, with a black fedora cocked to one side and slightly forward. Saul Friedman had made his fortune in retail over the decades: shoes, clothes, souvenirs. He could sell shit. He'd had three restaurants, three wives and three daughters who were also tall and lean. His face was the ethnic prototype of the Russian Jew. His voice was as low as his head was high and he'd sing at any major function he was invited to whether asked or not. He was Tevye in Denver. Like I said, he knew everyone and he knew real estate and he knew how to get attention.

We took him for dinner at Gildersleeve's and asked his advice. He called us the next day and said to meet him at an address downtown between Larimer Square and El Chapultepec.

Saul was waiting, black suit with white open-collared shirt, lid tipped rakishly, his back to the door, watching folks walk by, returning waves and nods. You couldn't keep him a secret.

He turned to us with his arms stretched wide, back arched, and nodded his head toward the narrow space with construction permits taped to the window and door, concealing everything that was happening inside.

"Here is your new home, gents. This will make you famous! This will make you rich!" (Modesty was always Saul's thing.) "This is the future home of Whiskey 'n Ribs, Denver's new craft Whiskey and Rib Joint. Opens in three months. They've agreed to your broadcast in the front window during the lunch hour once a week for a year. You can have a speaker out front so everyone will hear you, and probably stop and watch. The publicity possibilities are endless. I can be your first and frequent guest. You don't have to pay me. Well, what do you think?"

Holy shit! What *did* we think? About the space and location, I liked it. I saw Edgar's nod, too. About Saul's guest appearances, beyond the first show, my stomach tightened. I'm guessing Edgar's did as well. Saul was such a force. How could we prevent a takeover?

Edgar caught my eye with a wink and I nodded.

"We like it, Saul. Here's the thing. This is such a tightly scripted show and you're such an extraordinarily busy leader in this city. Maybe we could impose on you for the first broadcast of each month where you'd do kind of a three minute cameo appearance, say, let the city know what breaking news you might have about new developments coming on line, or your favorite new restaurant or bar. Hey, people would start to talk about that. If you had the time, of course."

Edgar is a quick-witted prince. You could see Saul's eyes brighten. His mouth scrunched into a *You might have something there, guys.*

We asked for a tour inside the space that went deep but was about the width of a doublewide mobile home. Carpenters were completing various kinds of cozy and imaginative seating nooks. The bar was long and narrow, with an oak framed mirror rising just short of the ceiling. Saul said it had been shipped in from some ancient pub in Dublin. Whiskey 'n Ribs looked like a place that might catch on.

We mentally measured the space by the arched front window where we would be broadcasting our show to the passersby and the city of Denver. We caught some people pressing noses to the window between the permits to see what the hell was going on. I'm certain none of them considered the possibility of a live radio talk show.

Thursday, May 4, 2017

Roxy dazzled us with her ability to speak in various voices, regional accents, or foreign accents and a broad range of ages. "For some of those guests that fall in the category of *made-up stuff,* I could be the live voice in studio or calling in."

Time passed quickly as we put together more scripts and segments. It was exhilarating, working without constraints. It was also exhausting to come up with lots of fresh ideas, then to go over them the next day to see which still seemed potent and funny. We began to break in the middle of our sessions, sometimes going for a drink or coffee. Or just a walk. Sometimes a drink or two seemed to loosen us up; other times it knocked off the needed edge. We were learning a whole new craft. There was an intoxication that came along with that.

The three months seemed like an eternity at first, but we needed every day of it to learn our roles, assume our new selves, for that was what we were really doing. Becoming a couple of guys that we weren't before. Morphing. Internalizing new personas. Integrating and accepting the new talents and skills we were acquiring or discovering. Tooling up. We were actually emerging into new phases of our lives. And we were doing it because we could, and we wanted to.

We opened files for various features such as new product introduction, breaking news, personal pet-peeves, particularly embarrassing situations, listener questions, and questions for listeners. Eventually we would add science and medical breakthroughs, reports from special correspondents, reports from contacts with ETs, personal advice inquiries, and, a file for what I'd term as Oddball Stuff that stood alone, unfit for any category.

One idea seemed always to lead to several others.

I confess that sometimes I felt overwhelmed by the possibilities and the effort that it took to keep that flow going. Other times I looked at Edgar and felt a dread coming on, like did we really have anything at all or was this just another case where a couple of amateurs got carried away with themselves. It was a pit-in-the-stomach time. Eventually we found ways to restore our confidence. Roxy was a lifesaver in this recovery from the doldrums.

Finally, it was time to record some of our segments for a gut check.

The small recording device that Roxy owned became our first trial at broadcast. How unnerving this felt. We stumbled and stumbled.

EDGAR: Well, this time our listeners have not disappointed. In response to our three questions last week, we have three finalists to chose from.

ME: Refresh us with the first question, Edgar.

EDGAR: Right. Here goes. The question was: should parents be allowed to refuse vaccinations for their children?

ME: Great question, Edgar. And who came up with the best answer?

EDGAR: Well, here was one specific answer from Hal in Westminster. Hal wrote: "Yes. If people are not allowed to refuse vaccinations, soon all the viruses will be extinct. And then, since nature abhors a vacuum, nature will create some super new virus that will be more dangerous and kill ten times as many people. Maybe even everyone."

ME: Sounds plenty logical to me, Edgar. Who could disagree?

EDGAR: As a matter of fact there were some who strongly disagreed. I'll read this one from Stephanie: "I am so stressed about this issue. I have three precious kids under seven years old. And I am so torn about what to do. I hear arguments from both sides. There doesn't appear to be an easy choice and I want to make the right choice for my kids. It seems like a real mess. I'd like to be persuaded that there is a right choice for our children. And for all of us.

ME: Obviously there is no simple answer, is there? And if there is one right one, it's important because we're all affected by what that choice is.

EDGAR: Maybe we need to get a virus specialist on who can straighten this out. Should we go on to the other two questions?

ME: I thought we were going to pick the question that most of our listeners answered, right? Besides, this isn't very funny, is it?

EDGAR: That's true, Jake. OK, then, let's move on.

ME: Right. And I see Roxy walking over with a sheet for you. What do you have Roxy?

ROXY: Can you believe it? BREAKING NEWS. Have at it.

EDGAR: Here it is folks, BREAKING NEWS: THE LATEST DEMOGRAPHIC STUDY REVEALS THAT SOME STATES ARE RED

AND SOME ARE BLUE!

ME: Interesting, Edgar. Is that like Red, as in the financial hole, and Blue, like in deeply sad?

EDGAR: Great thinking, Jake. Color seems to mean many things. Red could be hot and blue cold, for instance. Something for our listeners to talk to their friends about.

ME: Sure seems like we have a lot of scientists in our listening audience.

EDGAR: Big minds are attracted to big minds.

Monday, May 29, 2017

The next hurdle had to do with hardware. What equipment did we actually need to broadcast? We planned to have microphones, of course, for all three of us. And a bleeper with easy access. What about sound effects, like a crying baby, or a sneeze or playing a statement or quote from someone newsworthy? Or, not newsworthy? We'd need a sound system for out front of Whiskey 'n Ribs. Headphones we presumed. And how the hell do you hook all that up to a radio station? Oh, and the small matter of a radio station. Edgar and I stared at each other. Roxy, as usual, answered, "We'll find a way."

This time we had the gall to call Paul. Paul was a much younger fellow that I'd met at a golf driving-range a month and a half earlier where we teed off adjacent to each other. On my third shot, I almost creamed him with a drive off the tip of my driver that barely missed him as he walked a couple steps forward to retrieve a ball he'd barely nicked with his five-iron. After emphatic apologies, we went for a drink in the clubhouse. It turned out he worked for Channel 10 and was responsible for all the equipment from in-studio to all the remotes. He spoke in a technical language as alien to me as Chinese. After a beer and an enjoyable chat, he returned to the driving range. I tossed my clubs in the trunk and decided I was way too dangerous to play any more golf. I kept his business card.

Paul agreed to lunch. It was worth every penny.

He told me of an old low power AM station that was barely functioning. AM 1480. The owners were considering selling it, or upgrading it and trying to resurrect it. It was the station Roxy had heard about.

He gave me a couple names and phone numbers. Roxy jumped on it immediately. And Paul offered to check on some used studio equipment.

Monday, June 5, 1017

Within a week we were the proud owners of three used Sennheiser mikes on adjustable booms, head-sets to listen to each other, an audio console which Roxy would operate. AND, an agreement that we could have a noon-to-one o'clock time slot on Saturdays on AM1480. We'd probably need a modem to send our broadcast back to the station for transmission. Also, a speaker setup to project outside the restaurant.

It seemed a great opportunity to get on the air without having to buy a radio station. We were rolling. As a reward to ourselves, we recorded another potential skit:

ME: Moving right along here, Edgar, we have a couple questions from our listeners. This one I think is for you: A young woman asks, What prompted your parents to have **you** *as a child?* (A burst of laughter from Roxy in the background)

EDGAR: Is that a hostile question, Jake?

ME: Hard to say. Do you think she knows something about you that most of our listeners don't know?

EDGAR: Impossible.

ROXY: (in the background) "Yes. She must."

ME: Just give it your best shot, Edgar.

EDGAR: Well, I was a love-child. So you could say I was an accident. Or mother was trying to force the marriage issue.

ME: And they did have to decide whether to have you, and they decided yes. That's says something.

EDGAR: But they were both practicing Catholics, so it doesn't really.

ME: But they did decide to get married, right?

EDGAR: But that could have been motivated by guilt and not love for what came out to be me.

ROXY: They could have given you up for adoption. Or even sold you on the black market.

EDGAR: This is becoming painful for me. I like the love-child answer. The problem is: Both mom and dad are dealing with memory loss, so I'll never be able to ask them. Why did you have to choose me for that question? Why did our listener have to ask it in the first place?

ME: All I know is, supposedly there are no coincidences. Somehow you were intended to get this question, Edgar.

EDGAR: Who says there are no coincidences? She could have just as easily asked you the question.

ME: But she didn't, Edgar. That's the point. The power of our broadcasts to get at the truth for our listeners.

*EDGAR: **BLEEP!***

ME: Quickly, let's move on to BREAKING NEWS, Roxy?

ROXY: Sorry, Edgar, I didn't realize you were so sensitive. Here it is from our news wire: BREAKING NEWS: THERE ARE MORE MOTHERS-IN-LAW THAN FATHERS-IN-LAW IN THE U.S. (She repeats the statement).

*ME: And with that for us all to ponder, we have reached the end of our hour. Thanks for listening. And thanks to our sponsor: **Glacier Pure Powdered H2O**, the amazing new product that's so easy to use anywhere you're thirsty. Yes, you simply add water, and drink. **Glacier Pure Powdered H2O.***

We've been live from Whiskey 'n Ribs . . . sippin' whiskey and simmerin' ribs. The essence of craft in Denver. Located downtown on the East side of Larimer between 15th and 16th.

Thursday, June 8, 2017

Of course, while absorbed in pursuing the dream of a radio talk show, there are many other realities occurring in our separate lives. In my case, I am still coping with a personal life that might require the help of a comedy writer with exceptional skill. Please bear with me.

I've been divorced for a very long time. I have two fabulous daughters in my life and for that I am grateful every single day. I've also had a few delightful women in my life. I did ask one to marry me. She declined. Probably wise on her part at the time.

With this new venture on my plate, I've found a new energy and vitality to express what I have inside. Talk about making up stuff, I'm making up more stuff than I ever dreamed possible. Don't ask me to explain where it's coming from, I'd have to confess there is a God or a universe working on my behalf.

I'm also aware that I don't have someone special to share this new endeavor with. It's just a sense hanging around a little more poignantly than I'm accustomed to. What should I do about it? Good question.

Today I've assigned two hours to work solo on questions to ask our listeners. I try to make them enticing enough that they will take a stab at an answer. Maybe get agitated at not knowing what the answer should be. We hope to have call-ins once we're on the air.

Here's a couple:

1. What is your biggest regret in your life?

2. What's the most important thing that could occur in your life today? (Kind of the genie-in-the lamp question.)

3. What's the biggest con you've pulled off in your life? (C'mon it doesn't have to be a bank heist).

4. If you could change your first name, what would you choose?

5. In your opinion, what would a library scandal look like?

That's not two hours worth. Some questions were quite lame. Others couldn't pass our *rigorous* standards of decency and propriety. For instance: When did you first notice your pubic hair?

Like I said.

I met Edgar at this week's bar on Gaylord for lunch. He'd been working on the same project so we compared notes. Being married for thirty-seven years, his questions were more directed toward relationships and the bottomless well of questions about how to make a long relationship still be fun. Good luck, Edgar.

Two that I found very cool were:

1. What would happen if you always laughed at your mate's jokes?

2. How do in-laws impact your relationship with your SO?

Now we had to generate some listeners.

Monday June 12, 2017

Roxy was at her computer working for her own clients when

we arrived. She wrapped up her project and lifted the lid off a box of her homemade English Toffee. Edgar asked how many? I didn't wait for her answer and lifted three pieces.

"What do you two think we should have as theme music at the beginning and end of the show? Or on segues between features?" Roxy looked at both of us, expecting something.

Edgar and I stared at each other, clueless. "Can we use anything we want? Will we have to pay for it?" My two questions.

"I don't want to use oldies from the sixties, I see way too much of that during the PBS fundraisers. I feel like I'm going back to a forty-second high school reunion. And afterward, I'm supposed to sign over my estate to the network. Then die." Edgar, piqued.

"I couldn't agree more," said Roxy. "Your turn, Jake."

"That leaves out the Bee Gees, then." I was at a loss. Finally, "What about Leonard Cohen? Would that bridge the age range, whatever that age range is?

"You're thinking, Hallelujah, The Radio Guys are on?" Roxy asked.

"Marvin Gaye? Asked Edgar. "That song where you hear the crowd noise at a party, and then he starts talking about war, too many people dyin' and we need peace and stuff. *What's Goin' On?*

"I don't know," answered Roxy. "How about Moby. His early stuff is pretty powerful."

"Whaling music, is it?" Me, a smart ass.

"We need something upbeat. Happy. Driving. Energetic." Roxy was serious. "It will either invite people to listen, or switch stations. It's their first impression of the show."

"The Star Spangled Banner," I offered, embarrassed as it left my loose lips. "Would I have to take a knee? Roxy, you know more about this than we do. Come up with some examples for us. I see what you're getting at. Something infectious. Maybe someday we'll be walking down the street and hear someone whistling our theme song."

We moved on.

It was Roxy, again, pushing us to think of how we're going to promote the first broadcast of our show. "As a core, I think we should use Pandora, Spotify, Facebook and other social media. I don't think we could justify free ads as a public service, although I'm counting on you two to improve the mental health of our listeners."

"So, let's make up some ads, with that in mind; improving the mental health of our listeners." Edgar urged.

"We can do it. Here or at the bar?" I asked.

"I say you each write some. Then go to the bar, look them over and bring them in tomorrow." Roxy finished the discussion.

Tuesday June 13, 2017

Like clockwork we arrived at our office at ten. We traded ad lines back and forth. Roxy took notes.

ME: Friends, are you tired of being on edge? Cranky? Lost? Unfulfilled? Well, here's your guaranteed cure: Saturday, at twelve noon, turn your radio to 1480 AM and listen to the outlandish wisdom and mind bending inspiration from the new show: The Radio Guys Talk. You'll never be the same again.

EDGAR: Are you feeling lowdown, blue? Are you thinking of hurling something fragile across the room? Are you out of anti-depressants and your shrink is out of town? Have we got a cure for you!

ROXY: Both possibilities. More.

ME: What's it worth to you if we could guarantee you a couple good laughs, maybe even a belly laugh? No matter the dumps you might find yourself in?

EDGAR: When was the last time you looked in the mirror and laughed wholeheartedly? Or even smiled? Maybe you have the curable disease of Grumpiosis Mytosis. Or even my favorite: Irritable Bowel Syndrome, a smile stopper if ever there was one. Well, we've got you covered every Saturday at noon with a free dose of The Radio Guys Talk.

So it went for a half-hour and we felt we had a direction that could appeal. Roxy urged us to develop a couple of other concepts that didn't remind potential listeners of their infirmities, and their bowels.

We went down the paths of: Daring listeners to laugh. Or, not laugh. Having lunch at Whiskey "n Ribs, where you don't have to sit across from someone you're tired of listening to. Even mood-changing or mind-altering radio without mushrooms or "brownies" or Coors Light. Among others.

We cautiously agreed we were moving forward. We had some fiber in our segments. Some piss in our vinegar. We became aware of how much content we needed to fill an hour at a pretty quick pace. Edgar suggested we have a segment whereby we'd play a very short musical phrase and see if our listeners could identify it, or identify the performers. Maybe three or four of them in each show. Just to take up some time.

Roxy asked, "What if no one calls in?"

I looked at Edgar, "We'd have to ad lib, admit our concept was a bust."

"I think we just have to have more backup materials. A list of questions, more sudden Breaking News, or . . . just make up more and more stuff. Just what you guys do."

There was a kind of forced chuckling that attempted to dismiss any worry that there would be a reign of silence on the airwaves, a dread which, at times, I'm certain, causes everyone on the air, live, to wake up sweating in the middle of the night.

I know I've mentioned how attractive Roxy is compared to what Edgar and I brought to our project. But her skills and knowledge. Her nerve and take-charge manner. These were our difference makers. If we failed as Radio Guys, it would not fall upon Roxy. Damn, we were lucky.

The owners of AM 1480 had invited us to use one of their ancient studios in the meantime to get familiar with the equipment and to rehearse our segments in a studio atmosphere. We jumped at the chance and went over every day or two to try out our stuff.

At our first opportunity, Roxy led us through the drills: manipulating our audio console, taking in calls, playing prerecorded segments, using recorded sounds from bleeps to groans, trying out various music segments and segues. And most important, helping us get used to a pacing that felt right. Something you take for granted as a listener. Like what a comedian has to do to give the audience a split second more to process and respond before moving on. What an education. All new stuff. For guys who were making up all new stuff.

Wednesday, June 14, 2017

While Edgar and I were trying to make up stuff that would make people laugh, Roxy was making us laugh at ourselves. She was mercifully tolerant, yet demanding that we push ourselves. *Too long; too obscure; TOO OLD, boys! There's a huge audience under fifty. And forty. And thirty. You want some of your audience to outlive you. And if you don't, don't worry, some will. And they will remember your show. If they listened more than once. And you don't want to have them be relieved at your passing.*

Brutal.

It's not that we took ourselves so seriously. I'd like to

think we're just from a different generation and we needed some upgrading and updating. Maybe I was being too charitable. But, we knew Roxy was right, about everything. And we trusted her. So we girded up under her guidance. She said to watch Colbert to see how to communicate with a wide age group. We did. It was a daunting challenge, not to watch, but to make any serious comparison to what our abilities were. Numbing and humbling. We dug in and pushed on. Any entertainment of hubris on our part was maybe the funniest joke of all.

Soon, we worked on a new aspect of our format, The Radio Guys Listener Poll. Roxy urged us to do this on-line given our overworked staff, namely, Roxy. That required a link which we would add to our website, which also was yet to exist. For the moment, it would be as follows:

ME: And so that brings us to some puzzling questions that we've gathered here in the studio. Some our own, others from listeners. And we're going to put some of them up on our website, radioguys.com. So you all can plug in your answers. What have you got for us Edgar?

EDGAR: Sure, well, you've always said that we're not a political program, but I have this from my wife, Margery, who is not political, but who loves betting. What do you think of this: What will come first, Donald Trump's divorce or his impeachment?

ME: Roxy, isn't that political?

ROXY: Only if it favors one party. A while back, in the time of Monica, I think you might have asked the same thing about Bill Clinton, right?

ME: Will some of our listeners feel offended?

EDGAR: I say we see what happens, let our listeners respond. Let's put a third choice: Neither will happen. Don't force a choice.

ME: Put it up on the radioguys.com. Let us know out there. Now I think we should take a word from our sponsor.

EDGAR: And that would be: POLITE INTERRUPTIONS, a daily message for those who never get a word in edgewise. Have you ever been in a conversation with one or more people, for example, where one person does ninety-nine percent of the talking? Or more? Are you too timid or sensitive to realize this is not a conversation? By any stretch of the imagination? Or worse, have you had to sit next to such a situation? Where it starts to grate on you, and you end up mad at all three people? Angry at the one who can't shut up and angry with the others who have no self-respect?

ME: Why, that happened to me the other day at coffee. I couldn't figure out who to yell at and I finally couldn't take it anymore.

EDGAR: Make a note, listeners. Here are some suggestions for you from Polite Interruptions:

1. Say, could I clarify something you just said?

2. I wish I could write this all down. Let me get a tablet from my car. (Alternative: Let me get a roll of toilet paper.)

3. Excuse me for a minute, I seem to have a twist in my colon.

4. How did you learn to talk for such a long time? You must have a hard time finding people who can keep up with you.

5. Would you like to know my reaction to what you're saying?

6. Do you have any friends?

7. Is your shit written down somewhere? I have to go to the bathroom and pull my hair out.

8. Why don't . . .

> *ME: Say, Edgar, could I clarify something you just said?*
> *ROXY: And I seem to have a twist in my colon.*
> *ME: All right, listeners, you get the idea. You don't have to put up with one-way conversations anymore. Polite Interruptions will send you a new escape clause everyday if you just get the Polite Interruptions App. It's free, and it will set you free . . . if you don't have the balls to speak up for yourself. Don't wait.*
> *EDGAR: Were you trying to say I was going on and on? Too long?*
> *ROXY: Oh, no.*
> *ME: Never.*

Saturday, June 17, 2017

On an overcast Saturday morning the three of us took a couple of our scripts and three folding chairs down to the Whiskey 'n Ribs' back entrance, using a key given us for when the construction crew was absent. Upon entering we were immediately enveloped by nose-hair burning fumes from the recent varnishing of the exposed wood.

After moving a huge exhaust fan close to the open door we turned it on high and stepped back into the alley for a breather. Fifteen minutes later I moved quickly through the construction site and opened the front door part way. We waited another fifteen minutes before hustling through with our chairs to the front window area where we set up like we might during a broadcast, Edgar and I side-by-side as if at a table, facing outward. Roxy to our left at the end of the invisible table, poised to see both outside and us.

"So, this is how it might feel. Of course all the signs and permits will be removed. What do you think?" I asked.

"I think the odor will kill us." Edgar, philosophically.

"It's already ruining my hair." Roxy, resignedly.

"C'mon. It's not going to be like this." Me, despondently.

I stood and turned upwards, taking the full arched window and the high, century-old ceiling tiles into consideration. The zinc bar was covered with heavy canvas, various tools and paint and varnish cans. A compressor and a pail with used brushes soaking in solvent were packed in a corner. Everything that was wood had been sprayed. The rest, some cushions and boxes of fixtures and glassware and other unknown objects were covered with plastic sheeting. All signs of progress as we moved closer to the launch of the restaurant and our show.

"Maybe the smell of ribs slow-cooking will overwhelm these fumes," I offered.

"We can only die once," said Edgar.

"Age before beauty, boys. I'm not ready to die yet."

"Let's run through one of our segments quickly. Just to christen the place. We can see who drops first." I thought it was clever enough to get a smile. It wasn't.

We sorted our papers to a short section that went like this:

ME: Why don't we take a break from our fascinating conversation about why women with pets are happier than women with husbands, and catch up on the breaking news. What have you got, Roxy? Roxy hands a sheet to Edgar.

EDGAR: Well, here's a white flag: Democrats ask for donations to determine why they've lost the election to Trump?

ME: Isn't that political, again?

ROXY: It is, a little. But read the second one, Edgar.

EDGAR: Yes, here it is: Republicans secretly poll party members to find out how and why Trump won the presidency. See, equal bafflement, Jake.

ME: Fair enough. Curious minds want to know. And, friends, this portion of the Radio Guys has been brought to you by, STAND UP GUYS, sports apparel and casual dress apparel for, well . . . Stand-Up Guys. standupguys.com will get you there.

EDGAR: And what will it get you, Jake?

ME: Good question. I'm sure it's not clothing to help you stand up. So that makes it a character and fashion issue, doesn't it? Are there any stand-up guys anymore?

EDGAR: No one I know. Roxy?

ROXY: I knew one in sixth grade, but he was a boy, not a guy.

ME: Well listeners, let's leave it this way until this is clarified. You guys know if you're stand-up, or not. If you have to ask, I'd be skeptical. Of course that doesn't allow for modesty, does it?

EDGAR: I'd just look at their web site. See if you like what you see. Nobody is going to question your legitimacy when you place an order.

ME: OK, then, let's end this show by thanking another one of our courageous sponsors: The Roger Federer Tennis Ball Refuzzing Machine. Patented to replace the worn-off fuzz with new, fluorescent yellow fuzz. Extends the life of your balls for years.

EDGAR: So from sunny Denver, broadcasting home of The Radio Guys Talk studio in the front window of Whiskey 'n Ribs, epicureans' choice on downtown Larimer, we say goodbye until next Saturday at noon. And, in the meantime, don't you worry about a thing!

Monday, June 19, 2017

And then I met Carly. For the third time. The first time was almost twenty-four years ago. I was crawling out of a divorce, in one bloody piece held together by super glue. Carly was the mediator in our failed reach for an amicable settlement. Details are unnecessary at this point. Scars heal. Memories atrophy.

Actually details might be helpful. To be fair to all.

Extracting consensus from the two of us, Mallory, now my ex-wife, and me, was like extracting cooperation while performing a dual root canal. My particularly mature contributions to the mediation process were a brooding silence followed by infantile sarcasm. "Don't think you can lord your PhD. in Child Psychology over my BA in Advertising."

And, after grinding my teeth while Mallory stated one of her killer demands, I finally snapped out of a faked doze with: *Uh, Mallory, would you mind restating that slowly, I didn't quite understand your full proposal. It seemed so . . . so generous.* (I swear I remember seeing Carly purse her lips in in a vise clench to ward of laughing. I know I did.)

That had nothing to do with my emotional immaturity, of course.

I was attracted to Carly. She was unaffected, composed and a delight to look at. Unfortunately I had already fallen for the realtor who was selling our house as Mallory and I excoriated the rules of civil verbal combat and paid Carly enough in the process to possibly purchase our house. She was too aware of the ghosts she would inherit to do such a ludicrous thing.

Our realtor, with fabulous legs, and a neediness that was formed during her recent separation from her husband, was a perfect connection for my battered spirit. Like many others that reject the advice to go slow and grieve and get your own life settled, we became instantly inseparable, essentially fucking our way through our hurting and lonely egos.

That lasted about two years. Then I ran into Carly again, at a book-signing for Christopher Moore. Turns out we both had read everything he had written. We went out a few times, and I really did like her. She, on the other hand, was on alert. She had seen too much of my complaining and whining and stubbornness during our mediation sessions and was wary. She also knew I had jumped into a new relationship before the marriage was legally ended, and she was one of many who had urged me not to do such a thing. She ended our little fling, fling in the diminutive sense, telling me I wasn't ready for prime time, a real romance. I told her I'd really done the work and was ready. She smiled kindly, and walked away.

Me, busted.

Which brings me, us, to this day. I stood right behind her in the checkout line at *Whole Foods.* God, how trite! "Hey, how you doin', Carly?"

"Hi Jake. Great! You?"

"Right, all's well."

Maybe I was caught off guard. Absolutely I was. But, she was more beautiful than twenty years earlier. Softer, eyes brighter. Mouth relaxed in a smile. She was next up and she had only a few items compared to me. I calculated there was enough difference in the amount we were each purchasing that she'd be driving away by the time I walked into the parking lot. So, in front of cashiers and customers I quickly lost all restraint and blurted, "Carly, I sure would like to get together with you. It's been a long time and I, um, um, sure would like to get together with you."

She tilted her head and looked at me. A wave of doubt washed across her face. I could see her mind shutting down. I panicked.

"No, really, I'm different now, (I'm pretty sure I sounded like I'd just been released from a correctional facility). I mean all that is behind me. I've reformed. No, I've put all that legal stuff behind me. I'm free. I uh, you don't have to worry, I mean, not that you ever did have to worry. So uh, it's such a surprise to see you, and I sure am making a fool of myself. Ha, ha."

I felt the sweat running down my forehead, and under my arms and I quickly thought of simply fleeing from my place in line, racing outside into the lot, and curling up in the cage of an empty grocery cart. Then, as if she were a Sister of Mercy, she touched my arm and said, OK, Jake, I'll wait outside and give you my number.

Just like that. And slowly the several customers and employees close by started to clap lightly, uncertainly, as relieved as I was.

"Oh, Okay. Great. Uh. Yeah, I'll finish here, and I'll see you . . . um, outside."

I was smooth. I was on my game. Actually, I was a sopping towel. I started to wonder if she'd agreed just to escape the ridiculous man behind her that was making a scene that would embarrass a baboon. I was a wreck, a wreck of my own making. That encounter took less than two minutes to strip away my composure, my self-confidence, and my dignity. I felt like I was trying out for a bit part in Dumb and Dumber IV.

I didn't care. I really didn't care. That's a lie. I did care. But she said yes. We exchanged numbers outside. We agreed to meet at Pearl's for happy hour in two days. I said thank you and great and then said the same things again. And then I shut my mouth, finally implementing damage control, and walked to my car.

Driving home, I was elated. I wanted to tell someone, share my excitement. But I didn't want to jinx the thing before we even got together to utter the second paragraphs in our reunion. (Reunion is probably a bit too optimistic. Perhaps an unlikely and acutely cautious encounter is more apt.)

Wednesday June 21, 2017

My "date" with Carly at Pearl's would prove challenging. I almost scraped sides with a parked Buick while maneuvering to squeeze into a parking space out front. Inside, I spotted her at a high table against the wall. She was clad in headphones, talking to someone, writing on a legal pad. I stood watching for a couple minutes, not wanting to interrupt. My anxieties intensified, I finally went over to her table and gently pulled out the chair, making strange hand signs to encourage her to pretend I wasn't there.

My first objective was to expulse the teenage personality with which I had made a fool of myself in the Whole Foods checkout line. The look on her face when she ended her call told me she was on high alert, probably having reconsidered giving me her phone number. Or, it could have been her phone call. I was to learn that her career path had taken her from divorce mediation to director of three halfway houses for adolescent drug abusers. She now had a lot of fires to put out on a daily basis. Plus, she was managing all the events and fund raising to keep the three operations running. It was hard to know how much these pressures influenced the serious face she offered.

"Hi Jake, sorry about that call. I came early, thought I'd get some work done. Maybe you might chicken out, or forget." She did smile, just a little. I'm sure of it.

"Well, I'd never forget. I've spent forty-eight hours reliving the fool I made of myself, asking you out, or however one could interpret my deranged performance. Tell me, why did you agree? Was it just to get out of there? Or, a surge of pity on a desperate man?"

"Or it could have been that I needed a good laugh and there you were, your stand-up routine unabridged." She smiled one of those wide, close-mouthed smiles that essentially says, "Your turn now."

"Any regrets? Other than refusing to get into a relationship with me, what was it, twenty years ago?"

"Very funny, Jake. You're probably thinking I've been pining ever since. When actually I had fallen for a man who turned out to be a good-looking, smooth-talking loser. I think he was unemployed more than not. He failed to show at most of our mediation attempts, no surprise. So, after hiring an expensive lawyer that ate up a generous part of the assets that I was trying to protect, I shifted my career to one so consuming that I don't have time for a relationship. So there, don't worry about your stand-up performance."

"Kind of a good news-bad news situation. Hmm. I guess I won't propose marriage like I was intending."

"Good read, Jake. So, tell me what you're up to? Still an ad-man?"

"Retired. I gave it all I had. I was getting too old to know how to pitch the millennials. And even their parents. I like not having hours, and bosses way younger than me. As the birthday card from my daughter stated so succinctly: *You're Old As Shit!* So, tell me more about what you're doing."

She did. Gradually relaxing as she listed what she liked and what she didn't. It seemed about half and half.

"I'm making a good living, not like I might in the private sector. But it seems to satisfy my helping gene. What they say about the important work not paying enough is true, Jake. I guess I've always known that."

"Do you miss the mediation work?"

"Not really. I think working intimately with people on life support was quite discouraging. Although I do remember that you made me laugh a couple times." She smiled. (See, I told you she was trying her best to smother a laugh at my antics.)

"Oh, that's good. Maybe I will propose marriage. You could work. I could make you laugh at the end of the day."

She choked a laugh. But at least it was a laugh, not a choke. I'm pretty sure. We agreed to meet again a week later, after her major fundraiser was history. We hugged; it felt great. I left with some hope lingering, still wondering if she might reconsider later, after recalling the checkout line incident one more time.

I drove home, stopping to pick up Chinese take-out, and, a couple blocks later, a half-gallon of ice cream. Life in the fast lane. I decided to keep my date with Carly a secret from everybody, for a while anyway. But, I was already way down the road in my fantasizing: Our first roll in the hay. Our first road trip together. Our first European vacation together. (I stopped short of children. And raising chickens together in our back yard.)

Slooooooooo-down, Jake! You've got a radio show to put together. What if Carly could be a guest on our show? What's latest in half-way house protocol? What if we announced our engagement on The Radio Guys?

SLOOOOOOOOO-DOWN, Jake!

Thursday, June 22, 2017

We began working intensely on the segment of our program we called Interviews with the Radio Guys. Here's where Roxy achieved star power. Here's where we discovered that we could expand our cast without expanding our cast. We recorded our first interview with the British Sub Minister of Economic Withdrawal, recently appointed to the Cabinet of the newly elected Prime Minister Theresa Mary May of England, or Great Britain or the UK, if you prefer. (I think there's some kind of an identity issue over there) Excuse the muffling in the beginning where the Sub Minister, Her Ladyship Camilla Wistlepink Birtwistle, is orienting herself to an interview she evidently had not been privy to.

SUB MINISTER CAMILLA: **Bleep!** *Who the bloody hell am I talking to? Radio Guys? Fuck whistle! Some heads are going to roll here, Bingston.* (Evidently Bingston was her Personal Secretary, at least for the present.)

BINGSTON (Reassuringly: Yes, Mum, well then, we'll sort this out won't we, Mum? We're actually on the air now. With the Americans. The man's name is Jake. His co-host is Edgar.

SUB MINISTER CAMILLA: BLOODY WANKERS . . .

(Silence for ten painful seconds, and then I attempt to smooth over any hurt feelings on my part and welcome Her Ladyship Camilla Birtwistle of Britain, or England, or whatever.)

ME: Good day, Your Ladyship. It's a beautiful day over here and I hope you're enjoying one there in your country as well. Thank you for taking the time to visit with us. We are thrilled, of course.

SUB MINISTER CAMILLA: Yes, I'm sure. And I'm thrilled to be awakened in the middle of the night to talk to you, Radio Guys, is it? (Roxy's impersonation of a pissed-off Sub Minister from way over or down under or wherever, was blisteringly right on. Edgar covered his mouth and I was thinking it time for our first commercial.)

ME: Oh, no, I guess our staff didn't think of the different time zone. Sorry. Kindly tell our listeners how do you function when you're on a different time zone than everybody else?

SUB MINISTER CAMILLA: What? Oh, cheeky, eh. Well, your listeners are not the center of the universe, or the world, sorry to inform you. A great deal of the world operates on our time zone. Perhaps you're the odd ones out. (to the side and muffled but audible) *"Bingston, your arse is in the hot grease of a fish 'n chips fryer."*

ME: Excuse me, Madam Sub Minister, how could I be so

foolish. Please accept my apologies. Let me ask you this. We're being inundated, or I should say educated, about the BREXIT situation. I gather you're right on top of this one. (Another aside: Who are these fuckwits, Bingston?) We hear a lot about soft and hard referring to BREXIT. Could you tell us about that? And also whether you prefer it hard or soft?

Edgar rises suddenly from his chair and leaves the studio, spitting as he goes. I'm alone to smooth out the ruffles between Her Ladyship the Sub Minister of Economic Withdrawal and Me.

SUB MINISTER CAMILLA: Mr. uh, Jake, is it. I sense you haven't a clue about BREXIT. Maybe you think it's some kind of a quinoa snack. And I suspect you and your listeners are much more concerned about the most idiotic President the world has ever witnessed than about the realignment of the political and economic relationships on the continent. We did have a national vote on this. We're a democracy, I'm sure you've heard, and we decided to reclaim some of the sovereignty that we'd relinquished in our relationships with our neighbors. It's quite a complex and arduous process. I'm sure your listeners would be fast asleep if I were to attempt a further explanation.

ME: (looking for Edgar and shrugging my shoulders at Roxy. Where was I to go with this fucking interview? Edgar reenters and puts on his headphones. I defer to him.)

EDGAR: Good morning, Sub Minister Birtwistle, I guess a very early morning. Sorry. I'm Edgar, one of the Radio Guys, grateful for your time and thoughtfulness. Maybe we could wrap up your excellent analysis with that last question about BREXIT: Are you in favor of hard or soft?

SUB MINISTER CAMILLA: (Muffled aside to Bingston) "See me after this monstrous cock-up is over. With your suitcase.) Well, Edwin, is it? Let me put this in a way that you and your listeners just might comprehend. Let's think of BREXIT as a

French baguette. I prefer it soft enough so that there is minimal hardship on any of our citizens. And that it is hard enough so that, should both of you ever be cleared to visit our nation, I will personally greet you at the gate and watch with great pleasure as Bingston shoves it up your rosy red rectums.

Silence.

SUB MINISTER CAMILLA: And since you two Rhodes Scholars probably need to bone up for your next interview, I will happily say good day to you Radio Boys. **Bleep,** *Bingston. March your redundant arse back here!*

BINGSTON: Of course, Mum. More silence.   1

EDGAR: Are we still on the air?

ROXY: We are. She rang off.

I put my face in my hands on the table. Roxy was slumped, removing her headphones.

ME: Whoa! Did we really deserve that? . . . For a Sub Minister she was a real piece of work, right?

EDGAR: She is no minister . . . Frankly I expected a little more from a government Sub Minister.

ROXY: Maybe she was just having a bad day. Or night, actually.

ME: Y'know, it must be a crazy place to live. I mean they don't even know who they are. England? The Brits? The Commonwealth? Great Britain? The United Kingdom, UK, Land of the Beatles? Impossible. (SILENCE FOR TEN SECONDS) *You know what I think? It's a real credit to us that we're just simply . . . Americans! I'm proud of that.* More silence.

ROXY: Or . . . Yankees. More silence.

EDGAR: Or the United States. Or USA. Or the US. More silence.

ROXY: Or the Lower Forty-Eight. Dilly Dilly!

EDGAR: So, friends, that might have been the first American talk show to interview a female Sub Minister of the UK.

And you heard it here on the Radio Guys Talk. She was a bit miffed, wasn't she? About the time zone thing, maybe? What say we move to the next segment of our broadcast? What will it be, Roxy?

ROXY: In this case, Edgar, it would be Breaking News. And I've just taken one off the wires. I'll give it to Jake. I think he's recovered.

ME: Thank you Roxy, Hmmm. OK, here goes. BREAKING NEWS! THE PRESIDENT IS ACCUSED OF SNATCHING A FEMALE BROADCASTER FROM ONE OF THE CABLE NEWS NETWORKS TO BE HIS NEW PRESS SECRETARY. Well, Roxy, interesting choice of words or word, don't you think?

ROXY: I know. I just hand them over as they come in.

ME: OK then, enough for that. Pretty self-explanatory, right? . I mean it could have said grabbed, I suppose.

Friday, June 23, 2017

We recovered from our bruising interview with Sub Minister Camilla Birtwistle of England during our second round of Happy Hour cocktails the following day. I twisted on my stool, checking for pain levels, "I swear it was like conversing with a claw hammer, my back is all scabs."

"I'm glad we're not negotiating with her over our license." Edgar shook his head heavily. "I don't think I'll ever look at a baguette in quite the same way."

"What should we send as a thank-you gift? Other than beef jerky?" Roxy smiled, as if she was having the last laugh on Sub Minister Camilla. "Why do they call her Mum, anyway?"

We didn't have an answer.

I offered, thoughtfully, "Could we send her some tea? Do they drink tea over there?

"Other than our wounds and inevitable scars, I think

we're cleared for ambulance chasing and driving in all future interviews. Roxy, you're my choice for a Purple Heart." Edgar led us in raising our glasses.

"Well, fellow conspirators," I shifted the post mortem to a cheerier topic. "As of today, we're well past half way to our opening show. Live and, unhinged. I think we're making great progress. I really do. What's your take?

"I like what's happening, too." Roxy was first. "But, we really have to take control of political content. Like you warned us, Jake, It's way too easy to go there. Now, we need to get to a full sixty-minute show. I don't think we know yet how it feels to go the full hour. It doesn't sound like much, but it'll feel like a marathon until we've done it a few times. It's the concentration."

"Maybe we should pre-record our first program. At least wait until the second one to go live." Edgar looked hopeful.

"Edgar, I think we can do it live." I said. "Even if we screw up more than once, listeners will cut us some slack if we just fess up to our amateur status. In fact, we should go into it expecting a couple gaffs or screw-ups or whatever they call it in the trade. We're human. Besides, we might not have many listeners. Maybe just a handful."

"I agree, Jake," said Roxy. "Edgar, look how you handled the Sub Minister. I mean that took agility. And confidence. You'll handle anything that comes along. Just remember how well you stayed composed when she referred to you as boys, as fuckwits. I mean you guys were pros!"

"You're absolutely right, Roxy. I guess I didn't hear 'fuckwits'. She said that, huh?" I asked.

"And she seemed quite familiar with the color of your rectums."

I split a gut and Edgar sprayed some of his mouthful of Guinness. In his choice of beer, he was siding with the Irish in their long history of abuse at the hands of England, or the Royal Tannenbaums, or whomever.

"She didn't think much of our President, did she?" asked Roxy. "Like she'd like to cut off his baguette, maybe."

Edgar instantly pressed his beer onto the bar, securing against spill.

"Remember, this is a politically neutral talk show. Maybe the only one in existence right now." I was half serious. "Should we get an interview with another British official? Don't they have a loudmouthed mayor of London or something?"

"I'm on it," Roxy smiled, an evil glint in her eyes.

Roxanne Buddington-Finch

Another aspect of Roxy's life was being mom for two high-school daughters, Kendra and Lilith. Two gorgeous girls, you couldn't help but agree. She was chauffer, chef and good-cop/bad-cop, depending upon the rising and falling of hormones, and the ebb and flow of relationships. The girls were smart as hell, and Roxy was smarter yet. It all worked. They got along. They fought and loved. As I got to know all three, I often gave thanks that we never found Rex.

Roxy, by her own example of energy and wit and moxie, brought out the best in Edgar and me. We had to be on our toes or she'd drop into silence, her head tilted, her mouth pursed and her eyes to the sky, waiting, until we felt her withdrawal, looked over at her and snapped out of our lethargy or daydreaming or whatever guys do when they think no one is watching.

Her expression was like a motherly parole officer. I can only believe she had some faith in our potential and she didn't want to see us blow it with the relaxing of discipline that accompanies retirement. Our response, each in his own way, was a dropping of our faces, busted like children caught picking their noses or pushing a vegetable under a napkin on their plate. After holding her pose until our eyes locked onto hers, her stare morphed into a smile that was so forgiving, our levels of guilt jacked above red line.

This situation always recurred, sometimes just days later. It's probably why we seemed to be making good progress, all in all. I wondered how I could have used her techniques to motivate the writers and art directors that worked for me in the ad biz. I don't think I was loveable enough to get away with her compassionate urging and her humorous nudging, especially while lacking her unquestionable brilliance. She was the kind of person who could make big things happen around her by simply being herself.

When I met her for lunch during Edgar and Marge's three-day road trip to visit their son, she filled in more details about her life, how she kept her drive and humor and wisdom firing on all cylinders, every day, it seemed.

"Some of it is just in my genes. Mom and Dad were goers. I guess I am too. I was one of those lucky ones who watched how her parents lived, and decided what parts fit me. They never told me what I should do. The message to me was: *You can figure it out. You know best.* That's a real gift."

"And you've made it work pretty well. Actually very well it seems to me. And by yourself."

"As soon as I was pregnant with Lil, my second, I realized I'd made a big mistake with my marriage. It wasn't working; it wasn't going to work. I'd seen my dad make some mistakes, mostly business errors, and he always seemed to face up very quickly no matter the situation. He stopped what he was doing, and moved on. He had no tolerance for being stuck or being unhappy. It was a big lesson for me. I think he was such a positive guy. He thought mistakes were something to learn from, not to be self-imprisoned by. Good notion, right?"

"Good, and unusual, unfortunately."

She told me how she got into her own web design business, how quickly she picked it up, and how fast it grew. "The weird thing is that I have such happy and healthy clients, that I actually have the time to do this with you guys. And this is really a good thing for me and it's so damn funny. I think we'll all live longer."

"I'd like to think that's true."

"So, Jake, a little more about what the Radio Guys thing means to you? Like why you didn't try this a long time ago?

I'd wondered about this, too. Was it just another thing that came along in the sequence of life events? Was it going to end, or expand?

"Sometimes I think the question is: Why in the hell did I try it at all? I don't think I was looking. I wasn't completely bored. Maybe I was starting to become bored. Talking about aging. Talking, talking, talking. I think I missed the adventure in my life, like I'd had before, and couldn't make up for it just by traveling and grumbling."

More thoughts came: "Maybe I thought that God had a little more in mind for me. Yes, I do believe in God, after not believing for much of my life. I try to keep it quiet. It's usually a conversation stopper. "Anyway it came to me one day, kind of out of the blue. I was sick of our politics, watching it endlessly, or talking about it. I'd watched the rise of Stewart and Colbert and Samantha Bee and John Oliver and several others. And they made me laugh, and they were smarter than anyone else in the country, and I thought how delicious it would be to be drinking their Kool-Aid. And . . . how there was no way I could do what they do, now or ever. And I laughed at the idea. But I loved the laughing. And one day I thought about doing a fake radio show, a podcast, for the sheer fun and hell of it. I was thinking in terms of maybe a twenty-minute broadcast from some imaginary location, an abandoned lighthouse, say, on some island off the coast at one in the morning. Something outrageous. That if it were a bomb, no one would know about it except Edgar and me. I had him in mind from the start. So that's it. It's moving along, isn't it?"

"You remind me of my Dad, your imagination. You get an idea, a notion, you don't talk yourself out of it, you buy into it a little more, and some things seem to fall your way, then they start tumbling your way, and pretty soon you find yourself doing things you never thought, never conceived you could do. It's magic, Jake."

"I like that. Like you stumbling onto our ad for Rex. That's enough to make me a believer."

"Thank you. I agree."

Later, while finishing Chinese on my deck, I thought about this conversation with Roxy. If our venture ended tomorrow, it would have still been the best adventure I'd ever embarked upon. Worth every ounce of effort. But it wasn't going to stop tomorrow. We had lots of shit to make up.

Gradually, as it always happens, my mind drifted to what we'd been doing, and to our interview with Sub Minister Camilla. She was right about our politics. And she was right about how we, on this side of the pond, don't give a shit about what happens over on the Continent. Unless, say, it threatens our source for Italian Montepulciano, or Belgian chocolate or secret Swiss bank accounts. Or if it resulted in a hard French Baguette shoved up our collective bottoms.

We are Americanos.

Monday, June 26,2017

With Edgar back in town, we three began our session at the unused studio, sizing up just where we were in the whole process and, mostly, where we needed to spend serious time. I must say the atmosphere and the tone of our discussion was way upbeat. We'd swallowed a lot in a short time, digested it, and we were owning our new levels of competence. With no illusions that we were going to replace Kimmel or Colbert or Fallon anytime soon. In fact, we agreed that our goal should be one complete, satisfying show that we could feel proud of, even if it was our one and only.

I mean, hell, no one was going to fire us. Unless we frightened customers away from Whiskey 'n Ribs. Our man-about-town, Saul, was working the media to be alert to a fantastic new happening in the Lodo environs. He would let them all be the first to know, once we were ready. I guess the downside of some good publicity was that we would be exposed. And, we could bomb. No more about that line of thinking. Not a word.

We didn't talk about it much, but I was impressed how well Edgar claimed his full part in this, my venture. Not that I didn't think he could. But, he had a streak of modesty in his kit that made him a better man. He'd been a civil engineer most of his life, Purdue University, and thirty-five years of evaluating, repairing, and overseeing the construction and reconstruction of new and used bridges, highways, entries and exits, sewers and, when he took a year and a half off from his profession, helping a group of his golfing buddies build a new golf course.

What made Edgar such a natural for the radio mic, in addition to his strong mellow voice that could melt hearts when he spoke personally with you, was the fact that he was the Big Book of Jokes. He had a memory that was cast like a prehistoric creature in amber resin, and he could pluck an appropriate joke instantly from its recesses. Talk about a source for material on a live broadcast. He was an escape artist with the ability to counterpunch. A secret weapon. He made my role easy.

By now it was apparent the three of us had solid chemistry. Through some great fortune, our egos were small, at least with each other. Maybe because Edgar and I were old enough to have been visited by numerous challenges, bumps in the road and basic exposure to life. Roxy was just a hell of a lot more mature and radio savvy than either of us. Praise the Lord and pass the ammunition.

We settled into our highest priorities.

"I think you two should have more setups to toss things back and forth with each other," began Roxy "An actual conversation. Ad lib. Wing it. For instance when listener's feed questions to you. Or in response to breaking news. You're both pretty quick and you should have more discussions, see where they go. See what comes up that can go on our Poll. Push things. Not long, but long enough to pull listeners in. Give them more to think about, or talk about." Roxy looked to us for reaction.

"I like it," answered Edgar, "but I think it will need some serious work. Just so we don't freeze up."

I added, "Roxy, you should be a bigger part of that. Push us. Add your own thoughts. Question us. You're smarter than we are, anyway. And you have a good sense of when to go on. And when to full-stop. And that will prevent us from just bouncing from one item to another, rapid fire, which, in an hour could be exhausting. Like trying to outrun a machine gun."

Edgar nodded, "So, we should come up with a bunch of questions or incidents, ad lib them, and record them. See how we sound. Get comfortable with it. I think it's harder than it looks. Except when Charlie Rose does it. Like magic."

"Roxy, you be like Charlie," I said. "Try to keep us talking." A half hour later, we were mic'd up and Roxy began.

ROXY: Now here's a question from a listener in Boulder. I think from a woman. She asks: "What personality trait do you most admire in a woman?" Take it away, boys.

EDGAR: Besides money, you mean?

ME: Of course besides money. I've been unmarried for so many years I can't remember what traits I really dislike. Wait a minute. I do remember. But that's not the question, is it?"

ROXY: No, Jake. What do you like the most?

ME: OK. I think money was a terrible answer. I think generosity is a better way to put it. You know, generous with compliments. Generous with time. Lots of ways a woman can be generous.

EDGAR: You're making me look bad. I was not being serious. Actually, a woman who laughs easily and laughs a lot is an amazing woman. My wife, Marge, is a great example. There. That feels better. That feels right. Jake?

ME: Affectionate. That's something we don't always admit. And since I'm not in a relationship right now, I can say that without offending anyone.

EDGAR: Why do I get the impression you're using our show as a dating service, Jake? That's already the second time you've brought up your marital status.

ME: I'm just sayin'.

ROXY: And I have a second question. If you could, who would be the one person you would rather be? Aside from our President, of course.

EDGAR: That's not fair. I'll have to rethink. Jake?

ME: Living or dead?

ROXY: I would suggest you live. It would help us finish this show.

ME: It's just that I think I'm such a great guy, why would I *change?*

ROXY: Edgar's right, Jake. You are using this show as a dating service. Radioconnection.com. You've got to answer the question, not avoid it.

ME: OK, that leaves out Robin Williams. So I would be . . . Tom Brady. He's got it all and he's still in a starring role. Hey, maybe we should have him on as a guest?

ROXY: I'm on it, Jake. Edgar, who would you transmogrify into?

EDGAR: I'm buying time here. Since our President is off limits. And I was never a jock. Too slow, too short, too nonaggressive. So I'll select Ira Flato, the Science Friday guy on Public Radio. As long as Marge could still be my wife. Hi out there, Marge. It's me, Edgar.

ME: Good move, Edgar.

EDGAR: I mean, he's in science and he gets so many interesting people on that talk about things I'm interested in. Yes, no question. Ira Flato. With my wife, Marge.

ME: Hey Edgar, one thing. I don't think it's fair that you take Marge. I mean that's picking and choosing, not going with the whole transformation. I, on the other hand, am willing to take the complete plunge, take on the whole package, even Tom's wife, Gisele.

So, that's how we started the process. Twice we came to a full stop, stumped at where to go with the conversation. Roxy edited those gaps out, figuring we had the agonizing discomfort well impressed upon us. She said not to worry, it'll happen again, it always does, to everyone. We listened to the recording four times. Roxy stopped it wherever a comment seemed useful. We weren't discouraged. And we laughed a few times. A good sign.

Tuesday, June 27, 2017

I sat down on my back deck, my second cup of coffee hot in my hands, no trace of a hangover, as content as a barracuda suspended in salt water, watching a massive school of fish quieting down nearby. If he had chops, he'd be licking them. He'd be making his move soon.

I wasn't ready to move yet, not with crumbs of a scone stuck all around my mouth. I was still awaiting the first sounds of an ambulance or a fire truck on the busy street in front of my townhouse. It was the confirming evidence that I was living an urban experience. It's curious how those sounds that initially were jarring become the urban version of white noise. Squeals of breaks, the impact of colliding cars, the yelling of passersby in the middle of the night, settling arguments with high-pitched profanities, the shattering of the occasional empty bottle. I think I'd go nuts back in the burbs, or any farther from the city center. Yes, I do see a shrink on a reasonably regular basis. But not for the urban cacophony. My relationship with my therapist is sustained by two reasons: Jan Baumgardner listens to everything I say, and she has a body that would challenge the designers of the Alfa Romeo. Oh, and she's the smartest person I've ever known.

Usually that's more than enough. And recently she's been a cheerleader for my crazy new venture. I like cheerleaders. But I've learned to be careful of new ideas, keeping them to myself until I felt bulletproof to such possible reactions as: *Why would you want to do that? Won't that cost a lot of money? You've never done anything like that, have you? Gee, I'd never want to do that? Don't you like what you're already doing?* And, once recently: *But, you're retired; you don't have to work anymore.* All with a noticeable paucity of encouragement, and the unsuccessfully veiled scold: *Why aren't you ever satisfied with the way things are?*

I've learned that ideas, good ideas, big ideas, are not

only precious, they're vulnerable in the early stages. They need to take root in your heart and become strong before you expose them to "well meaning advice".

Except with Jan Baumgardner. She comes prepared with a watering can and fresh topsoil to nourish fresh ideas. There are no *shoulds* or *should-nots* in her vocabulary. She's a hopped-up cheering section. I would never bet against her.

She starts every session with her prayer, in the form of a joke that usually relates to her profession. Yesterday she began: ***My therapist said that my narcissism causes me to misread social situations. I'm pretty sure she was hitting on me.*** Then we're off and running.

Bolstered by yesterday's session with Jan, I catch myself smiling between sips, actually laughing when I think of our last session at the studio, our attempt to have more of a conversation between the three of us about something we had no idea about. Yes it was bullshit, made up, fantasy, maybe partly true. But, it was so damn much more fun than many of the conversations I overhear in my life, going way back and right to the present. And, as far as I know, it's harmless. And to the extent that I can laugh, it's got to be good for me. No, I'm not an idiot savant. An idiot, maybe .

When my kids were young I recall how much I disliked the phrase "I'm bored." It seemed to come all too frequently, and they'd expect a ride to the mall or something else to *entertain* them. *To be entertained* was the nectar, the morphine drip. And, of course, I'd say something brilliant like: Why don't you read a book? Or, do your homework. Or something else with an equally distinct tone of disapproval. I disapproved of their boredom.

Of course I have to admit that boredom has often been my complaint. I'm bored. My way of dealing with it now? Make it seem absurd, crazy, ridiculous. Hopefully, at times, endearing. Create a new reality in some way. Occasionally it works.

Back to my deck chair. What I've gradually concluded is this: It seems to me, that my whole life, my careers, education, family, relationships, wins and losses, have been leading inexorably to this new adventure. To have a radio show. To be a talk show host. To be a radio guy, on my own terms, to sink or swim, but to carry it out some way, some how. And, it's gathering steam. I reach for the train whistle cord and pull down, hard. Look out, cows!

To dream, or not to dream? To be, or not to be? Aren't those the real questions? It seems to me they are always our choice.

Hold on there. I think I just felt the inveterate drop in my stomach when something seems wrong. About that joke Jan kicked off our session with yesterday. Was she implying that I had too huge an ego? And, that she thought I thought she was hitting on me? Shit, I hate these doubts. I'm too old to be human. Jan is straight ahead if anything. Maybe I'll ask her about it next time . . . only if I really need to.

Wednesday, June 28, 2017

The first item on our agenda when we met at the studio was, well, making an agenda. For the day, and then for the next couple weeks and the few days before the first broadcast. Roxy had a checklist; we each had a copy.

"My intention was to go through each of the things on this list, check them off, complete them or put one of us in charge. You with me?" Roxy was in high spirits. She proceeded, "So, first we have the name of the show. We've been using *The Radio Guys.* You OK with it?"

"I am, but are you OK with it Roxy? You're a huge part of

it. You OK with "Guys"?

"Unless you want to call it Guys and Dolls? But that sounds sappy. I'm good with "Guys.""

"OK with me, said Edgar.

"How about *The Radio Guys Talk?* Says a bit more about what they might expect. I'm OK either way, though." I said.

"I like *Talk.*" Roxy looked around, caught our nods and checked off item one. "Next I have: how do we dress? Denver casual? Special T-shirts? Sport coats? A skirt? Hoodies?"

"If it's really hot in the window, can we peel off our shirts?" Edgar, avoiding the dress code.

"What about something casual, but sharp? Like Rugby shirts or blazers? Enough to suggest we didn't just get out of bed, or fall off the turnip cart. Even a sharp dress shirt with jeans. We're not the swamp people." I had a sense of it in my mind, but not a specific solution.

"Shaved?" Roxy again. "How about make-up? It's radio, but our biggest audience might be on the sidewalk outside the window. At least until it catches on and the world is glued to *AM 1480, The Radio Guys Talk.*"

"Don't people expect faces made for radio?" asked Edgar. "I can live with shaving and a dress shirt. One of Mr. Rogers' sweaters. Makeup? Not so much."

"Roxy, do we really need to consider makeup?" I pleaded. "We all get a little sun this time of year. We're not pasty white."

"Dress shirts, a nice top for me, shaved faces for you, maybe a classy sweater, no makeup. Sold." Roxy made notes and moved to the next question.

"Introduction? Who does it? And How?"

"I've been thinking about that. I mean, Edgar has by far the best voice between the two of us. But, what about you doing it, Roxy? Kind of unexpected. You've got enthusiasm, energy, you're easy to understand."

"You mean like a circus ringleader? Edgy in some way, right? I could work on it and let you judge. Otherwise, I agree, it should be Edgar."

"Although it's Jake's show, his idea. I think he ought to do the intro." Edgar seemed embarrassed.

"Not a chance." I responded. "Either of you make a better vocal impact. I need time before my brilliance shines through." I tugged at a nonexistent bow tie

Roxy continued, "OK, I'll work up a couple routines. Next, we need to work out how we move through the show. Who makes segues; moves us to the next topic, etc. So far we've shared making transitions, like, *It's time for Breaking News, or It's time for a word from our sponsors.* I think one of you should have the main responsibility. I can signal to you, hold up cards. I think it should be you Jake. You have a good sense of where we're going. Keeping it moving. You're an ad guy. You know how to get someone's attention, and keep it, and when it's time to shift gears."

"That seems good with me, Edgar?" I turned to my partner.

"I need to rest my star vocal chords anyway. Maybe we should have them insured? What do you think?" Edgar, never a simple answer. Well, hardly ever.

Roxy marked off another item. "I will make up some signs to signal you Jake. Plus we'll each have a fairly complete outline in front of us. Plus, remember this is what our headphones are for. We can talk without the audience hearing.

She moved on. "Next, how do we interact with the live audience out front. They can hear us. At this point we can't hear them. Probably that will be the case all the time, unless we rig up some way to take a mic outside. If we want to."

"We can read lips, sort of," I offered. "We can respond to

them if we want. See how it goes," said Edgar.

"I could play a brief crowd track, a roar, polite clapping, whatever would contribute to the humor. Something inappropriately enthusiastic to what is actually taking place." Roxy grinned. "You'll get the hang of it. I've never seen you two at a loss for words. Except for those couple brain freezes when we tried to record normal, scintillating conversation between the two of you. Ha, ha."

"I was acting normal. Edgar left me hanging in the wind." (I can play the victim role with the best of them). "I'm sure I'll have the opportunity to return the favor."

"Not the golden rule, Jake. Turn the other cheek, I say," said Edgar.

"OK, then," Roxy stood. "That's my list. Hey, we're getting stuff done, right?" She stacked a few papers on her desk as she powered up all the studio equipment so we could begin recording more unrehearsed, abnormal conversation between the three of us. It was becoming normal, this abnormal stuff we were making up.

Thursday, June 29, 2017

We were smack in the middle of recording a segment of our show we would call, *Useful Advice to Our Listeners, or Not,* when we spotted the statuesque form of Saul Friedman, raked fedora and open-necked white cotton Henley, untucked, standing at our studio window, for who knows how long. We ceased our struggling routine and motioned him to the entry door.

"Good morning, fellows. And lovely lady." He swept low toward Roxy, ever the lady-killer. "I'm just stopping by with a few ideas for your show. It's just around the corner, am I right?" "Saturday the twenty-second, if all goes right with the restaurant."

I smiled, but my radar was on hyper alert, wondering what "ideas for the show" meant.

"Well, I stopped by the restaurant. They're interviewing for all positions and it looks like they're on schedule for soft openings the Monday, Tuesday and Wednesday before that. With the big private opening on Friday evening. I guess you guys have talked about not being there for opening night, even though it would help your publicity."

"I think they'd prefer to not complicate their opening. It's OK with us,"

"Anyway, I think you need some promotional materials. Stuff I can hand out, for one. And stuff Whiskey 'n Ribs can hand out to all their customers. Provided they like your show and don't mind being identified with it."

I responded, "We're having a dynamic sign painted to remind passersby of our show when we're not there. It'll stand on an easel inside the front window. I think you're right about cards and some kind of easy handouts. Or stand-up cards by cash registers for anyone willing to display them. Maybe with small takeaway cards with show details. Something Saul can use. I think we've got time."

"Give me some copy and I'll get on it. Also invitations for the media to be there for our first show, right? What else, Saul?" Roxy asked.

"Sounds like you guys know what I'm talking about. PR releases. Maybe something a little crazy. You know, a marching band, a Goodyear blimp. Maybe some radio spots on several stations. I think handing out cards or something on Saturday to people already downtown would be great. Getting a crowd at the front window would attract more people."

"We're on it, Saul. Thank you for keeping us on task." I

poured on the gratitude, hoping it might bring our business to a close. Not so fast, Jake.

"What was that you were reading before I came in? Not your show stuff, was it?"

Boom! I became as territorial as a lioness with cubs. My hackles rose like those of a prize rooster. I felt the steam rise. Sure I had more symptoms but you get the point. I flashed over what Saul might have overheard. We had been struggling with a new segment, shy on substance, and probably enthusiasm. Still, I responded to the 911 call to my professional remove.

"Yes and no, Saul. What you heard was part of our process to explore new concepts. It's rough. Very rough. We have learned that we have to risk the unknown to discover the really good stuff. You heard some of that process. To the extent it was the three of us talking, exploring, mining, yes, it could become a part of our show. But, not until it glows like a uranium find. If uranium glows. I don't know if it glows, actually."

I noticed that Saul's look of consternation remained, the stern parent, ready to offer unsolicited advice. I left no opportunity for the stern parent, or overzealous critic to be heard. I seized the air space.

"In fact, Saul, we're behind schedule on our rehearsing today, and we have lots to do. So I wouldn't worry if I were you. We're working things out. But, I do really appreciate your help with our promotional materials. We will get you what you need, and we take seriously what you do in this community. It is marvelous and there's no one who does it better. Thank you for stopping by. It's good seeing you."

I'll call you as soon as we have something, Saul," Roxy said.

"Right then." Saul hesitated a long couple seconds, then evidently read between the lines of what I was saying, if I hadn't been clear. "Ok, keep up the good work."

With Saul's departure, Edgar chimed in. "We did sound pretty rough. Do you think the segment is worth pursuing? He's an odd duck, isn't he?"

"He means well." I answered. "I've learned that you have to be very careful who you ask advice from. It's not just my thin skin. Trust me. And I agree it's a rough concept, or it seems to be. I say we scramble on some promo ideas for Roxy and give the Helpful Advice concept another try tomorrow. I'm thinking it's the questions that need to be raised to a higher level. Maybe more *out-there?* Maybe more provocative? Maybe just funnier?

During the next three hours we developed our promotional theme to launch The Radio Guys Talk.

>Who is ***Clint Eastwood*** listening to?
> **The Radio Guys Talk**
>AM 1480 Saturdays. Noon to One
> OUTRAGEOUS RADIO LIVE
> Front window,
> Whiskey 'n Ribs, Join us.

The campaign fleshed out with: Who is Yogi Berra listening to? Who is Lady Gaga listening to? Who is Phil Jackson listening to? Who is Richard Nixon listening to? Who is Vladimir Putin listening to? Who is George Carlin listening to? Who is Clark Kent listening to? Who is Stephen Colbert listening to? And on and on. It would be short and swift. Hopefully under the radar of lawyers and agents representing any of the living or the estates of the deceased in the campaign. If we caught some heat or after we'd been on air a few weeks we could resort to a Word of Mouth Campaign and change the cards to:

WHO WILL YOU TELL ABOUT:

THE RADIO GUYS TALK   AM1480
SATURDAYS NOON TO ONE
OUTRAGEOUS RADIO

So, oversized business cards. Counter displays for checkout. Maybe bumper stickers, eventually. Saul would have his handouts and we could start handing them out the week before as well.

Friday, June 30, 2017

My second date with Carly, as related to Edgar and Roxy in a moment of reckless self-disclosure, provided me very little relief. First a little background info to prepare you: I've tried, over the years, to fully grasp the many reasons for my lack of successful relationships with women. At least long term relationships, including my marriage. Is it simply that I haven't evolved beyond the *Me Tarzan/You Jane* level of maturity? Here, see my cave. Scratch my back hair. Become my love slave.

Notice, I didn't say, please. I haven't arrived at the begging stage yet. I'm sure I'll get there.

How would I rank myself on the maturity scale for a retired ad man? Pre Neanderthal? First off, I think it is important to know where you're located on the grid of human evolution, that long line of creatures delineating our stages of evolvement. I'm pretty sure I'm just to the right of the one whose knuckles still brush the ground, with tail lopped off. Makes me wonder how I ever got a BA in Advertising? Actually, it doesn't. Still, I don't apologize for the cards I've been dealt, nor for the choices I've made.

With this appealing baggage, depending on *your* location on the evolutionary grid, I did some thoughtful planning before my date with Carly. First, I would assure her that my age, ten years older, was not a problem. I could still climb the stairs to my bedroom without breaking a sweat. Also, my parents never suffered from memory loss even at the very end. At least to the best of my recollection.

One confession to Edgar and Roxy was: I've long been a sucker for beautiful legs and a stunning smile. And these things that I covet, eventually aren't sufficient enough in an adult relationship and I move on?

My daughter, Jennifer, told me not long ago, "Dad, you've had some really neat women in your life. Just not the right one yet."

Bless my daughter's generosity.

In any event, my conversation with Carly was utterly enjoyable. I loved the things she said and the way she formed her mouth and lips to say them. So, in my mind, it's completely understandable why I cracked. Why I blurted a proposal of marriage. Why her beautiful mouth hung open, her eyes awaiting some plausible explanation for the bomb that shattered the delightful chat we were having. "You frighten me, Jake!" seemed so unsurprising, compared to my question.

As I said, after my blurt of a proposal to Carly, there followed first the deadly silence. The, "You frighten me, Jake!" actually was a pretty smart reaction. Who, in their right mind wouldn't bail, or immediately book a long trip to Varna on the Bulgarian coast of the Black Sea? To place them a considerable distance from my derangements.

As I realized how appalled she was, I attempted a feeble explanation about me having a loose tie rod. Lacking an airline ticket, she simply rose, grabbed her purse and walked intentionally to the exit.

Later in the evening after our abbreviated second act, I stopped for a drink(s) at Illegal Pete's. Frequently I land there in summer weather where great ideas readily occur as I gaze through the dazzling sunbursts created by the misters, and I jot these gems down while draining copper mugs of Tequila Mules, creating pages of notes in several foreign languages I'm quite unfamiliar with. As you would expect, these inspirations require agonizing deciphering the following morning.

My summarizing brilliance?

Maybe I should look closer at my knuckles to see if they haven't been dragging on the ground recently.

Monday, July 3, 2017

While the rest of the country prepared for the Fourth, many in transit, many a long way from home, Edgar and I spent the morning in solidarity with those Americans who didn't have the day off, who couldn't extract an extra day in the society that penny-pinches it's vacations and time-off in the fear that people will become complacent, even decadent. Or, perish the thought, might even achieve greater mental health.

But enough of one of my long time pet peeves. Edgar and I elected to suffer with the deprived. And sought to plumb the depths of wisdom worthy of our long lives.

What did we come up with that was worthy of our sagacity? Well, we explored the various ways we could tease the wisdom from the great universal law of Cause and Effect. This is what survives:

BEAR SHIT METAPHOR

1. If a bear shits in the woods, will we hear the tree fall?

2. Bear no shit; tree no fall.

3. If a bear couldn't find the woods, would the trees just stand around?

4. If a bear had the runs, would a tree lose its bark?

5. If a bear were plugged up, would a tree's sap thicken?

6. If we couldn't hear the bear shit, would we hear the tree fall?

7. If a dozen bears shit in the woods, would we hear a grove of trees fall?

8. If you met a person who thought up things like this, would you call 911?

9. If you've read this far, would you embrace other metaphors about woods and forests?

10. If you've read this far and considered going to the woods to take a dump, where would you place yourself on the human evolution chart?

11. If you've tried to recount your own version of this metaphor, would you admit it to someone you were trying to court? Or to someone you worked for?

Now, there you have clear evidence that we're still sharp and with it. "Hey, Edgar, who called the ambulance that just pulled up out front?"

Wednesday, July 5, 2017

Roxy arrived at ten sharp with a plan for the remaining days leading up to our first broadcast. "We're going to do start with a fifteen minute outline. Perform it. Listen to it. And repeat it.

Next day, twenty minutes. Same thing. You can revise the material, add some, delete some. Whatever moves you. When you reattempt a segment or even a joke, you'll see how you can do it in a completely different way. You can change the tone, the timing, the tempo and the exchanges back and forth. You will become masters of the universe in no time."

Edgar and I stared at her. She was so confident, matter-of-fact, about our abilities. It sounded great. Could we believe her? For the first time I wondered if we'd been drinking our own Kool Aid too much. It was a stomach feeling. I recalled it from the many times I had to give a major pitch to a client or a prospective client. Usually it followed a sleepless night and it stayed until the first few sentences came out of my mouth. My dry mouth, to be more exact. Sure, I got much better with it over the decades, but it never disappeared.

I wondered how it would be on our first live show? Sweaty? Maybe lockjaw? Maybe thick tongue? Or, maybe momentary blank mind? I've experienced all of these, ranging from dispiriting to harrowing. What about cardiac arrest? Maybe we *should* pre-record our first show. I reconsidered.

Power on, we did. Here is the second version of the abbreviated show we recorded that afternoon:

ROXY: *And now we return to the Radio Guys, Jake and Edgar, for the second half of our broadcast from the front window of Whiskey 'n Ribs right here on Larimer between 15th and 16th. And we begin with a question from one of our listeners.*

EDGAR: *Fire away, Roxy.*

ROXY: *A Constance Phlegm writes in: What qualifies you two to have a radio show?*

ME: *Hmmm. Is that simply a question, Edgar? Or is it a challenge? Why am I taking it personally?*

EDGAR: *It's a simple question. Constance is just curious.*

And I would answer that by far the most important thing is looks. And, Constance, if you're listening, we'll put you on a list for when we print up glossies of ourselves, Roxy included.

ME: OK, I'll go with the curiosity angle. I'd say life experiences. You and I have more than a hundred years of life experience between us. That's why we have so much to say. So much to offer.

EDGAR: And modesty.

ME: Exactly. No hubris in this studio. (In my headphones I hear Roxy.) "Constance Phlegm is on the phone. She says she meant, what qualifies *you* two? She asserts that chimps would be an improvement."

ME: Well, Roxy tells me that Constance Phlegm is on the line and she is evidently questioning our bona fides as radio performers. Maybe she thinks we should have some kind of license or degree or something?

EDGAR: Who is she to cast aspersions? Hey, Constance, if you could see us, you might notice this finger I have pointing skyward. And it doesn't mean we're number one.

Back to my headphones and Roxy. "Jake, I think if you look through the window at the crowd gathered, you might spot an agitated lady with her white hair tied in a bun. She seems to be returning your finger signal. Maybe you two need to ratchet it down a little so we don't get in trouble with Whisky 'n Ribs."

I stared at Edgar as he scrunched his face. This is the kind of publicity we don't need this early in the game. Or ever.

EDGAR: Just kidding, Constance. Oh my gosh, what a misunderstanding. This does mean we're number one. All of us. We're all number one. And we don't have a license to be hosts of a talk show. In fact, we need good people like you to make this a successful talk show. Thank you for becoming involved.

ME: And of course, it's obvious that looks aren't

important. You can see for yourself. (My lame smile and limp little wave were all I could muster. Pathetic).

EDGAR: Maybe Roxy has a second question for us? Roxy?

ROXY: I sure do. It's from another woman. She asks, At what age should men not be allowed to appear shirtless in public?

ME: Sweet Jesus, Roxy, she's not out front with the crowd, is she? (I'm scanning the gathering for a woman with a nasty grin).

ROXY: This is a write-in question. (I shake my head at Edgar).

ME: Now this isn't just curiosity, Edgar . . . there's a clear implication that she doesn't want to see shirtless men in public after a certain age. Like it's something unseemly. Hideous.

EDGAR: Hrumph. I should be offended. But, she might have a point. I'm not so comfortable taking a close glance in the bathroom mirror in the morning. I think she does have a point. What should we do, come up with an age?

ME: Don't cave so easily, Edgar. This is a slippery slope. Eventually men of a certain age could be confined to their homes from sun-up to sundown. Will we have to wear a white shirt and tie when we're mowing the lawn? Won't we be able to expose our painted bodies at football games? And baseball games?

EDGAR: That's serious man stuff. You're right, Jake. No one's going to keep me from beating my blue and orange chest while I'm booing the refs. Or spilling a beer on the guys below in front of me. That's basic man cred.

ME: That's more like it, Edgar. Stand our ground. We're losing all our advantages in the work place. Women are being elected willy-nilly. Women are getting into universities. Men are being dragged in for marriage counseling. We've got to draw the line somewhere.

Roxy, in our headphones, "Maybe you two should dial it

back a little. It looks like it's mostly women in your live audience out front. And they appear to be troubled by your comments deriding women.

EDGAR: Just kidding. Of course I was kidding. Just trying to generate a little discussion. (The window group is watching carefully, waiting to be convinced). *My wife is my favorite person in the world. She treats me like a king. OOPs. I meant we love and respect each other, completely. Head to toe.*

ME: I think you've made your point, Edgar. I would just like to add that I love women. All women. In fact, I was married to one, once. We got along famously. Until we didn't. Well that's another story. Say, let's do this. We can't possibly come up with a reasoned answer to the listener's question; we're running out of time. Why don't we put it up on our phone poll, Roxy? Something like: Is there any age beyond which men should not appear bare-chested in public? We can give some of the results on our next show. Let everyone weigh in on this . . . social issue.

EDGAR: I'm getting the slash across the neck signal from Roxy, friends. It's time to wrap up. Thank you for joining us, The Radio Guys, and Roxy, of course. We'll return, armed and dangerous, next Saturday at twelve noon, on AM 1480. As we say around here, Chill or be chilled!

Friday, July 7,2017

This just happens to be my birthday. My attempt to postpone it another year met with the same lack of success it has the past five years. It's like people are locked into the unnecessary annual-to-the-day fixation on birthdays. It's so punitive. Even if we're not in the mood. Even if we don't have a party planned. Facebook will not let us forget. No way to lighten up, cut some slack in the actual date or even the month. Talk about a hard taskmaster.

This month I'm getting ready to launch a brand new venture in my life, and then along comes my birthday and I'm reminded that I better haul ass as my clock reels off minutes and hours that I'll not have again. I don't even think people off-the-grid can escape this presage of the Grim Reaper. I look in the mirror and recite several hundred times: *I'm not getting older; age is an illusion. In fact, me and my life coach are going to beat this aging thing, beginning with ignoring my birthday. Fuck Facebook. I'm taking the road less traveled . . . without birthdays. You watch!*

And, I'm going to call Carly since I haven't heard from her. I'm certain she's waiting for me to call first. Call it intuition. I mean, she's very bright. Surely she knows I was intentionally trying to impress her with my absurd joke. It's what guys do, right? It's how we shoot our way out of our tired life patterns, the paper bags that keep us on an even keel, ruled by predictability and repetition.

When we shoot our way out of our several paper bags, we shine with pure brilliance. I know Carly knows this. Maybe I'll wait through the day, give her a chance to call and confess she was overwhelmed with my moment of comic artistry.

On second thought, I think I'll call now. Take the high road. Forgive her for not catching on to my wicked one-liner. She'll be so relieved. I won't let her beg for forgiveness for one brief shining moment. *"It's OK, Carly, sometimes I surprise myself. I can be too sophisticated, cutting edge, in my humor. Like all big thinkers I need to rein it in on occasion."* She'll see that. She'll get that. Right? What am I waiting for?

I dialed. Finally her voicemail with the usual invitation to leave a message and number. Fair enough. But then, "Unless this is Jake. I don't know who you think you are, Jake? Or who you think I am? But I didn't find you amusing. You denigrated a very sacred thing to me. You must think I'm stupid. You disrespected me. Then you laughed when I got up to leave. That doesn't work for me. I don't need that in my life. I don't need you in my life. I hope this is clear."

Whoa! Harsh! Hmmm. Like I said, she's smart enough to catch on to my humor. She's still playing hard to get. Making me sweat. Notice she didn't say, *Don't call me again, Jake.* That's a come-on if there ever was one.

I marched around my kitchen and living room, surely there was something I could eat or drink or kick to make me feel better. Maybe a mirror that needs to be resized with a chisel. Who am I kidding? I screwed up big time. She was as final as a light switch. She had every right to be afraid of me; I am like a drone with a loose tie rod. I think I should send flowers, lots of flowers. And a letter cosigned by my shrink, Jan, explaining the loose tie rod thing. Maybe I should retract my proposal of marriage.

Monday, July 10, 2017

For three days I've waited for Carly to ring me up, mea culpa, throw herself at my mercy. She must be sick or out of town. Maybe she lost her phone. It happens. She might not even have my number at this point.

I sent an SOS text to my shrink, Jan Baumgartner. As I walked to the restaurant, (she agreed to see me for half of her lunch hour, the only time she had that day) I harkened back in my mind to the joke she kicked off our last session with. The guy who completely misinterpreted what another person said. Because he was so embalmed in his self-centeredness. Was that me she was speaking about? And now I'm going to explain my predicament, having shocked a lovely woman with my outburst, and thinking she would soon come crawling back.

Jan was already seated, a glass of iced tea just delivered,

and she looked at me like I was a child who had left his backpack on the bus, or his lunch on the kitchen table.

"So soon, Jake. Here I thought you were on a roll. Tell me what's up, and then we'll order."

I did, leaving a few ugly details out, whereby she tilted her head, waiting for more grim admissions. No glossing over how I created my own crisis, especially on her lunch hour.

She kept her head tilted until I admitted every sordid, embarrassing, juvenile detail. Even the argument I had been having with myself about how Carly would come crawling back. That was the worst. Then, nodding her head knowingly, she laid out the joke she said she'd just heard that very morning:

The pharmacist asked me my birth date again today. I'm pretty sure she's going to get me something.

She signaled the waitperson over to take our order. All I could think about was that she had me in mind when she told the joke about hitting on me during our last session. And now I'm feeling humiliated. Not by Jan, but by me. I ordered dry toast and water. Then I canceled the toast.

"OK, Jake. Don't go dunking your head in the swamp." She'd never said anything quite like that before. "I know you're embarrassed. But this is nothing serious. You're not thinking about what you're saying in this encounter with someone you quite fancy. Does that fit?"

"It's terrible. But it just came out. The proposal, I mean."

"Yes. And then you got wrapped up in how she might come to forgive you your comments, which I don't believe you really apologized for, because she'd be crazy to not be crazy about you."

I didn't know what to say. Jan's scalpel moved quickly to

my tumor.

"Here's my thought. You're mixing your conversations with someone you kind of like, with the scripts you're writing for your show. You are still planning on your talk show, aren't you?"

I thought about this as I took a deep breath. Was that true? Was Jan trying to let me down easily? Or was I just a self-absorbed *rube?*

"Look, Jake. You didn't get to where you are in life by being an idiot or a jerk. You have good friends, a great professional record of working with all kinds of people. And I think you're a thoughtful guy. But, you've had some not-as-successful experiences with women. Not all bad, but, for whatever the reason, no really long term ones, except for your marriage which wasn't so good at the end. Am I right?"

Jan's Greek salad arrived. My water glass was still full. I thought about reordering the toast.

"I *think* you're right. I hope you're right."

"I am right. You aren't psychotic. Not pathological. You just have some bumps with women that you haven't worked out. It's more insecurity than inability. Maybe your humor is an attempt to disguise your lack of confidence. We can work on that. In the meantime, think back on the sequence of your thoughts from the moment she got up and left you on your date. From not knowing how to react when she was obviously offended by your joke. Right on through the mind game you played in your head about whether she'd call you with an apology. Think about how your daughter might have reacted in a similar situation. You have a good relationship with her. Think of what kind of apology she might expect."

I nodded my head. I almost felt hungry enough for toast. Almost.

"You're trying to write funny, outrageous stuff, Jake. For

your radio show. Maybe not for making a good impression. Especially with a woman. Now, get out of here, I need to take care of my salad. I'm not worried about you, Jake. You're a good man."

Sheepish, but, relieved, I thanked her, took a gulp of my water, and walked to the exit, waving daintily as I pushed through the revolving door. Man, that was intense, unnerving and reassuring, all in about twenty minutes. Thank you, Jan Baumgardner. I walked all the way home thinking about how I could have done it differently, and what I'd say in a letter of apology.

But, was my proposal of marriage just a joke? I'm not so sure.

Thursday, July 13, 2017

I saw it was Saul calling. I wondered if he had second thoughts about our conversation a week or so ago. I think he was perplexed about what he witnessed in our studio. Maybe appalled. Oh, well.

"Jake, I've got a great idea for you. Got a minute." Evidently he wasn't withdrawing his support.

"Absolutely, Saul, pour it on."

"I just got off the phone with the editor of *The Westword* and I pitched him the idea of two new businesses uniting downtown, you and the Rib place. I think he'll do a feature on the two of you. He said he'd have someone contact you. The guys name is Tony. I think it's a great idea."

"Thank you, Saul. Good thinking. I'll wait to hear from Tony." Saul said good-by. He's a busy man. Tony Fournier called thirty minutes later and we set up an appointment for the next morning in our studio. Roxy brought bagels and vegetable cream cheese.

Tony looked younger than twenty-five, a smart white shirt with a tall formation of hair like the young basketball players just drafted by the NBA. Shaved up from the ears straight vertical to the top. A gold cross on a chain, rich brown eyes, he was a young black man bursting with energy. I liked him immediately. "Well, you know my boss is high on the idea of doing a story on a new radio program hooking up with a new restaurant downtown. I'm not sure he thinks it's a combination made in heaven. He's a skeptic, which you almost have to be in this business. But I think we can have some fun.

"Let's do it," I said.

"Good. I decided to keep the interviews separate. So you're my first. Let's talk about your radio program. How did it start?"

I answered, "Kind of out of nowhere. Both of us are retired, completely new to broadcasting. Roxy has some experience producing with her college radio station. She's holding this together as we cut our teeth."

"And it's a talk show, right. Like Bob and Ray? Or Oprah, with two Oprahs?"

I looked at Edgar; he seemed more than content that I continue. "Bob and Ray, Tony? That's way before your time. I didn't think anyone under sixty would remember them. Don't tell me you know about Arthur Godfrey, or Don McNeill's Breakfast Club?"

"I know *of* them. I was a communications major in college. That's probably why my boss put me on this. Pretty much anyone who eats can write about a restaurant. That's an exaggeration, I'm sure you know. So what makes your talk show different?"

"It might help to tell you what it's not. First, it's not a political talk show. There's enough of that out there, twenty-four seven. And it's not about show biz, or sports biz or biz biz or news biz; except for our own take on breaking news.

"Got it. So what is it?"

I continued. I was starting to feel uneasy about this part; it was the first time we actually told someone, who was probably going to inform lots of someones about what we were trying to do. What we thought was our best shot at making this a successful go. What if Tony frowned? What if his editor squashed the idea as lame? What if this punctured our high-flying balloon, whooshing out all our hot air?

"Go ahead, knock 'em dead, Jake." Edgar sensed my hesitation.

"All right. We have a talk show designed to do one thing. Make people laugh. Because it's not political, everybody is fair game, especially ourselves. In fact, maybe we should change the name of our show to the Radio Guys Laugh. How's that sound?"

Roxy flashed a thumbs-up. Edgar nodded. A possibility.

"That would be clear, unambiguous." Tony was writing like crazy. "Sounds like a decent idea. It's a big challenge, telling people you're going to make them laugh, then trying to deliver. I tried stand-up open-mic in college. Just a few times, enough to find out how terrifying it is."

"I don't think we would even consider that." Edgar added, emphatically. "Although, we are going to allow listeners to watch us through the front window while we're broadcasting. At least until Whiskey 'n Ribs slips us pink slips."

"Are they hiring you?"

"No. They agreed to give us a year of one-hour Saturday slots in their front window. No contract. Just handshakes. Saul Friedman set it up. He thinks highly of them. We had the same impression in our meetings. I think Edgar and I would agree that if we flopped, we wouldn't hold them to their commitment."

I meant this. I couldn't imagine being unwanted if we bombed then continued to embarrass ourselves on their premises. "I might consider housesitting in various remote locations in the world."

"So that adds some pressure, doesn't it? But you don't have to be financially successful with this, right?" Tony looked around at the three of us. I realized more acutely how close we were to our first live broadcast. I tried to shift my mind to the fact that we had a limited financial exposure in this whole thing. Unless of course, someone took us to court for something we said on air. Maybe I should reconsider the personal liability policy I canceled when I left the agency. I would call my insurance agent.

"That's true," said Edgar. "I guess we only have our own self-respect on the line. That's not nothing. But we concluded that not trying this was really more damaging to our egos than trying and failing."

"What kind of humor? Who would it most resemble? Who makes you guys laugh?"

Roxy raised her hand, "They're both funny guys. And they play off each other extremely well."

"Thank you, Roxy." I looked at Edgar for suggestions

"Without avoiding your question, there isn't anyone in particular that we're trying to emulate. There are so many great funny people. Maher, Colbert, Fey, Stewart, John Oliver, Silverman, Poehler, Bee. And on and on. Hey, Bob Newhart is still on occasionally. Probably some of the smartest people in the country are comedians. We're not even considering ourselves in their league. That in itself would be very funny. For some reason, I think we have something to offer. We'll know in a few weeks, won't we, Tony?"

Then I ticked off a few examples of our "breaking news" approach and he nodded approvingly. He asked a few more questions about our backgrounds, strangely inquiring if we had criminal records. Maybe he was looking for a shot on the Radio Guys Laugh. Maybe he was already laughing at our chances. At least I hope he was laughing.

When the article appeared one week from opening, we grabbed about fifty copies, thinking we'd find places to post the page with the two quarter-page features. *Radio Guys join Restaurant Guys in New Venture.* And, *Laugh While Dining.* Tony wrote an intriguing article, not promising what he didn't know. He admitted that none of us had criminal records and he thought we had great comedic heroes. The photo in the magazine, two photos side by side, taken from a perspective of us facing off: Us with headphones talking into our mics, facing off against cooks sipping with ladles from their pots.

Thanks, Tony.

Friday, July 14, 2017

Eight nut-tightening days, at least for Edgar and me, until we go live. The three of us shared a bottle of wine at Vendome for lunch. Then one more. It was lovely under the canvas awning, amidst pots of stunning flower arrangements and the mellow and cheerful voices entering the imminent weekend.

"We've had a good week," said Roxy. "We've come a long way. You two amaze me. I'm glad I saw the ad for Rex."

"I am too. We'd be scrambling for ways to back out of our contract without you."

"To us and to our big adventure." Edgar raised his glass after refilling all three.

Roxy leaned back, her wine glass resting in her lap, her face moving into the sunlight. "I think taking the afternoon off was brilliant. Then the weekend. It'll give you guys a chance to refresh. I'm going to paddle my own canoe. In this case a paddleboard. On the Chatfield Reservoir. Two girlfriends have been begging me to teach them." She was unfairly beautiful in a natural way. If it were a TV show we were embarking on, she'd be the only one on camera. Edgar and I would be her invisible off-camera sidekicks.

"What do you two need to do starting Monday?" she asked. "How soon can we rehearse at the restaurant?"

"I'm waiting to hear back. I called yesterday and asked if we could be there from Wednesday on, during their rehearsals for the Private Opening Friday. Make sure all the equipment works, including the outside speaker."

Edgar shifted in his chair. "I think we should finish our outline or script or whatever you call it by end of day, Monday. We need to time it, review it, revise it. Whatever. One question I have, Are we using any of the stuff we've recorded along the way?"

I answered, "I think we've got more than enough newer stuff to fill the show. What do you think Roxy?"

"I agree, but it's up to you. There have been some really good segments. You might think about that over the weekend. Maybe some of the intro ideas and the openers deserve to be looked at. Just so you two are very comfortable with how you begin. On the other hand, being nervous isn't all bad. Being flat is. So just prepare yourselves to succeed. It's a mental state. You guys have the ability, no question."

"Thank you." I tipped my glass to hers. "So we show up Monday morning with whatever our thoughts are and knock out an outline, right?"

"Right", said Edgar. Roxie nodded confidently.

As we stood to leave, she opened the shopping bag on the ground and handed us smaller bags filled with our oversized business cards, counter tents and the mini posters with our "Who *does Clint Eastwood listen to?*" campaign.

"Start handing these out tomorrow. I have lots more ready at the studio. Oh, I forgot to tell you. The Radio Guys Talk now has a website and a Facebook page. So long, boys."

I took my time walking home. The sidewalks became busier with rushing folks escaping offices, heading to their favorite watering holes or seeking transportation out of downtown. I headed toward Panzanos for a Tin Cup Manhattan. Friday afternoon is one of my favorite times to be living in this growing, robust city, one that offers sunshine most any day of the year.

Monday, July 17, 2017

Ten AM. We all show up with visible effects of spending at least part of the weekend outside, the Colorado sun intense enough to generously employ SPF 30. I had arrived ten minutes earlier in time to make coffee and cut in fourths a variety of donuts.

"I want you to know that my bag of promo materials is gone. All our biz cards included. My wife did her share, more than half, so I need to reload." Edgar was quite pleased with the effort. "It was interesting how people looked at the stuff, then turned to me to ask questions: What is this all about? Are you part of the show? I admit it felt good to say yes to that question."

"I'm out, too. I think the stuff we posted looked good, Roxy."

"Well, you guys wrote it. And I have more in my car." Roxy stood, lifting her coffee, "I suggest we move into that old conference room. There's a huge white board on the wall and we can outline all the segments of our first one-hour. Put as much down as we can, stand back and take a hard look."

We followed her, toting the plates with donuts. I could

already feel the coffee/sugar surge. Under the fluorescent lights of the shabby room with the long Formica table, dappled with numerous cigarette burns from the pre clean-air era, Edgar and I sat while Roxie marked the white board into twelve five-minute spaces. "Why don't you two give me ideas of what goes in each space, starting with the beginning. Just to see what we've got. We can erase and move things around. I think this will give you a better idea of how much we can squeeze into each five-minute slot. Get an idea of pacing, what follows what most easily.

"I like it." I nodded. "Could you type it up for us?"

"That's my plan. We can make adjustments each day up to Friday. That'll give us two days rehearsing it."

"And you're still thinking that Jake and I won't know all of the items we'll be reacting to?" Edgar bent his face like the whole notion of us not knowing was dangerous.

"I still do. There have to be a few things you might not be specifically prepared for. Like in the listener question segments or the Breaking News segments, for example."

I thought about this, too. We'd done this a number of times during the rehearsals, Roxy slipping us fast ones. Mixed results, but also I got her point. Faked surprise is not complete surprise. At this point I was OK with it. "Let's do it."

We proceeded, beginning with, of course, Intro and Welcome. Roxy wrote in a just legible size, making sure we included every little thing that came to mind. It seemed like a lot for five minutes, but after about twenty minutes we began to consolidate.

There was the welcome, the introduction of we three, the rather loose ground rules of the show, most specifically the "political free zone", and the thanks to the folks at Whiskey 'n Ribs for risking their reputation and their future on their association with our profoundly untested and unproven experiment.

We were filing our flight plan.

By one o'clock we'd finished slotting segments in each space. Eventually we could see how to best sequence them, sometimes with a specific title or a script idea, like where we ask the audience questions: "What's the biggest con you've gotten away with, ever?"

After our lunch break, we worked on segues of all kinds, planned or unplanned, rescues and escapes. Roxy said if we get comfortable with the various ways to move along, so we can do it unconsciously, then we can handle the unexpected, figuring there would be those moments that would require brilliant and necessary rescues. She took us through possibilities such as when our mics go out, brain freezes, coughing jags, dry mouth, potty breaks, stumbling on pronunciations, fainting, our outlines falling to the floor, sneezing eruptions, even a drug bust outside our show window.

We learned that sometimes just laughing out loud at some loss of control or composure was the most natural thing to do. Hey, we're just rookies in this business.

As we walked out the door, Roxy reminded us that the burst of radio ads on Pandora and Spotify had begun that very morning with the two recorded commercials we'd done for *"What's so and so listening to?* In this case: Madonna and Yogi Berra. "Be careful, who knows how many people you'll run into will ask if you're the Radio Guys?" She was extremely optimistic. Or just makin' up shit.

We laughed. The first workday of launch week was under our belts.

Tuesday, July 18, 2017

Although I caught several of our radio ads on Pandora and

spotted a few of our flyers posted in coffee shops and various grocers and retailers, none of us were accosted on the streets by curious potential fans demanding autographs. Why should we be surprised? You have no idea how much media exposure is required to wedge your way into someone's consciousness. Besides, our promo spots had no pictures. Remember, we had faces for radio.

But, I thought the spots were good, and maybe they'd catch on over time.

In studio, with Roxy's printed notes and a rough outline, we went to work. At her suggestion we used the outline first, with no notes to flesh out the segments. It was frustrating. We were trying to do it essentially from memory. We were terrible. She said she expected that, and we stumbled through again, with little improvement.

Then she gave us our more extensive notes including some segments fully written out. It was so much easier and I could see why she'd put us through the utter frustration. When we were done, we loaded all our gear into Edgar's wagon and unloaded it at the restaurant, covering everything with plastic to shield from dust and other contaminants that still filled the air.

We continued passing out counter cards and business cards with our show times to anyone we encountered.

Wednesday, July 19,2017

We were impressed walking through from the back entrance, two painters were doing touch up work, fans were blowing fumes out the front and back doors. It was spit and polish beautiful, imaginative design to the detail, gloss you could see your face in. The bartender and her assistant were carefully arranging the booze on the backlit shelves, with the working bottles on the first level all along. A great track of beach trance pulsed through the space.

Roxy immediately focused on her equipment, checking connections, testing sound volumes, positioning mics. I unrolled the red velour backdrop with our logo centered just above our heads when we were seated. Gold letters were sewn onto the fabric, ready to be draped from a crossbar on Saturday morning.   Next I checked the two easels placed right inside the window glass displaying posters announcing our show, the time and the station. There was already a large silk banner in place at window center announcing Whiskey 'n Ribs Grand Opening Saturday.

Things were coming together.

"What say we go through a few random segments; we might as well get used to the equipment in the new space?" Roxy opened her arms to the table where everything was in place, inviting us to be seated, hidden from view from the restaurant by the red banner.

Below the window was the drilled opening where we could slide our cord to the outdoor speakers during the broadcast. There was a clever closure on the opening to keep out the weather and bugs post show, depending upon the season.

"Well done, Roxy. This is terrific." I said.

"Couldn't be better," added Edgar. Can you believe it? We're really organized, right? And still there's time to refine any potential glitches."

Edgar was right on both counts. But could you ever prepare for all contingencies in the real world?

We began at the beginning: Edgar welcoming listeners and window gawkers to THE RADIO GUYS TALK.

Thursday, July 20, 2017

The day before the Whiskey 'n Ribs private opening Friday evening, and two mornings before our twelve-noon launch, we arrived at nine AM. The kitchen and wait staff and bartenders were moving at high speed, the smells from the kitchen were intoxicating, the orders shouting out loud and clear. Cooks in white, wait-staff in black with black fedoras. One of the managers was handing out red nametags clipped to a large board where they all hung. Each waitperson was taking a brief oath to return them to the board before leaving. They were laughing about it, but you could tell it was dead serious. There was an air of competence and professionalism about the operation.

We spent the next hour listening to rumbling bass tracks Roxy had put together. We were thinking of something that was arresting, with an energizing beat, perhaps a suggestion of jaws, without causing someone to go into panic attack, and, when Roxy lowered the volume, we could talk over it and be understood. We went through Duane Eddy, Pearl Jam, I am the Resurrection by Stone Roses, and others.

In two hours we'd all agreed on a two-minute bass track. As a reward, we stood and watched over our backdrop into the restaurant. The entire crew was moving in a tight order drill, commands effortlessly given and received, waiters pushing through the two, one-way swinging doors. Appetizers, entrees and sides being delivered, empties being stacked and returned to the kitchen. Cocktails reordered, wine poured, water refilled, questions answered, desserts recommended and ordered. Effortless hustle, a tray dropped and immediately attended to, bills asked for, cards given, questions about the bills, questions about the service, compliments, a customer sick, almost fainting, the two owners, checking each table, thanking the customers, gently asking for feedback, tell your friends if you liked what you ate.

This was a crack team of many. Sedulous but relaxed, ready and willing, customer is always right, we're here to make this the most relaxing, enjoyable, savory and memorable eating-out experience of your lifetime. No exceptions.

Did we have as much chance of success as they did? It was just a nagging tic in my eye. Insistent. We faced each other with a kind of bulging-eyed *EGAD!* expression.

Friday, July 21, 2017

Friday was their day. Whiskey 'n Ribs would unveil itself to their invited guests at their private evening opening. We elected to stay away and not be a distraction.

We decided to stay apart from each other as well. Saturday the 22nd would come soon enough; we would show up at eight AM. I do think we had prepared in earnest. Were we too old to be nervous? I wish. I think I walked ten miles through the downtown area later that day. I took a pocket size notebook and a pen in case I recalled something important. I handed out more cards and posted more mini-posters. I don't recall much else, probably because my mind was someplace else. Twice I thought about calling Edgar, to see how he was doing. I thought better of that idea; we're both old enough to know what we needed, and we would ask for it if we were concerned. Roxy was paddle-boarding on the Cherry Creek Reservoir with her girlfriends. My mission for the day was to get a good night's sleep. Predictably, like the old days before a major presentation, my mind roared through the night, relenting for a mere two hours during which I stole some uneasy sleep.

I retured at ten. Those two hours began about four AM.

PART II

In the beginning, it was just a crazy idea.
It was crazier to think we could pull it off.

Jacob Finnegan

Saturday, July 22, 2017

Two young men were setting the chairs down from the table-tops when we pushed through the back entry on Saturday morning. The private-opening flower arrangements were still looking fresh and colorful and the two women behind the bar were polishing glasses as they were pulled from the dishwashers.

We walked through carrying our stuff: folders, brief cases and our shirts and blazers on hangers. We greeted the staff as nonchalantly as anyone following the priest from his cell to the gallows, although I doubt anyone with that destination would be forcing fake smiles like Edgar and me. Roxy wore a white blouse and, looking smart and sexy, a fabulous pair of jeans.

Once we'd set up, moved the Grand Opening sign to the side, checked the sound system, the phone, and the folders of paperwork we carried, we took a pit-stop while Roxy unveiled the croissants and coffee she'd picked up on the way in.

Talking in our non-radio voices, we carefully went through the show script. It was difficult to not use the volume and tempo we'd been working with for almost three months. In fact it was scary; nothing sounded very funny when we said it in calm, laidback voices. I was relieved when we tossed our pencils on the table, nothing more to note.

I can't remember exactly how we bided our time for the next hour and a half, but I do know I questioned the whole cockamamie notion that we could pull off what we said we were going to pull off.

And then it was 11:45, finally, and the clock was noticeably speeding up. Roxy was talking to us through our headphones as she straightened our collars and tugged our blazers into place.

"You guys look absolutely terrific! This is going to be great!"

And then there were five minutes to go. Then three. Then one. No more shuffling papers. We fumbled with how to fold our hands and watched the curiosity seekers pause while strolling past, some coming up for a closer look, others standing by the curb as though they didn't dare approach this cage of monkeys during feeding time. Our bass track announced the shift in reality: From practice to performance

"Ten seconds, boys." Roxy, all business. "Five, four . . . Edgar!"

Edgar: Good morning, Denver. And welcome to a brand new Radio Adventure. You are listening to The Radio Guys Talk. He's Jake and I'm Edgar. And for those of you in our live audience, there's Roxy, the eye candy and the brains that drive this whole show.

So far, so good.

ME: Thank you all for tuning in to AM 1480 or coming out to Whiskey 'n Ribs, the fabulous new eating establishment on Larimer between Fifteenth and Sixteenth. We're right in the front window and if you're anywhere downtown, head on over.

EDGAR: Well, Jake, I see several of our friends loitering outside in front, and a few of the new friends we met while putting this show together over on Gaylord and in the AM 1480

Studio. And quite a few new faces, welcome. It looks multi-generational to me, that's good, right Jake? (Edgar waves to the several in front who can hear us, though we're limited to lip-reading.)

ME: *It's just what we'd hoped for. All comers are welcome.*

It's also apparent that Saul delivered on his efforts to alert the media; there are three TV crews with their mobile sky dishes, reporters and cameramen right out front. It must be a very slow news day.

EDGAR: *Maybe you can explain exactly what this show is all about, Jake.*

ME: *First let me mention that Whiskey 'n Ribs, who have generously, and fearlessly, you could say, welcomed us to broadcast from their front window each Saturday from noon to one . . . is one exceptional restaurant. Come in for lunch, or dinner. Happy Hour at four. If you go inside you'll see the backs of our heads, which some say is our best side.*

EDGAR: *And just what is our show, anyway?*

ME: *Well, it's a talk show. Between us and between you and us. We don't have many rules, but there is ONE. This show is a political-free zone. A safe haven from politics. That's right. We decided there's enough of that going on elsewhere. And, we're pretty tired of it. Maybe you are, too.*

So, instead of pitting us against each other, Edgar and me, you and us, making us edgy, grouchy, irritable, or even rageful, our intention is to make you laugh. That's right. Laugh. At us. At yourselves, at others. That means everyone is fair game. Except for politicians.

EDGAR: *That's taking a lot of material off the table, Jake. Can we get away with it?*

ME: *I think I see some heads outside nodding in approval, Edgar. A sure sign of enlightenment, don't you think?*

EDGAR: *I think you're right. And don't forget to mention*

that anyone dropping by can fill out a coupon with your name and email address. The winner at the end of each show receives a coupon for a free double-shot of their top-shelf craft whisky to use any day of the week.

At this moment Roxy reaches over, sliding a sheet of paper in front of me with the heading: BREAKING NEWS! I hold it up toward the window then quickly turn it back and begin reading.

ME: OK, Roxy has handed me a Breaking News announcement and here it is: BREAKING NEWS: NEW STUDY REVEALS THAT IT'S ALWAYS RAINING SOMEWHERE. Let me repeat. (I repeat).

EDGAR: Hmmm. You're saying 24/7? 365? Right?

ME: That's how I read it. Breaking News.

EDGAR: Well, is that a Meteorological law or something?

ME: Isn't Meteorology what the weathermen and women study? And aren't they wrong about half the time?

EDGAR: That's what I'm thinking. So maybe it's raining only about half the time 24/7, 365. And, why do we listen to the weather reports, then? Do you, Jake?

ME: Only when I'm thinking of playing golf. You, Edgar?

EDGAR: Only when I'm cooking out. So you don't play golf if there's a chance of rain?

ME: Oh, sure I play. I just wear a rain jacket.

EDGAR: So maybe this study should state that it's always raining somewhere in the world, at least half the time.

ME: Weather forecasting is fraught with error. We know that for certain. Was this really Breaking News, Roxy?

ROXY: I just pass on what's handed to me. Maybe we should move on. We're not getting very far, are we? Does it look like rain outside, Edgar?

EDGAR: A chance, maybe. But I'm not cooking out today, anyway.

It's then that I notice Edgar squinting frontward, into our gathering crowd.

EDGAR: I'm watching a pretty woman outside who seems to be pushing her way to the window. Boy, she's intent on breaking through. Careful out there.

Then I search the crowd. And, forcing her way, jumping and waving, twisting and elbowing to the window . . . is Carly.

ME: Sweet Jesus, Edgar, it's Carly. (I mumbled almost inaudibly.)

And, finally, she's pressing her hand against the window, turning her hand over to expose a ginormous diamond, the size of a Smart Car, on her forth finger left hand.

She yells something that I can't hear, but how can I not read the way her beautiful lips form the words, "Hi Jake! How's it going?" I wave sheepishly at Carly, Carly with her full, stunning smile. She widens her eyes and tilts her head and I lip-read: "Thank you, Jake!" Then she turns and twists her way back through our adoring fans, by now thoroughly annoyed, and enters the area between the curbs where she proceeds to skip in a large circle waving her hand in the air and eventually bringing the slow- moving traffic to a halt.

Of course, all news cameras present have turned from our front window to the much more fascinating breaking news on the street. A few seconds pass, then one polite tap on a horn, then a couple more, and now we have a car-horn brass section blasting everyone outside to cover their ears. We have no difficulty hearing the horns through the heavy plate window. Holy shit!

I smile wanly, trying to catch my breath. I turn to Roxy for help. Is it time to retrieve our interview with the new Sub Minister of Economic Withdrawal in The UK, Camilla Thistlepink Birtwistle?

We are well into panic mode. I am recalling the half

written letter of apology on my desk at home, urged by my therapist, procrastinated by yours truly. I'm aware that everything seems to be slowing down in my mind. What I see is in slo-mo. And my hearing shuts down. I glance at Roxy as she is rapidly issuing commands that I can't hear. Edgar is nodding his head in slow motion, eyes on our street circus.

And then I see Carly moving slowly to the front of the blocked cars. One-by-one the horns back off. She stands directly in front. She raises her index finger to her lips in the Big Silence sign, gently nodding her head. Then she forms her hands together in the Namaste position, slowly bows, then yells to the many stalled and perplexed drivers, "Thank You. Peace Out!" She turns, jumps onto the far sidewalk, and casts one rainbow shaped wave at us. She then resumes skipping down the sidewalk out of sight.

The crowd begins cheering at the non-interpretable event that just graced the first fifteen minutes of our first broadcast. The cars slowly creep forward, honking lightly and politely, the drivers with something to pass on to whomever they encounter the rest of the day.

Edgar heroically marches on.

EDGAR: Hey Jake, who was that babe with the engagement ring directing traffic out front? She sure looked like she was talking to you. Didn't she say Thank you, Jake? Did you have something to do with that ring? Did you ask her to marry you?

ME: Well, uh, no I didn't. Yeah she was someone I know. Yes, she was really excited, wasn't she? (I might as well have been drooling or sucking on a lemon.)

As my mind is returning to present sense, I hear Roxy in my headphone attempting to fill the several-minute dead space on our broadcast, informing listeners that an unexpected activity was occurring a glass window away from our restaurant studio, causing a traffic jam and blasting the air with horns. It doesn't look like anyone is being threatened. An attractive blonde is celebrating something or other. Then urging Edgar to break with a message from one of our sponsors.

I look at Edgar, who was running his finger up and down the first page of our show outline. Finally finding a separate sheet that flutters in his hands as he pours over the script.

ME: *Okay then, Edgar, tell us who is bringing our listeners the first quarter hour of The Radio Guys Talk.*

EDGAR: *Perfect timing. We are brought to you by Nefertiti Cosmetics, the magical ultra hydra makeup with the mystical ingredients that adorned and preserved the Queen of the Nile. Today it is their ground-breaking facial makeup, containing not only pigment polishers and ultra defoliants, but also mosquito repellent for your undistracted enjoyment of all outdoor activities, from hiking to biking, and from picnicking to rolling in the hay. Is that right, Roxy?* (Roxy smirks.) *So, keep the mosquitos at bay, and attract the men to stay. Nefertiti Cosmetics and Shampoos. Say, Jake, wasn't Elizabeth Taylor Nefertiti? In the movie, I mean?*

I have regained full motion of my mouth by now. I'm seeing in real time, and praying my muscle memory has returned my voice to it's normal octave. Sweet Jesus, this might be our last show. The clock set in front of us reads: 12:23. It seems like we should be wrapping up.

ME: *I think you're right, Edgar.*

Roxy continues the bailing operation.

ROXY: *Thank you Edgar. So, I just want to inform our listeners who are wondering if we planned all the events we've experienced already. No. Absolutely not. Like we promised you, this is live, improvisational more than scripted, and, well, we hope you're enjoying it.*

ME: *Roxy speaks the truth. Had we planned all this, several men in white coats would be escorting us to an emergency vehicle that just arrived out front. Meanwhile, it appears that camera crews from three TV stations will just love running some of their footage later. I warn you to keep your children from watching.*

I can feel eyes burning into the back of my head. I turn around in my seat and look up. I am right. In addition to one of the reporters with a mic held downward, Sebastian, one of the owners, is staring into our "booth". His bewildered, strained grin begs an explanation. I open my mouth and no explanation escapes my lips. I return his pained grin with an equally pained expression. I turn back to The Great Unraveling.

EDGAR: *Well, Jake, things seem to have settled down. Thank you, Roxy, for deftly finessing the unexpected. Perhaps we'll have a clearer explanation from Jake later about what just happened. She sure was happy to see him.*

I gave Edgar a feeble cut-off sign across my neck. Then I heard Roxie in my headphones: "Let's try another Breaking News."

ME: *So, all you listeners out there, are you with us?* (a majority chorused, Yeah! Which was easy to read.) *Wonderful. And I've just been alerted by Roxy that we have another BREAKING NEWS. The only news you'll hear that you can really trust. Guaranteed to be true. That's right.*

As I pray that Roxie has a good reason for ANOTHER Breaking News, I reach for the paper that she extends to me and glance over it.

ME: *Thank you, Roxy. So, here goes: BREAKING NEWS! THE UNITED STATES IS NOT AT WAR WITH BELGIUM! That's right, WE ARE NOT AT WAR WITH BELGIUM!*

EDGAR: *Well, that's a relief, Jake. You know that brings*

up the question: When was the last war the United States won?

I tilt my head, glance at the window for inspiration, consider whether this crosses the political boundaries, and throw my hands up as I shrug.

ME: I'm pretty sure we won a war in Grenada. You know the one we conquered with our Air Force and Special Forces?

EDGAR: You might be right there, Jake. I guess we should avoid any political innuendos, right? I mean it seems like we've been in lots of wars since then."

ME: Let's just savor the victory in Grenada. What's next Roxy?

ROXY: OK, boys, this is where we ask our listeners questions. We'd like to know what our listeners are thinking. What they've got going on in their lives?

ME: So we have selected three questions. And you just have to answer them. For those who send their answers in, we'll select the most interesting answers and read them on the air next Saturday. Of course, that assumes there will be a next Saturday for The Radio Guys Laugh.

ROXY: Not to worry, Jake. We'll be back! For you listeners, if you want us to know your answers, mail them to The Radio Guys Talk, PO BOX 9797 Denver, Colorado, 80214. So Edgar, what's our first question?

EDGAR: Here it is: What is the biggest con you've ever pulled off? Hmm. Are we talking about Ponzi Schemes here?

ME: Not necessarily. And, if you don't want your name read, just make a note of it. We're not trying to bring down another Bernie Madoff. Just something you've pulled off that you'd like us to know about. Consider it an opportunity to confess. Maybe you're a twin who switched places with your twin on a date? Or on his or her wedding day? Whoa! Or you pulled a con on your Match.com dating page. Big or small, we're interested. We're not interested in your police record. Or, those things you weren't caught doing that were criminal acts.

EDGAR: Unless you think they're funny, of course.

ME: Here's the next question: Why do worms come up out of the ground? Boy, that's a science question, isn't it? These are questions for any age, aren't they? Ask your kids.

EDGAR: There are no rules, about these questions. Otherwise we wouldn't ask them. So let's hear your take on why worms come up out of the ground?

ME: That leaves one more question. And, here it is: What job do you wish you'd pursued, but didn't? So, kind of a regret question, right?

EDGAR: I always wish I'd been a bartender for a while. Engineering didn't quite give me the laughs I would have enjoyed. In fact, I could still do that, couldn't I? I could teach these younger bartenders how to make a real cocktail. An Old-Fashioned, the old fashioned way. Not these Frou-Frou drinks with eleven ingredients they're taught today. Same with a Manhattan.

ME: Let me know when you get that job, Edgar. I'll bring my retired barfly friends in for a test. OK, that's our three questions for listeners this week. What's the biggest con you've pulled off? Why do worms come up out of the ground? And, What job do you wish you'd tried? Send your answers to The Radio Guys Laugh, PO Box 9797, Denver 80214.

ROXY: Looks like some of our live audience is scrambling to write down our address. I think they have something to say.

It seems like we're back on track. All of Roxy's possibilities for problems that we'd prepared for hadn't included the doozy we'd absorbed.

And then we heard the scuffling back in the restaurant. Dishes crashed, a couple of women shrieked, someone yelled, "Grab him!" I tried to ignore the escalating commotion, we had a fucking radio program to do, and, unlike all the rehearsing we'd done, you couldn't just start over on this one.

ME: (A bit uncertain of myself) *So, the next segment of our show, by the way, is brought to you by* **Patriot Pill & Pea Splitters.** Hmmm . . . so this is a combination splitter I'm guessing. One splitter does it all.

EDGAR: *I think this show is giving me a **splitting headache.** Could this **Patriot Splitter** cure my headache?*

ME: *Why not, Edgar? It says" multiple uses" on the package. Hey, could it also include shooting? Pill shooting? Pea shooting? It states right here: Fast, easy and foolproof. Do your splitting the **Patriot** way.*

EDGAR: *That's reassuring, Jake. Well, this brings us to our new product discovery section. We're constantly on the lookout..* . another crash. Another yell to "Watch out, he's got a gun." And the extended noises that could only mean people were diving for cover. Edgar resumed . . .

And today our new product is: **Mousetrap Reloader.** *It says here . . . it is designed to help you reset a mousetrap after it has smooshed a mouse, and it's . . .*

And then the squad cars squealed to a stop out front.

I could walk you through what happened, blow by blow, from a looking back perspective. And I will, at some point. Let me just say proudly, we managed to keep the Radio Guys Talk broadcasting throughout the next fifteen minutes, including the chaos as the cops subdued three men who had entered the rear exit and had begun grabbing women's purses and men's wallets until two of the women on the wait-staff and one of the owners, and a cook with an eight-inch carving knife, and then a couple of diners took them on. The gun proved to be intimidating, but not effective, and no shots were fired. We continued to broadcast while watching the police march the robbers out the door in cuffs, and hustle them into squad cars. There was a roar of approval from the inside customers, and then a roar from the outside listeners, some of whom were interviewed by officers until it was established that no one out front had seen anything happen. There were still eight minutes of our show yet to broadcast. We'd gone through the resetting of mousetraps, an interview with the Assistant Hockey Coach of The East High School women's hockey team explaining why girls can be more than goalies, a weather report from the hottest city on the planet, an announcement for our coming new segment on morons, oxy-morons, that is, and we were beginning our third interruption for Breaking News.

I read the sheet handed to me by Roxy.

ME: BREAKING NEWS, here it is, folks. CONTRARY TO CONVENTIONAL WISDOM, POLLS SHOW THAT PEOPLE IN THEIR FORTIES ARE OUTLIVING PEOPLE IN THEIR FIFTIES. Hmmm. Let me read that again. (I did.) *Does that sound right, Edgar?*

EDGAR: Why not? They're younger. They haven't died yet. Sure.

ME: But more could happen to them before they die, right? EDGAR: Maybe we should put that up on our listener poll. We can do that can't we Roxie? See what our listeners think?

Roxy: I'm on it. So you can respond to The Radio Guys Listener Poll by simply going to our website: radioguys.com. Click on the poll section and type in your comment and press send. We'll settle this question, won't we Edgar? Jake?

ME: I hope so. It looks like our live audience outside has some thoughts on this. They're waving frantically, but we can't hear them. It appears that all but one of the police vehicles has pulled away out front.

We briefly inform our listening audience there was some major action taking place on the other side of the curtains behind us while we continued our broadcast.

ME: We'll have more to tell you next week about the

extraordinary events that have taken place within our very first broadcast. Provided I'm off my meds and released from interrogation and whatever else is necessary to right my mental ship. You listeners in the Denver area will probably see and hear lots about this later today. There was enough media activity down here to cover the Invasion of Normandy.

EDGAR: That's for sure. The good thing is, no one was hurt. And you listeners and the gang out front have stayed with us. That's very gratifying. What's next, Roxy?

As Roxy guided us into the last minutes, I looked up and recognized, how could you not, Saul Friedman, staring at us from the near curb, duded up with a yellow double-breasted sport coat, a purple fedora cocked slavishly and a lavender ascot tucked into a purple dress shirt with a white collar.

We'd gotten a call from his nurse in the ER Friday evening; he'd broken his foot during a Tango lesson at the Merc Café and was unlikely to make it to our first broadcast.

But there he is.

He raises an aluminum crutch, leans back and lifts his encased right leg just high enough for two camera crews to spot him. (Saul never misses a chance to be caught on camera.) He smiles and pumps his left thumb. Is it possible he actually enjoyed the chaotic opening of our first show? Or is he relieved that his accident prevented him from damaging his reputation with a guest appearance.

I wave back and join Edgar in the wrap-up.

EDGAR: We'll join you again next Saturday at noon, don't forget. Stop in at Whiskey 'n Ribs. The food is fantastic and there's always something exciting going on. He raises his arms and waves to the outsiders who return the farewell.

ME: That's right. Have a great week! Tell your friends. Live high or die. Thank you, Roxie for saving our bacon.

Then, as the bass track rumbles, we three slumped.

Edgar removed his headphones and held them in his lap. I rubbed my eyes, as if to erase a scary dream. Roxy crossed her arms, tilted her head and exclaimed, "That was one fucking radio talk show. All I can say is, one fantastic fucking recovery, boys!"

I shook my head slowly, "Was it really a recovery? Or did we merely slow the sinking of the Titanic?"

Edgar broke into a giddy, coughing laugh. "Who was that gal with the big rock, Jake? You've got some splainin' to do."

"Yes, Jake. I've never seen you unravel like that. This oughta be good."

Roxy remained with her arms still crossed over her chest, but her grin was evil and about to erupt.

"If I told you I needed to go feed my parking meter, could we cover this later?" I lamely offered.

Patient silence. The only noises came from the restaurant where the chatter was lively, the laughter was cutting loose, and the two owners were leaning over the red curtain, grinning down at the exhausted Radio Guys crew. My gaze around our "studio" revealed a diorama of unidentified alien species.

"Absolutely amazing," said the one called Sebastian.

"Don't tell me you guys planned all that?" chuckled Rocco. "We can't handle all the people who have come in to eat. We're giving free drinks if they'll return later. Can you believe the PR we're getting. Did you see all those cameras?"

"We want some of the same stuff you've been drinking. Or, smoking." Sebastian turned to handle a couple customers who wanted to have menus signed and dated.

"So, we're not fired? Canceled?" I asked cautiously. I was frankly disabled with neuron warfare within my brain and body. I was also reaching for a temporary lifeline to escape having to *splain* the Carly saga, truthfully. I'd prefer a skillful rewrite of the entire episode: My innocence or simple misunderstanding run amok.

Rocco laughed, "As long as no one was hurt. I don't think we could have paid enough to hire a band or a circus or a low flying airplane doing barrel rolls down the Sixteenth Street Mall with banners and smoke trails at two hundred feet, and have this kind of impact. Positive impact. I mean, our staff, especially the two women who jumped these guys, is being interviewed and filmed for features on the news tonight. They are heroes. And like I said, so many of those outside are trying to get seats. This is how legends are born."

"So we're not canceled?" I was still processing Rocco's exaltations. I looked to Edgar and Roxy in disbelief. They both shrugged, like *OKAY, no problem. Contract extension accepted and signed.*

"And we're just hitting our stride, I think," teased Edgar. "Always a little rusty the first time out. It's what we expected, sort of."

"Nice going, folks. Good PR, huh?" Next to Rocco, the unforgettable face, with a hand in a yellow sleeve, touching the brim of his purple fedora, was the smiling face of Saul Friedman, the man who brought out the media in numbers that far exceeded the anticipated importance of the opening of a restaurant and the inaugural broadcast of rookies on a low watt, almost defunct radio station.

"All in a days work," Saul knew he had delivered big time. "I had a hard time finding guys to pull a fake holdup though. Something about potential gunfire. I'll try to spice it up when I'm on your show next week."

The purple hat backed away

"So he was kidding about the hold-up, wasn't he?" asked Rocco. "He just told us he'd leaned on a couple stations to send out reporters."

"You never know what you'll get with PR. But you know you'll get something with Saul." I said with an affirming nod. "Hey, it was his doing that connected you and us in the first place. That's something we would have never come up with. Don't hold it against him."

It was all true. And we're still standing. Or sitting, on our chairs. Heartbeats slowing down. In a makeshift window studio, our first broadcast, signed off. With an hour of mischief, chaos, humor, and whatever else occurred, to digest, and later lie awake replaying in-between nightmares.

Later in the weekend.

The media did not disappoint. In one way or another, the Sunday Post and the Saturday TV news splashed the slow news weekend with excessive coverage of the Grand Opening hi-jinx. The paper had two articles, one titled: *Grand Opening Stops Traffic.* The other, *Waitresses Overpower Robbery Attempt.*

Channel 8 focused on an unidentified woman with suspected connections never revealed, carrying out some ritual or celebration that stopped traffic in front of Whiskey 'n Ribs, a brand new restaurant in downtown Denver during their grand opening on Saturday. The reporter linked this event to the radio broadcast inside the front window of the restaurant that seemed to be gathering an agitated crowd on the sidewalk. Again, that was unexplained, except that no blood was shed. Readers were left to imagine a standoff something on the level of the 1917 Russian Revolution.

In the second article, the waitresses overpowered the robbers, *unfortunately* without a shot being fired. And the three thwarted robbers were led quietly in cuffs to the paddy wagon. In one paragraph our broadcast was described as a misdirected attempt to hype the grand opening, absent giant inflatable creatures beaconing passersby to check out the menu. I thought about writing the editor and asking for an acknowledgement of our show's name and broadcast schedule. I set that notion aside. What's the point?

We fared better on TV although most of the footage was on Carly's escapades. She wasn't identified. And, oddly, the camera crews didn't chase her down. Maybe because she was obviously in good shape and obviously faster than a crew running with all the gear. They didn't quite connect her to our broadcast other than showing her elbowing and thrashing her way to and away from our window.

After the arrest of the thieves, there was an attempt to get a comment from Roxy and she deftly deflected any knowledge with a shrug and a great and helpless smile. Edgar and I were ignored by all. Praise the Lord.

The good news: So far the traffic-stopping woman was unidentified. And, we were green-lighted for a second show.

Monday, July 24, 2017

I had, with uncanny foresight, made an appointment with my guru/shrink, Jan, for the Monday morning following our inauguaral broadcast. I was hoping we could share the laughs and rave reviews of our first show. Maybe she could talk me down from a lofty ego trip. Or tell me she was ready to leave her fantastic boyfriend just to be with an emerging media star. Not so fast, Jake. Obviously, our conversation would be more complicated than that.

For one thing, she recalled hearing Edgar question me, on air, about the woman flashing the engagement ring at me through the window and then proceeding to stop traffic and orchestrate it's resumption, on her terms. She also commented on the change in my voice during that episode, and my silence as Roxy took over in explanation of what was happening. I couldn't get away with being on a potty break, or collapsing from food poisoning, though I considered both strategies.

"Of course that had nothing to do with the woman you asked to marry you, did it, Jake? The one you were going to apologize to?" Her smile and vocal tone blended a balance of kindness with the reminder of an adult scolding an adult child with tender reassurance. Of course I was embarrassed.

"I started writing the letter. Actually it was half done." Weak.

"She's quite a woman, Jake. Very attractive from what I saw on the news. Maybe a good thing she wasn't interviewed."

"Amen. You're right about that. I guess I'm lucky that the back-story didn't leak. Her story. About my antics. None of those reporters chased her down. But it's only a matter of time, don't you think?"

"Maybe. How fast can you deliver your apology to her?"

"Pretty fast. I have a big incentive, don't I?"

"Well, unless, you want to ride this incident into follow-up stories in all the media about the wild life and excesses of the new talk show host in Denver. Notoriety could boost ratings, right? Or spoil the laid back image you guys are attempting to portray. You are trying to pass off as stable adults, are you not?"

Jan coughed in her hand, enjoying my predicament just a wee bit.

"I'll pursue the apology route, immediately. Maybe it will work. Maybe her fiancé will prefer some anonymity for the two of them. Maybe."

With time of the essence, we ended the session early, after some talk about the show. Excepting the Carly incident, she was very positive about the parts of the show in which I was present and accountable.

"The three of you are made for each other on air. You can tell you like each other, you're all very adept at what you're doing, especially given your inexperience. You're likeable, too. Frankly I was impressed. And you'll get better."

"Thanks for listening, Jan. And for treating me with kid gloves this morning. On with my feeble and tardy apology."

Home at my desk I read through the unfinished letter of regret, quickly springing to mind all the unplanned events that earthquaked our first show. It was no longer a question of nerve to contact Carly, it seemed like a combination of cover-up and salvage pled into a written ceasefire.

Then I calculated the amount of time to get to her place, the strong possibility she'd not be home, the ticking of the clock, and the growing possibility in my mind that some ambitious reporter was leaving no stone unturned trying to unearth a scoop.

I reread my letter, signed it, and called her cell phone. Once again I got her voice mail. Once again her message to leave a message and a number. And then: *And if by chance this is Jake, I think I already thanked you. I had been sitting with a marriage proposal from a very fine gentleman when I agreed to see you. You proceeded to insult me, but you caused me to think about the man who had asked me to marry him after really getting to know me. I called him and thanked him and told him I was wearing his ring. For that I say thank you, Jake.*

Ouch! Not only did it sting, it was humiliating. It didn't take me long to phone back, listen to her condemning personal message once again, wondering how many others had or would hear it, and apologize in every way I knew how. It was a no win for me, unless it caused me to look at my own behavior, again. But I did mention that she caused quite a bit of excitement Saturday, and she looked beautiful as she conducted her horn orchestra, and I didn't blame her, and I deserved every intended comeuppance, and I pleaded with her, begged her, to remove her voicemail addendum as an expression of mercy. Then I walked my letter across town to her mailbox.

I never called back to see about the voice mail. She never called back to accept my apology. My next days would take me at unexpected moments to review my location on the chart of human evolution.

Wednesday, July 26, 2017

Our trio continued preparation for our second Saturday broadcast. We'd assigned ourselves the task of writing new ideas and content on our own. I was relieved because it postponed my interrogation about the Engagement Ring Mystery. In the midst of the stress of anticipating a follow up article or mention on TV about the woman who stopped traffic, I had dreamed up numerous explanations that placed me in a better light. Than the truth.

However, when we sat facing each other in the studio, I couldn't come up with anything as preposterous as the truth, which they most likely wouldn't believe anyway. Nor would they abandon inquiry. They nodded with each sticky admission.

"So go over that part you skipped, Jake, the why-you-did-it part, your proposal," Roxy was like a Scotland Yard bulldog interrogating a purse-snatcher with a hefty bank account. "Our public wants to know, Jake."

I took another deep breath, glancing at Edgar to call a halt to the inquisition. Edgar's eyes lit up with glee. I read it as, No way, Jose.

"I didn't tell you about that part; I was too

embarrassed." Still they waited. "The honest truth is that I don't really know why. It really seemed to burst from my mouth before I realized it. It actually felt right. Honest. Until I saw the horror in her face. I mean was it so bad? Wasn't it at least a little bit funny? Or am I just warped?"

"Was this the first time anything happened between the two of you?" asked Roxy.

"You mean other than when she was our mediator in divorce proceedings way back when? Or when I asked her out a short time later? Or when I made a hybrid fool of myself trying to ask her out in front of a stunned group of shoppers in the Whole Foods checkout line a few weeks ago? You mean like that?"

"So you do have a *history*." Noted Roxy. I let that sink in. What the hell.

"I guess you could say that. Quite an unusual one. Did she see me at my best? How do I answer that? Was I making a joke of the whole thing? Am I an imbecile? Bad at timing? Desperate?"

I could answer all those questions with a *Maybe, but?*

"But what if that's how I felt? What if somewhere deep inside I knew that was what I wanted? After so many years of hiding her way back in my mind, I was simply acting on my deepest consciousness?"

I looked at them pleadingly. They were staring at each other grimly. This was worse than *True Confessions;* these were my partners in a new venture. They were discovering that I was a closet loony. And I had opened that door.

"I rest my case. Tell me I'm at least trustworthy in our venture." After a pause and a kindly smile, Roxy said this: "I trust you completely, Jake. And I don't know about your real feelings for this woman. A couple things occur to me. One, if these are your true feelings, it's likely not over yet, unless you can put her behind you. Two, if word gets to the media, it might mean a continuation of the saga that began during our first show. You could be a hometown celebrity. Or weirdo, even. Not all bad. Not all good."

"Yeah, radio show wannabe insults woman with a marriage proposal on first date."

I hung my head. Edgar must have felt he didn't need to add anything to Roxy's comments. A one-gun firing squad was quite adequate.

I continued, "I know, I've been worrying about that, that's why I apologized profusely. I'm hoping no one calls the media if they recognize her on the news. But she is quite lovely. I absolutely promise I won't do anything so foolish again."

In less than thirty seconds, my two cohorts exploded in laughter.

"Jake, the worst that could happen is that this blows up, we become famous or infamous. Or ignored. What does it matter? We did our best and more on our first show despite absurd interruptions. We've lost only a small amount of money, and we've created something special, even if it is short-lived." Edgar was laughing unremorsefully. "This is what we've been working toward. Making people laugh. Let's move on. Let us give you a hard time when the going gets tough. Maybe you should have a segment on advice to the lovelorn." He upped his laugh volume.

I felt better. What the hell, I asked myself. I really wasn't being devious, or offensive. Was I?

We moved on. Their stuff, unhindered by scandal, was far richer than what I brought to the table that morning.

By one o'clock we had roughed in our outline on the white board. It was loose but with enough sprouts of new material. We rehearsed what would become a new interview, and some new questions for listeners. We toyed with an advice section for the lovelorn. It proved fertile. Lastly we decided how much to inform new listeners about the broadcast *interruptus* that likely caused them to give us a try on our second attempt.   We   were   regaining   our   reckless, unshakable confidence. Arriba!

 Friday. July 28, 2017

Beware of free advice. Especially if it's preceded by, "I'm not telling you what to do. But . . ."

Roxy took us through our listeners' responses to our three questions on our website. In addition, we asked how they liked the show? You might say there was some piling on. "You shoulda had less talking and more humor; "Don't bring on girl's soccer coaches, people are more interested in golf or tennis; "I don't know why we can't call in about politics. It's a free country, isn't it?"

There were a few more. But you get the drift. And I'd be unfair if I didn't mention that a few folks wrote: "Nice show." " It was different." "I'll sure listen again."

God bless you.

We tried to calculate how many actual listeners there were in addition to the live front window audience. Hundreds? Fifty? A dozen? Sobering unless we were way off. But, we were buoyed that we got some response, and, hey, we were bound to pick up a few more after the mindboggling publicity. That is, if people remembered for a whole week.

And, so far, no story about the identity of the woman who stole the show. Surely some people were thinking she might make a follow-up appearance. We did work on some ways we might respond. We hoped it would not be necessary.

Saturday, July 29, 2017

We heard our first applause as we shuffled through the Whiskey 'n Ribs and the set-up crew welcomed us with apparent appreciation. High fives aren't a bad start to the day.

By eleven-thirty there were a few more curiosity seekers, and one TV station likely looking for another flash-mob experience. There were a few faces I recognized. Several brought cards or tablets to communicate with us through the heavy plate-glass window. Also, there was a police officer standing on the far curb, most likely primed to call in reinforcements.

As The Radio Guys with blazers settled in, Roxy arranged her setup to conveniently slide a screen over to conceal herself during a planned phone interview. We had good money riding on that segment.

So, enough talk. Let's TALK.

EDGAR: Good morning, Denver. Good morning listeners. And good morning to all you listeners gathered out front of Whisky 'n Ribs on Larimer between 15th and the 16th Street Mall. Welcome to the Radio Guys Talk. Or, laugh! I'm Edgar, next to me is Jake, and our producer and brain trust is Roxy. We're glad to be back after our uneventful maiden voyage last Saturday. Oh, maybe some of you caught the bits of news about what happened.

ME: By the way, not to worry about any of that kind of thing recurring. There is a police officer right across the street. And he's huge and fierce and all business. And, it's great to see familiar faces out there, and many new ones. Edgar, it's like we're on television in a way. Without being on television, right?

EDGAR: Right. Well, we have a lot in store for you today, so let's get moving. Roxy, what's first?

Roxy slides a couple typed sheets my way.

ROXY: Last Saturday we asked our listeners three questions. And we had quite a few answers to select from. Here's some we thought were the best, or most unusual.

ME: And let me assure you that we are totally unqualified to pass judgment on these answers. So, please keep that in mind.

It's amazing how quickly the gathered audience stands to attention.

ME: Here was our first question: What is the biggest con you've ever pulled off? And here is the one we selected. I might add the listener requested anonymity. I think you'll understand why. "The biggest con I ever pulled off was getting my sisters to deliver my daily paper-route for twenty-five cents. There were 52 homes and it took about forty-five minutes. I collected thirty cents from each customer each week.

Well, it sounds like a slumlord in the making. What's your take, Edgar?

EDGAR: That's free enterprise isn't it? Probably not covered by child labor laws. I get the anonymity. There might be some scores to settle.

ROXY: Maybe everybody came out all right. And they were actually doing some work. The two sisters.

ME: Was that the era of the five-cent candy bar?

EDGAR: Did he say how long this went on?

ROXY: You have all the info we received. My question is, was it a con, or just exploitation?

ME: Maybe we should put that up on the RADIO GUYS LISTENER POLL. A CON or EXPLOITATION? Or an APPRENTICESHIP? Or, a miserly paid INTERNSHIP.

EDGAR: I think intern has kind of a smarmy connotation now. Or is that too political?

ME: Yes. Lets move to the second question we asked. That would be: Why do worms come out of the ground? (I shuffle the papers) *And it looks like there are two equally brilliant answers.* (I watch our outside listeners concentrating) *The first answer: Worms come out of the ground to suntan. Ah, good thinking. I hope they use sunscreen. At least SPF 50. And, the second answer: The worms come out of the ground for Happy Hour. There you have it. How about those submissions!*

ROXY: *Looks like our window audience approves of those answers.*

EDGAR: *I can't see a moral issue in these answers. Or in the question. My choice would be Happy Hour.* (Most of the audience gives a thumbs-up).

ME: *Which brings us to question number three: What job do you wish you had pursued but didn't? I'm sure that doesn't include exploiting your sisters for your paper route. Or for your lawn-mowing business.*

ROXY: *What about pole dancer?*

ME: *You could still get away with that one, Roxy. And that's a compliment.*

EDGAR: *I'd come see you. It would be my first time, of course. Boy, I suppose I'd have to tell Marge.*

ME: *Well, here's what our listeners wrote: By the way, four said bartender. One said Cable TV installer. One said foot model. And one woman said jockey. There were many others. So we had a difficult time deciding. An actress. A rock-band singer. Another said an exterminator. No details on that one. One said a card dealer in a casino. Another said a car dealer in Reno. Hey, was that the same person?*

EDGAR: *You can see the variety from our listeners. Just remember, it's never too late. Well, unless you're on the pole dancer track. Thank you all for your submissions. Personally I wish I could have driven a bulldozer or a wrecking-ball crane.*

So far, so good. The background noises in the restaurant were reassuring, the traffic out front moved unhindered, and our "groupies" were behaving like normal adult groupies. We smoothly segued into our new segment.

ME: OK. We have a new segment in our show. We call it OXYMORONS for Smart Listeners. Now, I'm sure most of you know that an oxymoron is usually two words that seem to be incompatible or self-contradictory. George Carlin made one famous when he offered: Military Intelligence. Then there was Business Ethics. Just some fun stuff to help us appreciate the English language, right? So we've gathered some for your consideration. And when we read them, we'll ask for a thumbs-up or thumbs-down from our street side audience. And, at the end we'll tell you how to send us your own favorite, or, better, one you've made up yourself.

Here we go.

ROXY: Jumbo shrimp. Or even: Fresh frozen jumbo shrimp.

We look at the audience. They seem to digest the concept and the example and one by one, give a thumbs-up. OK. But will this get to be funny?

EDGAR: How about: Advanced Beginner?

ME: Seems like a positive response. But a lot of puzzled looks. Like where is this going? (A few nods from our listener/watchers.) *So, maybe you folks out there want more. Something more unusual?* (A few more nods.)

ROXY: Here's one: Non-working mother. (OK, more laughs from the animated faces outside, especially the women. Probably best to end on an upper.) *Jake, what have you got?*

ME: (I slide my finger down a list in front of me, and stop) *Does this qualify? A little pregnant?* (The gods smiled on that one and most of our viewers laughed.) *Well, that was a try on our part. But we want to know if you want more oxymorons. So let us know by sending in your choice for next week. You can do this by going to our website radioguys.com. Your vote counts. Leave us your vote and/or your oxymoron.*

We looked at each other, sensing we needed to jump-start the show. I was actually thinking we needed another robbery attempt.

ROXY: *All right now. We've got some BREAKING NEWS in, boys.* (She hands over a sheet) *Edgar, here you go.*

EDGAR: *What have we got here? BREAKING NEWS: DIVORCE IS INCREASING AMONG MARRIED COUPLES. Hmmm. That's pretty interesting. And, you heard that here first.*

ME: *Why is that interesting Edgar? Where else would divorce increase? Are you trying to pull one over on us?*

EDGAR: *Well, among Catholics, for one. Or senior citizens. I'm just sayin', these observations are subtle. Intriguing.*

ROXY: *The data says what the data says. Are you quarreling with the data, Jake?*

ME: *This is moving too fast for my brain. I know that something isn't right. I'll get back to it later.*

EDGAR: *OK, Jake. Well I know our listeners enjoyed our new product segment last week. The product to help you reset a mousetrap after it's smooshed a mouse. Hey, was that when we were interrupted with the attempted robbery right behind us? We didn't finish that one, did we?*

ROXY: *Yes, Edgar, I can't find the copy anywhere. Lets move on.*

EDGAR: *OK then, here's a real lifesaver for you. Another new product. It's called the **Significant Other App**. Got your attention, right? The Significant Other App will help you remember not only key dates for your beloved, but maybe a special phrase to show you care. Or, excuses for forgetting to buy something, or make reservations for something. Or didn't come home the night before. Hmmm, there's a sticky one. Or overdrew from the joint checking account.*

ME: *Or stumbled over his or her name, or the kids' names, or that you have kids. How about forgetting to ask about the sport scores over the past four months? Or that you forget to mention you invited mother for dinner for the fourth consecutive Sunday afternoon.*

EDGAR: Hey, how about anniversaries. Or reminders that your SO commented about something she or he liked when you were window shopping. Or that you promised you'd be home on time. Or needed to plan a weekend getaway. It's endless. You keep loading up as something comes up and it makes you a hero. Check it out. The Significant Other App. Maybe there's a way to mention you heard about it on The Radio Guys Laugh, and you might get a discount. Or, Honorable Mention.

*ME: Could it remind you to **not** say something, or **not** do something about a sensitive matter? Like don't cook that dish again that way? Or, you got me a toaster last year for my birthday. Or, an ironing board. Or schedule another fishing trip when she's dying to see the fall colors.*

EDGAR: Absolutely, Jake. I see unlimited possibilities to improve the quality of your relationships.

*ME: Let us know how the Significant Other App works for you, friends. And now we'd like to let you know that we're brought to you by **Pickle Me Elmo**, the Great American Gherkins that deliver real Pucker Power. Let me add that Pickle Me Elmo brand pickles have won more awards than any other pickle brand, not only in Denver, but clear across the country. In fact this company has an entire building along side its pickling operation just to display all it's awards. More silver, bronze, plaster or ceramic pickles than books in the Denver Public Library. That's saying something, isn't it Edgar?*

EDGAR: Impressive. And a great connection. Perhaps readers really like pickles?

ME: Hard to know, Edgar. But we like them and that's the truth. Pickle Me Elmo, folks. Get some.

EDGAR: Roxy, tell our listeners about the next new section of our show. This is one they won't want to miss.

ROXY: Some of you listeners who went on our Website, radioguys.com, noticed we put up a new feature. The Radio Guys Advice to Listeners. We invited listeners with issues or problems they'd like us to help them with, and we'd select one each week and have you share this by phone so we can help you out with masterful advice. Well, we received more than several from which we selected Ms. Elmer Johnson. And, we have her on the phone: Good morning, Ms. Johnson. I'm turning you over to Jake and Edgar.

EDGAR: Hello, Ms. Johnson. Welcome . . . Ms. Johnson? Are you there?

MS. JOHNSON: Are you talking to me?

EDGAR: Yes, Ms. Johnson. Why don't you tell us about your situation?

MS. JOHNSON: What situation?

EDGAR: Uh, you wrote that your neighbor tried to poison your dog.

MS. JOHNSON: Oh that.

EDGAR: Yes. Why don't you explain that to our listeners.

MS. JOHNSON: Can I talk now?

I'm looking around at our live audience, shrugging what do I do? They seem to be yelling but I have no idea what.

EDGAR: Yes. So your neighbor tried to poison your dog. How do you know?

MS. JOHNSON: Because my dog is sick.

EDGAR: Ah, and did you see your neighbor do this? (Edgar swipes his brow like maybe we'll get this conversation out of lockdown.)

MS. JOHNSON: No, but I know he did it. I know it was him. He's always complaining.

EDGAR: About your dog, right?

MS. JOHNSON: Of course my dog. He hates dogs. He hates

my dog.

EDGAR: And when did this happen?

MS. JOHNSON: When I let Biscuit out to do his one-two at night. He calls me on the phone. He yells at me to keep my dog inside. Like I'm supposed to keep him inside for ten hours.

EDGAR: What does he say?

MS. JOHNSON: My dog is a she.

EDGAR: No, your neighbor. What does he say?

MS. JOHNSON: He says shut your dog's pie hole. Can you believe that?

EDGAR: Is your dog barking then?

MS. JOHNSON: Of course she's barking. How else would I know she's done? (I'm starting to think this is bordering on funny. Our audience out front appears to be dying with suggestions as to how to handle Ms. Johnson.)

EDGAR: So you wait until you hear your dog barking, then you let her in, right?

MS. JOHNSON: Of course! Why would I leave her out after she's done?

EDGAR: OK, Ms. Johnson, I think we're getting a clear picture now. Well, thank you for sharing your problem. And for being interviewed. Roxy what's next?

Edgar places his head flat on the table, exasperated. I can still hear Ms. Johnson breathing on the phone. She hasn't hung up. She breaks in.

MS. JOHNSON: So what should I do about my neighbor?

ROXY: (Disconnecting the call) *Well I think we lost Ms. Johnson. That was a challenging issue, to be sure. And so we move to our next topic, reminding you as we go, to trade your anti-depressants for the twelve noon Radio Guys Talk every Saturday and lift your spirits.*

ME: That's right, Roxy. By the way, as you will notice on our website: radioguys.com, we are going to offer Radio Guys *tank tops and t-shirts starting next week directly after the show. We'll set up a table outside where you can get a special deal for $20 each. Cash. We'll have several fashionable colors for our fashionable listeners. And caps are coming down the line.*

I notice some thumbs up outside. It's good to imagine our listening audience that's not out front is having as positive a reaction to our broadcast. So I ask:

ME: Any of you listening on your radios, please let us know how you're liking our show. radioguys.com and leave us your feedback. You can help us make it better.

As I look over at Edgar, expecting to hand off, I see he has just raised his head from the table and is massaging his temples. I also glance outside where some commotion is occurring. Not the squad car or the traffic-jam kind. But there is a white sign waving over the heads of those lined up close to the window. I'm straining to read it as I try to identify the woman waving it. It's not Carly, Judas Priest. Wait, oh no. I turn back to Edgar.

ME: Edgar, there's a woman out front waving a sign. Frantically. And I think, I'm pretty sure, it's someone you know. I can read the sign now. It says: Edgar, don't forget your hemorrhoid pills, honey! Holy shit, Edgar.

EDGAR: Oh, no. It's Marge. She must be off her meds.

He drops his head once again to the table. The audience turns around to check out Marge. Some appear to be laughing hysterically. I'm checking the clock, hoping we've moved closer to the end. Roxy is going through our outline, deciding what would best fill the remaining minutes. Then I notice the yellow derby hobbling by on the decked-out dude with matching yellow waistcoat and slacks as he passes through the gathered listeners, heading to the entrance and pushing the curtain aside to enter our space and take a seat. Edgar recovers enough to remove his head-set and hand it to Saul. I'm relieved to have him show up a little early for the 2-3 minute segment we'd allotted for him. We might have to have to rein him back in for the next week, but for now, he was a welcome sight.

ME: Well, listeners, while Edgar catches his breath and recovers from Marge's delicate reminder, our good friend, Saul Friedman, has just arrived in our studio. Now, for those who don't know Saul, or know of Saul but have never seen him, I need you to picture him over your radio. Saul is, by far, the most stylish and debonair celebrity to ever walk the streets of Denver. Let me attempt to paint a picture. Because he is, first of all, a visible legend in this city. His elegant deep yellow Derby tops off the matching yellow waistcoat as he glides along. Then there's his electric blue silk shirt with a slightly deeper blue silk tie. Matching yellow slacks and what appear to be black patent leather dress shoes. I'm not doing him justice, but I will add that he is a very debonair and studly man. Thank you Saul. How did I do?

SAUL: My, Jake, that was over-the-top. I thank you for the enthusiastic embellishments. Not many men would take the interest or the time. It's good to be on your show. It's a bit quieter than last week when I was hobbling out front in an ankle cast.

ME: I must agree with you and I am a little relieved, although Edgar's wife seems to have some mischief in mind.

SAUL: She does, doesn't she?

ME: So, listeners, what we're planning to do is have Saul join us when he can to offer you new insights about what's happening in Denver in the cultural and dining areas. There's no one here that knows this better than Saul. So, what have you selected for today, Saul?

SAUL: Well, this one is easy. We're sitting right in the front window of Whiskey 'n Ribs. And let me say that this is one of the best new restaurant concepts to open its doors in Denver in quite some time. The two owners, Sebastian and Rocco, have honed their craft for over 21 years combined, in Memphis, across Texas From Snows in Lexington to Franklins in Austin, and also in Kansas City. You'll find Memphis-style dry-rubbed pork ribs, Texas Braised Beef Brisket, Pulled Pork and Pork cheeks. Try their Aleppo Pepper and Cherry Gravy. If you don't fancy meat, they'll grill fish exquisitely. I've known these boys since they were in school. We're lucky to have them back here.

ME: And, Saul, tell us about their Whisky. They distill it here, is that right?

SAUL: Actually, they distill it about two miles from here. It's ninety-four proof and it's very special. Have a shot, up or on the rocks or in one of their famous classic cocktail recipes. And some of you who appreciate great cocktails made the old-fashioned way, like a Manhattan or Old-Fashioned or maybe a Derby Julep, will be thrilled to discover those rich tastes still preserved. They even offer a tailgate sipper for those headed to see the Broncos or the Rockies. You will really enjoy this place.

ME: Thank you, Saul. We look forward to another one of your recommendations very soon. Restrain yourself from the Tango until you're completely mended.

SAUL: You boys, and your beautiful producer, have a good week now.

I'm checking out Edgar, who seems to be firing on all cylinders. Roxy is watching me, waiting to guide us into the home stretch. I look down at our sheet, just a few options not yet crossed out.

ME: Well, we managed to get most of the important items covered today. We didn't get to ask: Why do most people have stage fright? Of course, as a listener you can easily see why we would be extremely nervous about turning on our mics. Looks like Edgar has recovered from his surprise visitor. Thanks for listening. And for visiting. Roxy?

ROXY: (As the bass track begins) Remember to go to radioguys.com. Let us know how we're doing. Make a list of those you want to get our tank tops or t-shirts for. Good afternoon, Edgar, Jake and everyone.

EDGAR: And remember, CHILL OR BE CHILLED!

It's more than gratifying to see the waves coming back at us as the crowd breaks up, quite a few lining up to come inside. It's even a bigger high when a couple of them inside look over our red curtain and ask for an autograph. I mean, it's fabulous.

As we're straightening up, replacing the large Radio Guys Laugh banner with the small posters on easels at the corners of the big window, Sebastian leans over giving us a high five and a super grin. "Hey, guys, pick what you want from the menu, we'll have it in ten minutes. You can eat in our office."

"Edgar, was that visit by Marge planned?" I asked, "C'mon, level with us." He looks up as if surprised. "It wasn't planned by me, I can tell you that. I had no idea. I'm going to have to get rough with her tonight."

"I can't tell if you're pulling one on us, amigo. But I'm glad it was on you this time. You handled it well, by the way."

"I timed how long your head lay on the table," Roxie said, "One minute and six seconds. That's seven knockout counts, in my book. I mean that's enough time for us to call 911. Way more than enough time."

Roxy nodded sternly. A feigned remonstration.

Monday, July 31, 2017

Yes, I had a first-thing appointment with Jan Monday morning. Call it insurance, or hand-holding, or a potential rescue if I crashed again on Saturday. I walked into her reception area feeling pretty good for the most part.

Jan gave me a hug and told me a joke. This time I could laugh. I even asked her if I could use it on the air sometime.

"Be my guest. I just picked it up online. I think as long as you don't imply it's yours, you'll be all right. You don't have to mention my name. Not that I'm afraid of what it might do for my practice, of course."

"Of course not. You let me know when you think it might help you. Maybe I could start with just your first name. Dr. Jan."

"Let's wait a few more weeks. I'll check with my insurance policy. Maybe I'm restricted from certain kinds of PR. Just being cautious."

Jan is so solid that I couldn't tell if she was pulling my leg in any direction.

"Jake, that was another good show. You recovered well, and I loved the interview with the dog owner. The lack of an answer to what she should do was perfect. That was a no-win question. Let the dog lovers and haters squirm a little. Accepting ambiguity is a sign of good mental health."

"You know how to make an old guy feel good, that's for sure. I'm getting to think we can handle most things. At least one of us can. I'm talking about Roxy, of course. And so far, we're not getting any hate mail. Actually we're not getting much mail at all. But some, anyway. And it's pretty positive."

"So, I guess the big question is: Carly?" She sat back in her chair.

"Well, it's still a big question. For me. One good thing is: nobody seems to have tracked her down. And that surprises me. That clip of her has been shown on TV quite a few times. One not so good thing is: I haven't heard one word from her."

"And?"

"And, well I admit I get a pit in my stomach when I do

think about her. I'd rate it a seven on a pit-in-the-stomach Richter Scale."

"You can live with it?"

"For now. But I hope I don't have to for long. I hope it goes away. Like she's gone away. I really don't expect her to call."

"It's never easy, Jake. There's no shortcut. Best thing is: Feel it. Then let it go. That's a ritual that might require many repetitions. I know you'll survive."

We small-talked for a while. She asked how we developed our material. She was genuinely interested. It was good for me to answer. It's always a bit mysterious how you create anything. And it reminded me of the evident chemistry the three of us shared. After a long career in advertising I'd seen creative teams come and go, struggle and fail, and, just often enough, jell and erupt in explosions of genius. Those were times when I agreed with Einstein that imagination trumps knowledge. A quite surprising belief for someone who has set such a high bar for brilliance in science.

We parted with a client/patient hug, always a moment of reassuring compassion with Jan.

Wednesday, August 2, 2017

After a few days off from radio prep, we were eager to reengage. I was even worried that we might not have allowed ourselves enough time to put another show together. We'd been drawing on some of the material that we'd accumulated over the past months, and there was always a chance we'd strike out in our sessions.

"Jake, I haven't seen anything in the media about Carly. Maybe the potential storm has passed," Roxy nodded.

"I'd like that."

"Maybe we should save that secret, until interest in our show flags," offered Edgar. "Although it seems like we're still ascending. From a very small base, of course."

"Let's just keep doing what we're doing. We don't really have much control over other people, anyway. Especially Carly." I didn't like the notion of using it to our advantage. That just didn't sound like it would go right.

"OK, let's get to work." Roxy, more serious. "I have one idea, for the science segment we sometimes do. A friend told me there are no rooms available in the state of Wyoming to view the eclipse on the 21st of this month, a Monday. Jackson Hole has been booked for more than a year. At outrageous prices. People are coming from all over the country, and the world. I'm guessing science nerds, mostly. What I was thinking is we do some kind of a skit. Maybe a remote. What do you think?"

"Would we do it on Saturday the 19th?" asked Edgar. "Two days before?"

"Or the week before?" I was liking the notion. "Like we got the date wrong? Or we're talking about who's coming. Or people who are heading up there in caravans or tailgate parties or, what if the eclipse failed? Betting on the eclipse. Or the weather and whether we'd actually see it from Wyoming?"

"Breaking News about the eclipse? Postponed? Hacked by Russia?" Edgar was in.

"Or, we preempt the event. Breaking News has Putin being hustled into a limo, heading for his historic meeting with PM Theresa Mary May at his dacha on the Crimea. He has info for her about what the European nations are planning in their negotiations over Brexit. She has information for him about Brussels hacking into his emails and discovering his plans to build a world-class theme park in the Crimea based upon the secret lives of American Presidents."

And on and on.

We shifted to the coming Saturday. By three o'clock we had enough rough stuff to sleep on until the next morning. I drove to a familiar watering hole in LoHi. I sat outside at a table with an umbrella and ordered a pint. Then I ordered a burger. Then I thought about the dating scene. Now you're probably wondering why I'm such a klutz with this dating thing. Well, maybe you aren't. You're probably trying to shout through the thick plate glass or across the bar, that I'm too desperate. Too needy. Too pushy. Or, too unaware. Or, too something. Maybe all of those things. Maybe that's why I've been single for some twenty-five years. Here I thought it was because I was devoted to my career.

I watched the arrivals, all ages, mostly way younger than me. Occasionally a few at my age level. I always wondered what their stories were. Eye contact rarely seemed to reveal much beyond uncertainty. This was the routine of online dating. I should know; I had tried it numerous times this past year through several mingle websites, mostly to no avail.

I tried rigorously to find excuses for my failures. I found that too often the photos were not current, some dated from high school proms, I'm almost certain. My photos were usually less than five years old.

Currently I am unaffiliated.

I didn't limit my approach to online. I left no stone unturned. I would cleverly hint to everyone I met that I'd be forever grateful if they would find me the woman of my dreams. As though I was joking, sort of. I was dead serious.

I hit on the gal who cuts my hair. She picked up her razor from the drawer, and waved it in a relatively friendly warning, like do you know what I could do with this? With a smile. I took that as a no, from Flo.

But Flo did recommend a client. Who has six dogs. Who can't stand to be away from them for more than a couple hours. My car wasn't big enough for us all to go out for coffee.

So far not much luck with matchmakers.

Then there is the attractive woman I see from time-to-time at the gym where I work out. From time-to-time. She seemed younger than me. I noticed the two dumbbells she was using for upper bodywork. They were five pounds more than what I could manage. I asked the young guy at the front desk about her. He said he couldn't tell me, wink-wink, because of privacy rules, that she was a former track competitor and sometime triathlete. I thanked him and decided I'd wait until I could at least lift what she could lift. It might take a while. Or more.

Thursday, August 3, 2017

Lunch with Roxy.

"Jake, I'm sure you'll find someone with the exposure you'll be getting from this show. I've no doubt. "

"Well, that makes one of us. And here's the thing, I still haven't gone a full day without thinking of Carly. I'm hopeless."

"Of course. But it's only been two weeks. In the scheme of things that's just healthy."

I considered my health. *Was I healthier thinking of Carly, or was I terminal?*

"What is your private dating like, Roxy?"

"Private, ha ha! Not really, Jake. I have a guy I see once in a while. Not serious. Not the one. But my life is full. My business. This caper. Great women friends. And two daughters. More than a person can handle and keep their wits. But I do pretty well. Here's my thing: I do honestly believe that, if I live as true to myself as I can, I'll find the right one. At the right time. That's it. It keeps me from panicking. Better than that, it keeps me in a pretty good frame of mind."

"Think it would work for me? That true-to-yourself thing?"

"I wouldn't give you any advice, Jake. Only you know what you need. But I would say this: If not true to yourself, who would you be true to?"

"It does come down to that, doesn't it? So, so simple."

I stopped talking long enough to let that notion sink in. It calmed me down, at least for a time.

Friday, August 4, 2017

Saul dropped by our session at AM 1480 studios just after lunch. He says he's got clients that want to buy ads when we're ready. They think it's kind of a status symbol for being hip. They would want a *Proud Sponsor Of* sign for their window or whatever. Hmm. What will this do for our current sponsors?

We kick around 5-10 second spots. Or just a mention of the Name with no further info. And maybe make it pretty expensive, just to limit it. This seems crazy. Brought to you by Simon and Samson, Attorneys at Law. Nothing more. We sit on it.

Then Saul says he could take a mic outside, interview one or more of our live audience. Scripted questions, of course. Throw out some questions that might get a laugh. We decide to give it a try. Tomorrow or the next week.

We quit Friday, relatively at ease about the next morning's broadcast. I head for Whiskey 'n Ribs for my first taste of their Whiskey at happy hour. And to reflect on the advice given to me by my psychological support network: Roxy and Jan.

The whiskey was excellent, truly. So were the two

women tending bar, Tracy and Zil, entertaining and delightful. Sebastian, one of the owners, stopped by to chat. He was still feeling positive about our relationship. "Yeah, several times this week, customers have asked when your broadcast is. We give them one of your cards."

I've had lots of positive feedback about my work career over time. Funny that Sebastian's compliment might have felt the sweetest. He refused to let me pay for the three shots I enjoyed before heading home.

Saturday August 5, 2017

It was so obvious, what Edgar was doing. He was bringing back the Paisley Tie. Yes. "For my entire working life as an engineer, the only way I could ever jazz up my stylish khakis was to change the color or design of my pocket protector. This might be the only thirty-year old tie in existence that still had tissue paper around it in the box. And, I've heard paisley is in, or at least making a cultivated run for fashion reentry. I'm taking a cue from Saul Friedman. Why not."

"Go for it, Edgar. You look fabulous. Your move next, Jake." Roxy smiled, checking out the gray open-collared shirt peaking from my blazer, nodding unconvincingly.

"Here comes your icon as we speak." I point to the stunning yellow derby bouncing across the street toward us. Saul, sporting his yellow waistcoat and matching slacks, made his uninhibited arrival. I'd expect nothing less. After all, he is appearing on a radio show. "He's early. I have a feeling we'll be trying the remote mic out front today."

By eleven o'clock a few of the passersby wave as we're going over our outlines and checking our sound. Roxy moves the card stand from the window corner closer to her so she can easily slide it in front of her when she does one of the voices in our planned phone interview.

Two minutes before show time she brings on the low-level growling base track that turns more heads toward us and cranks up our own adrenalin, even if unnecessary. She gradually amps it up to the point where you know something has to happen. I think this track is a great move. My feet are tapping. If I could hum in tune, I'd be growling myself.

High noon.

EDGAR: Good morning, Denver. Good morning all of you listeners wherever you are. Thanks for joining us. We're the Radio Guys. I'm Edgar, he's Jake, and the one you're most happy to be looking at, or hearing, is Roxy. As you can see, she's wearing our new Radio Guys Talk tank top that you can buy outside after our show. (Roxy stands and turns around) *We come to you from the front window of the fabulous new dining spot, Whiskey 'n Ribs, on the east side of Larimer between 15th and 16th right downtown every Saturday at noon. Thank you for joining us. And for all of you standing in front of our studio window, thanks for showing up this Saturday morning with the threat of showers any moment.*

ME: We have a terrific show for you. Follow-ups with many of your postings on our website and some new segments that will get you thinking. Roxy, where do we begin?

ROXY: That would be with who pays the bills. Edgar?

EDGAR: And our sponsor for the first quarter hour is Dale's Saddle Restoring Kit. If you have saddle sores, there's a good chance that Dale's Saddle Restoring Kid will soothe what ails you. We'll have more on this rear flank salvaging treatment later in our show.

ME: One thing that amazes me is that so many of you contacted us on our web site, radioguys.com during the week.

Keep it up, we want to know how we're doing and what else you'd like.

ROXY: Right, Jake. For example, we thought maybe the OXYMORON segment we tried out might have fallen flat. But not so fast, guys. We had lots of submissions of your favorite or made-up oxymorons. Remember, an oxymoron is two words that seem to be contradictory. Like jumbo shrimp.

ME: And here are a few of the many you added to our list. MANDATORY OPTION. I like that one. And, PRETTY UGLY. That's good. (I look at the listeners outside the window. They seem to be patiently interested). Here's another: EXACT ESTIMATE.

EDGAR: Ah yes. As an engineer I remember being asked to perform that impossibility many times.

ME: OK, three more: NEGATIVE GROWTH, and GOOD GRIEF. And last, DEAFENING SILENCE. We all have heard that one. Good work listeners. We've got some highly intelligent listeners out there, right Edgar?

EDGAR: Absolutely. But you can't take their loyalty for granted. Really bright folks expect good things. Interesting and entertaining things. We are doing our absolute best. Jake?

ME: Miracles can happen. Which brings me to our new topic: we're calling it ADVICE TO THE LOVELORN. Now, having been utterly unsuccessful in my own private life regarding this area, I think I know about some of the struggles with relationships. So, I'm going to bring in by phone, an expert that can help sort out some of your questions about love and loss. And I'm happy to welcome by phone (Roxy has mostly concealed herself by now) Dr. Nadine. Good morning, Dr. Nadine. Thank you for joining us. And you're calling from where?

DR. NADINE: Why ah am calling from Hope, Arkansas. Razorback country. But you probably already know that.

ME: Yes I do. Great football team. And, Dr. Nadine, we have several questions from our listeners to get your opinion on.

Can we start?

DR. NADINE: *You sure can, Sweetie.*

ME: *A woman asks: What if he forgets my birthday? For the third year in a row? Hmm. I guess many of us could relate, right, Dr. Nadine?*

DR. NADINE: *Yes, but that's no excuse. Here's what your listener should do. If he forgets your birthday, then you forget his Saturday. The day he's got a golf outing, you take off early and leave him with the kids. That puts a little more balance in things. An eye for an eye, y'all might say.*

ME: *Well, that's quite direct. And, Dr. Nadine, what if there are no children?*

DR. NADINE: *Well, you simply rearrange your relationship. For example, you just cut him off.*

ME: (I'm thinking of the non-subtlety of the good doctor. But the folks outside seem to be connecting. At least the women). *And I guess I should ask the logical next question, what if there isn't much going on to cut off?*

DR. NADINE: *Well, Sweetie, you move to Plan B, or in this case Plan C. You begin by sending yourself flowers. You tell him they came without a card. Ask him if he sent them. See if he lies. Pretend you're mystified, but in a way that suggests you have some inkling. Like, "Gee I wonder, oh no, that just couldn't be." You take meticulous care of the flowers when he's around. Pinching off the dead heads, watering them, commenting on how much you like them. Ask him if he thinks someone is stalking you? See how that might work?*

ME: *One way or another, you turn the tables don't you, or twist the knife, Dr. Nadine. Very interesting.*

EDGAR: *I think next time we could have a question from one of our male listeners. We all know there can be two sides to the story. But we sure appreciate the thoughtfulness of Dr. Nadine. I can see the women out front are smiling and talking to each other.*

ME: They certainly are. By the way, we are required by radio law to tell our listeners that we are not responsible for any advice given over the phone or on air, no matter how effective or ineffective it might prove to be. Even though Dr. Nadine is licensed by both the National Association of Paranormal Psychologists, and, Standup Channelers for Lost Relatives and Pets. Isn't that right, Dr. Nadine?

DR. NADINE: Correcto, Jakie. (I can see Roxie skillfully easing the screen back to put herself in full view.)

We move through a New Product Feature, this time it's an App that teaches how to drive a car in seven different languages, and instructs the learner while at the wheel. Our discussion ends with speculations about whether this App will be outmoded once self-driving cars are no longer speculation.

ME: OK Roxy, what comes next?"

ROXY: (As she slides a sheet in front of Edgar.} *This just in, Edgar with the BREAKING NEWS.*

EDGAR: What do we have here? Hmmm, BREAKING NEWS! GROWING INCOME GAP BAFFLES POLITICIANS IN WASHINGTON FOR THE THIRTY-FOURTH YEAR IN A ROW. (He repeats it and sets down the paper.) *Gee, there's some consistency for you.*

ME: Great point, Edgar. You know how we hate surprises. We don't pay our representatives to be bouncing all around, trying this and that.

EDGAR: That's right, a steady hand. A firm grip on the wheel. No monkey business.

ME: Exactly. Stay the course, I say. And how much credibility can you give those numbers, anyway? If it was as bad as those numbers indicate, wouldn't there be a lot more complaining?

ROXY: Thank you Edgar, that's our BREAKING NEWS,

folks. And I notice that our good friend Saul is heading out front with a remote mic. So maybe we can get some thoughts from our fabulous fans. While he's getting organized, why don't we remind our folks out front that we'll have Radio Guys tank tops for sale right after the show. Twenty dollars. All colors and sizes. They're very comfortable, cutting edge and all. And you can help us promote this show. Thank you so much. Oh, and next week, we'll have T-shirts.

ME: Also remember, that if you'd like to be a phone guest on our show, say in our personal advice segment, go to our website: radioguys.com and you'll see how to give us your information and your question.

EDGAR: It looks like Saul is all set up outside, in fact he's stepping up to a woman who is carrying a sign.

I notice her white hair tied in a bun as she looks up into Saul's face with a straight back and a pointed chin.

SAUL: And whom do we have here? (She muscles a stern smile and thrusts her mouth to the mic as she also turns her sign so we can all read it.)

I sense a scrotal tightening as Edgar and I absorb the sign just as the woman answers Saul with: "My name is Mildred Fillmore. And I have a question for these two Bozos."

I also notice that Saul finally catches the provocative sign Mildred is hoisting over the crowd which now is focused on her and her banner: FREAKS AND PERVERTS. And for the first time I see Saul Friedman stumbling with what to say. He feebly observes, "That's a pretty outrageous accusation, Mildred."

By then Mildred has taken charge.

MILDRED: It certainly is. I just have one question for these two perverts. When was the first time either of you had sex with a human being?

That's when Edgar and I lock eyes with each other, our

minds ricocheting off all flat and curved surfaces, scrambling for shelter or holy intervention. A quick glance at Roxy provides no escape. I do the manly thing and yield to Edgar the opportunity to handle this delicate inquiry and preserve our show's threatened dignity.

ME: Well, I have never lived on a farm, so I think I should turn this question over to Edgar. (Who, as far as I know, never lived on a farm either).

Saul is looking at us, firmly holding his remote as Mildred exhorts, "See. Look at them. PERVERTS!"

Edgar freezes for the moment; I'll never know exactly all the options he was considering. Later he told us he was coping with a high-speed spin between two general positions: Was Mildred trying to get us to admit to bestiality, or admit to our first human sexual experience to deflect that possibility, but still embarrass us with the disclosure?

With a wet brow and armpits, Edgar finally replied with masterful grace and agility.

EDGAR: Well, I'm proud to admit, that after my first experience with you, Mildred, my next experience was with a woman, my high school sweetheart, who later became my wife.

As Saul steps away from Mildred, we watch her face contort into Munch's *The Scream.* Or a reasonable facsimile. Inside we can't hear any sound from her, but we can't avoid noticing that many of our listeners out front seem to jump simultaneously.

Fortunately Mildred turns the opposite direction from the restaurant entry and stomps away just as the law officer is crossing the street to our side. Inside I am marveling at Edgar's genius. That's why I knew he'd be fabulous at this. I pressed my hands together and bowed to him. Later I would bathe him in accolades and pick up his bar tab for the coming week.

ROXY: Saul is rejoining us inside so we can hear his tip of

the week. I wonder what he has in mind for us? There is no one in
Denver who has his pulse on what's going on like Saul.

And I remind our listeners that we are going to bring
you special pre-coverage of the Eclipse on our Saturday
broadcast the 19th of August, just two days before the actual
eclipse. On Monday, the actual day of the eclipse, we'll have a
special podcast including a remote from an international
expert covering the event from Jackson Hole Wyoming where
folks from around the world are gathering to view this event
with the clarity of the sky distant from city lights. Mark that
down. You can connect with our podcast on our website:
radioguys.com.

As the bass riff rumbles under our farewell, Roxy
apologizes that our time is up and we'll catch Saul the following
week. She ramps up the volume and we remove our headsets,
lean back and, I'm almost certain, each shake our head in
bewilderment and gratitude.

Rocco leans over the curtain behind us. "Great job, guys." He
reminds us to order lunch and to use his office. As we shuffle
back through the full crowd of diners, several wave at us, and
even cheer moderately as though we'd just slayed a modestly
sized dragon. It still feels great.

Saul was waiting for us, dropping his head as we
entered. Was it good to see him slightly humbled? Maybe. But,
thanks to Edgar all had ended reasonably well.

I stood there, a big grin on my face. "Saul, why in God's
name did you hook up with Mildred?

"I didn't see her sign," Saul apologized immediately.
"She was alone, nice posture, stood out with her white hair."

He failed to admit, in front of Roxy, that Mildred had a
great front porch.

"Did you get her number? Invite her for a drink here?"

Edgar was enjoying this. Saul was squirming to regain his regal stature, his downtown glam, his sartorial pulchritude. Saul had let his guard down in what should have been his natural role as Denver's hip urban personality. Would it be his last chance to be "the man-on-the-street interviewer"? No. He would return elegantly in the future, charming revealing comments from listeners and watchers wanting to have a little thrill from dipping their toes into the live broadcast world.

"Does anyone know, or want to admit why Mildred is so hostile to us?" asked Roxy. "I wonder if she wasn't the one who wrote us asking about our credentials to be radio talk-show hosts. Someone from your past, Jake? Edgar?"

"Absolutely not me. I don't know any Mildreds. Or Millies. Or Millicents. Not one." I felt defensive.

"Doeth ye protest too much, Jake?" Edgar grinned. Saul stepped back, his face relaxing.

"No! No! No! Just because of that little incident with Carly, you guys aren't going to hang this one on me." I wasn't surprised at this turn. What are friends for? "Anyway, here's my question, Edgar, how did you come up with your stopper? It was brilliant. And so believable. She had no idea who she was messing with."

"I was very impressed," said Roxy. Saul nodded affirmatively. Edgar grinned, "I could have admitted it was all true, farm life could tempt that early experience. Variety is the spice of life. I thought about it. And then I thought about Mildred being my second non-human experience. The one that turned me toward female humans. But, I thought that was getting too complicated and I had to get at it, fast."

Roxy roared. Saul removed his yellow derby and bowed. I shook my head in wonder and Rocco entered his office with four cold beers and assurance that our lunches were on the way.

Monday, August 7, 2017

"Don't tell me that wasn't scripted, Jake. That outdoor encounter skit is a regular part, maybe the most outrageous part of your show."

It was eight forty-five. Jan had squeezed me in ahead of a couple that was now waiting in the lobby. She had a "don't give me any bullshit look on her face."

"I'd like to be so clever as to take credit for our outdoor gymnastics. But I'm not nearly that smart. Maybe you can give me your hypothesis."

"I don't have one. Without getting woo woo. I can only speculate that you and your sidekicks   have the uncanny ability to attract these things. You would know more about that than I do. That woman on Saturday was really hostile. Why for you guys? I really wonder. But I don't have an opinion. At least one of you might know, or will discover the connection. Or you're just in her sights as someone who represents greater issues. Like the media. Or men who attract adoring fans. Or change in downtown Denver. Or something more obscure. Maybe one of you looks like her father, or a man who spurned her. Anyway, you handled it well, though I don't think it left her in a very good mood. My only advice would be, if she returns on a mission, I'd alert the police officer you said was assigned to your broadcast. By the way, having a police presence says something for your efforts. Something good for the most part."

"I honestly don't have a clue about Mildred."

"And, no word from Carly?"

"No word."

"OK then, Jake. You're on your own. I've got clients waiting. You're good to go. Hug me and keep up the good work."

I walked half a block to a new coffee shop I hadn't tried. It was scattered with people but the line was short. I carried my latte to a long high table in the center from which I could see what was happening at most of the tables. Already laptops were plugged in or resting on auto rechargers. I enjoyed speculating about who was running their business enterprise remotely. Interior design, real estate, interviewing potential employees or investors. There was an animated group of Lyft drivers at a large round table sharing tips on how to beat the system and max their commissions and fees. And, others doing classwork or preparing for exams. Or, just sitting like me, contemplating my navel.

On this morning my navel seemed interested in considering the past four and a half months, from when I first broached the radio idea to Edgar, to the present with three shows under our belts, a downtown window broadcast setting where we were still welcome, and the unusual opportunity we had with a live audience of a few dozen that probably outnumbered our actual radio listeners. We had a rich opportunity for feedback from those outside.

As I marveled at the coffee drinkers' purposefulness at whatever they were doing, I thought several things. One, we should be very satisfied at how far we'd come. Sure, we'd been on air for less than a month. Sure, we had a few screwy episodes out front of our window. And, sure, we were doing all this on a shoestring.

But that should not diminish our achievements. There was good intelligence and wit and chemistry between the three of us. And with Roxy, we'd struck gold.

Personally I felt terrific, other than my non-relationships with women.

I wondered how much a change I'd made in my life about a year earlier had helped in this whole venture? What

I'm talking about is that I stopped watching cable news, and about ninety percent of regular news. That has done wonders for my temperament and my thinking. I know what is going on, how can you not hear blips and pieces now and then. And I still read the New Yorker, though it is far less enjoyable for me as the political reporting and commentary is painful, and I skim through in no time.

When we made the show a politics-free zone, I was wondering how that would play out. The temptation is there everyday to take a poke at someone. It's so easy. Thank God there are comics like Colbert and Bee and Oliver who do this exquisitely, much better than I ever could.

When we started writing material in Hillary's former campaign office, we frequently had to remind ourselves: No Politics. The amazing thing to me is that there is still plenty in this world to laugh at. We are the most amusing specie, other than monkeys, who don't really speak a language we can understand, though they do seem quite apolitical.

And once we realized that there was plenty to laugh about, we simply went at it. And, I will say, it's extremely liberating and gluten free.

Is it for everybody? Of course not. If you've got nothing going for you, then absorbing and digesting and regurgitating the news is a lot to give up. But, if you're not the faint of heart, I highly recommend it. A close friend of mine told me recently, "If I don't plan to do anything about it, I don't bring it up in my conversations."

I do occasionally find myself in range of a news broadcast, though if I can politely excuse myself, I do. And what I've noticed is that at least ninety percent of it is speculation. What is (or was) he or she thinking? Why did he do that? What will he, she, they do now? What will happen? How will they react? How will you feel about what they might do? Enough speculation to lick your finger a thousand times, hold it in the air and check for wind direction. Then the listener has a chance to repeat this speculation all day, whenever in a human encounter. It's the kind of thing that, at best, produces blisters on your ass, and the chemical changes in your bodies that result from fear, uncertainty and inaction.

I do check out Charlie Rose on occasion. And also reruns of The Bourne Identity flics. I also enjoy conversations with actual people who have other things to talk about besides political speculating and handwringing. They're out there, in numbers. And maybe some of them are making merry at noon on Saturdays in front of Whiskey 'N Ribs.

But, mostly I feel lucky that I've thought about other things that have taken my energy and imagination places I'd never dreamed about. That's been a very good thing.

Saturday, August 19, 2017

EDGAR: Good Morning, Denver. Welcome once again to THE RADIO GUYS TALK. And this morning, just as we reminded you last week, we have a special program on the eve of THE ECLIPSE. So relax, unless you're driving, and sit back, unless your standing on the sidewalk out front here at the Whiskey 'N Ribs restaurant on the east side of Larimer between 15th and 16th in downtown Denver. Jake, how are we covering the Eclipse two days before it actually happens?

ME: Good question, Edgar. And thank goodness we've done our homework. At least Roxy has.

EDGAR: Speaking of Roxy, we should let our audience know that Roxy is in Jackson Hole, Wyoming as we speak. That's where all the accommodations have been sold out for over a year because of the amazing view unhindered by city lights and other light pollution.

ME: And in about twenty minutes we'll join Roxy with some of her amazing contacts and experts on all that surrounds the eclipse. But first, a word about the folks who sponsor this special broadcast.

EDGAR: And that would be our friends at SunGAZE Eyewear for Eclipses and Nuclear Bomb Test Viewing. Let me just say this: these folks really understand what is needed to protect our precious eyes, right, Jake?

ME: Absolutely, They made ours for us, and we're wearing them now so the fans outside our window can see for themselves. Ours happen to have bright yellow frames with the Radio Guys Watch and the date of the eclipse, August 21, 2017, printed across the top front of the frames. Each lens is four inches in diameter to assure protection, and there are many options from a Kraft paper lens with a pinhole in it to an obsidian crystal lens like we are wearing. They're stunning folks. A fashion statement with total protection. Edgar, you were commenting on them this week when they arrived at our headquarters."

EDGAR: I sure was and so was Roxy. She said that the big question long after the eclipse has eclipsed, would be: Where Were You When You Were Wearing Your SunGaze Eyewear? And if you don't have yours, head for any major retail parking lot in Denver, and look for a car with an open trunk and a sales representative standing with these glasses on waiting to serve you. If you don't see one, try a different parking area, maybe around a major mall for example. It'll be worth the search.

We proceed with a segment on the issue of how and how much do hackers get paid for what they do. Which leads to conversation about whether hacking is good or bad. Is it simply a question of who's side you're on?

Then, some feedback from our listeners on our website, especially the conversation with Dr. Nadine. It seems there is boundless creativity about additional ways to "balance" the situation when your "significant other" forgets your birthday. For the third year in a row. One sly idea was: *Pick any day you know is not your S.O.'s birthday and greet him or her in the morning with a song and a card and effusive affection. When he/she says, but it's not my birthday, you act crushed. "Yes it is. I know it is. I never forget your birthday, Sweetie." Then you press your hands to your cheeks in a look of horror, and realize, "Oh no, it's . . . it's . . . oh yeah, it's his (or hers). I'm so sorry. My mistake. Yours is . . . maybe suggest another wrong date, depending on your level of malevolence. Oh well. We all make mistakes."*

All in all, we were getting more contact from listeners. That was good, and it helped us segue from one week to the next.

This week there was also an inquiry about the woman who stopped traffic with her engagement ring on our first broadcast. We didn't respond on the air to that one, better to let sleeping dogs lie. Or awkward breakups die. Instead, Edgar discussed his wife Marge's method of soft retaliation when he missed her birthday or their anniversary. She served him his two least favorite dishes alternate evenings for a week.

Next we brought in our Denver raconteur and restaurant connoisseur, Saul Friedman, who skillfully and deftly took us on a savory mental tour of Mexican restaurants and street food vendors to discern the absolute best cheese enchilada in the city and surrounding neighborhoods. Saul said it's easy to make up a "nouveau" presentation of a Mexican staple for the food snobs (Of which I am one! He admitted.) But if you can't fry an egg perfectly, or deliver the perfect enchilada, I don't return.

While delivering his soliloquy he removed his yellow derby and replaced it with one of the huge, glittered, Mexican sombreros sought after by the aging tourists coming out of a souvenir shop and returning to the cruise ship anchored off Cozumel. I thought he was making a run for *"the most interesting man in the world"*.

Finally, it was time for our really big remote extravaganza.

ME: Thank you, Edgar. And now out to Jackson Hole where Roxy is standing by. Hello, Roxy. What do you have in store for this unusual preview of the eclipse.

ROXY: Good morning, guys, and listeners. First off, the weather report for Monday is encouraging. Less than 10% chance of showers. So that's good. Now, I've been working the past two days with an amazing woman, Simoni Hayek. Simoni is a special News Correspondent for Al Jazeera Radio and Television based in Beirut, Lebanon. Her special fields are science and military arms development. I've enjoyed getting to know her and I'm extremely impressed with her knowledge and international take on the eclipse. Simoni, say hi to Edgar and Jake.

SIMONI: Hi Radio Guys.

JAKE AND EDGAR: Hi, Simoni.

ROXY: As you know it's quite crowded up here this week and Simoni has been staying, with her engineer, adjacent to one of the original motels up here called The OLAS MOTEL. OurLipsAreSealed. It's very quaint and, more interesting, is who is staying in the twelve double rooms. Simoni?

SIMONI: That's right, let's see, there are representatives from Turkey, China, Germany, Norway, Canada, Brazil, Israel, Iran, Russia, and, oh my goodness, uh, South Korea, Saudi Arabia and India. I think I have them all.

JAKE: I guess the question would be, why? Why all these people in Jackson Hole? Surely there are other places where more is going on?

SIMONI: Well, here's what I think. This is a place where they don't think your SA or CIA can bug all their conversations. I'm quite certain that most of these people are spies for one country or another. In fact, when I've covered other international gatherings, like governmental security, for example, I've seen more than a few of these people. They turned up here with reservations made by themselves, not in the name of their governments. All of a sudden they're side-by-side at the OurLipsAreSealed Motel. What a place to sniff out foreign intrigue. A reporters dream. And I'm right next door at the YourSecretsAreSafeWithUs Motor Lodge. I'm the only media person there.

ROXY: Simoni believes that she's being used as an unaware outlet for some of these "spies" to leak information to the world or even to the White House. Especially the bogus information. So I know that you and our listeners are going to be amazed.

EDGAR: Wow! We're talking real scoops then, aren't we?

ROXY: I think so. In fact Simoni sat down with me this morning with some pretty amazing information. Simoni, will you tell them what you told me, please?

SIMONI: Sure, that seems to be my role here. Well, here goes. By the way, I will file this with Al Jazeera right after your broadcast. About six-thirty this morning I get a knock at my door and it happens to be the intelligence officer from South Korea. He says, that as we speak, the Prime Minister of England, Teresa May, is secretly flying to Putin's Dacha on the Crimean Coast. Evidently Putin has hacked the strategy for how the European Bloc is going to negotiate Brexit. Huge Hack, I'd say. And, get this: in exchange, the PM is giving Putin a list of phone numbers of the escort services the White House is using in DC and certain foreign cities.

ME: Tasty stuff, I'd say. I suppose they'll have to change the numbers once this gets out, though.

SIMONI: Nothing stays the same.

ROXY: That's not all from the man from South Korea. Tell them, Simoni.

SIMONI: Right. He loves to gab. Then he told me, real hush, hush, that The Supreme Leader of North Korea, Kim Ill Bung, based in Poonang, has authorized an entire field of rockets to be launched carrying a massive amount of Kim Chi into the atmosphere to clog our satellite warning systems including the Star Wars Anti-Ballistic System that Reagan supposedly put up there somewhere. That icky stuff sticks to anything.

EDGAR: Sticky shit, is it? Well, you won't clean that up with chop sticks, will you, Jake?

ME: Well, I can only wish that moron from Poonang a ruptured spleen.

EDGAR: This Simoni is really wired into that motel. Looking out at our listeners, I'd say they're buzzing. It's pretty sexy to be the first in the know. By the way, we do have some Breaking News here, Jake. It kind of fits with all that is going on in Jackson Hole right now. Here it is: BREAKING NEWS, THE WHITE HOUSE IS ON HIGH ALERT EXPECTING ALL OUR ENEMIES TO TAKE ADVANTAGE OF THE ECLIPSE IN THE MOST DANGEROUS WAYS. (Edgar repeats and slides the paper to the side.)

ME: Stands to reason. Hard to trust anyone anymore, right Edgar? Maybe this is a good time to bring up the issue we talked about yesterday and the day before. You said, and I agreed, that the eclipse definitely needs a name. Even if only for the thousands, maybe millions, of expectant mothers who might want to name their babies born on August 21 after the eclipse. It's too late to get our listeners to weigh in on this name so we went ahead and picked a name from over a hundred suggestions from the three of us.

EDGAR: I'm glad Marge and I aren't in that expecting group.

ME: Me as well. Not that I have a choice at this time.

EDGAR: So, everyone, since we live in a time of celebrities, both good and evil, we picked a name that mirrors one of the characteristics of the eclipse, in this case the precious few minutes when it is in the perfect place. The only name we know that has had such a dramatic and abbreviated tenure on the world stage: The winner, it's gotta be: THE MOOCH.

ME: THE MOOCH. Hired on Friday as White House Communications Director and fired ten days later. Anthony Scaramucci. Perfect!

ROXY: But what about the name for babies. You can't be serious.

ME: Hmmm. Maybe just Eclipse, for them. Or Clipper? Or Skipper? But we have to stick with THE MOOCH. Where were you during THE MOOCH?

Outside the women, most of them, seem unsatisfied. The men are laughing. Edgar attempts a rescue.

EDGAR: Maybe our listeners can get to us on our website, over the weekend and we can make an announcement on our podcast Monday about an alternate name.

The women nod vigorously. We move on with THE MOOCH for the present.

ME: By the way, listeners, our good friends at SunGAZE protective eyewear for eclipses and nuclear bomb tests, have generously offered to pick up the rather substantial costs of our remaining broadcast today in order that you have uninterrupted coverage of The MOOCH prelaunch direct from our hookup with Roxy in Jackson Hole. Thank you SunGAZE.

And what else do you have for us, Roxy?

ROXY: This just passed to us from the Canadian Representative at the OLAS Motel. It's about the weather.

According to NASA, if, on Monday morning, the weather forecast shows that more than half the country will be under cloud cover, the White House has ordered the eclipse to be rescheduled so that more Americans will have a chance to see it.

EDGAR: OK, fair enough. That seems like a very democratic policy. At lease half of Americans should be allowed to see the eclipse. To see THE MOOCH, agreed?

ME: By the way, listeners, be sure to send us a photo or selfie of yourselves in your eclipse eyewear. We'll announce the most interesting and the most glamorous selfies on next Saturday's broadcast. Back to you, Roxy.

ROXY: In line with that, last night I saw Madonna on Celebrity News wearing an eclipse helmet with built in goggles. Fabulous yellow just like ours. Now, let's shift to the science aspect of our coverage. I met several experts at a round table discussion yesterday and one of them, Dr. Dieter Deuter, Professor of Astro-Physics, from the University of Hamburg, Germany is right here. Thank you, Dr. Deuter, for spending time with us.

DR. DEUTER: You're wery velcome, Fraulein Roxy. I am wery pleezed to be here.

ROXY: Dr. Deuter, l . . .

DR. DEUTER: Ya, Fraulein Roxy, pleeze to call me Dieter .
. .   ROXY: Oh, Dr. Dieter, well yes, uh, many people are concerned about potential problems that may arise because of the eclipse. For example, at your discussion yesterday, a colleague of yours from Tehran warned that the magnetic field created by the eclipse will reverse all the clocks in the world, even the digital clocks. This is quite alarming. He maintained it will cut into the hourly wages of those who punch in and punch out, and interfere with start and finish times for all timed competitions. On the plus side it will allow us to review mistakes we've made in the past, such as stock market trades, undo those

decisions and make different ones.

Quite disconcerting isn't it, Dr. Dieter?

Dr. Deuter: Pleeze, just Dieter, Roxy. I sink we are getting aqvainted by now. Vell, I listened to zee Professor Komenie, he loves to talk, and zee truth is: he has a brain the size of a Pistachio nut.

ME: Whoa, aren't Pistachios a major export from Iran, Dr. Dieter?

DR. DIETER: Ya, but I don't eat zem. Zay are an inferior nut. Just like zee Professor Komenie.

ROXY: Thank you, Professor, for your insights. I'm sure our listeners will be relieved.

EDGAR: It seems that fears are ubiquitous as far as The Mooch is concerned. Just like back in 2000 when the pundits shouted the sky would be falling. What else do you have up there, Roxy?

ROXY: Well, I have Simoni Hayek, our correspondent from Al Jazeera back with us. She has been accumulating bits of news and has also brought us another guest expert, Carson Spool, Director of Science for Everyone, a non-profit organization that attempts to bridge the gap between the scientific community and the layperson. He attended a panel of experts yesterday to bring us some of the varying theories related to eclipses. It's quite fascinating, all these different scientific ideas. Director Spool, what have you been hearing that we should know about?

CARSON SPOOL: Good Morning. You know I've heard everything from the flat earth kind of ideas, to the view that oysters and clams were formed from the arced shadows of past eclipses going back to the beginning of water. But here is one with merit. Numerous scientists are debating this one and it's important because of its implications for our future survival.

ROXY: Please fill us in, Director Spool.

DIRECTOR SPOOL: It has to do with the missing piece of

Einstein's Theory of Relativity. The piece Einstein always predicted someone would discover and employ to smooth over the bumps in his profound historical theory. In layman's terms, it's where the law of gravity takes a time-out to restore it's own equilibrium. If gravity weren't restored, the planets in our solar system would begin to stretch the pull and move farther and farther from the sun. The surface temperature of each planet would fall. Ultimately the law of gravity would be fractured because of the extreme cold, and the planets, released from its hold, would proceed up to speeds of imminent meltdown. This could all occur in less than three hundred years.

ME: That's quite alarming, Director Spool. Have you corroborated this, uh, theory, with the scientific community?

DIRECTOR SPOOL: You must understand, this is brand new science, cutting edge. The literature is minimal but I've checked several postings on Wikipedia and I believe there will be growing support as testing data and computer models yield more evidence. It's coming, is all I can say. Of that I am quite certain. We have to find a way to reduce the stretch of gravity's pull or we could find ourselves up shit creek.

Edgar and I stare at each other. Shake our heads, wondering if this should prompt a BREAKING NEWS ALERT? Or let our good audience come to grips on their own? We move on.

ME: OK, well Roxy, we're getting close to the end of this special pre-coverage of The Mooch from Jackson Hole. What are some of the loose ends you and Simoni have heard the last couple of hours? I'm guessing there's plenty of gossip within and about that group staying at the OLAS MOTEL. Some lips that are not so well sealed. Could that be right?

ROXY: Yes, there seems to be some seepage. Again from the Canadian spokesperson. He reports that the White House is strongly considering rescheduling The Mooch, by a couple days, regardless of the weather, to undermine the credibility of the scientific community to predict anything, including global warming. Just sayin'.

SIMONI: I've also heard a rumor from the Belgian room #7 that the wobble in The Mooch is a result of huge and constant deficits in the budgets of Europe and the United States.

EDGAR: That's just what I've been wondering. About the wobble, that is. Thank you both for the wealth of information and the stories that don't ordinarily see the light of day. Absolutely fascinating. Thank you, Simoni. Thank you, Roxy. We'll see you for our podcast Monday.

Both Edgar and I look over our notes, including our final breaking news item. I indicate to Edgar that it's time for his professional voice.

EDGAR: It's BREAKING NEWS time once more. Our last one that relates to THE MOOCH. So ready up out there. BREAKING NEWS: ON MONDAY, DURING THE MOOCH, ZIGGY MARLEY WILL RELEASE, SIMULTANEOUSLY IN JAMAICA AND MIAMI, A NEW REGGAE ALBUM CALLED ECLYPSO. (Edgar repeats, slowing to emphasize *Reggae Album called Eclypso*). *That music brings back a lot of great memories, right, Jake?*

ME: Absolutely. And for all you Bob Marley and Ziggy Marley fans, here's a little trivia from Wikipedia about the Marley family: Bob was born in Jamaica to Cedella Booker and Norval Marley. He was a white Jamaican from Sussex England whose family claimed Syrian-Jewish origins; she was an Afro-Jamaican. Ziggy, Bob's eldest son, is married to Orly Agai, an Israeli of Iranian-Jewish origin. Boy, Edgar, I would love to see those family trees.

EDGAR: No kidding, makes mine sound like a sapling with no branches.

ME: OK, folks. Thanks for joining us once again. Be with us Monday as we follow The Mooch on our podcast. Link to it on

our website, radioguys.com. And we hope to see you again next
Saturday at the same time. Take us out, Edgar.

EDGAR: Have a great week-end, friends. And remember,
Chill or Be Chilled. (And the Almost-Jaws bass riff rolls out as
we wave at our on-the-street listeners.}

It's just Edgar and I and Saul who have lunch in the back
office of Whiskey 'n Ribs. Our first real remote behind us. No
bombshells outside the front windows.

"Hey, this seemed pretty OK, given it was only our fifth
show," I commented.

"That was just one hour out of the week, and I'm
drained," said Edgar. "And Roxy was doing the heavy lifting.
How do those people do daily talk shows, some for three
hours?"

"Good question. I'm happy we started out this way.
Maybe even end up this way. Especially with most of the
comedy writers working for our government in DC."

Saul added, "It is exhausting, I can see. Thank all the
non-secular powers for the gift of Roxy. Did you think the
enchilada report went OK? I know you were probably
expecting a more straightforward review."

"I thought it was great, Saul. And after reading about the
Marley family roots, I'm thinking we should spread out into
much greater diversity and unusuality, if there is such a word."
(Edgar shakes his head; there isn't such a word).

The owners, Rocco and Sebastian step inside their
office. "Great show, guys. Saul, maybe sometime you could do a
little tutorial on craft whiskey, kind of like your search for the
perfect enchilada. There are several other good distillers in the
area. You know, a rising tide raises all boats, right?" suggested
Rocco. "Sounds good to me," I responded.

We savored our pulled pork and a couple beers before
parting ways. I had a great feeling about the show. Then I

started searching in my mind for what might blow up in front of us. I hate it when I do that.

Monday, August 21, 2017

The Mooch.

What struck us most as we did our podcast during The Mooch was hearing some of the passion with which people described their experience. How they were moved, awed, stunned even. I talked with a man who was making plans to take his family to view the 2025 eclipse and praying that he'd live to see the one in 2045. This kind of reaction was enough to threaten any cynicism that might remain among the Radio Guys, almost.

Roxy was back for our real time podcast. She had more stories, several unmentionable on air, about the buzz in and around the OLAS Motel. As of this hour, there were no disappearances or homicides among any of the temporary residents there.

There was a puzzling sense about the astonishing interest in The Mooch; so many people wanting to look at what we weren't supposed to look at. Is that a basic tenant of human nature? Kind of like the porn curiosity? Or opening your eyes before you've finished counting to twenty in hide-and-seek? We just can't help it?

Or, do we just want to know, and in this case, see. I mean actually seeing stars in the sky close to the eclipse in the middle of the day is quite amazing, right?

As the bass riff rose in volume, we welcomed our listeners, several who stood outside, a few with SunGAZE eyewear for eclipses and above-ground nuclear-test viewing. They were constantly looking skywards, and then checking us out. We wore ours, but didn't look up, because we were inside our front window studio.

We began.

ME: Well, Edgar and Roxy, it seems that we will mostly be making announcements about what we hear from around the world as well as locally and nationally. And Roxy seems to have a stack of things already. Where do we start?

EDGAR: OK. Right here in our fabulous city of Denver, there's a Home Depot upon whose roof is a large and growing gathering of lookers. They've utilized a huge array of extension ladders or been assisted to the heights by a number of rental power-lifts if they were unable to climb to the roof. Where they aren't supposed to look at The Mooch.

ROXY: From poolside at his Mar-a-lago Palace in Palm Beach, the President and his immediate staff and the Russian Ambassador are glancing skyward for something, his staff perhaps anticipating a floating pink slip. And the Vice President is standing by somewhere in case he's needed for something. The rest of the White House staff has been given the day off to watch The Mooch with their families.

ME: Well, that's reassuring. I'm sure the White House staff has been working overtime to prepare for this event, especially with the possibility of having it rescheduled. By the way, what do we hear from Poonang, North Korea?

ROXY: So far the barrage of rockets carrying Kim Chi has yet to be launched. On the other hand, the Supreme Leader of North Korea, Kim Ill Bung has announced he will destroy South Korea. No details on the how, yet.

ME: Keep us posted, Roxy.

EDGAR: Well, here's a list of things, not quite breaking news, about other related eclipse events: China has announced a new fragrant tea, Sacred Flower Eclipse Tea. I doubt if the name, The Mooch, will catch on over there. A patisserie in Nice, France is serving up a Chocolate Eclipse. And France has authorized the naming of a recently developed wine grape, Vin de Lune. And, get this; in the spirit of international cooperation, the White House announced from Mar-a-lago Palace that the U.S. is building a Nuclear Stealth Bomber, thus informing the world that the skies are no longer in contention. They belong to the U.S.A. And don't forget it. Now there's something, right, Jake?

ME: We're no pushovers, are we? A sky for a sky. Kim Chi doesn't have a Chinaman's chance. Does that make sense?

EDGAR: Sure, like a riddle. It's all cosmic funny business.

ROXY: I think we knew earlier that England had canceled any political events or celebrations surrounding THE MOOCH as it was almost certain to be raining and no one would show up. But, a major London outdoor retailer has redesigned the mackintosh with a special eclipse insignia that is being sold madly throughout the ill-weathered isle.

ME: Well, that's the spirit. And I have this news flash, not completely breaking news, that several southern state legislative bodies are scrambling to have the eclipse, that we call The Mooch, officially named, The Jefferson Davis Eclipse.

EDGAR: Never underestimate our patriotism.

Roxy hands Edgar a sheet.

EDGAR: Thank you, Roxy. Here is the BREAKING NEWS: SO FAR, NO ONE HAS BEEN DIRECTLY KILLED BY THE MOOCH. That is really amazing. (He repeats the headline) I can't help but wonder if there will be some deaths. I mean people are going to be looking up, even some drivers, I'm sure.

ME: Do you think there will be lawsuits? Can you blame it on The Mooch? Or will people be held accountable?

EDGAR: It is an act of nature. But, still. If someone falls off the roof of the Home Depot, is anyone liable? Like if one of the lifts tips over? Or a ladder rung fails? Or someone simply falls over the edge while searching the sky for Kim Ill Bung in a hot air balloon.

ME: Good to worry about, Edgar.

ROXY: Well, boys, here are a couple new items that might give you pause. From an observatory in Palm Springs, actually a telescope in a high rise, a photo has clearly shown a picture of a rocket soaring across the dark center of The Mooch with GUAM painted across it. Yes, Guam. On a rocket.

THE MOOCH came and went. We began to wrap up. A few non-sensational news items trickled in but people were drifting away from out front and we imagined our radio listeners were doing the same.

The national media attention began to shift to the President's scheduled evening address from pool-side about what he thinks of Afghanistan. What will he say? Followed by what did he mean? Followed by, what will that mean? And then, does he really mean that? Or How should we feel about what he might mean? Then, a later media review about what do other countries think he meant? And how will what he might have really meant play out at home and abroad? And what might the president's supporters think about what he said? And will that help or hurt his standing and popularity? Finally, "experts" will be called upon to speculate if the eclipse had anything to do with his announcement about what he might do about Afghanistan? And then, there will be varying opinions in Afghanistan about what he has said he thinks about Afghanistan and what he might do.

We might even catch a few candid comments here and there, such as: who really gives a flying fuck what he says or what the pundits think he's saying.

In the end, there will be no end. The news will repeat the most dramatic speculations all night long, and then repeat them in the morning for anyone who hasn't had enough, or has nothing going for them or is in media and is charged with keeping the speculative fires burning 24/7. My lasted speculation is that eighty-seven percent of the news is speculation.

We will not be covering the Afghanistan Speech. We won't be reviewing it on our Saturday broadcast. We are a politically free show. Unless, Kim Ill Bung's Kim Chi payload is launched into the atmosphere and interferes with our broadcast hookups, and we see him sailing over Denver in his hot-air balloon. Then it becomes personal.

All said and done, our podcast took about fourteen minutes to set up, sixteen minutes to watch our outside audience watch the eclipse, and twelve minutes to debrief our radio audience with breaking news regarding the eclipse.

We estimated our live audience out front at about thirty-five listeners, and a wild ass guess that our podcast audience might have been as many as fourteen listeners. We could have had them all over for dinner to get their reactions.

PART III

Early on I was full of myself. More
recently I am full of baloney. I'm
much happier being full of baloney.

Jacob Finnegan

Monday, August 28, 2017

Roughly five months have rocketed by since April Fools Day

when I dropped the absurd idea of a radio show on my good friend Edgar. That's hardly enough time to learn how to make a good Bolognese sauce, let alone muscle through six one-hour talks shows designed to hold listener interest and to make them laugh a bit.

Our follow-up show, August 26th, to The Mooch Podcast, swept up the odd contrails that inevitably follow a major international event. In the case of The Mooch, nothing should surprise.

Roxy compiled a list of unremarkable Mooch trivia that we enumerated on the Saturday broadcast. For example, on the following Wednesday, several spies were caught hiding in the White House. It turns out they had snuck past White House guards who were looking up at the eclipse, some with their special glasses on, and several (rumor has it that our President was among them) who thought the warnings were simply a scam to sell protective eyewear. Those several are now under serious treatment to save their eyesight. And they will most likely need to seek new careers outside of the security industry.

On the southeastern side of Manhattan, more specifically on the bridge connecting to Brooklyn, a young male comedy writer named Archie, was attacked by a small group of thugs for refusing to argue with them about whether an actual eclipse had taken place. Archie was quite OK with the actuality of the event, The Mooch. Evidently the thugs were not.

Twenty-eight percent of the people who watched the Mooch were skeptical of its reality, thinking it was an illusion perhaps manifested by dark forces that had no appreciation for cosmic funny business.

Ripley's qualified The Mooch has having the largest international audience to watch an event that you weren't supposed to watch.

Dr. Nadine had no opinion about The Mooch, but she did declare that it was *Paranormal*, and it could foul up, even further, relationships that were on the rocks. Unless, of course, those people, who know who they are, could get an appointment with Dr. Nadine, or, at minimum, read her latest book, *Recoupling Uncoupled Couples*.

ME: *Well, it looks like our stalwart listeners here on the sidewalk came through all this unscathed.*

I wave at them, so do Edgar and Roxy.

EDGAR: *Thank you all for coming out. This is our seventh Saturday broadcast, and I, for one, am promising that I won't talk about The Mooch anymore. Not one word. It's time to move on, right?*

ME: *Unless you're one of the young mothers who named their newborn after The, uh, Mooch. May you have no regrets.. I'm sure your child will thank you for it later in life.*

EDGAR: *After they return from an ashram or a few years in an asylum. I'm joshing, of course. How do we finish the show today, Roxy?*

ROXY: *Well, first with a message from our sponsor. And then an announcement from our New Product source. And, finally, and I can see his yellow derby bouncing along down the other side of the street, our man-about-town Saul Friedman. I'll bet he's got a great idea about where our listeners can enjoy a new culinary experience.*

EDGAR: *OK, this segment of the Radio Guys Talk is brought to you by our friends at Fresh and Breezy. They have a new product, another product to solve a real problem. It's called: Driver's Window Savers, and it's not for preventing the breaking of your windows by a rock or hitting a low-flying goose. It's to prevent against unsightliness when you have to spit, and, after looking around so as not to be recognized, you hurl a loogie sideways only to realize your car window is still closed.*

Edgar pauses to see if there are horrified looks on the faces outside our window. I look at him with slight apprehension. Have we just lowered, for the umpteenth time, our bar of good taste?

EDGAR: You can find these moist paper window savers at your supermarket or any of the auto supply stores near you.

ME: What makes this a special product, Edgar? How does it work?

EDGAR: No rocket science, Jake. It comes in a packet like lots of wipes, although this packet is in the shape of a garbage truck, so it's easily recognizable. You merely remove one of these Window Savers and quickly rub over all the embarrassing evidence, and the ultra absorbency and the special chemical fluid instantly restores the clear shine.

ME: Sounds like a miracle, Edgar. Thanks to our friends at Fresh and Breezy for another way to improve your day.

ROXY: If you haven't noticed, Jake, it looks like Edgar has a new fan club outside. I can see at least half the women are wearing paisley ties. Quite fashionable, I'd say.

I notice the new paisley that Edgar has, then, sure enough, the number of women donning a version of same. Then they raise a banner that sums it all up: WOMEN WHO LOVE MEN WHO WEAR TIES.

ME: Wow! You do have a fan group, a very attractive one, Edgar. You must be flattered. An engineer with a fan club based on your sartorial flare. And none of them have pocket protectors.

EDGAR: I had nothing to do with this. Maybe they're making a statement that very few men in Denver wear ties anymore. Denver casual has become the gold standard for Denver men, it seems. I'll bet less than twenty percent of men have worn a tie in the last two years. Maybe women would like to see their men dress up once in a while. But, hey, I am pleased. Imagine me, having any remote chance of such a following.

ROXY: Hey, you're a stud, Edgar. And you're right. You can't tell a brain surgeon from a carpet salesman based on how they dress. And you thought you had a face for radio. Maybe there's a TV in your future. Why not?

For the first time, I gave that some thought. A radio show, also on TV. Certainly there were many of them already, especially in sports broadcasting. But, us? Don't even think about it. Then, again, that's not keeping an open mind.

Conveniently, Saul slides into a chair next to Roxy, sets his yellow derby on the table. He nods approvingly at Edgar, and waves to the women who like ties.

Surely Edgar won't give Saul a run for money in fashion. Then I wondered, what will Marge think about women chasing Edgar? My guess is she'll love every minute of it. And she'll be telling all her friends.

I looked at Roxy as Saul went into his eloquent exposition about Pho, the Vietnamese noodle soup meals traditionally sold all along Federal Avenue. They'd been expanding in popularity, moving into the suburbs and even downtown. Saul pressed his opinion that it was worth the drive to Federal where there were dozens of Pho Restaurants that offered a real cultural experience, and a wide variety from chicken or shrimp to tendon and tripe and the common experience of having to listen carefully through the Vietnamese accent. Finally he offered several interesting names for Pho restaurants, first enunciating the correct pronunciation of the word: FUH. His choice was one he'd read about in Seattle called *WHAT THE PHO!* (Do you suppose their customers would adopt the acronym WTP! among knowing friends?)

As Saul was finishing up, I noticed Roxy had a concerned look on her face. Then she shook it off and moved into a quick reminder that we would have The Radio Guys Talk t-shirts for sale after the show. In nine colors.

When Roxy began cranking up the bass riff to signal we were coming to the end of our show, I had a sense of satisfaction about how comfortably we worked together. Our first two shows, with all the embarrassing interruptions and panics, seemed distant. Was that because we were more confident? Or just the lack of unexpected disruptions? Time would tell, of course. But I felt the confidence that a relief pitcher has when he knows he's got all his stuff working and he's confident he can get the next three batters out and preserve the W.

Monday August 28, 2017

This was the first Monday morning that I didn't have a session scheduled with Jan; she was out-of-town. She told me she needed a break from her clients' struggles to devote to her quirky, for a woman, I think, passion for fishing. In this case fly-fishing. She stayed at a hot springs spa in the mountains and fished her days for rainbow and brown trout, which she released and then ordered in the fine dining restaurant that fed the guests. There was one other woman who shared her passion and they met up each year about this time. This fly fishing buddy was also a psychotherapist and Jan told me they unloaded all the crazy encounters they'd had with clients the past year, pouring out their annual chance to laugh out loud at the absurdities of the human condition as we attempt to re-rudder our life courses. All of this anonymously, of course, in deference to HIPPO.

For some reason, she hadn't mentioned our radio show to anyone, probably not risking the remote possibility that one Mildred Fillmore, might interrupt another broadcast with accusatory evidence that our show was endorsed by at least one psycho ninny. I did, however, muster the courage to compliment the woman triathlete who could out lift me with barbells at my local gym. I couldn't think exactly how to interrupt her rigorous routine, so I just assumed when the time came I'd say the right thing. Wrong! What would you expect?

"You look like you've done this before," I said, trying to make sure she took me seriously. *I mean, seriously?*

Her look expressed silently that this wasn't the first time she'd heard my lame come-on. And it hadn't impressed her on any of the previous occasions.

She, however, expressed compassion for my paralyzing awkwardness. What is it about trying to get a date with a woman you don't know, without ever saying, *Hey, I'd really like to have a date with you?*

"I have done this for years now. Is that what you really want to know?"

"How did you guess that wasn't what I wanted to know? I have a finely developed skill of saying something really stupid when I'd like to talk with a woman that I don't know. Unfortunately it seems to come naturally. My name is Jake and I have seen you here many times and I think you're attractive and I never had the guts to make a fool of myself with that clever pickup line and ask you out."

"Well, Jake, that's a mouthful. Are you married? Are you financially stable? Have you ever served time in prison? Are you conservative or liberal? Do you have children? Let's see, that's good for starters."

"Geez, that is a mouthful, isn't it? Actually, thank you for the questions. At least I have something to talk about that doesn't sound stupid.

"I'm divorced for almost twenty-five years. I'm retired from an advertising career. I don't owe any money. No prison, yet. Ha, ha. I'm pretty liberal, and I have two daughters who are smarter than me. But they seem to like me."

"Interesting, Jake. My name is Elizabeth. And what would you like to know?"

"Uh . . . (Brilliant start, Jake.) Well, I know you've done this workout thing before. Many times, it's obvious."

I was enjoying her facial expressions. Her laugh lines were lovely, though hesitant. Her teeth were beautiful. And her brown eyes were clear and warm. I took a liking to her. Right away. And, I DIDN'T ASK HER TO MARRY ME!

I continued, "I guess the same things, as a start. Are *you* married?"

Elizabeth tilted her head, as though measuring whether she wanted to have this conversation proceed. "I am married. In fact I'm in the process of a very contentious divorce. So, you might not want to go further with the questions."

Still resisting the ridiculously tempting notion of responding with, *Will you marry me as soon as you're divorced?* I said, "I guess that could mean a lot of things. Could we have coffee or a drink sometime and talk further?"

"I think that would work. What's your last name, Jake?"

"Finnegan. Jacob Finnegan. I'm sure you've never heard of me. No reason to."

Just shut up, Jake. Take her seriously.

"*I'm* leaving town in the morning to visit one of my kids in Chicago. Why don't you give me your number and I'll call you when I get back. That'll give you time to reconsider. Back out if you'd like."

"Sure. Maybe I'll get cold feet. But don't count on it."

I gave her one of our *Radio Guys Talk* business cards. She took it without looking at it, slipped it in her workout shorts and reached to shake my hand. It seemed very uncomplicated. Why do I always make it so difficult?

Wednesday, August 30, 2017

After the three of us worked on new content for four and a half hours, Edgar and I drove downtown, parked behind Whiskey n' Ribs and walked through the kitchen to the bar. We were the first to order, about a half hour before anyone else showed up for Happy Hour. We sat around one corner of the bar, easy to see each other as we talked.

"Interesting that Saul says he can get plenty of the local businesses to advertise on our show. I worry that it'll kill our current fantasy sponsors just by an overload of ads."

Edgar responded, "I agree. But, even if you and I don't need an income, I think we need to get Roxy something. We can't let her do what she does and in good conscience not pay her." I nodded in agreement.

He continued, "I'm not sure what that amount should be. Maybe we could start with something the two of us could handle, and gradually increase it."

"I like that. We could start the first of October. Have a special party to let her know how much we like working with her."

We sat silently for a while, savoring the whiskey. I was considering our good fortune when the thought popped out, "You know, I've been thinking about our show being a politically free zone. I didn't know how that would work, what with all the outrage and the angst and the division that exists around the country."

"You think we should open up to comments on the political swamp?" Edgar perked up as he quizzed me.

"Not at all. I've just been really surprised that there is so much else to make fun of, or to laugh at. And I am really feeling better not taking sides or a poke here and there. It's a big change for me. I'm guessing my blood pressure is seriously lower, though I haven't checked."

Rocco and Sebastian walked into the bar area, checking

to see who was working and stopping to greet us.

"How's it going, guys?" asked Sebastian. "I liked your coverage of The Mooch. How did you get all that stuff out of Jackson Hole? I couldn't tell how much was legit."

"Don't spend too much time trying to figure that out. We sure don't." Edgar reached to shake their hands. "Are we still in your good graces?"

"No question. There seems to be a growing interest in your show and the fact you're on air right in the front window of a downtown restaurant. Our restaurant. Any idea how many listener's you have?" Rocco asked.

"Pure guesswork," I answered. "More than a dozen, I hope. All we know is that quite a few people are standing at the front window on Saturdays and some of them are regulars. You've probably noticed Edgar's fans: *Women Who Love Men With Ties.* But, I'm sure you could ask five hundred people randomly in Denver before you'd find one who knew about the show."

"Maybe, said Sebastian, "but we know there are lots who come in and ask about the studio you've set up. We always encourage them to give it a try."

"Thank you." I said, "We're just talking about having seven shows completed. It's a small number, but it takes a lot to put them together. And we're laughing at the notion that we've actually pulled it off this far. The force must be with us."

"Got any outrageous things planned, like those two women who quite dramatically stirred things up?" asked Sebastian.

"Not really," I answered. "You know we've told you none of that was planned. Honestly. We couldn't risk that kind of thing. What if it really went south? Shit, someone could get killed. Maybe us."

Sebastian laughed like he got it. But there was also a

hint of suspicion that we weren't coming entirely clean. They walked out, making hand signals to Claire, our bartender, that our tab was on the house. Life is very good right now.

Edgar and I picked up where we left off. Should politics still be left to others?

"I might be accused of ignoring some real important stuff that's going on, but there are so many people covering it, some good, some bad, and it's so much a part of peoples' conversations that I have no idea what to add to it. One thing I know is, I can't do much about our politics unless I'm really working on it, spending money and energy, and I know there will be a time for that. And I'll jump in. In the meantime, I'd rather talk and think about something else. In this case, something outrageous."

"And my wife thinks we're outrageous, and funny, and she's always talking up the show."

"Good for you, Edgar. Tell me, aren't you enjoying this whole thing?"

"Like I never believed possible. Pinch me, Pasqualini."

"Pasqualini?"

"I think he was some famous Frenchman that said something famous? After being tortured in a Chinese prison."

I laughed. "I don't know about that, but I can feel something coming on about him. Poor guy. A new sponsor, maybe?"

"That's how it seems to happen, isn't it?" said Edgar. "Some word, some phrase, some odd notion, that's how we get our material, isn't it?"

I laughed again. "For a man with almost forty years of civil engineering under his belt, you pick up on the whole process quite nimbly, Edgar. Isn't it nuts?"

"Nuts!"

We parted ways a half-hour later, Edgar headed for one of Marge's home-cooked meals, I stopped for take-out, Thai, in this case, and a half-gallon of ice cream. As I sat on my deck finishing my meal, I realized that I hadn't thought of Carly for almost a whole day. Until that very minute. It was a mixed bag. In the end, there was a pang as I thought about her moving on, and realized I wasn't completely out of the woods. Maybe I needed to find something funny about my dilemma to help me move on?

Another thought to explore for our show, maybe. After all, I was doing a segment with Dr. Nadine about relationships, matters of the heart.

Saturday, September 2, 2017

The low rumble of the bass guitar settles us down and we prepare to begin as Roxy brings the growl to an attention grabbing level, then quiets it quickly as she nods toward Edgar.

EDGAR: Good morning everyone. Welcome to the Radio Guys Talk. A modest little talk show where we intend to take your mind off whatever might be troubling you. Thank you for listening. And for the enthusiastic listeners gathered out in front of our broadcast booth in the front window of Whiskey 'n Ribs downtown on Larimer between 15th and the Sixteenth Street Mall, welcome as well. I am humbled to see a number of beautiful women wearing classy neckties to support my efforts to upgrade my appearance by wearing ties for the first time . . . well, since I got married. That's about right. And I love the banner you carry, WOMEN WHO LOVE MEN WHO WEAR TIES. You're very special. On my left is my partner in crime, Jake. And next to him, the brains, the class, the eye candy, that drives, maneuvers and fuels this show. Roxy is the one I'm bragging about. And she's about to tell us what we have lined up for you today.

ROXY: *Good morning everyone. Great intro, Edgar. How'd you get so fly?*

EDGAR: (Befuddled) *Fly? Uh . . .*

ROXY: *You know, cool, sharp. Sassy. Don't worry, you can take it as a compliment.* (she laughed) *We'll talk later. You're right, we have a great show including a visit with Dr. Nadine, an on-air interview with a budding celebrity, and some of our regular segments like New Products from The Wall Street Journal, and, questions from our listeners.*

ME: *And you just handed me a couple of new oxymorons from our listeners. Let's quickly get them up there. Remember, these are two words that are used together with obvious incompatibility. Here we go with one sent in by a woman who said we could use her name, Jane Doe. So, thank you, Jane. She says she just went to one of these for the first time. A Poetry Slam. Hmmm. Poetry Slam. What do you think, Edgar?*

EDGAR: *That's a good one. Obvious though, if you're into poetry. It's a gathering of angry, outraged poets looking to settle their grievances. What else could it be?*

ME: *Sorry Edgar, obviously you're not into poetry. Are there any engineers who are into poetry?*

EDGAR: *I never brought the subject up while on site as an engineer. Although I seem to recall a few roses are red verses from childhood. What words would rhyme with hydraulics, or abiotic, or racking course?*

ME: *Well Jane tells us that it's a gathering where poets read their own work, and eventually the audience, mostly other poets or family and friends, votes for who they liked best. It's very civilized, Edgar. Unlike civil engineering, maybe.*

EDGAR: *Engineers are more into opera.*

ME: *Thank you, Jane. Now, here are a couple more. The first from a woman just returned from a long weekend of family camping, in the rain. You'll get this one, Edgar. Happy Camper.*

Right folks, Happy Camper?

Outside a few fist-pumps confirm agreement.

And two more: Good Grief. Something we all use. And, another one that most of us use, maybe with a little more amperage, Holy Shit!

EDGAR: We decided that we could use that one without bleeping, like someone did on Oprah, right?

ME: We did. So thank you for sending these oxymorons to our website, radioguys.com . You know this is the segment that refuses to die. Our listeners, at least a vocal portion of them, continue to send them in. And we will continue to respond.

ROXY: And now, a word from our sponsor for the first quarter hour: our friends from **Gluten Fix Supplements,** *the folks who provide you with gluten, if you can't find meals or food products that are not gluten free, or if you live with someone who follows a gluten free diet, and you go along with it, rather than have to fix special dishes on your own. With Gluten Fix you can eat gluten free, with plenty of gluten to maintain your normal levels.*

ME: There's a response to every need, isn't there. Really, I don't know if I should eat gluten or not? Maybe I'm too old. Even bacon is being suggested as an addition to so many dishes. Of course I come across it most frequently in Bloody Marys where they offer bacon infused vodka, and an actual slice of bacon that is somehow stiffened and stuck standing side by side with the dill pickle and Serrano pepper. Breakfast in a tall glass.

ROXY: I don't think that has anything to do with Gluten, Jake.

EDGAR: Roxy has just handed me a BREAKING NEWS! bulletin. Thank you, Roxy. Here it is, folks. BREAKING NEWS: YOUNG PEOPLE HAVE DOUBTS ABOUT WHETHER SOCIAL SECURITY WILL BE AVAILABLE FOR THEM. Let me read that again.(he did) *It didn't seem very funny to me.*

ME: You're right Edgar. My kids tell me that. They don't have much faith in our government, it seems.

ROXY: My kids definitely don't. For a large part of their lives they've seen dysfunctional leadership in our nation's capitol.

EDGAR: Just like the steam engine, maybe? It's there, until it isn't.

ME: Here's a sordid notion. Our representatives are waiting for more and more of our people not to expect it, Social Security. Then they don't have to vote against it, it will just not be in the budget some year. Poof!

EDGAR: This is getting into politics, isn't it, Jake? Our no-fly zone. And, it's not very funny.

ME: You're absolutely right. Let's move on. The joke is on no one.

EDGAR: Well, here's something we never counted on.

He points across the street where a tour bus is unloading. A banner on the side reads, **Radio Guys Talk**. As the passengers disembark, it soon is apparent that most of them are wearing fancy ties. Even most of the men.

Roxy stands to reach a note being passed over our backdrop.

ROXY: For our listeners, there's a bus unloading in front, and those debarking are wearing ties. Obviously this is related to Edgar's cult of Women Who Love Men With Ties. And I've just been informed they have reservations for lunch here at the Whiskey n' Ribs, after our show ends. There are seventy-two of them. Evidently they belong to group called Action on Saturdays. A Denver-area group.

ME: Let's see, that almost doubles our radio audience. Welcome everyone. When Saul gets here, we should get him to interview someone from this group.

Edgar waves, holding up the ends of his paisley tie. Some of the new arrivals respond in kind.

ME: I hope this show meets their standards of action. They should have been here for our first couple shows.

ROXY: I see that our celebrity guest has arrived. He's just getting settled.

We shuffle the chairs and hand him a headset as he takes a seat.

ROXY: Our guest comes to us recommended by our friend, Saul, who caught him at the Comedy Pub, just a few hundred yards from here, two nights ago. He refers to himself as a stand-up wannabe. But Saul says he was impressed.

EDO was born in Ljubljana, the capitol of Slovenia. He immigrated to the U.S. twenty-one years ago. He is an American citizen now and he was, and still is, a professional artist, a painter, who sells his landscapes across the country. Welcome to EDO DOBNIK, everyone. Sporting a six-dollar haircut, a shirt with airplanes doing acrobatics against a sky blue background, and a week's growth of beard that is headed in no particular direction, his hands are decorated with a full palette of paint smudges, and his smile is tight from so many years concentrating in front of an easel. A youngish man in oldish appearance. He fumbles with the headset. And catches himself from tipping sideways as he glances around, staring mostly at the gathering crowd.

EDO: Looks like the word got out about my appearance here. (He smiles weakly, but a few of our razor sharp audience outside catch his humor and laugh.)

ME: Hello, EDO. Yes, you must be used to this by now. The crowd adulation, I mean.

EDO: Last week when I arrived at another comedy venue to open for a stand-up act, there were only four men sitting in the place. I said hi and asked them where they were from. They looked at each other then said, "I think we have the wrong place. We thought this was an AA Meeting."

ME: Not much of a bar crowd, was it? So, EDO, you refer to yourself in this background sheet as a Fine Artist and a Stand-Up Striver. What does that mean? And by the way, you have a very distinctive voice, beautiful accent. Great for radio.

EDO: Thank you. Well, I guess it means I've selected two careers which have very little financial stability. So far I've gotten to the point where I do a few minutes to open for a headliner. I guess that's the striver part.

ME: And you want to be a headliner, I take it.

EDO: Of course. That's my goal.

ME: Well let's back up here. Why stand-up comedy? Did you try it in college?

EDO: No. Closest thing to performing was blowing a horn in the marching band. I was a natural introvert. In fact I was excellent at being non-social. Even non-existent. I was so damn good at being awkward, that at some point along the way, I began to nurse this skill.

ME: I guess it didn't interfere with your painting, then.

EDO: True. Painting is a very solitary profession. But then, after twenty-five years of trying to act like an adult, I was attempting to have a conversation at a party with a woman who was desperately trying to separate herself from my awkwardness, my presence. I eventually blabbered, "So I guess you're not thinking of getting married to me." She laughed. In fact she laughed so hard she choked and sprayed red wine onto her white tank top and all over her hands and arms. I didn't know what to do, brush her boobs or call 911. And I started to laugh. You could call it a spiritual moment. I was so uptight, so stiff, so awkward, I just had to laugh.

And that was the beginning. My second creative career. I just knew it clear as a glass of gin. A revelation. I kept laughing while my wine-sprayed and momentary conversationalist slipped away with friends to somewhere she could borrow a clean top, *or, more likely, just leave. I never saw her again. Now, don't tell me you've located her and she's in back to greet me and tell me she's never been able to get over me.*

ME: Not quite, EDO. But I'm sure she's listening. How could she ever forget you? So your comedy shtick is self-deprecation?

EDO: Self-immolation might be more accurate. Sometimes it gets the audience on my side. There are people who identify with self-pity, I guess. Awkwardness is my Co-Pilot, my bumper sticker.

ME: So two careers with financial insecurity. Why? Comedy is tough, unless you become a Seinfeld. I can imagine painting is the same, unless you turn out to be a Picasso.

EDO: You know, I've asked myself that all my life. I guess I never inherited the sensible gene. In fact I don't know what that would feel like. I've been a part-time security guard, a ticket-taker at theaters, and a dozen other dead-end jobs that keep popcorn in my kitchen and fast food wrappers strewn with pizza boxes all over my living room that doubles as my studio. It's a glamorous life.

EDGAR: I'm listening to you, EDO, amazed at what you've taken on. How has it changed you, this comedy career?

EDO: I don't exactly know. Maybe I've had to look at my awkwardness so intensely that I've almost befriended it. To the point where it doesn't cripple me. You know, if you can stand up in front of a bunch of strangers, and try to make them laugh, it's about as frightening as standing up in front of a firing squad without closing your eyes.

ME: I can imagine. So, how do you get to be a headliner?

EDO: You tell me. I've been waiting around for several years. No one has asked me yet. (Pause) *Come to think of it, maybe I do know. Could it be just as simple as, first, having enough drop-dead material? Like why I'm more comfortable dating cousins. Or why I only have sex after baseball games. Then, when I get the audience with me, I just keep on talking. I simply delay welcoming the headliner I'm warming up for.*

ME: What could happen?

EDO: I don't know. But I'm going to find out.

ME: We thank you, EDO DOBNIK. You can see some of the positive reaction out front here. Tell us, what is your best killer line?

EDO: Well, I can't do it here. I only do it when I see an attractive woman in a white blouse holding a full glass of red wine. Our viewers are clapping and yelling though we can't hear them. As EDO works his way awkwardly through the opening in the backdrop, I notice Roxy staring out front, squinting, straining her eyes, in fact. She breaks her trance, returns to her notes.

ROXY: Dr. Nadine is with us again. And I have her on the line from Hope, Arkansas. Her latest book is Recoupling Uncoupled Couples.

ME: And how are things going in Arkansas this morning?

DR. NADINE: If you mean, how is my new book selling, I can say it's a landslide, although we don't exactly have landslides here in Arkansas. (Her Arkansas drawl immediately establishes her as someone a cultural thousand miles from Denver.) *You could say it's started a recoupling landslide down here. And it's moving out over the country. I'm sure you can buy it in Denver. Or, on Amazon.*

ME: Well tell us, are there just a lot of couples out there who are separated, or divorced, uncoupled as you say, and want to get back together but don't know how to go about it?

DR. NADINE: All of those reasons, plus often a lot of pressure from friends and family, especially if kids are involved, to give it another try. You know, folks down here don't really like the notion of divorce. It's just not the way it's supposed to be.

That's why I spend so much time talking about getting people talking again. Creating a bridge to overcome unrequited love. If you're not talking, the next stage is walking. Away from each other.

ME: I see. Well, since this segment on Advice for the Lovelorn, is mine, I thought I'd ask you about something that has frustrated me. On-line dating. I've been single for way more than twenty years and I haven't been successful on several major online dating sites.

DR. NADINE: Here's the thing. Most men don't really know what women want. Sure, some of them want financial success in their mates, most of all, but, and this might surprise you, some of the really good ones want a man with a good, a great sense of humor. Even the real religious ones.

ME: And how do you get that across before you actually get someone to respond to your site?

DR. NADINE: Well, come on now. You have to write something funny. Or get help writing something funny. Of course, if you're not funny, that will only get you one meet-up. Then you should move on to another thing that you think is endearing about you. Cat got your tongue? Ask a friend or two. Don't have any friends? Well, I guess you could make something up. But, really, that will only go so far.

ME: I guess that makes sense. Mating isn't for everyone, is it?

DR. NADINE: You can't force matrimony or hegemony I always say. Pets are always good.

ME: So you think I've been going about this the wrong way, then?

DR. NADINE: Of course. That's gotta be the case. You're a handsome man with a highly engaging personality and an enchanting voice. You're just not putting the right foot forward.

I'm starting to think Dr. Nadine has me confused with

the mellifluous voice of Edgar. At this time I make the decision not to bring up my disastrous offer of marriage to Carly on our first date. Why bring up something quite so embarrassing? It could only go south. Maybe to Hope, Arkansas. I don't think it could propel me into a new career like it did to EDO Dobnik.

ME: Thank you, Dr. Nadine. We wish you well with your efforts to recouple people. By the way, something I've always wanted to know: Why is Arkansas, pronounced Arkansaw?

*DR. NADINE: Well, there's a very good explanation, Jakie. Some folks claim it all started with a typo when they were printing the first state records in 1836, the year we became a state. Just look at your keyboard. Notice how close the S is to the W. But, a keyboard typewriter didn't exist until the 1860s. So the real story is that a very proud and adamant young typesetter, Will Clinton, insisted on the phonetic spelling **saw.** His reasoning was that everyone would misspell the new state, and confusion would reign. Well, the governor wouldn't go along with the upstart typesetter, and the documents were reprinted with the **sas** ending. You might be interested to know that in many parts of the state, the elementary schools teach the **saw** ending because the parents are tired of having to explain the unexplainable spelling to their kids.*

ME: Well thank you. Very interesting. So keep us posted about Recoupling Uncoupled Couples.

DR. NATINE: I'll be delighted. Remember, what goes 'round, can go 'round again.

I'm shaking my head as I spot Roxy, focusing again outside our window. Her expression is uncomfortably distraught. Then I see Saul's yellow derby bouncing along on approach.

EDGAR: Here comes our man-about-town, Saul Friedman. He's grabbing his remote mike and headphones, ready to risk his neck outside interviewing some of our onlookers. Good morning,

Saul.   Saul sets his derby aside to accommodate technology, and quickly moves outside with his gear.

EDGAR: Saul, maybe you could find out about this group that arrived by bus to see our show and to have lunch here right after. Their group is called Action on Saturdays. Who's in charge of the Action on Saturdays group?

Several turn and point to an attractive woman, above average height, auburn hair, and seemingly ready to laugh at the slightest excuse. She's wearing a bright blue top over white slacks and blue deck shoes. Saul moves right to her.

SAUL: Hello there. And you are the leader, I see. Your name, please.

LADY: My name is Mary Helen, and yes, I'm kind of the organizer of Action on Saturdays. We're a very social group and we like to check out interesting things and we have a great time doing it.

SAUL: And you picked the Radio Guys Talk show.

MARY HELEN: Yes. The daughter of one of our members happened to see it when you were covering the eclipse and said we have to come down here. So here we are.

SAUL: Are there any qualifications to be a member?

MARY HELEN: You have to have a sense of humor. And you have to be able to arrive at our bus prior to departure time. This is our second year.

SAUL: Well, you have a fabulous smile, I guess that qualifies you, right?

MARY HELEN: It was my idea originally. To give me an excuse not to do housework or yard work on Saturdays. We've grown fast, over seventy members now. Our bus had problems this morning, otherwise we'd have been here right from the beginning. But I see why it was recommended to us. A show that makes me feel good about being alive.

SAUL: Well, thank you, Mary Helen, for bringing your

group, Action on Saturdays, to our show. I hope you enjoy. And laugh. And I know you'll like "Whiskey "n Ribs.

Roxy is leaning toward me, talking through our headphones, a stressed look. "Jake, something is weird. There's a very odd, strange man out there. I saw him last week. And I think I saw him near my house the other day. He didn't look the same, but I think it's the same guy. Creepy."

"Which one is he?"

"The one in the navy baseball cap, and the gray sweatshirt and the huge aviator sun glasses. I can't read what the shirt says. He's right by the curb. Ick."

"Maybe we should have Saul check him out. Saul can you hear this?"

Saul nods and forms a circle with his thumb and index finger. Edgar is also searching out front. Saul thanks the Action on Saturdays group for joining us. Then he moves toward the weird guy, greeting several others on his way.

SAUL: What a lovely crowd of people. Let's find someone who's not wearing a tie.

He casually sidles up next to the weird guy, raising the mic to his mouth.

SAUL: Here's a fine gentleman without a tie. Sir, welcome. How did you happen to come here for The Radio Guys?

The stranger almost panics. He is too hemmed in to hightail it, but he definitely would like to disappear. As he keeps turning his head, looking for some way to avoid Saul, he also senses all the eyes turned toward him and concludes he has no choice.

WEIRD GUY: Vell, I yust vas valking by. I vas curious, I am guessing. Eet ist fary unusual, no?

SAUL: Well, I can tell you're not originally from Denver, where are you from?

WEIRD GUY: I am from Svitzerland. I am touring and I

never seen a radio program like zees one.

SAUL: What is your name, sir?

WEIRD GUY: (Now frantic for an end to this conversation and an exit.) *Meine name ist Hans Grueninger. Yes, sank you, I must be going.*

SAUL: Thank you, Hans, for chatting with us. Enjoy your touring. And now back inside for the finish to our show. Jake.

ME: Well we seem to have many interesting listeners and watchers here on this Labor Day Weekend. Good work, Saul. Edgar what's next?

Roxy exhales, her troubled look confirms she knows him from somewhere. We'll find out more when the show ends.

We move through the last third of the broadcast. New Products from Wall Street. And finally our last segment: three questions we ask our listeners.

EDGAR: So, get your pen and paper out, folks, or your phone, this is the time when we ask you, three questions. These are questions you can ponder over the coming week. And here they are: First. What is the course you liked the most in high school? (He repeats)

Got that? OK, now the second question: What word or phrase makes you squirm in discomfort? (Again, he repeats)

And the third question: What would you do if the fiancé who dumped you at the altar moved in next door with married mate and children? There you have your assignment. See what comes up for you. Usually we're really surprised at your answers. Post your ideas on our website: radioguys.com .

As the bass sounds slowly intrude, we remain silent until Edgar signs us off with his mellow reassuring voice. His last words: *Remember to do your homework. And, hey, we're in Denver, get high in the Mile High. Thanks everyone.*

Roxy looked wiped. I felt wiped. We moved back to the Whiskey 'n Rib's office where we ordered pork sandwiches and cold beers. The gal who took our order said she heard our ad, *Who Does Lady Gaga listen to these days?* on the radio. Very sly, she said.

Edgar asked Roxy, "Is sly like fly?" Roxy answered, "We'll talk later, Edgar."

Saul limped in a few moments later. "I tried to catch that guy. Well, follow him anyway. He was really in a hurry. He turned corners twice almost immediately. My ankle is still mending, so I lost him. He was definitely strange."

"Well, I know who he is. He's definitely trying to disguise himself. I met him in Jackson Hole. He was the Prof from Germany who threw the Prof from Tehran under the bus. Called him a hazel nut or something. A pistachio, it was. Then he kept trying to get on a first name basis with me. It felt weird, like I was being hustled all the time. I'll listen to that broadcast and get his name. Yuck!"

"I remember how he tried to persuade you that the two of you were best friends. How did he get your name and all that?" I was becoming more concerned.

"I gave my card to that woman who helped us up there. Simoni. I guess she passed it on. Maybe she couldn't tell one weird guy from another in that motel. I'm sure he was very persistent."

"You think we should inform the police?" asked Edgar?

"It's not a bad idea," answered Saul. "Get that name first. I don't know if they'll do anything. But I can ask down there. I've got a couple friends."

"The main thing is to be on the alert. You said you saw him in your neighborhood, Roxy?" I asked.

"I did. I wouldn't have thought anything of it except I remembered a guy who resembled him at last Saturday's show.

This is too weird. Thanks for getting him to talk, Saul. He couldn't lose his accent. That's what gave him away." Roxy took a gulp of her beer and leaned back in the chair. We agreed to let the show content rest until Tuesday since Monday was officially Labor Day and we were all laborers. When Sebastian and Rocco came in to compliment us on the show, Rocco asked if we'd be willing to autograph menus for the seventy-two diners from the bus who would be soon be occupying all the seats.

"That pretty woman in blue told me that several had asked to meet you all. Pretty nice, eh?"

"Very," I said. "Next it'll be hand imprints on the front sidewalk. Come get us when it works best for you guys. We'll eat slowly. The foods pretty decent here, you know." I smiled, thinking that except for Roxy's new problem, this had been a great seventh show.

Tuesday, September 5, 2017

Roxy erased the white board in the AM 1480 studio while we refilled our coffee cups and cut up croissants from Adele's Pastries. She was in better spirits. Saul had called her to get more information before he headed into the police department to check out the man that had introduced himself to Roxy as Professor Dieter Deuter up in Jackson Hole.

"Maybe I'm just overreacting about this whole thing. Maybe he's just a strange awkward guy who has a crush on me. That thought is horrifying, though. Yuck!"

"As soon as you hear from Saul, let us know," said Edgar. "I will. Let's move on for now. We have a clean slate to fill for Saturday."

During the next hour our ideas began to make it to the white board. At the same time we talked over the last broadcast. Our concern was how long we could continue an interview either on the phone or on site and still keep our audience with us?

We listened to the call with Dr. Nadine, and the interview with the standup striver, EDO DOBNIK. That had gone on for almost seven minutes.

"I think it was amusing enough, though," said Roxy. "Maybe there is no arbitrary time limit as long as it keeps moving. You guys seem to have a sense for that. I didn't feel like signaling that we needed to wrap it up."

"But you would if it was dragging, right?" I asked.

"I would. And the call from Dr. Nadine, too. That was trickier. I didn't know exactly where it was going. Even though I was doing Dr. Nadine. That was the strangest thing I've ever done."

"I hear you. The hard thing for me is to forget you're the one doing the voice. I have to really ignore that and believe I'm talking to the real doctor. It is important that I don't look at you sitting there hidden from our audience behind that poster on the easel."

Edgar added, "It's like talking to two people at the same time if we look at you while you're doing an impersonation."

"We've got two phone segments listed for next Saturday," said Roxy. "I think we should spend some time working them out now. Especially the one with two guys from Chicago that are bringing their bathtub gin to Denver. I think it could be a good interview. I need to work on a youthful male voice. About thirty-five years of age. My concern is losing my voice if it goes too long. Then what do we do?"

"We fake a failed telephone connection, tell our listeners we'll try to reconnect later." Edgar shrugged, like no problem.

We tossed ideas around. It's crazy how that process works, one thing leading to another. It is a team effort, but you have to keep pushing, not settle on one idea, so you can weave an interview together with enough twists and turns that you know will get a rise. Once again I commented about how relieved I was that we only had one show, one hour, each week to create.

"Imagine a daily show. Or even one three-hour show. Actually I don't think I could do either. I'd have to be smoking something or snorting something, and I don't think the results would be very good."

"You never know until you're faced with it," said Roxy. "But I agree. It would be a huge stretch. I have no idea how many people work on a weekly or daily live show in New York or LA. But it has to be dozens."

We also dreamed up a new sponsor: *The Haberdashery Shoppe,* in downtown Denver, would be providing Edgar with his stunning ties every Saturday. We'd need Saul to help us with some brands and styles to give it credibility. Maybe we'd actually find someone who did have a clothing business and a great line of ties who would be interested. And, why not a drycleaner that would be willing to launder my blazer following it's weekly punishment from our prep on Saturday morning as well as the stress of being on air? I recalled the stress I felt during the failed divorce mediation when Carly tried to help my ex and me withdraw to neutral corners. And that brought to mind, of course, Carly, and how I made her laugh back then, at least once, and how she'd had the last laugh two months ago.

We generated another celebrity interview for the coming Saturday. It might evolve into a series of "celebrity guests" in town performing or whatever, and eating at Whiskey 'N Ribs. A natural tie-in, we thought.

It could be a Kardashian perhaps. In this case, a distant cousin, Vinnie Kardashian. Hard up for elusive celebrity attention, shunned by the tightly knit clan of, some would say airheads, that are on one cable channel or another, twenty-four-seven. There's no telling what he'd be willing to leak if he knew just one other person might hear it. Might identify with him.

We discovered that although his wife just had another baby, his marriage is on the rocks, his mother is on trial for murdering his father in the garage with a garden hoe, and he'd been caught by the IRS for not paying taxes the past ten years. Surely here was a man worthy of public sympathy and support, or, scorn and disgust. Such fun.

This was a job for a local actor with enough makeup to create sleeze, and still appear a hair credible. Roxy would make some calls. Our repertoire was expanding. The Radio Guys Players were in the embryonic stage.

Saturday, September 9, 2017

Our Saturday show rocked. We had a Vinnie, like no Vinnie could be. He was despicable, vain and irritable. He dished some dirty laundry about his supposed connection to the Kardashian clan that drew audible groans from our street-side audience. Edgar and I squirmed as Vinnie dove into his dumpster of disgust to verbalize that all of them had police records, seven children had been given up for adoption along the way, and sitting at the dinner table was like eating with a mob of whiners, backbiters and unbearably dull talkers. Enough to drive a man to consider a sex change operation, as well as a last name change. Vinnie was glad to be out of the putrid mist of their environment.

Edgar and I challenged him about most of his claims, scrambling to fend off defamation lawsuits before the Dashians got word of our show. *"When was the last time you were with them? (He couldn't remember exactly, except it was for one of their birthdays) Do you have proof of your relationship with them? (Not with me. But why would I lie?) Have you ever really met one of them or are you trying to play on their name? (I don't need to play on their name. I have a career of my own and it will be bigger than theirs in the end).*

Vinnie was nimble, if repulsive. He delicately walked the line between providing a good disclaimer for us, and still suggesting a grain of truth to his stories. Well maybe less than a grain.

We brought him to a close as the thumbs-down responses of our viewers became audible, even through the thick plate-glass window. We segued to a commercial for Out Damn Spot, by Monster Brands. *The super detergent for the most defiling stains and disfiguring blemishes on all surfaces and fabrics. Redact the dark and dirty.* Out Damn Spot seemed an appropriate response to Vinnie K.

Also made by Monster Brands: Felony Ice Cream and Felony Chocolate Syrup, so good to taste and a crime to waste.

We did not see Professor Teeter Totter. Later, unfortunately, we would find out he was watching from the lobby of the huge condo building across the street.

The rather strained interview with Vinnie had the viewers outside scratching their heads, and shaking them as well. Vinnie clearly had stretched the limits, the boundaries of any sort of taste. Vain, unkempt and impolite. Hardly a guest we would invite back. I assumed any radio listeners we had were likely questioning our judgment. I took the occasion to rescue.

ME: Well, I see outside that some of you are wondering about that interview with Vinnie. In fact we'd like to know what you're thinking. Did you enjoy it? Like him? Should we invite him back? So we're putting this up on our Radio Guys Listener Poll for you to weigh in on. Tell us what you think. How was our interview with Vinnie Kardashian? Just go to radioguys.com.

Unwilling to wait until they connected with our website, almost unanimously, thumbs down dominated the gestures of our viewers.

Undaunted, we next offered up a, topic for our listeners to also respond to: **What should be allowed on planes?**

EDGAR: I guess the first question I have is should people be allowed to use cell phones on planes while they're flying? Now that's a pretty straightforward question. What do you think, Jake?

ME: That's an easy one. My answer is NO. NEVER.

EDGAR: My, no room for accommodation, huh? Are you against people staying in touch?

ME: NO. I'M NOT! I'm against sitting in tight quarters having to listen to one half of a phone conversation with a fellow passenger who is talking in a loud voice because he or she is afraid they need to overcome the distance of thirty-five thousand feet. It's the cell phone Law of Inconsideration. (Yes, it is a word)

EDGAR: So it's the volume of the voice?

ME: No it's the inconsiderateness about it. And if the person on the phone whispered, it might be even more annoying. Like they were talking about me behind my back. Or planning something illegal, or asking how to get off the plane or how to set off a bomb.

EDGAR: No wiggle room on this, right, Jake?

ME: Boy, this is a hot-button, isn't it? Maybe it's because I already have long legs and the airlines have squeezed out so much legroom that I'm always ready to react when the person in front of me starts to lean back into my knees. And don't suggest that I should pay extra for more leg room unless you're willing to raise the issue of over-sized people needing to pay for two seats. Help me Roxy, I'm making a fool of myself.

ROXY: Hey, Jake. I'm pretty small and I don't enjoy flying much anymore. I get that you don't want to experience any more discomfort or intrusion as a passenger. I forgive you.

ME: Thank you, Roxy. I'm really not a monster.

EDGAR: OK, then. What about this? Should dogs be allowed on planes?

ME: How can I say no here in Denver? Everyone has a dog here, except for me. And my ex-wife . . . she's probably got one by now.

EDGAR: So it's another NO?

ME: I'm ok if they ride in steerage, with the other luggage. The dog . . . and the passenger, even. Please not next to me in my seat. Edgar, this isn't going well. And if dogs are allowed, why not cats? If someone is allergic to dogs but requires an animal companion, what about iguanas? Or a raccoon . . . or a snake? Where does it stop?

EDGAR: I take it you're against dogs with phones, then?

ROXY: I think Jake is being honest. And he's likely to catch some heat from this. Why don't we put this on our Radio Guys Poll. See where our audience stands on the issue. It's quite a touchy one, I think.

ME: Thank you. I can see by the expressions on our outside audience that it's time to move on. So let's open up this question that Tim, age fifty-three, sent to us. It's a doozer, I might add. It seems that Tim, who was not living in Denver when this happened three years ago, is still plagued by it and wants our take as to what he should do? He writes, "I bought a lottery ticket when the amount was up to fifty-three million dollars. I've never won anything, really, but I always write the ticket number down somewhere, and tuck it into my wallet. Then it happened, I saw the winning number when I stopped back into the store where I buy my newspaper. I couldn't believe it. It was my number. I almost had a heart attack I was so blown away. I raced home to *get the ticket out of my pants in the closet. They weren't there. I looked everywhere. I called Dorothy, my wife, at her work. Where are my tan khakis? I asked her. I was so worked up I could hardly talk.*

"They're where they always are after I wash them. In the dryer."

I raced to the basement and pulled the clothes from the dryer. Yes, the ticket was in the pocket, but totally disintegrated. Almost dust. No possibility to read anything. I was absolutely horrified. I leaned on my hands and felt sick.

Enough about that. You can imagine. I have tried so hard not to let it affect our relationship. But, it has, and I don't know what to do about it? Obviously she didn't do it on purpose. But she didn't pull it out of my pocket either. I love her. But I often get testy when there's a question between us. Or when I'm frustrated by something else. What would you do? And, what should I do?

ME: OK, Edgar, let's hear your take on this one. What should Tim do?

EDGAR: Let's see. If Marge had ever done something like that, what would I do? After I'd tied her to a chair in the basement with her head under a dripping faucet. For just a couple of months. That might sound like an overreaction. But you have to understand that Marge's idea of a practical joke is to stitch across my socks about three inches up from the toes and then listen to my reaction when I'm in a hurry to dress in the morning.

I've never come up with something to get even with her. Maybe I just don't have that retaliation bone in my body. Part of it is I hear her giggling in the other room when she hears my grunts and groans, and, well, I just love the sound of her giggling.

ROXY: You're a teddy bear, aren't you Edgar?

EDGAR: Maybe. But I've never even considered what the

loss of big money, like fifty-three million bucks, might mean. So I don't have an answer for Tim. But I guess you could say I feel his pain.

ME: What if it was just one million, Edgar? Roxy? Would it be any easier?

EDGAR: Might be harder. A million is a lot of money. Most of us would be thrilled to have it. Fifty-three million? It's almost incomprehensible.

ROXY: So what about Tim? Any good ideas? We don't know exactly, but it sounds like his marriage is OK but for this lottery fiasco.

ME: Sounds like a poll question. We're getting a lot of questions up there this week. But it's not like it was intentional, and if he loves his wife, he's got some work to do about forgiving her. Or, maybe that's not quite right. She didn't do anything that requires forgiveness. He left the ticket in his pocket, right? And should she have to be responsible for that?

ROXY: Now you're talking, Jake. And aren't there all kinds of tales about how big winners sometimes can't cope with huge winnings and it changes their lives in unexpectedly bad ways? They can't handle it.

EDGAR: I'm pretty sure I could handle it. (Edgar's huge smile and a quarter turn of his head convey a lack of conviction.)

ROXY: I'm with Jake. Tim, laughter might be the best medicine. There's nothing to forgive, and you're miserable because you're stuck and don't know how you should feel. But it's not how you'd like to feel, I can tell. I know you can work on that, Tim. Thanks for asking us. And with that, it's time to wrap up this Saturday's edition of The Radio Guys Talk. Edgar, take us out.

EDGAR: Thanks to our listeners and the growing crowd that stands out front on Saturdays to follow the show. We'll continue to deliver great weather to you. Sweet Jesus, what would we do if it was pouring rain from noon to one o'clock? We'll work on that this week. Maybe there's a way we could protect you all, just in case.

ME: *We thank all of our sponsors this week including our new ones: Felony Ice Cream and Felony Chocolate Syrup. Give them a try; it's a crime if you don't. Next week our man-about-town, Saul, will be back from a vacation. We'll find out where he was and what he did. And, keep up these conversations on our Radio Guys Poll. Just go to our Web site: radioguys.com.*

Roxy starts bringing up the bass track. She reminds everyone outside: "Hang around for a few minutes, I've got Radio Guys tank tops and T-shirts, including new colors.

EDGAR: *And remember . . . Chill or be chilled.*

We leaned back in our chairs, each of us. "Lunch time." It was Rocco, leaning over the backdrop. What a terrific idea. So would a couple cold beers. We straightened the papers in front of us as Roxy carried a box of merchandise out front to sell. It reminded me that Edgar and I needed to talk about paying Roxy. Pronto.

Monday September 11, 2017

My morning check-in with Jan, my shrink who just returned from a three-day vacation bone fishing in the Florida Keys, was very positive. I heard about a couple of her fishing catches that were every bit as glamorous and exciting as Steve Irwin, the Aussie Crock Hunter, whose frequent skirmishes with sharks and marsh pythons entertained, until he met up with an inhospitable stingray in shallow water.

It was her passion that was enchanting and irresistible. And it caused me to wonder if I was pushing myself enough in this life of mine. Could I compare anything with her passion for fishing? Her face lit up as she exuded a boundless energy as well as a harbored calm. It was something for me to think about. Also something for me to ask her about.

"How did you find this passion of yours? I think I want some of it?"

"That's a big question, Jake. Because I don't really know the answer. It didn't come instantly. In fact I had to be away from it for some months before I even thought much about it. Then one time I sat with a date in my living room, it was in December I think, snowing outside, and I described the fishing I'd tried with an instructor, and then how it felt when I actually had a strike, lost it, and then had another strike.

"He seemed hopelessly disinterested. I don't know if it was me or the fish. I, on the other hand, refilled my drink and talked on, realizing I really missed fishing, and I was going to make plans the next day to go somewhere and fish. That was the real launching, I think. Now it's my mental escape, and my go-to place for guaranteed pleasure and adventure. How's that for an answer, Jake?"

"It's a great answer! I'm wondering if I can climb on that wagon with the Radio Guys? I mean I like it. But do I like it as a passion? Or, just something new that's kind of fun to do?"

"Those are good questions. About anything, at any time. Aren't they some of the questions avoided in the "unexamined life"? I think taking a look is a good thing, Jake. Something no one can do for you."

We ended with me telling her I was going to meet up with my new interest, the weight lifter. We'd made a "sort of" date for when she returned in two more days. If we were still interested? She would ask when she called.

I thought I was still interested; my thoughts of Carly had been slightly rarer and briefer lately.

Thursday, September 14, 2017

When I look back on my first date with Elizabeth, there were a few things I would change. First, I would have chosen a different place than Whiskey 'n Ribs. Not that it isn't a great place, but I'm certain she thought I'd created a set-up. Everyone came up and said, Hi, Jake; Great show Saturday, Jake; People keep asking how to get your autograph, Jake. All great to hear, but Elizabeth looked bewildered.   We took seats at the bar and began our conversation. "So this has something to do with your business card, right?"

"I should have warned you. It's where we do our show at noon on Saturdays. And it's a brand new place and I thought you probably hadn't been here."

"And you're on the show, then?"

"Yes. With Edgar and Roxy. It's a talk show of sorts. I'm not surprised you haven't heard of it. We're just getting started and people are probably stumbling onto us. A few people anyway. We're getting responses on our website. And a modest sized group usually shows up in front on the sidewalk. We try to make people laugh."

"Laughing is good. Who's the funny person?"

"Well, there's Edgar, and Roxy and me. We all try to add to the humor. Edgar, he's a natural. He can remember a thousand jokes. And, he's quick on his feet. Roxy is also our producer, but she can create characters with her amazing vocal skills. I'm just along for the ride."

"So it's a talk show on Saturdays at noon, then."

"That's right. But, Elizabeth, I didn't invite you down here to talk about our radio show, though you might not believe that. I really thought you'd like this place. The owners and the staff are absolutely great."

"No, that's all right. I can use an abrupt change of place and topic. I'm worn out from the life I've been living lately. It's like a slow death."

"I wondered. I think you described it as a very contentious divorce. No fun, is it?"

"You've been there, I take it?"

"Yes. But maybe there wasn't as much at stake to use the word contentious. It was messy, childish, on my part, and maybe the rancor we felt helped to clear up any doubts of why we were going through with it. And crush any thoughts of giving it another try."

"It's amazing how it can turn. From high expectations to get-me-outta-here."

She did finally allow for a brief smile. She also slumped for a moment, catching her breath. "Before we go any further, I'd like a drink. I can see the bar is well supplied."

"Right. Sorry. Uh, Nell, when you have a second, help us with drinks. And this is my friend Elizabeth."

Nell is almost six feet tall, graceful, short black hair, and dark eyes that stare right through you, force you to take her seriously. She delivered our first round and dropped a compliment to Elizabeth. "I'm sure you can do better, but Jake is pretty harmless."

Two gulps for me and two sips for E. We resumed our conversation with my question: "So, in your situation what exactly does contentious mean?"

"There are several things, but one in particular. I think Daniel is hiding assets from the proceedings. Lots of assets. My guess is somewhere out of the country."

"Aren't there legal requirements to reveal all assets in a divorce?"

"Yes. And I know them well. But he's a smart guy, and I think he's been doing it for a long time. And so far no paper trail to track them."

"How long has this been going on?"

"I served papers on him almost three years ago. He has

stalled every step of the way as far as providing information on his finances."

"How close are you? To knowing about all his assets?"

"About half, I think. It's my best guess, although we never looked closely at each other's personal savings or investments. Just our joint assets. Now it's the principal of the thing. I've made estimates, lots of them, and I think I'm close to being right. And it really pisses me off that I have to keep spending huge lawyer money trying to get him to come clean."

"I won't ask any more, unless you want to talk about it. It's none of my business, but thank you for giving me some idea what you're going through."

She shrugged, as though she was used to it all by now. But I could see lines on her face that I hadn't noticed at the Gym. She was paying a price for her suffering, for her insistence on fairness.

At that moment she tipped back her glass of Pinot, downed it and set it down with a decisiveness that called Nell over.

"Another, just like the other, please. And you, Jake, another beer?"

"Of course. We can also look at the food menu. Should we eat at the bar or in back, Elizabeth?"

"I don't care, but I'd like to see the back rooms. I can smell that the food might be very good."

We were guided to a table for two against a brick wall. The candle was quickly ignited, our drinks were delivered and we toasted each other and moved into more biographical exchanges. She'd been a marketing VP for a major food company; I'd never had contact with them since we had a client with competitive products. "I quit that job when my kids hit high school. I had to get reacquainted with them before they were gone on their own. It happens very fast. I think my son was gone by the time I faced up. My girls are OK. Linda is having her first child around Christmas. The other one, Mattie, is beginning a Ph.D. program at CU. All three are pretty smart, and so far none has been in serious trouble. That's a pretty good record, don't you think?"

"More than pretty good. Your son?"

"In law school at DU. I don't think he likes it, but he'll have to decide. His name is Nathan. He played La Crosse there during his undergrad years."

We ordered another round and some pork sandwiches and salads. I was thinking of how I might usually proceed at a point like this on a first date. I could tell we were pretty different in temperament. She was easy to look at. Her first facial expressions tended to be very serious and her voice was a bit flat. But I liked her openness and I assumed her divorce process was having a seriously heavy impact on her attitude about life.

I didn't feel any pressure to make something happen. That was new for me. I thought it might be nice, great, to sleep with her. And usually that was enough to keep me hustling. But that wasn't enough this afternoon. I felt at ease, hardly inclined to make a crazy and inappropriate jump-shift to this question: *Elizabeth, after your divorce is finalized, would you agree to marry me?*

I took some credit for that restraint, but, honestly, I just didn't feel like asking. So how much credit could I give myself? I found myself eager to eat, maybe have one more beer. And I searched my mind for something funny to say, to entertain both of us. And nothing was coming. I swallowed hard, then took another swallow.

"Jake, I know I'm kind of a load right now. I feel like I'm plodding with heavy boots, dragging my past right behind me. I appreciate you asking me out. But I'm not sure I'm ready to even think about something after my divorce. My heart's not in it. And I think you're a pretty interesting guy. You've got lots going right now, much more than most guys your age, and I'm not implying you're so old. They are usually quieting down, coasting, burned out, maybe. You've got life and energy in you. I think I'm just not up to it. I'm stuck in my own pity, kind of in an endurance mode. I'm not happy about it, believe me. But it's with me every hour of every day. I think working out is the one time I feel alive. In fact, I've been thinking of entering a marathon, or more likely, a half marathon. It might really help me."

"You don't have to apologize. I'm probably not a good catch right now, either. Most of my energy is consumed by the show. And it's all new. Lots of adrenalin, and it's all I can do to come up with some of our material. I think we should enjoy our meal, another drink, and whatever happens, happens. I do think you're a cool lady. Just underwater right now. And your idea about a marathon seems like it might make sense."

Saturday, September 16, 2017

Our man-about-town, Saul, showed up about an hour early, back from vacation, his yellow derby lighting the way. While we were shuffling our papers and reviewing the sequences, the two actors that Roxy had lined up for one of our interviews were going over scripts, making notes as they found places to interrupt the flow with comments or questions. Edgar and I read some of our questions to get them used to our pacing and that was it. I had wondered if we should have had a rehearsal a day or two before the show, but Roxy assured us that these two actors were really pros and were doing it because it might be a fun gig. Hey, she knows her stuff. That's enough for me. A few deep breaths and the low rumble of the bass track pumped energy into the broadcast space, and turned the heads of our gathering listener/viewers toward our window. That thirty seconds of rumble performed miracles, at least in my case, creating the mood and tone and sense that we were serious and competent about what we were about to do. We couldn't control all of what might happen, but we knew each of us would attempt a rescue if something went awry.

EDGAR: Good morning Denver. Good morning all you great folks out front here at Whiskey 'n Ribs, a most fabulous place to sip and dine, right on Larimer between Fifteenth and the 16th Street Mall. Welcome to the Radio Guys Talk, a political free talk show where we try our damnedest to make your day contain a little laughter. As you might have seen, Saul, our epicurean maestro, is back in his yellow derby. He's prepared to come out front for an interview or two with you folks. Roxy, what's on our program this sunny Saturday?

ROXY: It's packed, boys. We've got your responses to last weeks poll questions. Dr. Nadine will be with us. Thanks to Saul's heads-up, we have a special interview with a couple guys who are bringing an outrageous concept to Denver. We have a new sponsor, and a couple oxymorons and, well, we'll see. Jake, who's bringing us the first segment of The Radio Guy's Talk?

ME: OK, last week we announced a new sponsor from Monster Brands. Out Damn Spot, the super powerful cleaner for just about anything. This week another Monster Brand product, Felony Ice Cream and Felony Chocolate Syrup are bringing you the first quarter hour of our show. Now, I want you to know this. This is sensational ice cream. I'm an ice cream junky, and I've tried three flavors this week because I know that I know ice cream. And this is the real McCoy.

Edgar: And what about the name, Jake? Felony Ice Cream? It does sound like a gimmick, don't you think?

ME: On the one hand, yes. But this ice cream really is

fantastic. And it is a crime if you don't try it.

ROXY: I know our audience doesn't fall for gimmicks. But, think of the next party you have for adults or kids, and since this product is just coming into Denver, think of the questions your guests will have about your clever, trendsetting dessert. I mean, don't we all want to be the first on the block, sometimes?

ME: Good point, Roxy. Of course I bought it because it is sensational.

EDGAR: Thank you, Jake. And here it is, just handed to me by Roxy. BREAKING NEWS. The news you won't hear anywhere else before you hear it right here on AM1480, The Radio Guys Talk. FROM CHICAGO. THAT'S RIGHT, BATH TUB GIN. HERE. IN DENVER. And with that BREAKING NEWS, here is Jake to introduce these two fellows who will tell us about this amazing development.

The two young men and Roxy are shuffling the chairs around us. She shifts the mics to accommodate them. They reach out to shake hands with Edgar and me. And we begin.

ME: We have our friend, Saul Friedman, to thank for bringing this new idea to our attention, before it actually happens. But it is no longer a rumor. And I'm happy to introduce these two young lads from Chicago, Ralph Capone and Tony Genovese III, to explain their new venture. Welcome Ralph and Tony. (They both say thanks and wave at the sidewalk audience.) *So, let me start with Ralph. This is on the legit, right? Bath Tub Gin? Right here in the Capital of Craft Beer and Booze, Denver, Colorado.*

RALPH: It's going to happen. We're here to announce that it's coming, before word leaks out. In fact we've had a small advance team out here exploring possible sites and buying up all the old bathtubs on claw feet they can find. We're negotiating between two sites right now.

ME: So, what kind of sites are you looking for?

RALPH: Well, one is an old building that was used for Ku Klux Klan meetings back in the twenties when the Klan practically controlled your state government. Maybe your listeners aren't familiar with how strong the Klan was here in those days; it's a very interesting history. (I watch the faces on our window audience sober up a bit and several exchange comments). *The other is in a structure that is a defunct public steam bath.*

ME: Very interesting choices. Trying to bring back a certain period, like Prohibition, I take it. So tell us about the gin and the bathtubs. Is that just the décor, Tony?

TONY: Not at all. The whole concept is called Bathtub Gin and Spa. It goes something like this: The product, Bathtub Gin, will be distilled with state-of-the-art equipment and the most extraordinary ingredients in the gin trade.

RALPH: We have been perfecting our gin over the past three years in Chicago. In blind taste tests, Gin-lovers tell us it is sensational.

ME: So it's different from other gins?

TONY: Absolutely! In fact I brought a bottle here this morning, along with some sipping glasses. You can see for yourself.

Tony pulls a bottle and five shot glasses from beneath the table. He holds it up for the window shoppers to see what appears to be a very old bottle with a label featuring a claw-foot bathtub with a gorgeous blonde waving as she steeps in the tub. He pours the glasses and places them in front of us. Each of us takes a generous sip, tipping our glasses toward each other. Roxy's eyes pop, so do mine, recognizing immediately that it is much stronger than the typical eighty-proof. Ralph proceeds with the business concept.

RALPH: So, like I said, the bathtubs are an integral part of this spa concept. Right now we have over seventy. (I glance at

Edgar and the outside listeners, the interest seems strong.) *It works like this: The tubs will be located side by side with enough space between for a Spa customer to slip by en route to their assigned tub. Upon dropping their terry cloth robes, they slip into the relaxing bath, seasoned with prize juniper berries, and look around to see what others are doing.*

ME: Of course they would.

TONY: Then they notice the cup holder with a crystal martini glass and a small carafe of dry vermouth. The tub is rimmed with various soap holders piled with an assortment of fancy olives, Gibson onions, lemon peels and tasty anchovies. You can imagine how reluctant they are to leave.

EDGAR: Wait a minute, now. You're telling me they're sitting in the buff in a tub of gin?

TONY: Not exactly. Unless they purchase our Premium Guest Package. Can you imagine that? Looking around and then cupping your hands in the divine brine and sipping this extraordinary gin.

It feels like we've just been put on alert. Questions fly through our minds, not the least of which are: *Do the guests shower first? And, what is the temperature of the gin?*

RALPH JUMPS IN: But Juniper Berry Infusion has many of the same soothing effects as bathing in gin. And, of course it's far less expensive. Now, here's how the gin comes in. See on this label, the suspended showerhead on a snake like hose. The client simply grasps the head, holds it over the glass, and presses a button. Out comes the Bath Tub Gin. If the client wants rocks, they're in the silver decanter hanging next to the soap dish.

ME: Whoa? (My mind goes back to the thought of naked people next to each other in bathtubs). *So they're in bathing suits? Bikinis? The clients? Edgar, don't tell me you're not conjuring up a remarkable image.*

EDGAR: I am conjuring what it would be like to stand up

in my birthday suit and glance down at the pickled wrinkles after spending several hours soaking in Juniper Berry effluence.

ROXY: I think I'm going to be sick.

TONY: We're working on this. First off, it's up to our guests. We're installing oval shaped structures above each tub, with shower curtains draped to give you privacy if you choose. But, we are hoping our guests will be able to have their martinis au natural when they desire. There will be enough space so you'll not feel like you're splashing each other when you get in or out or refill your glass.

ME: So splashing distance determines how close you are to each other?

RALPH: And, of course, the guests choose the location of their bathtub.

ME: It seems like you two have thought of everything. This sounds like another first for Denver and Colorado. It's a bold idea.   RALPH: One other thing. For any of you who are a little bit timid about a community gin bath, you won't have to tub it in order to drink it. Bathtub Gin will be sold in recycled bottles with the label featuring one of the old tubs with a ring around the inside, proving the gin is the same as that served to all those who have sipped and splashed in one of the antique tubs.

ME: OK. Well, move over all you craft brewers and distillers. There's a new bootlegger in town.

EDGAR: I suppose I'll have a dirty Martini.

ME: I'm upset by the image of you standing after three hours in any tub, Edgar.

ROXY: I still think I'm going to be sick.

It feels like the right time to segue to some shorter material, though I think the extended interview survived pretty well.

ME: Why don't we see what our listeners said on our Radio Guys Listener Poll, Roxy?

ROXY: First let me remind you we're brought to you by Felony Ice Cream and Felony Chocolate Syrup. It's a crime if you don't try them, friends.

EDGAR: Fits right in with Bath Tub Gin in the tub, don't you think?

ROXY: Don't go there, Edgar. So, our first poll question was about our interview with Vinnie Kardashian. Should we invite him back? And our viewers pretty much nixed a return visit. Although one person clearly appealed for more Hollywood Dirt.

EDGAR: That's your department, Roxy. You seem to have the pulse of the celebrity culture.

ROXY: I'll consider that, I don't like bragging about unseemly things. Our next question was about what should be allowed on planes, beginning with: Should passengers be permitted to use their cellphones for conversations during the flight? Jake, you gave a flat NO to that question. No wiggle room.

ME: I did. Still do. It's a sore point with me.

ROXY: Well, you were with the majority, Jake. But about twenty percent of our responders said there should be exceptions made. Like if there's an ill friend or relative back on the ground. Or if they discover they forgot something, like turning off the water filling the tub.

ME: I refuse to be drawn back into this, Roxy. It makes my head hurt. How in the hell do you make exceptions? And how long should they allow phone contact? Until the ill friend dies?

ROXY: Just sayin', Jake.

ME: Grumph.

ROXY: And next, Should dogs be allowed on planes? Jake, here again you were pretty adamant. But you pleaded for mercy because most everyone in Denver has or loves dogs. On this question, most people allowed for the exception of Service Dogs. Evidently people think that some passengers are really in need of these animals to travel. As far as other animals, Jake, you're pretty much in the majority, especially with regard to reptiles.

ME: Thank you.

ROXY: So that brings us to Tim. The man who said he lost fifty-three million dollars when his wife laundered his pants containing the winning lottery ticket. This was a tough one. And our listeners offered many suggestions. They were extremely compassionate with both Tim and his wife. And most of them offered suggestions to heal, forgive, forget and move on. In fact we had only one comment that suggested that revenge or punishment of some kind was the appropriate response. Just one listener.

EDGAR: I like that. It's time to let go of what's interfering with their happiness. Jake, you're not the one who sent in that comment about holding her feet to the fire, are you?

Roxy laughed. So did our audience. I liked the laughter, but I still felt like I had been reasonable about what should be allowed on planes. I mean, I love cell phones. Now. I admit I held out longer than most adult males. And I love it when people connect with their hurting friends. Just not on planes. Is that asking too much?

ME: Help me, listeners. I'm not an unfeeling monster. I'm not an animal hater. I'm really a soft touch. Most of the time.

ROXY: And thank you listeners for taking time to voice your opinions. It really adds to our show. We've got one of our regular guests coming up on a phone interview. Jake, why don't you prepare the way.

Roxy is straining to see out the front window. I know she's worried that her German professor friend might be lurking, probably in some sort of disguise.

ME: And who else but our good friend from Hope, Arkansas, Dr. Nadine. (I glance at Roxy who gives me the thumbs up.) *Hello, Dr. Nadine. How are things in Hope?*

DR. NADINE: Well, they're just fine, y'all. And, you're gonna love this. I just bought a flesh-eating Venus Flycatcher that sits on my table when I have sessions with clients. (I catch a few hands flying to faces in our outdoor audience.)

ME: Now that seems like it would frighten people, Dr. Nadine.

EDGAR: I think Marge would like one of those. She hates flies.

DR. NADINE: Well, Marge is not alone. But that's not the reason I have my Flycatcher in therapy sessions. You see, most of my clients are somewhat afraid when they enter into a counseling session. Afraid of a hundred different things. And I use my Flycatcher to show them they have nothing to fear.

ME: You've lost me there, Dr. Nadine. I guess I'd expect that your clients would be even more upset. More scared.

DR. NADINE: That's because you don't understand, Jake. It's called transverse psychology. Some experts refer to it as elliptical transverse psychology. (Edgar is staring at Roxy behind the poster on the stand. His hand is over his own mouth, anticipating his loss of control to laughter. I bite my tongue, not having a clue where Dr. Nadine could be headed.)

ME: And this Elliptical Psycho technique works?

DR. NADINE: Why it most certainly does. You see, the way it works is the client is reminded, by me, that there is no reason for a full grown adult to be afraid of just sitting down in a quiet room to chat. Even the fly, so little, yet so brave, is unafraid to step into the open Flycatcher simply out of curiosity. Then I very gently shame the client out of their fear. "Come on, now. How can you, a big adult, be afraid of just chatting? Why even that little fly is braver than you are. See where I'm going, Jake? Elliptical Transverse Psychology. It's the rage down here in Hope. I'm actually a pioneer in the field.

ME: So it's shaming that works, huh? Isn't that going kind of counter to most theories of helping people cope?

DR. NADINE: You must know that nothing stays the same, Jake. We evolve and our professions evolve. We aren't in Kansas anymore. Freud is long past pushing up daisies.

ME: Hmmm. I guess I have lots to learn. But, it seems to me a little like bait and switch. I'll work on it. Let me remind our listeners out there that Dr. Nadine is the author of the new best-seller in Hope, Arkansas, called Recoupling Uncoupled Couples. How is that going Dr. Nadine?

There's a pause. I'm thinking I offended Dr. Nadine.

DR. NADINE: I'm glad you asked, Jakie. I have launched work on a brand new book, a new concept in couple's therapy.

ME: Wow. You're always coming up with something, aren't you? What will you call the book?

DR. NADINE: Yes I'm a busy lady. The working title, and I think it's going to work just fine, is: When Recoupling Sucks.

ME: A sequel, I take it.

DR: NADINE: Absolutely. I've discovered that most people can never go back. There was good reason for their split. Period. That's all she wrote. Actually, it's all that I wrote. Save your money. For the book. It's almost done.

ME: Well, very interesting. Thank you so much, Dr. Nadine. We'll look forward to the launch. Thanks for joining us. And now we move on to what's next. And I see Edgar giving me the high sign.

EDGAR: We have our good friend, Saul, outside, mic in hand to check in with one or two of our loyal listeners that are actually viewers as well, right outside the front window of Whiskey 'N Ribs, a great place to sip and eat. A most fabulous place. Come by and enjoy. (Roxy reemerges in view. I don't think anyone notices.) *Saul, it looks like you've found someone out there. Who is it?*

SAUL: Thank you Edgar? I do have a lovely young woman,

as you can see. She's wearing a paisley tie, in your honor, I'm sure. And what is your name?'

CELIA: Celia. Just Celia.

SAUL: And where are you from, Celia?

CELIA: Guadalajara. Mexico. (Saul glances toward us; you can see the wheels turning) *I've lived in Denver for thirteen years. I love it here. My kids love it here.*

SAUL: Well I'm happy for you. You said you had a question for our Radio Guys. Why don't you go ahead and ask.

I felt the growing presence of sweat. Would this bring ICE out of the shadows? This was a political free zone and we wanted to keep it that way. Fortunately, Celia saved us, sort of.

CELIA: Thank you. Well, I've heard several of your shows, maybe most of them. And I keep wondering: How much of your show is actually true? Or maybe I should ask: Is anything on your show true?

ME: Well, Saul, you sure can pick out the one's with interesting questions. Let me see, who can I turn Celia's question over to?

EDGAR: Not me. I'm pretty sure it's all true. Unless you've deceived us, Jake?

ME: Roxy, then.

ROXY: The show was your idea, Jake. Sounds like a slam-dunk for you.

ME: I know the answer, of course. I just need a little time to properly explain it. Maybe we could begin our next show with my answer. (I look outside, every pair of eyes is on Celia. She is firmly shaking her head. *Negatory!*)

ME: That's what I thought. And I'm looking at my watch, and I know Roxy is about to trigger the bass rumble that signals we're at the end except for sign-off, so let me try this on for size. And, brevity: The line between Truth and Fiction can be Wiggly and Porous. True is in the eye of the beholder. There. Thank you

Celia. Thank you Saul. We'll clarify that next Saturday. I hope you'll be here. (I notice that Celia is trying to wrestle the mic from Saul. I am hoping she's too good-natured to draw blood.)

As per custom, after slumping back in our chairs, relieved, a few deep breaths, and the familiar invitation from Rocco or Sebastian to order lunch for back in their office, Edgar and I rise, slower than Roxy, stretch and head back to eat and decompress. I glance out the window where Saul is chatting with Celia. She seems in a good mood. Somehow I think she'll be back next week, pressing us in her quest for the "truth" about the Radio Guys *Truth.*

I can hardly blame her.

As we place our order, Saul joins us, a sheepish look on his face. "You probably think I look for trouble with these interviews, but it's not true."

We say nothing.

"Really, that wasn't a bad question. She just called attention to what most people must think about your show. You have to admit that you're rarely flirting with too much truth in your on-air tales. And people can't possibly think it's all true, right?

We still say nothing but let our faces drop as though we're appalled that Saul could actually think we were making up shit.

Then we laughed.

Saul turned to Roxy. "I checked again with the police when I got back from Miami. Nothing new about your stalker, Dr. Whatsit. Sorry. Maybe he took a hint."

"I thought so too, but today, I had that nasty sense that he was still around. I didn't see him, or recognize him. But I felt the same yesterday. It's a real yucky feeling."

Edgar and I looked at each other. We'd talked on the phone Wednesday about this very matter. I faced Roxy, "Edgar and I think we should hire someone for surveillance to see if we can catch this guy. Especially now that you believe he's still here. Maybe take matters into our own hands. What do you think, Roxy?"

She didn't say anything right away, but she was tearing up. Finally she wiped her eyes, "I just wish it, he, would go away. I'm so sorry to drag you all into this. I'm sure I'm safe. But I hate this. This is only supposed to happen to big name celebrities, not to the producer of The Radio Guys Talk."

She forced a coughed laugh, shaking her head, trying to chase it all away. "And I don't even know if he's dangerous or harmless."

"I'm going to make a few calls, see if I can find someone to do some work on this, Roxy."

"Oh, I don't know. I really don't want to burden you all with this. The police have the information. Let's just wait another week. I can manage. I'll be careful."

Saul moved to speak, "What if you did something during your show about this. Told the audience what was going on. Let them know how it was affecting you. Sort of educate them on what's it like to have a stalker. Maybe have a cop on to talk about what they can and can't do."

Edgar responded, "And, there's a pretty good chance this Deeter Dotter guy would hear the broadcast and maybe get out of town. That would be great. Maybe we could get some media people to pick up on it. Spread the word so he can't ignore that he's being hunted. What do you think, Saul, Jake?"

Saul, "I think its good."

"I do too. I'm sure there are other people in our city that have had this problem, or still do. Roxy, do you see any downsides to the idea?"

"I just hate to detract from the show. It's supposed to make people laugh and this sure won't do that. Could we wait a few more days? See if he shows? Shit, how could our attempt to cover the Eclipse lead to something like this? I simply interviewed him for a few minutes. Sure he seemed kind of weird. But I thought he was just a little too full of himself. Not that he was some kind of prurient."

"I'll make some calls. Saul maybe you could ask someone at the police department if they would appear for a short interview, or even if they think this would be a good idea. I still think it is."

"Thank you all for being concerned about me. I'll pay close attention this week. I'm sorry for the trouble."

The cold beers were delivered though I thought Roxy could probably use a shot or two of whiskey. It felt like we were all in this together now. It felt right. And I was keenly aware of what a special crew we had become. I hoped it felt safer to Roxy.

When I finally arrived home, I noticed the text message from Elizabeth, the weight lifter. *Hi, Jake. I heard your show. I liked it; it gave me a lift. Elizabeth.*

I thought about whether to respond. We'd been pretty clear that this was not the time to start something between us. I felt good about that. And maybe I was making too much out of her text. It's a tendency of mine. Finally I sent a simple response. "Thanks, Elizabeth. Glad you enjoyed it."

Then I thought for the rest of the day if I should have been more suggestive of something, more interested. Maybe I should give her a call. I didn't.

Monday, September 18

By the time I'd informed Jan about my first date with Elizabeth, including how we ended it with a comfortable departure and no expectations of continuing any romantic pursuit with each other, and Jan was nodding approvingly at how mature we had been, and I was considering stopping right there, feeling like a sensible adult, mostly, and I did stop talking but felt a definite inclination inside to spill the rest of the beans, and Jan asked, "Well, Jake, it sounds quite sensible. Is that where you left it?"

I hesitated, felt my heart beating faster, and dropped my eyes, knowing I needed to cough up those beans.

"Actually, not quite. I did text her again. I thought, what's the harm, she just gave me a compliment, not a love letter. I just said, "I'm glad it made you feel a little better." No smiley face, no emojis, not even a thumbs up."

"And?"

"And, she texted back, *Maybe we could get together sometime and talk a little about how you come up with your ideas. Your funny stories.*"

"Oh." Jan raised an eyebrow.

"Okay, we have a coffee date for just that purpose this Thursday. I regretted it the minute I offered the idea. Why do I do that? Just when I feel clear about it, I let my insecurities, that's what I think it is, my insecurities take over. Like I'm reaching for a life boat."

"Sounds like its not quite all done, Jake."

"But it sure seemed like it. She's not ready, I'm finally feeling more OK on my own. And I'm having a blast with our show."

"Well, it's not the end of the world, Jake. You've not proposed yet. Have you?"

"No". My shoulders slumped. "Sorry to bother you with this, Jan. I really wanted to talk to you about something else, something that Roxy is going through."

"What is it, Jake?"

I proceeded to explain the stalker that was frightening her. What we'd done so far and what we considered doing on the air. As usual she asked great questions. And offered exceptional wisdom.

"Whatever you do, Jake, make sure Roxy is completely on board. You're asking her to go public with what is probably not only a threatening situation, but, I'm almost certain, an embarrassment for her. At some level she feels like it was something she did that brought this all on."

I got the message loud and clear.

We parted. Once again I counted my lucky stars that I'd found Jan and she was willing to work with me.

Wednesday, September 20.

Our studio session began with me informing Roxy that I'd found an agency that could provide surveillance. They suggested they cover, discretely from eight in the morning until ten in the evening for a two or three day period. All Roxy would have to do was let them know when she was leaving her home and where she was headed so they could follow or transfer contact. "But, Roxy, you know it doesn't make sense if you're not completely comfortable with this. Just say the word either way."

Just getting it out in the open seemed to relax us. She even laughed a little. "You mean like Popeye in the French Connection?" "That's what we had in mind. With the lid, of course."

She paused for a moment, looked down at her open hands. "Well . . . you know how much I appreciate this. I'm just hesitant about doing it right today, since I haven't actually seen him for what, two weeks? I'd like to let it ride at least until I actually see him again. I'm willing to take the risk. He really hasn't tried to harm me. But, I am willing to bring it up on our show because I think it would be a good thing for other women. Even have an officer come on to let everyone know what the police face in these kinds of cases."

"Sounds good to me. You seem to have great instincts about this. Please keep your phone with you," said Edgar, "and call either of us any time."

"Thank you. Now, lets get to work."

And work we did. New sponsor ideas, new poll questions. And new features. We worked for almost three hours, then looked at the white board which was full of new material, or suggestions to be developed. Thinking up stuff can take it out of you. Even though the time flew.

Roxy had her clients to work on. Edgar and I went to Whiskey and Ribs where we met up with Saul. He had some thoughts on how to fund Roxy with paying sponsors. We still didn't see how that would work with our own non-paying sponsors that were a popular part of our show.

Saul had the answer.

"What I propose is this. I can get, instantly, at least a dozen of my clients that would pay just for the novelty of sponsoring your show. Just to "be one of the first" to sponsor it. And, so it doesn't interfere with your proprietary sponsors, all you would have to do at the very end of your show would be to have one of you, maybe Roxy, add something like, *And we'd also like to thank so-and so,* then put in five or six names very quickly, *for their financial support.* That's all. Change it every week, Once a month for each. Start with $200 a month to be mentioned. Twenty-four clients, that's about $50,000 a year. You've had a great start with your show. People want to brag that they're in on it."

"It sounds pretty good, Saul," said Edgar, looking at me.

"I agree. If you've got the clients, Saul. I really don't

want to get into that part of the business. If you think that amount will fly?

Saul reassured us, "For not much money we could hire someone to handle the financial part. Let me get people signed up, I don't expect a problem."

I felt comfortable with his proposal, "I really don't think it will affect the integrity, or lack of integrity, with our regular sponsors. Especially if we don't have to have any kind of tag line or promotional copy for these people. Great thinking, Saul."

We then brought him up to date on Roxy's decision to postpone surveillance for her stalker.

"I hope she's right," he said. "She's a smart lady, but this guy is kind of sick, I think."

We sat silently, ordered another shot each, and Saul informed us that he had found a woman from the police department that deals with stalkers and she'd be delighted to join us on air. We thanked him and knocked back our shots.

"Let us know about your clients who will advertise, Saul. We're informing Roxy we're going to start paying her something right away. We'll gladly cover it, right, Edgar?"

"Absolutely."

Saturday, September 23, 2017

As Edgar turned the key in the rear entry to Whiskey 'N Ribs promptly at eight AM, we practically stumbled through the restaurant to our broadcast setup. Inside the curtain we turned to each other, each ready to blurt out about last evening's news. What had happened was astonishing. It seems our nemesis, Mildred Fillmore, was at it again. This time she was arrested for crashing a fundraiser, a cocktail party for social workers. The fabulous thing was that the guest speaker was being taped for future use. It wasn't so fabulous for Mildred when the cops were called to interrupt her takeover of the presentation, the camera still rolling.

Roxy, with her hands pressed to the sides of her head, exclaimed, "I could not believe it. She attacked social workers for meddling in the parenting of children, no matter how abusive or irresponsible the parents had been. And she railed against foster parenting and counseling for kids in school. She's nuts."

"I'd love to know her story," said Edgar. "She's got to have some horrible history. I wonder what will happen to her."

"I had the notion to gloat when I saw her arrested." I chimed in, "But it was really pathetic. My only question is if she is dangerous? Has she got any record of violence or property damage?"

I had watched the documentary-like clip of Mildred ranting with a microphone until the police gathered her in and led her out to a squad car. By then she'd been yelling about all kinds of meddling in the lives of families. "I guess what she did to us was a warning of things to come. Disturbing the peace around an already disturbed radio show."

"You *would* bring up the thought that we have a disturbed show, Jake." Roxy stood in a scolding pose, hands on her hips, looking great in jeans.

We caught our breaths and began setting up the show.

"I'm guessing she won't be showing up out front anytime soon," said Edgar. "She seems to have her sights set on much bigger targets. We were just a warm-up."

Roxy continued, "Should we make some kind of joke on air? Like we've just been informed that our special guest, Mildred Fillmore, is unable to appear today because of a conflicting engagement?"

I liked the sound of it. And, at the same time, felt the pit in my stomach about getting a laugh at the expense of a person who definitely has some problems.

Roxy reconsidered, "I say we hold on that for now. See what it feels like halfway through the show."

As usual, she was right.

As eleven-thirty approached, we got serious. As serious as you can be when you're making up shit. Edgar snugged up his new paisley tie, I slipped on my navy blazer from the back of my chair, and Roxy brushed back her hair into a ponytail. I wondered if we would attend to any of these details if we were simply broadcasting from an enclosed studio without our crowd of outside viewers.

Then, Edgar lifted a twenty-pound dumbbell from below the table, performed a few curls with each arm for our audience, and returned it to its place. Next he interlocked his fingers and bent them backwards to the point where I worried they would snap. This was a new routine for him, and he was receiving a fawning response from his growing group of fans who aped his paisley with their paisleys. They also responded with their own curl motions and knuckle cracking. He finally raised his arms high, in an all out stretch, and waited for their almost instant response. After dropping his arms, he shook his head, rotated it around, and generated an overall shake of his body. Edgar was introducing a new form of radio yoga/jumpstart that I thought would inevitably evolve to warm-up DVDs for all women wearing paisley ties. Why not? Edgar could pull it off.

Finally, Roxy punched in the bass track and the energy filled our space.

EDGAR: Good morning, Denver . . . good morning all of you listening on your radios to the Radio Guys Talk. And good morning to all of you who've gathered outside our studio window in the front of Whiskey 'n Ribs, a most fantastic new place in town to sip the finest craft whiskey, and savor the most incredible ribs and pasta and salads and desserts. We're on Larimer between Fifteenth and the Sixteenth Street Mall.

ME: Thank you Edgar. I see your fan club of Women Who Love Men in Ties is filling the sidewalk. Maybe later in the show you can repeat your little preshow warm-up routine with the barbells that is already catching on down here. It's impressive to say the least.

EDGAR: Thank you, Jake. I'm building up my strength in case we're ever asked to increase our show from one to two or three hours.

ME: Well, I don't expect that to happen any time soon. But who knows? Roxy, what do we have for our audience on this fabulous fall day?

ROXY: As usual, we're packed with good stuff. Breaking News. Listener questions. Saul's fabulous culinary tips, and who knows what else. One thing I'm pretty sure of, we won't have a reappearance of the woman, Mildred, who made quite a scene down here a month ago. She has a conflict in her schedule. Evidently she was arrested for disturbing the peace last evening at a fund-raiser for social workers. I wish her well and hope she gets the help she needs.

My mouth dropped open as Roxy did exactly what she cautioned us against. She knew we'd react and looked at both Edgar and me, shrugging her shoulders and twisting her head like, "Did I just say that? OMG!"

ME: And I see that this first segment, Questions from our Listeners, is brought to you, whoa, it's brought to you by Dr. Nadine, and her new book, When Recoupling Sucks. Thank you Dr. Nadine. Not only is she a featured guest, but she is now a sponsor. Let's see what she says here on the book cover. I don't think I can replicate her Hope, Arkansas accent. Here goes: "Once again, I've been working on breakthrough therapy concepts to help my clients and my readers. I have always tried to help people in relationships improve their skills and techniques to enrich their lives as couples. And when couples break up, I moved quickly to a therapy program and a new book, Recoupling Uncoupled Couples. It has been a great success. But, in the process I've discovered that most people can never go back. There were good reasons it didn't work out in the first place. And if that applies to your situation, make sure you get my new book, being released right here in Hope Arkansas, today, called: **When Recoupling Sucks**. *It's a crash course on stopping your efforts to recouple when you discover that this effort is going nowhere. There are skills to help you put on the breaks, retreat to your rabbit hole, raise your arms in a victor's pose, and halt all attempts to continue on a course that will surely result in more pain and suffering. Watch for it. When Recoupling Sucks. It could be a lifesaver for your happiness.*

EDGAR: She does it again. Seems she's always on the cutting edge of therapy for couples, right Roxy.

ROXY: She's a nimble woman. We'll ask her more the next time she's our guest.

EDGAR: And before we move into our New Product Section from the Wall Street Journal, I have some BREAKING NEWS! from Roxy. So here it is: BREAKING NEWS: BOB DYLAN RELEASES A NEW ALBUM ARRANGED WITH ONLY A HARMONICA AS BACKGROUND SOUND: IT'S CALLED: NO BELL FOR ME. That's right: NO BELL FOR ME.

ME: It sounds like a dirge, doesn't it? Is it just because he didn't want to travel to Stockholm to deliver his speech and accept his award? Until he did, of course.

EDGAR: Never underestimate the man from the Iron Range of Minnesota. It sure doesn't sound like Mr. Tambourine Man. He can't be put into a box, can he?

ME: He sure can't. Okay, this is a good time to move to our New Product segment from the Wall Street Journal. Take it away, Edgar.

EDGAR: This product is a perfect fit for us here in the Denver area. It's from a company called Leaf Magic. And here's how it works: You all know we live in such a dry climate here, that we never know what our trees will do as far as fall coloring is concerned. Especially right here in Denver. While up in the mountains you can pretty well guarantee the aspens will glow with yellow, gold and orange about now. Not so much in Denver. Mine are still green, and too often they go from green to brown. And the same with other trees, like ash, and maple and even the Gingko that amazingly drops all its leaves on a single day.

ROXY: This sounds like an impossible challenge, Edgar. I know you have something in mind, though.

EDGAR: Listen to this. The folks at Leaf Magic will fix your leaf problem, at least the color problem, with an amazing product that acts as a makeup artist for your trees. If you're unhappy with the color or lack of color, you need one of their leaf color enhancement kits. It's called Jack Frost-in-a-Jug. Here's how it works. In this kit is a plastic jug with a spray nozzle, and the jug is filled with a solution that accepts any of the enclosed color packets: shades of yellow, shades of orange or shades of red. You make your choice and pour this rather gloppy color batch into the solution, then attach your garden hose and spread the huge plastic sheet to protect your lawn from being radically decorated. Turn on the hose. Point the nozzle to the top of the tree and firmly squeeze the trigger. The color solution clings to the leaves, until snow or a good rain or a strong wind brings the leaves down. The amazing thing about this invention is that the color is applied in varying shades, so it doesn't look like you simply spray-painted your leaves in one solid color.

ME: Wonders never cease. Is it on the market, Edgar?

EDGAR: It says it's in test market in New England and Tennessee. Seems to me they should be testing it in Denver.

I check out Roxy, who seems to be on high alert, staring out the front window. Immediately I clench up, thinking she's spotted her stalker, Dr. Teeter Totter. I quickly pan the crowd. What I do see is a very energized woman, with trailing black hair, a sporty red fedora and a large hand-painted poster on a wooden frame that she's carrying high overhead, one side visible to us, the other visible to the street, moving from one end of the crowd to the other and back.   Edgar catches what's going on, and squints as he leans forward. The sign is hand-lettered but clearly legible. As the carrier turns toward us and shifts directions I spot her oversized paisley tie with a red background and her huge smile with overpowering red lipstick. I read, along with the rest of the crowd: I'M GOING TO SLEEP WITH THE GUY WITH THE TIE TONIGHT!!!

The crowd gives way to her and starts cheering, looking back to Edgar for a reaction. By this time he's deciphered her disguise and is shaking his head. "No way," he says with his mic pushed aside, "It's Marge. I cannot believe her. Then, he shoves his mic back in place, and raises his hands, helplessly.

EDGAR: What can I say, I've never seen this woman in my life. But, she is quite attractive, not my type, exactly, but . . . sometimes you have to shake up your routine, right? Maybe if she would return after the show, I could get her name and phone number.

For the briefest of moments, I notice Marge jolt at Edgar's come-on. Then she turns toward him and sticks out her tongue, leaving everyone just a little confused.

Roxy laughs and I'm relieved that we have a less threatening stalker to contend with. Then she informs our listening audience what the fuss was all about.

ROXY: For you listeners who must wonder what just

happened, let me explain. A most attractive woman, dressed to turn heads, just marched back and forth among our live audience outside our studio window, carrying a sign that read: I'm going to sleep with the guy with the tie tonight. Of course that would be our beloved stud, Edgar. And you heard the rest. What you didn't hear was Edgar's comment that this woman was his wife, Marge, in disguise. More on that later, right Edgar?

EDGAR: What can I say? Guys with ties rule! See what you listeners are missing when you're not out front of Whiskey 'n Ribs at noon on Saturdays.

ME: I don't think you're fooling anyone, Edgar. And to think I was accused in one of our earlier broadcasts of using this radio program as an on-line dating tool to patch up my less than active love-life.

ROXY: There you go, Jake. You did it again. Shameless flesh peddling. Of yourself. Thank God we have smart listeners.

EDGAR: Enough. Let's move on. How about another BREAKING NEWS! flash from the Radio Guys. Here it is: LESS THAT ONE PERCENT OF PEOPLE OVER FORTY LIE THAT THEY ARE OLDER THAN THEY ACTUALLY ARE. (He repeats the statement)

ME: So, that seems reasonable. Right? When we're young, we want to be older. When we're old, we want to be younger. Where is the cutoff point? At what age are people pretty much content with the age they are? Roxy, lets put that on our Radio Guys poll for next week.

ROXY: I will. And I'll ask my two daughters. I'm guessing they liked being thirteen, because then they're teenagers. And I think they look forward to twenty-one.

EDGAR: I think after my thirtieth birthday, I always had a dread for the next decade. Forty. Fifty. You know.

ME: That's why we hang on to thirty-nine and forty-nine. Of course I'm not concerned about getting older. That's because

I'm still forty-nine.

ROXY: There you go, Jake. Trolling for women, again. At forty-nine, they're in for a huge surprise. (She laughs into her mic, relishing me on the defensive). *What do you think about people being able to find out our age online? Anyone's? Kind of gives us no where to hide, doesn't it?"*

EDGAR: It's like publishing national secrets. I bet it's got people more upset than the Pentagon Papers.

ME: That tells us something about your age, Edgar. Many of our listeners don't know much about the Pentagon Papers. Or the Deep Throat era.

ROXY: It is kind of an invasion of privacy, though. Yet, should age be such a sensitive issue? Should we spend so much time and money trying to be or look younger?

ME: Yes. And I'm sticking with forty-nine.

ROXY: And I'm looking forward to what our listeners say on our Radio Guys Poll. Let us know out there.

As we shuffle papers for a few seconds, the yellow derby bounces easily across the street toward us. Saul has arrived. I let our listeners know that he has a special segment coming up about his recent exploration into the menu of smaller epicurean delights. Small can be exceptionally tasty.

Awaiting his entry to our studio, Roxy fills some space with our segment that will not die.

ROXY: This isn't breaking news, but I'm here to report that our listeners continue to post new Oxymorons on our website. So in response I'm going to mention a few of them. As you'll recall an oxymoron consists of two words utterly incompatible or contradictory with each other. Until they are found effectively used side-by-side. We've used military intelligence as one widely used to illustrate this delightful figure of speech. And the first one is Passive-Aggressive. You all know Passive-Aggressive, right? (Our viewers nod) *And our second one is: Non-invasive Surgery. Or, how about Mercy Killing? Familiar, right?*

EDGAR: It's what happen when one of our jokes bombs. You've heard that on numerous occasions. In fact I think it once described an entire segment.

ROXY: Let's not dwell on that painful memory, Edgar. And here is our third for this week: Copycat nonconformist.

EDGAR: Sounds a little like an independent groupie, doesn't it?

ME: Or, an original copy. I guess that's pretty obvious, yes?

ROXY: One thing for certain, this viewer segment is alive and well. Thank you for contributing. And welcome to Saul, our man-about- town who joins us with interesting discoveries and recommendations each week.

Saul moves some chairs around, sets his derby on the table and sits down, nodding at each of us and waving at those outside.

SAUL: Good day everyone. It seems very alive around here. Can I add one of those oxy-morons to the list? From my line of work? How about, Healthy Desserts? Of course there are some. A few that, at least, are more healthy or less unhealthy than others.

ME: Like maybe an apple?

SAUL: That works. Anyway, today I want you to think tiny. That's my word. Tiny. And the food I'm talking about is a small herring, otherwise known as a sardine. It's something that's not a regular item on most tables in this country. But it's huge, even more than anchovies, all around the world, particularly around the Mediterranean from Morocco to Spain and all the way up into the Baltic countries. Okay, before you run out and fill your cart with cans of sardines, let me tell you about a new restaurant over in the Highlands, a Croatian Restaurant, family run, by Croatians, who else, and it's called Sea Delish.

This week I stopped in and tried their very simple and healthy sardine sandwich. Now, sardines are a great source of omega oil. They're stacked on a baguette or flat bread, with green peppers, a huge slice of red onion and a cucumber yogurt sauce. Really, it's to die for. The perfect combination, of course, includes one of several international beverages served ice cold. That would include aquavit, from fig and cardamom to grapefruit and lemongrass. Or, try Ouzo, or Vodka or Grappa, or Raki, or even Galliano. They offer them all at Sea Delish. I also had their special plate of pasta and sardines with killer seasoning.

Now, say you'd like to try some sardine dishes, salads or aperitifs at home. You need only go on-line to SAVEUR, spelled s---a---v---e---u---r, for incredible sardine recipes including sardines and lemon grass salad, sardine matzo ball soup, and stuffed and grilled sardines. Check it out. The delicious and tiny sardine waits to please you, along with cold wine or iced cocktails like a White Cosmo, or a Scandinavian Bellini. Or a super- dry frozen martini.

EDGAR: Thank you, Saul. A real catch, right?

SAUL: A healthy and tasty catch. And, by the way, I heard one of your radio commercials on Spotify last night. "Who does Clark Kent listen to on the radio? The Radio Guys Talk. I liked it. Cool.

ME: Thank you Saul. No time for you to do one of your remotes outside this week. Next time. Roxy, bring up the bass, it's all about the bass . . .

She does and I'm in a pencil-tapping frame of mind; the whole show felt good, and I leaned back as Edgar took us out, reminding our listeners to weigh in on our poll questions, send us their questions, and support our sponsors. And, *"Chill or be chilled."*

Roxy scooped up all the loose papers and let the bass track play on, even after we were signed off the air. Edgar stretched to see if Marge might be hiding off to the side, ready to take a bow. Roxy carefully scanned the crowed for her stalker, and I just waved at various folks outside who made eye contact. What a kick!

We adjourned to the back office; one of the wait staff took our lunch order. Saul apologized that he had to meet a client who was downtown, but, as he bid adieu, he took me aside and said he had eighteen clients signed up for mention each month for two hundred dollars a pop. I shook his hand vigorously, forgetting his age and how thin he was. "Fantastic, Saul. Really fantastic." I passed this info on to Edgar just as Roxy entered.

"No sign of the Hamburg Doctor. That's another whole week." she raised her hands together proclaiming a small victory.

"Great news!" Edgar reached with a high five.

I added, "And we've got more good news. You're on the payroll, Roxy. Saul has signed up eighteen of his clients to advertise on the Radio Guys. And you will receive two thousand dollars a month beginning next week. And, just know, we still consider you underpaid, and we want to sign you to a no-trade contract."

I thought she was going to break down, her eyes popped, her mouth dropped, she could not believe what I said. It was perfect. I welled up, maybe Edgar did too. It was one of those moments when you feel good all over, when you feel blessed by what's going on in your life.

When she'd wiped her eyes, all she could do was blubber a moment, until she finally squeaked out a grateful, "Thank you so much."

It was better than watching a lottery winner, simply

because she more than deserved it.

The beer and the pulled-pork sandwiches arrived and never tasted better. Roxy immediately admitted she lost it with Mildred Fillmore and last night's arrest for crashing the fund-raiser for social workers. "I don't know what happened, I really had no intention of mentioning what we heard on the news. Then, something took over. I thought it might be really funny, and I could acknowledge it but in a way that offered sympathy. I feel awful."

"I wouldn't lose any sleep over it, Roxy. It was and is funny, and we're all about funny on our show. And she brought it on herself."

Edgar didn't seem at all concerned, except for Roxy.

Monday, October 2, 2017

I sat in Jan's office waiting for her early client to finish. It had been two weeks during which she'd been down for the count with the flu. "Sorry about last week, Jake. I was sick enough that I couldn't listen to your show and actually laugh. But I could tell it was funny. Clever. I'm well now. How are you?"

"I am as well as you could expect an old man with a teenage mind to be."

"Explain, Jake."

"I, uh, have gone out twice with my weight-lifter friend, and, I really don't know what to say. I kind of like her. And I feel guilty about changing my mind from when we broke off like real adults should. And the other thing, maybe more important, is for a couple days, not back-to-back, let me say, I didn't think of Carly. I really didn't. But, on those other days she always came to mind. Isn't that progress?"

"It's always progress when you move past the panic stage. Are you past the panic stage?"

"I think so, but I'm afraid to say for certain. You know me by now."

"So, tell me what you like about the strong-armed woman? What's her name?"

"Elizabeth. And I've actually built up enough strength to lift with her curls at the gym. She's relaxing a little. From the pressure of her lawyer trying to get the complete financial holdings of her husband. Evidently some more of it has come to light and it seems like maybe he'd like to settle. Before they uncover even more, is my guess."

Jan nodded her head very slowly as if waiting for the hammer or something equally substantial to fall.

"Right, so I can lift with her. Not much to brag about. I don't think she really cares if I can or not. She doesn't tease me. About anything. I'm not used to that. I worry that she doesn't have much of a sense of humor. Maybe because of what she's going through."

"Well, what do you like about her?"

"Well, she's a good questioner. She asks about our show. How we come up with stuff. I'd say she's befuddled about how we do what we do. She does say it lifts her up a bit. That's nice. I've yet to hear an outburst of laughter from her."

"Do you know why she's getting a divorce? What her life has been like in her marriage?"

"Not really. I feel like I shouldn't pry. Maybe wait until she volunteers something."

"Probably smart, Jake. Like she said, she wasn't actually looking for someone to get serious with. You just came along with your track suit or gym shorts, and liked her looks and interrupted her solitude."

"I do find her attractive, even when she seems kind of remote. What do you think, Jan? Should I push harder?"

"What feels right, Jake? Are you in a hurry?"

"It's a funny thing, trying to hold back from my normal pace. I don't want to rush anything. I'm not used to that. But I don't want her to think I'm a dud. In case she really does come out of her gloom when her divorce is final."

"I could suggest ways to ask her if she's interested in becoming more serious, but why? She's willing to spend time with you. And you're not sure how you feel. Plus, she's coming out of a marriage, and even that isn't final."

"So you think I should hold back?"

"It seems like you're asking yourself that question. What's your answer?"

I took a couple deep breaths. I could sense my answer swerving back and forth. My inclination was to push forward, like I've always done. But, even as I sat there, I noticed that I had doubts. I reminded myself that after one date I was pretty clear that I didn't have strong feelings for Elizabeth. I didn't want to push for something that I would regret. And have to undo it down the road. "Right this minute I will say I should go slow."

"Okay. Maybe if you gave yourself ten dates with her, without making a move on her, or telling her you're falling for her, or releasing all your romantic charms, you'd know a lot more. So would she. What do you have to lose? It doesn't sound like you're competing with anyone.

I felt like a teenager with hormone issues. And Jan was the adult. What I was thinking was whether I wanted to sleep with Elizabeth even if it didn't work out between us. I wondered if I could postpone that possibility for ten dates. "Well, what if I do want to have sex with her? That doesn't fit with this waiting period does it?" "You have to decide that, Jake. And, she has to decide for herself."

I thought back about how I rebounded after my divorce, even before my divorce was finalized. It was water under the bridge, but it probably prolonged the time before I was really fit for a longer relationship. Then again, we did have a lot of fun.

"Maybe this is a good time to experiment. Like you say, what do I have to lose? Except maybe a roll in the hay. For a while, anyway. And I am an adult. Aren't I, Jan?"

"You are, Jake. And a man."

I left her office without total resolve. It would take me a while to really decide what I wanted. I decided to have two dates, then see what it felt like. After all, I was an adult, and an adult should be able to rein it in for a couple weeks?

I opened a checking account for The Radio Guys, a joint one with Edgar. We each deposited two thousand dollars so we could write our first paycheck to Roxy after the next show. By then I figured we'd have some money coming in from Saul's clients.

Our next two shows were devoid of major incidents. The question came up about vacations. We had a pretty lean staff, in fact zero staff as Roxie was as vital as I or Edgar. But each of us felt the need for a break. The answer seemed to be reruns. Which meant we needed to alert the audience, especially those who showed up out front of Whiskey N' Ribs. We decided to inform our fans on the 28th of October that we'd be doing a repeat on the following Saturday, November 4. We also consulted with Rocco and Sebastian and Saul.

We began to record spots to insert during the rerun to remind that we were on vacation, and would be back the following week. The repeat show would be broadcast in our same location, and we had life size prints of the three of us in sitting position mounted on Styrofoam to be placed in our normal seated locations. It felt like an excellent solution to a needed break. Saul even thought his clients wouldn't object paying for their names to be mentioned during our absence. "Like I said, you have a local cachet that these clients want to be associated with. This might even be special, 'Our spot ran during the first vacation the Radio Guys ever took, and we sponsored a rerun.'"

So, we each made our plans to be gone for a Saturday. We set about preparing for the 21st. We were managing our affairs just like adults. Well, almost.

Then, on Thursday, about six o'clock, Roxy called me. I was driving home and I could tell she was upset.

"Jake, I know he's here. The fucking stalker guy."

"Where are you, Roxy?"

"I just got home and I know he was watching me when I was walking from the store. I'd gone out after I finished with a client and when I got about a block from my home I could just feel that he was around."

"I'm in my car and I'll come over. Do you want to call the police?"

"I don't know. What if I'm wrong? I didn't actually see him."

"He probably doesn't think you saw him, right?"

"Right."

"OK, I'll be there in five. If he does come to the door or you see him, call 911. I'll come in the back way."

When I arrived at Roxy's address, I drove all the way around searching for a man outside or in a parked car. I didn't spot him so I parked on a side street and walked to the rear access of her complex and knocked on her back door. She peeked through the window instantly and let me inside.

"Thank you, Jake. I'm sorry, this could be nothing. I felt certain down near the corner. But I never did see anyone. And no one has walked by except a small group of kids with their backpacks."

"I didn't see anything either. But, I'm glad you called. That's exactly what you should do."

She walked back to the edge of her front window and looked up and down the street with no results. "Jake, please join me for a drink. We can sit where I can still watch out front."

"Delighted to. What are you offering?"

"You name it. Beer, wine or anything with gin, vodka, whiskey or tequila."

"Tequila on rocks, please."

With our drinks in hand we sat in the living room, at angles so each of us could look toward one end of the block.

"What should we do, Jake?" My kids are studying with friends and will be home about ten. I'll call them, maybe pick them up."

"I've been thinking. We could call the police. In fact I think we should, even without an actual visual on the guy. They'll send a cruiser by a few times, at minimum."

I made the call. We continued our serious conversation.

"Okay. It feels to me like he's been gone for a few weeks and just returned. I do trust my instincts. And I'll be very disappointed if my internal alarm isn't right."

We had a second drink and Roxy was straightening the office-portion of her living room where she did the website work for her clients. She pulled an ingenious curtain across in front of the alcove when she was done and the work setup disappeared. I kept watch into the darkness out front, seeing nothing on either side of the street and no cars or trucks moving by at slow speeds. Finally a squad car did cruise by, slowing during the entire pass down the block.

"Jake, what do you think about having that police

woman on this Saturday, the one that Saul contacted?"

"I like the idea. If your Doctor Teeter Totter is around, he'll probably listen, don't you think? Maybe he'll get scared and leave town again. Maybe for good."

"I don't know if he'll leave forever, he's still around after almost two months. Would you call Saul?"

"I'll do it right now."

Saturday October 21, 2017

By Friday morning Saul had made arrangements for Police Lieutenant Gail Jimenez to appear on the Saturday show. Roxy hadn't heard any strange noises around her condo, and she was pretty relaxed as we prepped for the show. We decided Lieutenant Jimenez would join us for the last quarter hour. Dr. Nadine would lead off the show, and would establish a lively tone and pace, an upbeat start.

The Good Doctor proved to be outrageous; Roxy could not be thwarted in her remarkable impersonations.

ME: Well, our thanks to Dr. Nadine. She does not disappoint, right Edgar.

EDGAR: Pure gold. It sounds like her new book is selling fast in Hope, Arkansas. When will we have it here in Denver?

ME: Like she said, it's supposed to be rolling out soon. Don't you wonder what she'll come up with next?

EDGAR: Maybe a cookbook? Quick meals for those in therapy?

ME: That would work for people whether they're trying to get into or out of a relationship. Win-win!

Edgar: I think it should include stiff cocktails, a must for before and/or after a session with Dr. Nadine. Or any other therapist, right, Jake?

ME: Unless it's an early morning session. Let's pass your

idea on to her, Edgar. As our radio coverage doesn't quite reach Hope. Not yet, anyway.

We moved quickly to some testimonials posted on our website by listeners who'd tried our sponsor Felony Ice Cream and Felony Chocolate Syrup during the past week. There were extraordinary claims of product excellence. "Felony chocolate syrup is the only thing I can offer my seven year old to get her to do her math homework." There were also postings that listeners couldn't find it in their supermarkets. We just said: "Be *patient. It's selling ahead of production capabilities.*"

Uneasily we wondered who was making up more shit: The radio guys or our listeners?

It became obvious that we were risking some customer blowback if they can't find a product that advertises with us. What we came up with was: *And we always remind our listeners that we can't be responsible for the availability of products and services that advertise with us. You can see we're a small group, and we don't have the time or money to check up on all product claims. We do our best and trust our listeners to maybe call before going in search of our client's products.*

Then, we had a phone call with one of the principles in the Bath Tub Gin project from Chicago. Ralph Capone gave us an update: *"We're shooting for February. You can imagine just the plumbing challenges we have. We now have ninety-six bathtubs. But, we'll be there. And, you probably heard, we're taking the old steam bath site for our distillery and spa."*

We moved into new products and questions from listeners. Finally, I turned to Roxy.

ME: Roxy, we have a special guest on next, and you have something to say by way of introduction.

ROXY: Thank you, Jake. So, all of you out there, I've had a real difficult time this past month and a half. I have a stalker that is scaring me and making me tense and ruining my sleep. I always read about stalkers chasing famous people, but I'm not famous, just ordinary like most of you. He showed up about two months ago out front, and was really weird, telling me that we were destined to be together, made for each other. Really icky. Our good friend Saul tried to grab him out front, but he had a cast on his broken foot at the time, and the guy ran away. We went to the police. They were very kind and have been helping in the search for this guy. I learned that there are more cases like mine than I ever would have thought. Maybe some of you have had this experience so you know what I'm talking about. I think the guy might have left the area for a while, but this week I sensed his presence once again. So I'm feeling the anxiety and fear again, and hardly sleeping. I called the police and they've increased patrolling the area where I live. Saul talked to them about having someone in the department talk about this on our show. At first, I said no. This show is supposed to bring some laughter into your lives and this is a real downer. But Jake and Edgar insisted it would be a good idea. Our listeners would understand. And I promise, we will make you laugh again . . . So, I am privileged to introduce Lieutenant Gail Jimenez. (Lieutenant Jimenez enters from behind the curtain and hugs Roxy and takes a seat. I notice that our window audience is absolutely fixed on her and Roxy.

ROXY: Welcome, Gail, to the Radio Guys Talk. I know you have worked with hundreds of women like me, maybe you can share some of your experiences with our listeners.

LIEUTENANT JIMENEZ: It's good to be here, Roxy. Thank you, Jake and Edgar, too. Well, what you're going through is unfortunately not so uncommon. We've had an increase in calls in Denver about stalkers and we have more than a hundred open cases right now. Most of them never reach the point of violence or physical harm, but sometimes they do. Nevertheless the emotional trauma is often serious. What you're going through is very frightening.

ROXY: The officers that I first contacted were very helpful and understanding and I know they were working hard on my behalf. What should someone do when they suspect someone is stalking them?

LIEUTENANT JIMENEZ: Exactly what you did. Call 911. We take these calls seriously, as you've learned. Don't wait to see if the stalker just goes away.

I look up and to the rear as our curtain opens at the corner revealing Saul holding his yellow derby in his hands. He spots Officer Jimenez and quickly backs out, an apologetic expression for interrupting. About a minute later, I notice a man coming out from the entrance to the condo building across the street. His head is shaved, his expression is indifferent, and his face is mostly covered by several weeks of new beard. He is wrapped in a puffy gray quilted parka. After checking for traffic, he warily crosses the street toward us. He steps up on the curb and stops. Roxy continues with her interview.

ROXY: What I'd like to know is who these stalkers are? What is it that causes them to latch on to someone, to almost become addicted with someone? That's what this feels like to me. Even to the point where they risk being arrested?

LIEUTENANT JIMINEZ: In some cases it is like an addiction. An obsession. The reasons are as many as there are stalkers. That's why it's important to contact the police, so they can get to the bottom of what is going on. And, Roxy, . . .

Roxy jerks her head toward the window, her eyes lock on the bald man in the gray parka. I can see her mind racing as she squints and tightens her face. She turns to me and points out front, hissing at me, "I think, uh, I'm pretty sure that's the guy. Oh my God!" She turns to Lieutenant Jimenez, "That guy outside, he looks different, but I'm sure he's the one."

Saul pokes his head through the curtain, and Roxy

directs him to look out front, "That's the guy, right, Saul?"

He stares for a few seconds and bolts for the door. There are many puzzled faces out front, turning this way and that, straining to see and to hear. Lieutenant Jimenez moves full tilt through the curtain. Edgar and I follow in pursuit.

As the crowd starts to agitate like an anthill someone has stepped on, the agitator, in a bright yellow waistcoat, angles through it toward the man in question. By the time the man on the curb realizes he might be in some kind of trouble, and starts to flee, Saul has wrapped around him like a six-foot-six-inch yellow boa constrictor that's been underfed. And like that powerful reptile, every bit of struggle by the bald man actuates Saul cinching tighter with his grip, even with his legs. It's over summarily, and Lieutenant Jimenez grabs the guy's arms one at a time and slaps on the cuffs. In one motion she is calling for backup as Edgar and I look on, amazed. By the time the man stands up, free from Saul's steel embrace, he has a terrified look on his face, and tears begin to run.

Meanwhile, back at the ranch, Roxy is catching her breath, watching every second of the action, her mouth hanging open. The Radio Guys Talk show is presently unattended, the airways are dead save for Roxy's deep breathing. Shortly the whoop-whooping of two squad cars penetrates our front window as they break to a stop out front. I run back inside and grab my headphones and tell Roxy to go check this guy out.

I spend some time explaining to our listeners the extraordinary event that has just transpired.

ME: Well, like we've said, we broadcast live, and, in this case, not one second of this was rehearsed or anticipated. You might not believe this, because some of you might think everything we do and say on this show is possibly untrue. And, there could be some slight justification for that. In this case,

Police Officer Gail Jimenez, came on our show to help inform you about stalkers, specifically in response to the stalker that's been stalking Roxy. The man the police have been looking for has just been caught and arrested outside. Our man-about-town, Saul Friedman, was the first to tackle this guy and take him to the ground. Lieutenant Jimenez has cuffed and arrested him and right now he's being moved to a squad car. No one has been hurt, I'm almost certain. And, I'm seeing we're about thirty seconds to the end of our show, and I don't know how to turn on the bass track to sign off. So, let me see here, thanks to these five sponsors who generously support our show: Second City Bank, Max's Auto Repair, The Comedy Pub, Donna's Mixed Drinks and Jenson and Johnson Legal Counsel. We'll probably post something about this interruption on our website: radioguys.com. Remember to chill or be chilled. Until next Saturday, be kind to each other.

Edgar and I went outside to mingle with our viewers, see how they were doing, and thank them for supporting Roxy and the show.

Roxy walked into the back office about fifteen minutes after Edgar and I sat down and drained our ice-cold beers. The buzzing we could hear among the full seating of guests in the restaurant surely resulted from what had happened out front. Saul entered just behind Roxy and she turned and embraced him with a bear hug. "You're my hero, Saul. You were amazing."

She sat and turned to me and Edgar, her face wet with tears. She blubbered as she began to talk. "It's so sad, so very sad . . . he was crying, sobbing . . . so sorry. . . he said he just wanted to be with me . . . he'd never hurt me . . . he didn't want to frighten me . . . just talk to me, that's why he waited until the end of the show, so he could talk to me . . . and be with me."

What to say other than we were so relieved this was over, and no one was hurt, and we sure do care a lot about each other. Sebastian entered the office wearing an anguished look on his normally easy-going face, "I had no idea. I gather you had planned to have this officer on. But to catch this guy? I don't know what to say. I'm just glad you're all OK."

"Thank you Sebastian. Me, too," said Roxy. "If you don't mind, I think I'd like a whiskey before I chase it with this beer."

"Absolutely," he answered. "I'll be right back."

For three people who do a talk show, there was very little talking for the next hour as we ate and lingered, enjoying the buzz of the customers, wondering what they were thinking, wondering what we were thinking. As we stole glances at each other, usually we just smiled and resumed sipping or chewing.

"All of a sudden, the show felt like I was on hazard duty; I can't figure how the whole thing happened, really. All because of the Mooch, right, Jake?" Roxy managed a smile.

"Ha, and I think that was one of your finest hours, doing the remote from that No-Tell Motel or whatever it was called up in Jackson Hole where those weirdoes from all over the world used the eclipse as a cover for their clandestine exchanges. You should get a Pulitzer for that, Roxy."

"Like I said, hazard duty. You just never know. God, I am relieved."

"You're amazing, Roxy."

"And thanks again, so much, for the raise. I really never imagined it."

Both Edgar and I called Roxy on Sunday to find out how she was doing. She sounded good, said she was extremely relieved and that she was about to go down to police headquarters to go over details about the case.

Monday, October 23, 2017

Three texts and voicemails requesting interviews greeted me Monday morning as I finished my coffee and left for a mind-bending session with Jan Baumgardner. I chose Tony Fournier, the Westword rep that had interviewed us while we were still putting the show together last summer. He had effectively introduced us with a compelling feature article and I felt like we owed him.

He wanted an interview primarily because of what happened with the stalker, but also as a follow up to his feature on the coupling of a new restaurant with a new radio show in downtown Denver. I told him, yes. We could meet this afternoon at three. I'd clear it with Roxy and Edgar, and we'd meet at the old studio.

On to see Jan.

"Well, Jake, quite a program. Congratulations." Jan was upbeat as she usually was. "I thought Roxy did an excellent job with the police officer. How is she doing?"

"Really great, I think. It's such a load off her mind. We're all getting together this afternoon. Roxy is at the police station again, right now, going over what actually happened. What a relief."

"Are you going to follow up with the police on your next show?"

"I don't know. We've got to hash that out. Any suggestions?"

Jan leaned back. "Not really. I think that decision is in good hands. You'll do what's right and what works. You're also the funny guys."

"Thank you. All I'll say is when the stalker was being taken down by Saul and cuffed by Lieutenant Jimenez, he really lost it and broke down, sobbing. It was sadly pathetic. I'll be interested in how Roxy reacts."

"Like I said, she's smart, and you'll do the right thing. And what's going on with you, Jake?"

I was almost taken aback. I hadn't thought of anything

else except what Roxy experienced. My stuff seemed insignificant. I had to think, why was I here other than to have Jan hold my hand as I attempted to move from adolescence into adulthood? Of course it was more than just that. Wasn't it?

"I feel funny about taking your time with my dating life, what there is of it. I mean I am an adult. You even said as much. And I should be able to handle my minimal love life."

I put on a big grin, pleading for confirmation. God, was I so bereft of self-confidence?

Jan chuckled, "You're more than able to handle your life, Jake. I have total confidence in you. And I think we should not meet for a couple months, barring some emergency. Or, unless I show up for one of your shows on a Saturday morning. Purely as a spectator."

At first I felt a wave of fear pass through me. Then, calm, of all things. I could walk the earth on my own for a while. I'd made a good decision about Elizabeth. Slow down, alter my traditional all-or-nothing behavior. Shift from tossing a stick of dynamite into the lake to assure I'd net a full catch instantly, to being content with sitting with a line out and a bobber for long hours of thinking and waiting. Christ, am I just making up more shit?

"Okay, Jan. I agree. I'll check in during the holidays. Meanwhile, know you've helped me immensely. Or even more."

I drove from Jan's office in Cherry Creek, to Pete's Kitchen on Colfax where I would order a breakfast/lunch meal of eggs, gyro meat, hash browns and English muffins. I sat, with my notebook open to write down things that occurred to me. On the left side of the spread I jotted down ideas for the show. On the other side, ideas for my life. With my mind relatively undistracted, the ideas for both pages flowed rapidly. I knew most would be discarded, but you never know for sure which ones will survive. I remember reading about the inventor,

Edison, who said that you should never let an idea breeze past without jotting it down. He maintained that ideas are so valuable, that losing even one of them is a serious loss. I had taken that to heart during my last years in advertising, and still do today. I don't have to rely on my diminishing memory, and I keep the slate in front of me clear and ready to receive more input.

Roxy had a meeting with one of her own clients so we didn't have time to talk before we sat down with our Westword Rep. He was still the high-energy, handsome dude. How could you not like him?

"Good to see you, Tony. Thanks in retrospect for your efforts before we went on air. To put us on air. You were damn important."

"You're welcome. It's been a pretty good ride so far, right?"

"Yes," said Edgar, "I think we'd all agree."

"So, what I'd like to do is a follow up, say a four month update. How you guys and Rocco and Sebastian have survived this partnership, what you've learned and where you are? And I'd like to start with what happened this Saturday with the arrest of the stalker out front. What that meant to you? And, of course, what it meant to Whiskey 'n Ribs. It's more than unusual."

I looked at Roxy, "Roxy, you just came from the police station. What's the status of the arrest?"

"I'm still thinking about what I want to say about that. It's tragic, in some ways, and I'm deciding how far I want to push it. Until I do that, I don't want to have all the stuff appear in the media. I'm sorry because I know people will talk and write about it on the air. There were several reporters down at the police station this morning pressing for information. It was kind of ugly. Sorry, Tony, I don't want that to become the summary, or even a major piece of our first four months in business. What do you think, Edgar? Jake?"

"I'll go along with Roxy," said Edgar. "We had other major events out front from the beginning. But they weren't really harmful to anyone, maybe a little embarrassing, like to Jake. I think we wait until Roxy sorts through this before we feed the sensational side of the media."

"Well, don't you think that these kind of crazy happenings out in front during your broadcasts have fueled your success? Got people talking about your show?"

"Of course, but most of those were just sort of outrageous, funny, even silly. And I'd like that to be the emphasis. Why people keep coming back."

Tony leaned forward, a question for me. "Well, I want this to go in this week's edition, which makes it hard to interview your fans. I have listened to enough of your shows to give my opinions, though. What say we move on, see what we come up with. How about how it works broadcasting from a restaurant front window? Is there stress with the people who own the restaurant?"

"Here's my take on where we broadcast. First of all, according to Whiskey 'n Ribs, it's helped their business on Saturdays, at least. For us, it's like being on TV. We have a live audience and we can see how they react every minute of every show. We get immediate feedback, it's like gold."

"I agree with Jake," added Edgar. "I thought it would be more intimidating. The window protects us, but we catch every reaction, and sometimes body and face tell you a lot more than what people say. So, I think it's huge for us."

Tony asked, "Well, what if you couldn't broadcast from there, would, or could, the show go on?"

"I sure hope it goes on. You can ask Rocco and Sebastian of course."

Tony continued, "I noticed that during your chaotic ending to the broadcast this Saturday, you thanked several Denver businesses for their support. What does this mean? For some of your *other* sponsors?"

"Obviously our "special sponsors" are very important to us. And we will continue with them, adding more as they become available. But we've also had local businesses that really want to support us and, even identify with us. So this is an experiment to accommodate both. We are very fortunate,"

We continued for the better part of an hour. It was quite enjoyable, after all we were talking about a new creation of ours that was still functioning and evolving and we were still pumped. Although we did remind Tony that we were taking a Saturday off to recharge.

Tony resumed, "So maybe a better question would be, how long can you continue with this? It does take a lot of time, I'm sure, and you have to wonder how long you can keep coming up with *stuff,* as you put it?"

Now that was a question we hadn't really considered or talked about. I actually thought of answering, *Hey, give us a break, Tony. We've just begun, really. Five months? That's not very long.* What I did say was: *I really have no idea.*

He turned to Edgar and Roxy.

They looked at each other. Both shrugged. Roxy released a hearty laugh that was great to see and hear. Edgar went along, easily. It was honest. Spontaneous. The best we could do.

Tony left, "Thanks guys, I hope you like what I put together."

The three of us stayed until Roxy filled us in about what happened at the police station.

"It was pretty awful. They are still holding Dr. Deuter. They want me to press charges and I am so effing torn. They did verify he was a professor at The University of Hamburg. Actually he's been on a six-month sabbatical. We had the wrong spelling of his name. As far as the information our police were able to get from Hamburg, he has no police record, which he swears is the truth. And he is so upset about what an arrest might do for his profession and employment. Especially a record as a stalker."

Roxy was genuinely upset, her hands were trembling and her eyes were watering again. "I asked Lieutenant Jimenez what she thought. She talked to him on Saturday and again early this morning. She thought he was being honest about his belief that he and I were meant for each other. He left Denver for almost three weeks after he'd been chased by Saul. He was disappointed I hadn't come to his rescue and he wanted to think things over, I guess. Evidently what he concluded was that he couldn't live without me. He returned to check this out, but didn't want to create a scene. Therefore the disguise. He was waiting for a good time to approach me."

"What's *your* take on him, Roxy?" Edgar asked. "It was certainly inappropriate no matter what his feelings are."

"That's what the Lieutenant said. She also said he was scared to death, and was so upset, and willing to go immediately to Hamburg and not return. She doubted he was violent or dangerous, but no guarantees. And, she said it was still up to me. She also said the evidence was a bit shaky: what I said about knowing he was near me but I didn't actually see him.

She leaned back and released a huge breath. "I am really glad it's over. I mean that he's been picked up."

"But you're not sure of what to do," I said, "which is very understandable."

"That's right."

"We'll support whatever you decide. You know that."

"Thank you."

I was about to shift our conversation to what we were planning during our week off, our Saturday off.

"You know," Roxy exhaled, "I've decided. I'm not going to press charges. The consequences would be too huge even if the charges were dismissed. He never actually hurt anyone. He was only trying to see me. And I want to put this behind me. If he's willing to get on a plane, that's what I really want. Yes, that's it. That's what is best for me. I don't think that I'm putting someone else in danger by seeing him released. I really don't. I'm going to see Lieutenant Jimenez and tell her what I've decided."

That's how it all turned out. Roxy took a good hard look at all that had happened, and made her choice considering what kind of harm might happen either way. She is quite something.

For the next three days we watched the listener posts come in, all in support of Roxy. Some offered personal experiences from their past, but most just encouraged her to get through the case and know she has lots of support. No one offered some kind of joke about the incident. We had a small but thoughtful following.

Saturday October 28, 2017

Our show was up-tempo from the start. After a spirited introduction by Edgar, and an expansive list of the show content, I introduced Roxy by thanking our audience for all the support she received during the week on our website. She took it from there.

ROXY: You know, that was a pretty shocking thing that happened last Saturday right out front. I want to thank

Lieutenant Gail Jimenez from our Denver Police Department for taking the time to help me talk about stalking and what it's like to be stalked. Thank all of you for weighing in with your opinions and support. I spent the weekend with Lieutenant Jimenez and other officers at the police station, going over everything about the suspect and the incident. In the end, I decided not to press charges. I decided he was not really a threat to me or anyone else, other than himself. I looked at all the evidence. No one had been threatened or harmed. He didn't have a police record." She took an enormous breath, *"So, I'm grateful to the Denver Police Department, and to all of you. I'm confident I made the right decision. And, now, it's time to laugh."* And she did start to laugh, just lightly. She is so damn appropriate.

It was also timely that we'd decided to take a Saturday off, the next Saturday. We spelled out how we would handle it, even to the point of telling our listeners the rerun would be broadcast right there from our usual place, and that we'd have replicas of the three of us in place if they forgot or decided they couldn't stay away.

ROXY: And, maybe you should make reservations inside for lunch on that day.

The highlight of our show was a follow-up call to Jolly Olde England and the Sub Minister for Economic Withdrawal, Camilla Thistlepink Birtwistle. Our intention was to find out how the Brexit was proceeding. The process of England withdrawing from the European Union. We reached the desk of her personal secretary, possibly Bingston. But, evidently Bingston, if he was still employed, was already occupied and Sub Minister Camilla was standing right there and picked up the phone in the absence of her secretary.

SUBMINISTER CAMILLA: "Yes, Good Evening."

We had decided that Edgar, with his smooth disarming voice, would have better luck with an interview than I had during our first chat back in July.

EDGAR: Oh, wonderful, Good Evening to you, Your Ladyship Sub Minister. I hope you are quite well. This is Edgar from the Radio Guys Talk show in Denver Colorado. Thank you for visiting with us.

SUB MINISTER CAMILLA: BINGSTON! What in the name of all the gods and saints is going on? (We hear the crashing of a chair, perhaps, then an anxious voice increasing in volume as he is now in listening range of the phone.)

BINGSTON: Yes, Mum, what is the question?

SUB MINISTER CAMILLA: This call. On your phone. I think it's those manky knobheads from the U. S., that radio show that called in the middle of the night last summer.

*BINGSTON: Oh. Oh. (*He responded to her withering inquisition.)

SUB MINISTER CAMILLA: *Yes, Oh! Oh! How did they get your number, Bingston?*

BINGSTON: Yes, Mum. I can't say, not from me. Some kind of a flopperoo in the steno pool, maybe. Wait, I've left the printer running, I'll be right back.

SUB MINISTER CAMILLA: (Muttering, but slightly audible.) *And a lot of bloody good that will do.* (Then yelling) *I don't know why I didn't sack you last time. So to whom am I speaking, again? I need to know who to say good-bye to?*

EDGAR: This is Edgar, Madam Sub Minister, Edgar Olson. I am so sorry to inconvenience you. I would be grateful beyond measure if you might chat for a precious few moments and we'll be out of your hair.

SUB MINISTER CAMILLA: Precious, my British ass. And you're not in my hair, Edna, or in any other proximity to me. So, ask me one question, and then return to your own hair, or lair, or wherever you reside.

EDGAR: Of course, Your Ladyship, how unthoughtful of me to make such a remark. It has an entirely different meaning on this side of the Pond, as you say. (I could feel her eye's rolling and blood pressure rising as Edgar tried to conciliate her with British colloquialisms.)

He continued: *Last time we talked about Brexit. How many of our listeners are interested, and now it has seemed to move off of the front page of the news over here. So I guess I would ask, How is Brexit, the process of England leaving the European Union, progressing?*

SUB MINISTER CAMILLA: Oh yes, how could I forget, you wanted to know about a hard Brexit, am I right?

EDGAR: Thank you for recalling. I am flattered. Especially with what must be an extraordinary schedule that you have.

SUB MINISTER CAMILLA: Way too busy for a phone interview with fuckwits. I also believe I told you where you could shove your hard Brexit. You do recall, don't you? I think I used the baguette metaphor.

EDGAR: Uh, yes Mum, I mean Ma'am. I think there was a misunderstanding there. Quite sorry on this end. But, I hope that it is going well now.

SUB MINISTER CAMILLA: Well, I think it's way over the heads of you and your listeners. (Aside: Bingston, get back here and relieve me from these twits, and then start preparing your letter of resignation.

BINGSTON: Yes, Mum. I'm sure there's a misunderstanding. We'll take care of it.

SUB MINISTER CAMILLA: There's no misunderstanding, except how these barmy arseholes have your phone number. There are enough tossers here in London.

BINGSTON: Yes, Mum. No shortage there. Shall I dismiss the phone callers?

SUBMINISTER CAMILLA: Oh, I can manage that, Bingston. I do recall, with pleasure, where I told them I would stuff their baguette were they ever to set foot on the tarmac at Heathrow. Watch, you might learn something.) (Back to the phone call) *All right, you have had your question. I suggest you listen to the BBC if you want to learn about Brexit. It might be a refreshing change from your twenty-four hour breaking news that is calculated to scare the twat out of listeners. Good day, then.*

EDGAR: Thank you so much, Madam Sub Minister Camilla . . . I think she rang off.

ME: Well done Edgar. You could not have been more courteous. I regret she didn't cover the phone when she made several comments to Bingston. I'm guessing if we attempt to contact her again it will be through a different personal secretary. She seemed upset.

EDGAR: Well, obviously not everything is tickety-boo on that side of the pond. Jolly Olde England seems a bit in the dumper. Or is it the UK? Or the British Empire?

ME: You should have asked Sub Minister Birtwistle. I'm certain she could have clarified that confusion.

EDGAR: True, I think she was just beginning to warm to me.

ME: What was she saying about the tarmac?

EDGAR: I'm not sure. Something about a spanking?

In the end we briefly thanked our new sponsors, then we all walked out front to help Roxy sell The Radio Guys T-shirts and tank tops, this time offering to autograph any purchases. Hey, we were still broadcasting since the twenty-second of July. We sold more than seventy autographed tops, ran out of several colors, and promised we'd be restocked by November 11, our next live broadcast. Eventually we returned inside for our post-show lunch. Saul was absent, having gone to New York City for a film forum and to sample some of the many new restaurants that were making Brooklyn a destination trip for lots of folks. A couple of the wait staff entered the office, asking if they could buy our T-shirts and have them signed. We gladly did so and refused payment. "You'll never know how much easier you have made our show."

"Well, what are you doing next week, Roxy, during our break in the action?" Edgar asked.

"I am flying to San Diego to visit a couple old girl friends, and walk the beach as much as is possible in four days. And, I'll probably eat some great Mexican food. I haven't seen these two for almost ten years. I can't wait. What about you two?"

"Marge and I are going to the Spa in Mt. Princeton to sit in the hot springs and eat fabulous food in their restaurant and soak until we're tired and ready to sleep in their fabulous beds with pillows made for giants. Marge has forgiven me for my remarks about trying out some different women when she appeared out front disguised as a different woman."

"You're a lucky man Edgar. As is my usual lack of planning, I have no plan. Actually I don't have anyone to do a trip with right now. Just like the past several years. Or, decades. I'm failing my responsibilities to get out of my rut."

Roxy responded, "You don't need a woman to get you out of town, Jake. In fact, you might find a woman out of town. Stranger things have happened."

"I know. I'll figure something. Maybe I'll watch Colbert, get some ideas for our show. Or, try some of Saul's eating recommendations. Don't worry about me. I'm an adult, you know."

We ended lunch and went our separate ways. I did have a pit in my stomach. I did need to get my mojo working. Or get another stack of mysteries at the library. The Radio Guys had become my life during the past six months. I was reminded of my work habits at the agency prior to my retirement. How it filled up my days, some of my evenings and even some weekends. I could lose myself in work as well as the best of them. Now retired, it didn't take long to realize that getting sloshed at various happy-hour stops everyday felt empty. The conversations became repetitive and predictable. And I started wondering about the effects that having just one more drink, or two, was having on my health and my attitude. But it had been a time-filler, something for my afternoons and evenings. Until the radio show.

Monday, October 30, 2017

By nine in the morning I'd made a plan. I called Elizabeth and made a date for Friday. If the weather was still decent we could take a hike in the afternoon. Later, I would cook for her. Then I packed some clothes and drove up to Grand Lake at the entrance of Rocky Mountain National Park and rented a room in the great old Grand Lake Lodge for two nights. I was one of four people staying there, it turned out. It was between seasons.

I planned to spend time coming up with show content, ideas that maybe we hadn't yet considered, while sitting on the fabulous front deck that overlooked the small tourist town of Grand Lake beside the lake fronting straight-up mountain peaks. I brought a recent book of short stories by Paul Theroux, a favorite author of mine. Like Graham Greene, he often wrote about interesting places in the world, far different from the U.S. They both enriched my life with their adventures and observations. As it turned out, I stayed a third night.

At the end of the day, I enjoyed a hearty beef stew in the dining room of the lodge and a couple cocktails that relaxed me beyond description. I realized I hadn't thought about Carly for almost two days. Of course that realization meant that I thought about her now. It always sparked a wave of jealousy, and a knot in my stomach. I know it might not have been the right match for either of us. We really never had enough time to determine that. I should say that I didn't. I guess that those couple times over the years that we did see each other, made such a delicious impression on me that I was certain we could overcome any difficulties.

My most recent response to dealing with thoughts of Carly was a series of positive statements about her. I would wish her well. I would tell myself that she had strong enough instincts to make the decision she made and that was an indication that it wasn't supposed to be. And the old saw that there were lots of fish in the sea. This one was far less persuasive as I had seen a lot of fish that weren't for me.

After dinner, I sat in a well-used rocking chair nearer the fireplace and read of Theroux's visit to Italy in his early twenties, out of university, student poor and aspiring to be a writer. His experiences, romances, encounters, reactions to the unique culture, the smells, the sounds, the people and the worn beauty of the small mountain towns transported me in my mind. And I longed for those days in my own youth when I didn't have the courage to risk such adventures. I was grateful that as I got older I started taking advantage of my opportunities to explore other parts of the world where people were experiencing a far different kind of living. I was fortunate to spend time in Nicaragua and El Salvador during their revolutions against dictators, in Cuba as it struggled against U.S. embargos and assassination attempts, most of Western

Europe, East Germany during and after the Wall, and, most interesting, Sarajevo, Kosovo, and much of former Yugoslavia. Add Greece and Lebanon, and many trips through Mexico and I felt grateful for my good fortunes.

I wondered what part all that played in ending up starting a radio talk show here in Denver. Maybe a powerful impression that we in the States are a relatively small part of the world. And maybe most of us, the white folks for certain, have not endured the struggles that many other peoples have. I guess it changed me. Sometimes I think I let it isolate me. Many of my attitudes didn't fit my former beliefs about this being the best the world has to offer, or that being American made me special. I couldn't jack myself up with that anymore. And I didn't know where that would take me now that I was no longer an ad man, no longer a businessman, no longer a blind patriot.

Don't get me wrong. I love my country for all the opportunities it has provided me. But my country has more potential and possibility and promise than to be constrained by the weak, paranoid snarl: If you don't like it the way it is, why don't you leave!

I wondered if the radio show was a reflection of "just wanting to have fun"? A stage maybe, to discover what was next. To explore something other than the current state of the nation. To consider what values I really wanted to hold on to, which I could release, and what has never occurred to me.

Crazy. What the mind comes up with when it isn't busy, busy. When there are fewer timetables and fewer obligations. When you choose to shed limitations you have imposed or accepted on your life, or your thinking. WTF! Why not start a radio talk show? Find out what you really want to think and talk about. Why not? It beats the easy routines. And I enjoyed a pretty interesting past.

But why just stop? Just because of retirement? Just because I don't have to work? Or, just because I'm getting older? Or, just because I don't have to prove anything anymore?

I mean, that's the point, isn't it? I don't have to stop. It's my choice. I've been gifted pretty good health so far. I can coast and watch myself age, and find ways to amuse or distract me. Or, keep busy, busy. Maniacally consumed. Crammed with what all until I die. Lots of things that don't demand my all.

Or, and this is a big OR, what if we turned our telescope around, forgot about aging, something we can't do much about anyway, and decided, chose, to look at what we've done before, all of it, as simple preparation for where we are right now. At a launching point or pad for what could actually be the most important time in our lives. We didn't live our life, simply to quit. To run out the days.

As I jot this down it occurs to me that this all makes sense, crazily. At what time in our life have we known more? Had more freedom? Had more time? And I'm not talking about a bucket list.

I remember seeing Jerry Seinfeld appear on Letterman when Dave was nearing retirement. Dave pushed him to reveal his bucket list. Jerry fended off, saying he was way too busy with new things. But Dave persisted until Jerry relented. He admitted that, under pressure from friends, he once started to compose a bucket list. He finished a page, sat back and read it. Then, he took his pen and scratched out the B at the top and replaced it with the letter F. Jerry is a very funny man.

In my mind that is a wonderful calling. To be funny. Newhart never cussed to get a laugh. (Check out his Stop It routine on Youtube.) Carlin began the defanging of the seven dirty words you can't say on television. Of course there is Colbert, Groucho,

Tina Fey and Dave Barry. Diller, and Hope and Paula Poundstone. Jon Stewart, Gilda Radner, Sarah Silverman, Eddy Murphy, Yon Yonson. Oops, he came from Wisconsin. Zang! There are so many. Hundreds.

I can imagine a most wonderful thing: A beautiful memorial, as large as the Viet Nam memorial, in our nation's capital, in memory of all the people who lived to make us laugh. Do you recall how our government sent USO tours to the theaters of war during WWII, Korea, Iraq, Afghanistan, and other dangerous locations? Who comes to mind? Bob Hope, of course. And many other comedians. Colbert went to Iraq, and while there had his hair cut, a buzz cut to identify with the soldiers. Politics didn't matter so much. And even a short break to laugh was so appreciated.

Rather, we endure the Washington gridlock, the self-importance, the lack of imagination, the party first, the country and the world last. How can you not reach the point where the only sane thing is to laugh? Out loud. At both parties, and their abuse of the system.

And so I find myself laughing. At all of us. At myself especially. For the majority of us have it so much better and easier than 90% of the people on earth.

Maybe our whining is another face of our "exceptionalism." We deserve everything, even though we have more than almost any other population has ever had. Except: humility, grace, generosity, curiosity and a sense of perspective about each of our lives compared to the rest.

Is it too unfair to admit we don't give a shit about what happens to other peoples in this world? As long as we're comfortable? What a seismic addition to what we honor, a memorial to humor. What enriches us and brightens our lives. I would go to D.C. to see that memorial. I would smile or maybe laugh out loud at a memory of what any one comedian did that made me laugh back when. What an antidote to the less than honorable or inspiring ways our politics runs our nation and impacts the world these days. I could spend all day.

Maybe a memorial to comedians would help unite our country in an effort to create a better society for each other. Many of our politicians take themselves too seriously, mostly fighting for reelection, rather than for the betterment of this country. They deserve to be laughed at. Sorry if I offend anyone. This is my best attempt at a nonpartisan observation. We need a change. A sea change. Part of that might be the ability to laugh at our elected government, so pathetically lacking in imagination and vision. Let's find a place where we can laugh together. And mourn together and celebrate together. That isn't all about war and politics.

Yes, a U.S. Memorial to the people who have made us laugh. And let's start laughing at ourselves. We have it coming.

There you have it. My rant for my country. I refuse to accept this as our best. So I chose to laugh. Join me?

Surely there are wealthy individuals who have had their lives enriched with laughter and would be willing to fund such a spirited memorial. Right on the Mall, maybe. Thank you, God, for funny people.

How did I get off the track there? Maybe that some people stay funny and alive, even after what we think should be retirement age. And they pay no attention to it, even if they've accumulated enough to sit back and nurse their bucket list and their next travel itinerary. They're driven by a spirit of energy and imagination to express themselves. They think they have something new and something next.

I think of Norman Lear, in his 90's with new shows he's piloting, new visions, new ideas, no time to get old.

So, you never know what you might come up with if you let your mind wander. Refuse to conform to what's "normal" as we retire. In fact, maybe *abnormal* should be the new retirement. Kick some ass; there's always some ass to kick if you just . . . kick. Maybe that's all I need, to have my ass kicked, even if I have to pay some one to do it. Get on with it. This life is truly my show if I want to make it so.

Tuesday. October 30, 2017

Well, that was quite a little rant that burst from somewhere last evening. This morning I wrote and read until noon, left my laptop in my room and trotted down the slope into town for, of all things, a Chicago Style Hot Dog slathered in mustard, and an ice cold Rolling Rock.

    Business was slow yet, in Grand Lake, Colorado. No ice for fishermen, no snow for snowmobilers and cross-country skiers. I hiked the town, checking out everything that was open. Near three o'clock I parked myself at a horseshoe bar where I sat, the only customer. An attractive fifty-something woman, brunette with a ponytail, an easy smile, laughing eyes, and a Periwinkle fleece jacket, poured my drink and made my day. We talked while I drank until five o'clock when the next customer finally arrived. He was followed shortly by his wife. They both ran a small gift shop in town, it turned out. I could tell I needed to stop drinking before I embarrassed myself. And I probably would benefit from an hour in the lodge hot tub. I stood, and, at the very last minute, introduced myself and found out that Catherine was the name of this lovely bartender. I also noted she didn't have a wedding ring. Something I was sure I couldn't say about Carly by now.

    I did soak in the outside whirlpool, with a cold beer close at hand. I thought more about Catherine, hoping she was a little older than my guess. She'd moved to Grand Lake a dozen years ago from Atlanta following a divorce. And she,

Catherine, (how in God's name could I talk with her for more than two hours without introducing myself?) worked as an accountant for several small businesses, and was very good at selling. She didn't need to convince me. She made enough to live reasonably well, she said, and she loved all the seasons and the hiking and skiing.

"I'd never go back. Do you think I'm stupid?"

She had a terrific laugh, low-key but with an infectious clicking sound that extended like a continuing chuckle. Very hard not to notice. Very difficult to forget.

Limp, after all the great heat, I struggled from the whirlpool up to my room and returned to the dining room before it closed for a savory plate of Chicken Alfredo and a side of vegies. Then I retired to read, lasting only a half hour before falling off. I actually considered I might pray thanks for this extraordinary day, something I hadn't done for years. Decades.

So I did. It felt good.

Before I tell you about my Friday with Elizabeth, a few things about that next afternoon across the bar from Catherine. I learned she was a young fifty-six year old. Her family roots were from Scotland, going back to the mid eighteen hundreds. She earned a degree in business from a community college while pursuing her divorce. She had no kids, thought her marriage was too shaky to bring any into the world. Much more mature and thoughtful than I've ever approached being. And, best of all, if I returned to Grand Lake, she'd consider going out with me. She said I seemed harmless enough. (That's the second time I've been defined as harmless recently.) Then her long low laugh as she poured a beer for a young local sitting further down the bar.

Friday, November 3, 2017

So, Friday afternoon with Elizabeth the weightlifter. We did our hike about ten minutes into the foothills west of the city. In a very short time I was in the role of follower. She might have been exhausted from stress, but she was in good shape and I was soon huffing. I quickly dismissed any thoughts I might have had about impressing her. Why I would have any, after seeing her work out over a period of months, was lunacy. But I did thoroughly enjoy the view of her from my follow-up position. Really, is that so shallow? Beauty? What I sometimes think makes the world go round? Don't women dress and act in ways to attract attention? Men do.

Anyway, this is not worth any debate to me. She has a great bod and she moves like an athlete. I hate to imagine how someone would describe my gait in my physical state.

We returned to my house, spent and sweaty. We showered separately on separate floors. Then I made us drinks, Martinis, actually, and we sat and talked and decided I wouldn't cook. Rather, we'd try one of Saul's suggestions. I had to twist Elizabeth's arms a bit, finally persuading her to try the Croatian place in Highlands called Sea Delish. The part that needed persuasion was their specialty: various dishes centered around sardines. I told her I was leery, too, hadn't tried it yet, but when Saul raved about it on our show, I questioned him after and he swore by it: Dishes with sardines.

So, at six o'clock we drove over and picked from a couple empty tables. I ordered the iced Aquavit, she opted for the iced Vodka. I'd say they served the purpose of moderating our fears about dining on sardines. And Elizabeth was smiling at the risks she (we) were taking, as we unflinchingly honored Saul's reputation for good taste, beginning with a sardine and lemon grass salad after we'd finished and ordered second rounds of our courage builders.

She asked about my visit to Grand Lake. She'd stayed

there years ago when her life was more tolerable. Not wanting to remind her of what she was going through, I asked her what things she had planned for herself when all the litigation was completed?

"I almost don't think of it. I'm probably spooked that it will sabotage these negotiations. But, you know, I should be thinking ahead. God knows I've lived in a state of emotional traction for several prolonged years. I think my friends are afraid to call me. I probably should think about something decadent, like an extended stay at a spa, maybe in France? Where people go to be healed. Yes. That's what I need. To be healed."

"That beats a season pass for the Rockies, right?"

"Yes. And it beats hunkering down in the legal system of high priced lawyers. Was your divorce this difficult, Jake?"

"Not as. I know it's always a stressful time. Ours was more a catfight than a fistfight or a battle of heavy weapons. My goal, in retrospect, was to make our mediator laugh at us. Of course, mediation eventually failed, not for lack of her best efforts. Funny, I don't think of it very often. Maybe too much time has past. Maybe I just don't have any regrets."

"My regret is waiting for so long to begin the process. That was my fault. I certainly had plenty of justification. That's what my daughters tell me, anyway. I think my oldest moved to Chicago to avoid seeing me suffer and struggle anymore. It was depressing for her, to all three of my kids. And, I think they really wanted me to get at it and stop complaining."

We moved from that to the theory I concocted up at Grand Lake, the one about seeing everything up to retirement as preparation for our greatest. The life we hadn't yet lived, the caper we hadn't yet pulled off, or the vocation or cause that would diminish all that came before.

"You mean like the best is yet to come?"

"Maybe. I haven't had an awful life. I didn't have a career that I hated, but was afraid to change. But, when I struck on this notion for a radio talk show, it grabbed hold. I thought it had no basis for success. It was just an idea. Like what we had to come up with for our ad clients. It was really all we had to offer them."

"And you were pretty good at it right, Jake?"

"I guess so. It never really felt like hard work. Coming up with ideas. And many were terrible, embarrassing. Thank God I worked with some very bright people who could tell me when my ideas stunk."

"How do you know when you have a really good idea? That's what I wonder when I think of the future. I have been reacting to my unhappy life for too long. I don't trust my ideas very much."

"I hear you. I'm not an expert. But maybe you start with small things. Like picking a sardine dish because you're curious. Or thinking about what you're very best at. Or what you get some enjoyment from. Like I said, I'm no expert, but I'm finding that I'm open to things that I never was before. The radio show might be only the first of many. Who knows? What was the first real job you had, Elizabeth?"

"Life guard. It wasn't exactly a real job, but I loved it, and I got paid for it. I was sixteen. I loved the sun. I loved feeling I was important, or doing something important. Protecting people in the water. I also found the courage to dive off the three-meter board. That took me half the summer, but I did it."

It was time to order our next dishes. We decided to split an order of pasta with sardines after seeing the size of the portions served to other diners. First they delivered a basket of hot garlic bread from a baguette. It was so delicious I could have lived on it. And we ordered a third round, once I said that all the bread and butter would absorb the alcohol and render us sober. You can see how the first two had clouded my wisdom.

"So, Elizabeth," I ventured a step into more personal territory, "do you think you might marry again?" As the question slipped all the way out, I regretted it as being very insensitive." "Gee, Jake, give me a break. I'm still married. I'm treading water. I'm about to eat fried sardines, and you're not very sensitive, are you??

She was scolding me, in jest partly, and she was smiling, and I felt like the enemy at the gate.

"I'm really sorry, Elizabeth. What an inappropriate question for you."

"Those are the right words, Jake. How can I be mad at you? I know you're not mean. And, I know I have to be able to handle some slights or comments that I'm not ready for. I need to laugh. Even at you sitting there like a guilty child caught with an open container of ice cream."

She raised her glass to toast. "Jake, you're OK. For a man." And she burst into laughter. Hopefully at my expense. And I thought she was wonderful.

"Well said, I deserve it. Maybe it's just cause I'm quite fond of you going here with me, and I just wanted to find out more about you. Anyway, thank you."

The sardines and pasta were magically seasoned. And I quickly forgot they were sardines. When the plates were cleared, I asked Elizabeth whether she wanted to try the sardine ice cream for desert, and she responded with dark eyes, a tilted head and, "Don't mess with me, Jake. I'm precariously managing my uneasy stomach from all we've consumed. And I don't think I can handle imagining such a thing and I know they don't have such a thing and you're just making up things like a kid trying to be obnoxious, and I don't want to give you the satisfaction of throwing up. So, retract it!"

I could see that she was trying to fight off all queasy feelings, something that I hadn't caught, but should have.

"Ouch! You really nailed me. I'm also an unrepentant wise ass. Of course there is no sardine ice cream!"

At another time I could have used a smart-ass comment like, "I was just too nervous to ask you to marry me." And we know how that has worked. So, I was making progress, like a turtle trying to cross a highway covered with ice.

"Thank you. I'm settling my stomach. I'm going to be all right. I'm telling myself this like my catechism drilling."

I paid our bill to a very lovely young woman with a heavy accent, most likely Croatian, I guessed. She confirmed it and said this was her parent's restaurant and she helped out while going to university.

"Tell your parents we will return. It was a terrific experience and I only hope my date will go out with me again." I smiled at Elizabeth. She rolled her eyes in return. And told the woman it was her first time with sardines, ever. And *this* man.

"We hear that quite often, the sardine part," she replied.

We drove to her house. I parked in front of the four-car garage set among various other Cherry Creek replications of English and Country French architecture. Quite elegant. In fact, regal. All I could say as I got out of the car and looked around was, Wow! I looked at her, and she shrugged, like yes, this is where I live. Don't ask me how or why. "It's just a house. A big one, yes. And we have help to take care of it. And my husband moved out until we settle. And I never considered a mansion in my future. And I definitely still don't. I'm ready to downsize, maybe to a studio apartment for a while. I'll show you around if you're interested sometime, Jake. But, it takes a lot of energy, and I'm really spent or I'd invite you in." And with that being said, she stepped up on her tiptoes, pulled my head down and kissed me soft and hard for more than a minute. I know it was more than a minute. Again, all I could say was, Wow!

I hugged her gently and said, "Thanks for a great time. I'd like to see you again, I'm not too concerned about your mansion. I might get lost in it. But, I'm overwhelmed by your kiss. Uh, so bye for now, Elizabeth."

I sat in my car for a minute or more before I slowly backed to the street. Wow! So that was my Friday with Elizabeth. And tomorrow, no show to prepare for.

Saturday, November 4, 2017. Our day off.

Well, I cheated. After my best night's sleep since the Mooch, I was rather lost with what I should be doing this morning. So, I wandered down to Whiskey 'n Ribs arriving about nine-thirty. There were no listeners out front, and the back door was open as the crew moved hastily about in preparation. The mouthwatering aroma from the hulking black smoker energized me. Sebastian and Rocco were rummaging in their office and looked up, surprised to see me. We had made arrangements for Sebastian to set up our stand-ins out front, and to turn on and off the broadcast made back in August.

"Hey, how are you guys? I'm not checking up on you. I had nothing to do so I thought I'd come down, and maybe do some of the work so you guys don't need to. God, it smells good. Do you ever get tired of that incredible smell of meat and sauce?

Rocco answered, "Only after I've stuffed myself. And that doesn't last for long. I think we can tell by the smell if the meat is perfectly done. It's always confirmed by Rodney inserting the thermometer in every single cut that's in the smoker."

Jeremiah added, "You're welcome to help, Jake, but let us do the electronics. Just in case there's a time when you guys can't make it and we have to improvise with an old show."

"Good thinking. I'll get out of your way."

I worked my way through the busy crew, greeting, shaking hands and generally being a wise ass. It would only take me a few minutes and I wanted to be gone before any of our fans showed. My task was simply to take our cutout likenesses from their standing position and set them up in our usual chairs. It took a little adjusting to straighten and tilt, and it was done.

I stood back and chuckled. What a lark this had come to be. I walked back through, waving and thanking the owners, and headed over to Sam's Number 4 for a huge breakfast. My mouth had been watering and needed attention.

Wednesday, November 8, 2017

At ten o'clock we three reconvened at the ancient AM1480 studio with ample bakery snacks to weather a hurricane. Edgar put on the coffee. As we parsed through our website to see what our public was saying or asking, we noticed several people had showed up on Saturday, not aware that we were off. There were a few smart-ass comments like Edgar and I looked better than in person, and how could we put on a talk show without opening our mouths? We jotted down the questions and comments we might work with. Then sat back and talked about how it was, missing a show, and what we did during our break. I admitted that I had two women I now liked, and I hadn't asked either of them to take my hand in marriage.

Roxy glowed with a radiant tan and the gossip she shared with two old friends about her "new life" in radio, and

Edgar described how he and Marge held hands while sitting in a small pool of thermal water that they had captured with piled river rocks in the stream that flows through the resort.

I told them my escape to the mountains was something I should continue. Then, we got down to business. A couple ideas for the show seemed promising. For example, a kind of radio séance where we interview deceased historical figures. Or, a tie-judging contest for Edgar's fans. Or, news from North Korea. And, more difficult problems to solve from our listeners. We discussed each of them briefly, added some, and began to work out our coming show.

Four hours later we were spent and the white board was plastered with words and ideas that were sifted, underlined, crossed out, and the survivors, well, survived erasure. Before we returned to our civilian duties I brought up the idea of advertising.

"We have some dollars coming in for Roxy, and maybe a little extra, and I'm willing to kick in some more, for some promotion to expand our listening audience from whatever it is, which I have no idea. What do you think?"

"I like it," said Roxy. I'll get some costs. We could do a saturation for a week on Spotify and Pandora."

Edgar agreed. "But I think we should also run an ad in Westword. Look at the article that Tony just put in about us. Pretty damn impressive. It fit so well with his progress report on Whiskey 'n Ribs. Sebastian said he thinks it's really helped their business."

"It's where lots of people look to find out what's going on in Denver. We could use a print version of our radio ads. "Guess who Simon Cowell from American Idol listens to? Or, Prime Minister Theresa Mary May?

Later that afternoon I received a call from Elizabeth. She was flying to Chicago to visit her daughter now instead of for Thanksgiving, when her father would "have" her. "I hope I'll get more used to this sharing of kids."

I could tell she was miffed, but she still sounded in better spirits. I told her to have a blast.

So, in a Machiavellian moment, I shifted my thoughts to Grand Lake and the fetching bartender I liked to call Catherine. Then I looked at the rest of my week, knowing we needed to rehearse our new ideas for the show. I didn't call Catherine. But I did text her: *Thank you for entertaining me on my visit last week. I look forward to seeing you again. Jake.*

You might disapprove of my seeming lack of scruples. I am in no position to shut any doors at this point. I'm cutting myself some slack.

Saturday, November 11, 2017

It felt like we were back in the groove as we finished going over our outline while listeners were gathering outside. The next thing we heard was that growling bass track that Roxy levered up on her refurbished Allen and Heath broadcast Mixer. She extended the run-up a full minute, to drive the adrenalin through our veins.

EDGAR: Good morning all you good people of Denver. We are back, and full of mischief. We are substituting for those cardboard cutouts that filled in last week. Great to see you out front here and hello to all of you who are listening on your radios. I'm Edgar, he's Jake, and the brains and the eye candy of this show, of course, is Roxy. It's wonderful to see you folks outside, pumping and waving. *So let's not waste any time, Jake. What's going on today down here in front of Whiskey 'n Ribs?*

*ME: Thank you, Edgar. I'd just say hold on to your hats.
Let's call this the recovery episode from our first week off. Let me
be honest, most of what we did on our time off, we can't share
with you, for obvious reasons, such as potential scandals and
having to make public apologies for sexual harassment. That
includes only me and Edgar, of course. We're working on a
statement for our listeners as we speak. I insist on complete
denial, my good friend Edgar demands full disclosure, a
politically correct heartfelt apology, and the offer to quickly
settle any lawsuits as generously as we can. Of course, discreet
payoffs are welcome.*

*EDGAR: Let's be cautious on the settlement thing . . .
Maybe we should ask our attorney.*

*ME: Right, Edgar. Prudence is important at a time like
this. So let's move on and let our listeners know that we're
having a contest that will run from now until the end of the year,
December 31. You will find a place on our website,
radioguys.com to post your five best guesses for who will be
brought down by women who have come forth with accusations
of sexual harassment. The accused must be public figures. Not
just some cousin, or neighbor or your mate, God forbid. They
have to be mentioned in Wikipedia to qualify. Right, Roxy?*

*ROXY: Yes, this Sex Pool, we're calling it, is the logical
outcome of all the outings that have been pouring forth. We're
offering prizes of The Radio Guys Talk clothing to our winners.
So take a look. No submissions after your nominee has already
been publically accused. And, the accusations have to be
mentioned in the national media. All fair rules.*

*ME: Now, friends, please don't think of this as merely
piling on. We've decided that there has to be somewhere in this
sorry mess for people to laugh. Maybe that's a reach, we'll find
out. We're even giving prizes for those who have been outed, kind
of a consolation gift, for providing us with news content. The*

prize shirts are being printed right now. They say: The Radio Guys Talk, Too Much.

EDGAR: *Well, that gets us back on track. Now, I want to thank all of you for sending your emails and comments to our website. It was great seeing your stuff coming in while we were gone.*

ME: *Except, there was more than one comment that Edgar and I looked better in cardboard than in person. And Roxy looks better either way than either of us. But, we admit, we agree with you.*

EDGAR: *Maybe we need more makeup.*

ME: *While you're checking that out, Edgar, let us remind you all that this first segment is brought to you by ROADKILL REMOVERS. That's right, and it has nothing to do with the Sex Pool we just announced. This is for your everyday encounter with creatures passed on. So you don't have to wait for the beetles and flies to do their nasty cleanup work.*

EDGAR: *Are you sure you have the right sponsor? I don't remember seeing this one.*

ME: *It's very recent. Came in last night, right Roxy?*

ROXY: *It did. With pictures of four hybrid vehicles jazzed up with their logos, and photos of their four Agents. They call themselves Deceased Creature Disposal Agents. It tells you a lot about them. How serious they take their profession.*

ME: *OK, then. ROADKILL REMOVERS. They offer a one hundred percent satisfaction guarantee.*

EDGAR: *Hmmm . . . I wonder how they work all that out? Like how they get paid? Or, where is the final resting place for these creatures?*

ME: *I'm sure we'll find out more, Edgar. Very good questions.*

EDGAR: *Looks like Roxy has handed me some BREAKING NEWS. Let's take a look. Okay. It looks like this comes from the headquarters of KIM ILL BUNG, SUPREME MILITARY COMMANDER, POONANG, NORTH KOREA. And it reads: NORTH KOREA NOW HAS A MISSLE THAT WILL REACH WASHINGTON, DC. Geez. Do you think he's bluffing?*

ME: He could be. Is that fair?

EDGAR: It's nothing to bluff about, is it?

ME: He's playing a dangerous game if he is.

EDGAR: And if he's not kidding, that's dangerous too.

ME: That's for sure. Maybe someone should warn him to wait until our Congress is in session and the President is in the White House.

EDGAR: What? What are you thinking, Jake?

ME: Oh. Well, I'm thinking that's the only way we'll ever get term limits. (Rim shot drum roll from Roxy)

Roxy raised her open hands toward the outside listeners, seeking help with what to do with her male conspirators. Then she moved on to an announcement.

ROXY: I've just gotten off the phone with Dr. Nadine. She was planning on being a guest this week, but she's lost her voice, almost completely. She's been on the fast track of selling her new book, <u>When Recoupling Sucks</u>, giving talks at every bookstore within a hundred miles of Hope, Arkansas. She said she's just been talking too much. Says people are fascinated with her new concept of couples counseling. Promises to be back next week. So, men, where do we go next?

ME: We wish Dr. Nadine a speedy recovery. She's obviously in high demand. Maybe we can still help our listeners. Roxy, why don't you pick out one of the questions they've submitted on our website, radioguys.com?

ROXY: Sure, we have several great ones to choose from. How about this difficult one: A male listener who asks that his name not be mentioned, for obvious reasons, wants to know what he should do when his wife's boss keeps asking her to dinner?

ME: Too bad Dr. Nadine can't weigh in on this. This could be dicey.

EDGAR: Is her boss known well enough to be in Wikipedia? He could be a candidate for our SEX POOL.

ME: What if she's encouraging these invitations? That is always a possibility.

EDGAR: Let's not go there. Let's take this question at face value. Should she resign? Should she threaten to report him to whomever takes these kinds of complaints? Should she tell him she's very uncomfortable with how often this is happening? She has a good marriage and doesn't want to jeopardize it?

ROXY: I have a dear friend whose wife was being asked out by her supervisor way too much. And she told my friend she was going to threaten him if he persisted. Well, he persisted and two weeks later, she came home to my friend and announced she was filing for divorce. Shit happens.

ME: You're right. So how do we answer our listener?

*EDGAR: I can't speak for Dr. Nadine, but my hunch is that she'd approve of something like this: Have your wife tell her boss that she's very uneasy with this situation, and give him a week to get the message, and if he doesn't get it, hire a stud weight-lifter type guy about her age, with the capability of a mean face, a snarl that would rattle the skeleton hanging in an anatomy lab, and have him show up at the place where they're dining. When your boss is eating, your "husband" hustles over and growls, Hey, you told me you were going to see one of your girlfriends. What the **BLEEP** is going on? You act terrified; your boss says, stutters something lame and inane, your violent "hubby" moves in on his face and says, "If. This. Ever. Happens. Again. I will punch your face into a bloodied cauliflower. And then, I will really hurt you." Then you cover your face and in a horrified response, you sob, "Yes, honey, this will never happen again."* Outside there is cheering. I'm thinking that Edgar surely must have Dr. Nadine in his headphones.

ME: *Brilliant, Edgar. I think Marge would be proud. Look out there. Looks like your fans are agreeing.*

ROXY: *Sometimes our very first instincts are the right ones. I hope this helps any listeners who face this sticky problem. And, Edgar, why don't you let our listeners know who has been bringing us the last half of our show.*

EDGAR: *Be happy to. And that would be: LAUGHING MOMMIES. Gee, I think Marge would have liked to be part of Laughing Mommies. Okay, Laughing Mommies are just what it says. A group of Denver Mommies who have decided on a way to cope with all the stresses and tensions and worries that they face every day. They get together and laugh. And, thankfully, now they are for hire. As laughers, of course. They will show up at your event after they've heard your needs. For example, an event where you're forced to listen to some gasbag go on and on. On cue, they start laughing in their group or sprinkled among the crowd. Often unnerving the pompous or boring speaker into fleeing the podium. They could dethrone any person who thinks a little too much of his or herself, preaching while fleecing the poor and enriching the rich. The Laughing Mommies can disrobe the most seriously self-absorbed and untruthful imposer on your time.*

ME: *I'm quickly liking the Laughing Mommies.*

EDGAR: *Or, let's say you're unsure of the speech you've written that you want to be funny. Laughing Mommies will float in your audience, and if the laughter fails to materialize, they will begin it for you. You can see all the possibilities. And imagine how good it feels to laugh at someone who takes themselves just a little too seriously. Go online, Laughing Mommies of Denver. I'm already laughing at the idea of using them for our show.*

We rolled on to the end, Roxy announcing there would

be a contest next Saturday for the woman who wore the most outstanding tie. In honor of Edgar's fans, of course. And it would be judged by Roxy, and none other than our sartorial expert, Saul. The prize: one of Edgar's never worn ties, still in the original gift box from a Christmas or birthday long past.

Afterwards, we followed Roxy out front with a replenished selection of tank tops and T-shirts in a full assortment of colors. We signed some of them, realizing that it seemed to help sales. Some asked us to date them, "We want to prove we were part of your original groupies before you became famous."

Whatever it takes. It is very flattering.

Our reunion in the back office for sliders and pulled pork was quite merry. When Rocco entered with three cold brews, he asked what we thought of having the cardboard stand-ins remain seated at the table during the week? Maybe dress up the set just a little, and make the promotional sign on the easel a bit larger. I looked at Edgar and Roxy. "Hey, it couldn't hurt.

"I'm on it," she said. "It needs a woman's touch."

We still hadn't decided on whether to have a Thanksgiving- themed show. Earlier in the week we discussed having a Thanksgiving celebration in pilgrim costumes, with Indians arriving with corn and turkey and other yummy things to relieve the extreme hunger of the Pilgrims.

Then, Edgar suggested we proclaim: *That from this day forth, all Indians, women and children included, will be shot on sight until they are pushed to the most awful, arid and unlivable land in the west of our country.* He ended with a post script: *"And this will not be taught in our American history books to our children, forever, except the part where the Indians take out Custer in a winner-take-all game of Corn Hole at the Little Big*

Horn Bar and Half-Way House.

Roxy rested her forehead on the table in the old studio. Edgar suggested maybe we should return to the drawing board.

Tuesday, November 14, 2017

Eventually we tabled, permanently, any kind of Thanksgiving-themed show. We figured that two preoccupations, the massive intake of food, and the obsession with an ever expanding four day shopping horror beginning at five in the afternoon of Thanksgiving Day, roaring through Black Friday and the weekend and on through Cyber-online-Monday would wring everyone out who participated in such foul humor and we should not remind them in any way that we were even aware of Thanksgiving. In fact, we made a mental note that next year, God willing, that Thanksgiving Saturday should definitely be a day for a rerun of an earlier show.

Thursday, November 16, 2017

The phone call came from Edgar at nine in the morning. "Jake. Are you familiar with how to use YouTube?"

"Hey, I have a Masters Degree . . . in Advertising."

"How could I forget? Well, Marge, bless her wicked little ever-lovin' heart, has messed with it, and with us. You better check it out. Just punch in Radio Guys talk about Korean Missile. Take a heart pill. If you've got your computer handy, or your phone, do it. Call me back."

Apprehensively, I follow instructions. I punch in Radio Guys talk about Korean Missile.

Shazam! There it is. A one minute twenty-seven second video of us, live, in our broadcast booth, the logo of the Radio Guys Talk just above our heads, as we're doing our thing, right on through to the rim shot drum roll.

Of course what stood out for way too long before the punch line about term limits, was the suggestion that the esteemed military commander of North Korea wait until that missile could take out most of our national leadership. At least that was my horrified take. I refused to watch it again. Instead I scrolled down about twenty viewers' responses. What a relief. There was one damning comment. "How could you communist traitors even think such a thing?" Ouch. But most came to our rescue: "Very, very funny; Finally something to laugh at; I'm still laughing."

I don't think I've ever been so relieved about something I said or wrote. I noticed there were just a few more than fifteen hundred hits. Not exactly viral, but I haven't a clue how so many people found this. It was posted late yesterday. Marge definitely has her mysterious ways.

I called Edgar back.

"Amazing," I began. "It scared me at first. Reminded me that what we say might end up anywhere. How'd she do it?"

"I agree. Marge swears it will help us. Maybe she's right. She had the idea and got the son of one of her girlfriends to video the last week's show on his phone. He edited it and, well, they just posted it. I only hope it doesn't prompt some sort of weirdo drive-by."

"Yeah, right. It's a good reminder that we don't get too political."

So, with Marge as our co-pilot, we were reaching beyond Denver. We had no inclination of what ramifications this might have.

Saturday, November 18, 2017

This was the coldest Saturday morning of our broadcasts so

far. The temp barely peaked above twenty as our bass track warned of whatever moronic mischief we would deliver. We had decided to present two new segments. After his eloquent intro, Edgar proceeded.

EDGAR: Now, it seems that during this past week, somebody launched a YouTube video from our last week's show. You might want to catch it. It just happens to be a one-minute and twenty-seven second video of our little discussion about the North Korean Missile that can supposedly reach our nation's capitol. Just go to YouTube and enter The Radio Guys Talk about North Korean Missile. Let us know what you think.

ME: As we move into this Holiday season, this segment is brought to you by the Significant Other App. This could be your lifesaver as there are so many opportunities ahead for you to make someone happy by remembering a birthday, often forgotten in the shadow of the other big celebrations. Or any special thing you want to do before it becomes lost in the melee of shopping, drinking and eating. So, get the app, load it with any reminders you don't want to forget, and relax into the calm and peace that is supposed to accompany this time of the year. Be a holiday hero, not a holiday goat. That's the Significant Other App. Download it free.

ROXY: I've just added out-of-town friends to this, so I don't have to send apologies for forgetting cards or phone calls.

EDGAR: And I know the pain of not being remembered. Marge's birthday is on the twenty-eighth of December. Yes, I have disappointed her in the past, and been reminded of it many times after. So I'm definitely into our sponsor's life saving reminder app.

ME: Okay, I think our listeners have the message, so let's get into our show with our first guest. She's on the phone from Los Angeles; it's her first time on our show. Let us say hello to Lorraine X. Hello Lorraine. And do I understand correctly that you are a LIFE COACH?

LORRAINE X: Hello, and thank you for inviting me. And yes, I am a life coach. Out here we say our job is to get your motor running down a better highway.

ME: An interesting way to put it. I imagine you've got your own motor running pretty well. How did you become a life coach? Through special training and education I would assume.

LORRAINE X: Actually through the best teacher of all: experience.

ME: Ah. Interesting.

LORRAINE X: My life had been one failure after another. Disaster, catastrophe, you name it. Addiction, Affliction and Infection, I sometimes refer to it. Bankruptcy, identification theft, left at the altar, shunned by my family, arrested for vagrancy and warned to stay away from young people. Was I a mess!

ME: So it was all that experience which prepared you to help others avoid such calamities and find their dreams?

LORRAINE X: Exactly. They say that until you've been in someone else's shoes you can't really relate to what they're going through. Well, I've worn more shoes than a hundred year old centipede. And I tell that to my clients so they can't say I don't really understand them.

ME: Wow! So, someone comes to you seeking help. Give us an idea about what they might be wanting.

LORRAINE X: Sure. It might be something such as a better self-image. Very important. What they wear. Where they hang out. Or how to be successful, starting with getting a job after they've lost three or four in as many months. Some don't know they need new teeth. And mouthwash. They're unable to get within five feet of anyone else. It's all self-awareness. And self-confidence. And some need organization. From people who are hoarders, and most likely won't seek my help, to women whose purses are filled with their life history and yet, can't find their car keys or lipstick. Or mouth wash. I've been through it all, except the teeth part. Good teeth run in my genes. And of course it's a must out here in California where everyone displays an enormous smile to mask his or her inner loneliness and self-loathing. You can't get on a bus out here without a fantastic, engaging smile.

ME: Wow, again. I had no idea. Edgar?

EDGAR: I'm shocked. Maybe you could tell us about your name. It's quite unusual. Well, I guess there was Malcolm X, wasn't there?

LORRAINE X: I knew you'd ask me about my name, X. Rather than some superfluous question about where I was from or how I got into this field. Oh, I guess you just asked me about that. Sorry.

EDGAR: No offense taken. I'm sure you get those questions all the time.

LORRAINE X: Yes, well, some people discover they might be in need of something as radical as changing identity. To help release the burden you've been carrying around. And one way that has worked with many of my clients, as it did with me, was a name change. Nothing will have greater impact on how you see yourself or how others see you as changing your name. Imagine. Even your friends have to rethink you. And sometimes have to struggle to recall your new handle.

EDGAR: So your name was?

LORRAINE X: Lorraine. But I didn't change my first name. The X stands for crossroads. Transition. Transformation. X marks the spot. It's a big deal for some people. After all, we weren't given a choice about our name way back when, before we knew who we'd actually turn out to be. You know, like we didn't get a choice of who would be our family. With your new name, you and your acquaintances might take you more seriously. And seriously, guys, taking yourself more seriously and respectfully is what it's all about. It will get your motor running down a better road to a more productive and fulfilling and prosperous life.

EDGAR: Well, that is impressive, Lorraine, uh X. Thank you for being our guest. And you can be contacted if someone Googles your name, am I right?

LORRAINE: Right as rain. Or, Lorraine, ha, ha. Great to be on your show.

ME: There you have it, friends. Something to think about. A name change, huh? Give us your thoughts on our website: radioguys.com. I need to catch my breath after that. Here I thought Lorraine X had something to do with being X-Rated. Roxy, what's next?

ROXY: Why don't I read some of the new questions we have for our listeners. A very short segment brought to you by Gluten Fix, the folks who bring you that special supplement for those who need gluten and can't find it anymore in the foods they love. With the holidays coming up, you can be sure some of your old favorites, from snacks to sides to main courses will be offered gluten free. Be prepared with Gluten Fix Supplements. Stock up today. Now, for our question: We want to know if you think drones should be used to deliver Christmas gifts? That's right, should drones be delivering Christmas presents?

EDGAR: I like the question. But, it really does have many implications, doesn't it? The whole Santa thing. Coming down the chimney. What happens to the reindeer? The enormous outdoor blow-up figures of all the Santa stuff? Will there be blow-up drones decorated with strings of colored lights?

ME: And what about the food the kids leave out for Santa? The children's books about the old fashioned Christmas? In fact, shouldn't parents have their kids weigh in on this question?

EDGAR: Many, many questions for our listeners. Well, we're eager to hear your thoughts out there.

ROXY: Then we move along to our new segment, inspired by last weeks breaking news from North Korea. That they have a missile that could reach our nation's capital.

EDGAR: Right, Roxy. And we've decided to call this segment: News From North Korea. Or, News from Poonang.

ROXY: It's all yours, Edgar. Start us off.

EDGAR: Here's the thing. Who really knows what's going on in North Korea? Our problem is compounded by the fact that our government insists on doing business only with people who speak English.

ME: Except, of course, if those countries are big and powerful, like China and Russia.

EDGAR: Right. Or, let's say they just happen to have a lot of oil.

ME: So, how do we get our intelligence, then, Edgar?

EDGAR: Simple. By eavesdropping on or hacking into our allies, like Germany, or Italy or England. Or even Canada.

ME: Well, what do our friends, our allies, think about that? Pretty nasty isn't it?

EDGAR: We simply have to. It's vital to our national security. Also, they usually have their reports translated into English. I mean, sure they complain. But what are they going to do? Shut down all of our Starbucks?

ME: I see your point. They're all much more vulnerable to violence from other nations than we are.

EDGAR: That's right. And, being bilingual has become a threat to our national security. Everyone who speaks another language is becoming suspect. Maybe they're communists. Or, Muslims. Or, or . . . Foreigners! We have to draw the line somewhere. Also, we don't have to put all our spies at risk like they do. Or, train them to speak other languages. Win. Win.

ME: So how does this fit with our efforts to help our listeners understand what is really going on elsewhere? Like in

North Korea?

EDGAR: Exactly. First of all, we contact North Koreans who speak English.

ME: Okay.

EDGAR: And, they must have some expertise that we're interested in. For example, in a few minutes we're having a guest from North Korea, a professor on leave right here at our own Metro State University. He's curious to see if a local talk show might be of interest to him. So, let's welcome him to The Radio Guys Talk. Professor Sing Park Choi.

From behind our curtain, an attractive-looking Asian enters, black hair, fit, and smartly attired in a charcoal silk suit. He gives a brief nod to each of us and to our outside audience, then takes a seat. *Welcome, Professor Sing Park Choi. Do I have your name correct?*

PROFESSOR SING: Yes, thank you.

EDGAR: And you're a professor of Business, correct?
PROFESSOR SING: Yes I am.

EDGAR: It's like an MBA program I take it.

PROFESSOR SING: It is. Exactly.

EDGAR: Great. Since so much business is international, I think our audience would be very interested in what you have to say. By the way, Professor Sing, your English is impeccable. I can't imagine how you have achieved such perfection. Tell us, please.

PROFESSOR SING: I've actually spoken it all my life.

EDGAR: Really. I had no idea they allowed that where you are from. Good to know. Still, you must be bi-lingual, yes?

PROFESSOR SING: Yes, actually, I also speak French.

EDGAR: Amazing. Truly. I hate to say it but some of us don't speak English nearly as well as you do.

Professor Sing nods.

EDGAR: And what should we know about how you teach

business?

PROFESSOR SING: Well, I offer courses in how American businessmen can be more effective dealing with foreign businessmen. What some of the different customs are, the importance of learning their language. Basic things that any smart person would want to know.

EDGAR: Gee. Makes sense to me. But I thought it wasn't possible for our businesses to have operations in North Korea?

PROFESSOR SING: Oh, it definitely isn't. But I help students with dealing with many other Asian nations.

EDGAR: Oh . . . I thought you were North Korean?

PROFESSOR SING: I am. I was born in Detroit. I teach at the State Tech School in Ann Arbor.

EDGAR: (Stares at Roxy, then me.) I'm sorry, this is confusing, I thought we had a North Korean professor who spoke English.

PROFESSOR SING: That would be me. I still have papers from North Korea. A North Korean woman who works in the office at Metro State called me and asked if I'd be willing to come on a talk show and talk about international business. Obviously there was a misunderstanding.

EDGAR: Oh my. I'm so solly, I mean sorry. Please forgive us. We need to be clearer, I think. Please accept a fabulous lunch on us at Whiskey "n Ribs, right behind us. It's wonderful and we thank you for your visit. You have shown us the importance of being bilingual.

ME: A good lesson, and Edgar, well conducted. I actually think he might be a pretty decent guy.

EDGAR: For a man from Poonang. A descendent.

Tuesday, November 22, 2017

Not surprising, the News from the North Korea segment fell short, like the missile probably would. But it still offered some unique possibilities in our minds. So, with a clean white board we tossed up ideas, some better, some worse.

Eventually the issue of U.S. intelligence gathering and drones began to mesh.

EDGAR: So it's true that our own Intelligence gathering is modest in it's results, and most of the good stuff comes from spying on our friends? With drones and hookers and other devious means.

ME: I guess so, Edgar. Some say we need more linguists; others say that's unpatriotic.

EDGAR: So we become reliant on hackers, then? And if so, shouldn't we focus all our efforts on being the "Hackers' Hacker"? Use all our bright young geeks, and a few of the old pro hackers. Once they're out of prison.

ME: I guess so. And where do the drones fit in?

EDGAR: That's the beauty of it. The hackers use the drones to listen in. And our military uses stealth drones to conduct war with missiles and rockets. And our entire military efforts will be focused on drones and specialists who run them, maintain them, assemble them. We would have them everywhere.

ME: So how do we have them everywhere?

EDGAR: Very Simple. The American way. We franchise them. ME: You're kidding, Edgar.

EDGAR: Not at all. Let's say, in China, we find some ambitious businessmen and women who want to earn some big bucks. Well, we just dig into our bottomless military and intelligence budgets, and finance, let's say, a noodle shop along some busy country highway, with a small camouflaged runway that leads up to the back door. Mount a locator or transponder in the pagoda shaped roof. And an outbuilding for hydrogen fuel cell storage.

ME: So you're saying that with a zillion or so drones, we will be safe and in the know.

EDGAR: And think of the savings in agents and training and ground forces and tanks and half our Air Force. And all our troops and their lifetime benefits.

ME: I'm catching on, Edgar. And we could have self-liquidating drones, and not have the cost of those cyanide tablets we give to our spies in case they are captured.

EDGAR: And drones are becoming very dependable. Maybe we'll even win a small war, bigger than our last win in Grenada. Why I can see us having stealth drones that no one could shoot down. We wouldn't need our jet fighters and our land battle weapons. Maybe just our rifles. This could signal a shift to the end of our crazy arms race . . . and all the weapons we have to make to stoke everyone's war machine.

ME: And keep our economy going.

EDGAR: But what happens if everyone has thousands of stealth drones?

ME: Hmmm. I guess we'd have to have bigger and faster ones. And faster and faster hackers. And many more trained operators. And anti-stealth technologies. And some huge super sonic jets with trawler type steel nets to grab the enemy stealth drones right out of the air.

EDGAR: Now it's making sense.

Thanksgiving Day, November 23, 2017

Both my daughters, age thirty-five and thirty-eight, returned to Denver for Thanksgiving. My Ex and I had never overcome our long festering feud enough to eat turkey together. So, our kids flipped coins, or something, and this year I got Friday and Mallory got Thanksgiving Day. Really, it didn't matter much to me. I think I was far along in my efforts to chuck the win/lose aspects of life. Except for the Broncos, of course. Edgar and Marge invited me over and I gratefully accepted. It was so easy being with their family. I relaxed, sipped and laughed at Marge and Edgar as they clowned with their boys, Marge making a huge thing about our new stardom on YouTube. "Your daddy's got a fan club and he just got a call asking him to help broadcast a boxing match. Can you imagine?"

I hadn't heard about this one. But, sure enough, it was true. The coming Wednesday. On Monday, Edgar and I would pour over boxing terms and strategies. The blind leading the blind. A sucker punch into a stiff upper lip . . . or something.

On Friday I would take my daughters, June and Jenny, for a gourmet experience at Whiskey 'N Ribs and an extensive tour of our front window broadcast studio with the cardboard cutouts of the Radio Guys. We also laughed about our emerging "notoriety" with the staff and owners. We ate and drank and quite soon they began to grill me about my love life. As they usually do. I even admitted the full story behind the outrageous opening day fiasco; the romantic breakup and the traffic-stopping demonstration out front. Even my compulsive proposal of marriage that was the deal breaker. I was happy to find myself laughing about all of it. I was making progress.

Jenny, always my staunchest supporter no matter what my screw-up happened to be, said, "Dad, she, whatever her name was, just didn't get you. That's all. Her loss. And we did see the YouTube video about North Korea. And showed our friends. You're doing great,"

"Now tell us *more* about the women in your life," smiled June.

So I did. As long as it makes them laugh at my expense, I'm for it. It's very therapeutic for me. And they're so damn much smarter than their old man about matters of the heart. I've always wondered about that, since Mallory, in my humble opinion, didn't seem to have one, and I, if I did have one, it seemed to be governed by pathological blundering.

Later in the afternoon, full of succulent food and abundant whiskey and wine, it was Uber time. They had finished updating me on their busy and, in their dad's opinion, quite rich and rewarding lives so far. They deserved it. Their heads and hearts were both in the right places. God, for a moment I wondered if I wasn't their actual father. I shall crush that thought if it reoccurs. As we parted, I told them we'd be live out front the next morning and they said they wouldn't miss it. I hoped we'd be fabulous.

Saturday, November 25, 2017

As the bass rumble achieved volume I saw my daughters emerge from their Uber, already laughing, at what I didn't know. Perhaps just the out-and-out absurdity of what their father was doing. They waved as they heard Edgar intone the welcome, adding their names to the general welcome to regulars and new listeners.

Roxy hands a yellow sheet of paper to Edgar and he glances through it.

EDGAR: Thank you Roxy. Our sponsor for our first segment, maybe a bit late, but certainly not for next year, or even the upcoming holidays, is from our new friends at Revival and Recovery Products. And specifically their amazing solution for our appetite pollution. Of course we overate, right? I sure did. Maybe a few of us even drank. And I'm still regretting my lack of control, even though it also happened last year and the year before. So, I won't be caught again without this amazing product. Complete Reclamation. That's right. Whatever you ate, whatever you drank, Complete Reclamation will make sure you awaken the following morning with no after-effects. You see, it is the most powerful anti-acid going, four times the power of the leading plop, plop tablets and, in addition, a mild but persistent laxative, all in half-dollar sized tablets that you can dissolve in water or eat like a Christmas cookie. It's amazing. Get some today. Complete Reclamation.

ME: Good work, Edgar. And thanks to the good folks at Revival and Recovery. I'll be interested to see what other products they make. And . . . we begin with BREAKING NEWS. And here it is. NECKTIE AND BOW TIE SALES WERE AT RECORD LEVELS IN DENVER ON BLACK FRIDAY. That's right. And I'll bet some of you out front are part of the reason. All of you who are part of Women Who Love Men with Ties.

Edgar waves. Thumbs up. And we're off on a show that gets a healthy Dr. Nadine back with the latest on her new book launch, *When Recoupling Sucks.* And, an energized list of questions for our listeners, including: How do we keep the Turkey in Thanksgiving? Unless you're a vegetarian.

It's a solid show, in the end, and June and Jenny help peddle shirts out front and join us for lunch in the back office where they fawn over Roxy like she's the most amazing woman they've ever met. And she is.

Monday November 27, 2017

I admit I found myself waiting for Elizabeth to call upon her return from Chicago. I never asked exactly when she planned to arrive. I just assumed she'd be eager to get back and get together. After all, her parting kiss felt like she was releasing all caution. At least it felt that way to me.

Edgar and Roxy and I were meeting at ten, Tuesday, so I had plenty of time to wonder and fabricate possible scenarios.

At four in the afternoon, no word, so I, calm as an irritated intestinal tract, called Grand Lake Lodge, and reserved a room for Tuesday and Wednesday. According to the young voice on the phone, I had my choice of almost, if not all, rooms. I thought it sounded pretty much like being alone in my house. Except for the reason I was heading there, to check in with Catherine to see if she still thought I was harmless enough.

Tuesday, November 28, 2017

Our meeting in the reflection of a freshly cleared white board and the tasty aroma of an entire Cardamom Coffee Cake brought by Edgar from a Swedish bakery, was the ideal counter to dropping temperatures. We kept cutting off modest pieces and devoured it with cup after cup of great coffee as though we were just emerging from a food fast for the past week. Which, obviously, we weren't.

Actually, the coffee cake eating pattern spawned a question for our listener's: Why do people always leave one piece of something on the plate at the end, no matter how much they'd like to consume it? What's your theory?

Maybe it was the coming holidays that fired us up. Knowing we had something to do that we were really enjoying, that would also distract us from some of the more corrosive and stressful pollution of the season. Mostly the commercial assault, I think. I should know, after so many years of trying to jack up the purchases for various ad clients' products. If there was anything I regretted about my career, it was the effort to keep people buying more, even things they didn't really need. I rationalized that we weren't forcing them to *buy*. They could make those choices. Still, we were employed to make them think they needed, really needed, to buy one or a dozen or a pair or a larger version of something they already had, or didn't have. The American Way.

Now I sometimes nursed that regret, knowing that there was a cost, moral more than monetary, distracting more than discerning, environmental more than endurable, of that effort to persuade people that they needed more stuff. Newer stuff. Questionable stuff. Stuff to make us feel better about ourselves. Stuff that we convinced ourselves we absolutely needed. Stuff we had to get up in the middle of the night after Thanksgiving to get in line for. I had been good in the game, made good money at it. And most of it had nothing to do with public service announcements. When I found myself in such a mood of remorse, the best I could do was shake my head, take a deep breath and get on with my life. Now I had a great distraction, our radio show, and I could laugh at some of the things I used to take very seriously.

I began, "Is there a way that we can make fun of all the buying that we do in this country? Even those who are really strapped for cash? I hate to moralize. But, have you ever thought of how many appliances, big and small, are tossed onto our junk heaps or landfills every day? For instance, how many TV sets are scrapped, even those that work? I'll bet that we dump more TVs per capita every day than any other country in the world. Surely we're number one!

"You think we can shame people into buying less?" Edgar tilted his head toward me like a wise grandpa just interrupted from reading the sports section.

"It sounds like that, doesn't it?" I answered.

"It's a noble objective, Jake," said Roxy. "Kind of a downer, though. Unless you've got a brilliant idea. How many video games should be enough for a family of four, say? Doesn't feel right to me."

"You're both right. It seems very parental. We're talking about being parental to the parents. I've always liked the line

used by Denver Water: *Use Only What You Need.* It's urging
without moralizing. Let's move on. I'm feeling like a
schoolmaster holding a switch over his students to keep them
in line. It makes me feel really judgmental. Edgar, it's all the
sugar in the coffee cake you so generously brought in. Unless
we get a real zinger of an idea, I say we drop this. Don't even
shelve it or put it on the back burner."

"By the way," Edgar announced, "I have prepared a list
of all the things I'm open to receiving this Christmas. I'll give
you copies, of course. I certainly can use a few new ties."

We laughed. Then Roxy offered, "Edgar, that might be
the best idea we could use. Talk about our own Christmas lists.
See where that takes us. Not just the "politically correct" list,
but what would really mean something to us. See what we
come up with. I'm almost out of olive oil. And there's a brand of
roller ball pens with fat grips that I like. Just for examples."

She continued, "Oh, and there's a brand of Sauvignon
Blanc that I love but don't buy because of the price. But,
occasionally I'd love to have a bottle. Or a case, actually. Ha,
ha." Winking.

She wrote the idea on the white board with a couple
more examples, then shifted to the coming Saturday.

Edgar began, "We've got some good questions out to our
listeners. And I think they've posted some good ones for us.
What if we do a back and forth with our listeners? Even if we
can't hear them? Get them more involved"

Thus began a thorough sifting of things our listeners
had sent in. Rich material, it turns out. And it pushed us to find
ways to make it funny on air.

At two o'clock, pretty much spent, we ended our efforts.
There remained some holes and some rough edges. We agreed
to meet Thursday morning. I was hungry, but I thought I could
wait until I arrived at Grand Lake, checked in, and parked my

sorry ass at the bar where Catherine, so enjoyable to watch, would fill my glass and lift my spirits. I hoped.

On the drive up I pondered that thought: *Lift my spirits.* Like I needed them lifted. Even after a great session with great friends and a wonderful visit with my daughters over Thanksgiving. Why in the hell did I need my spirits lifted? It led to some soul searching. And I didn't much like my answers.

Was I so needy? How could I not be thrilled about what was going on in my life? What was missing? I was doing something that I really enjoyed. I was creating . . . stretching abilities I didn't know I had. Concentrating on positive things rather than negative things. And it seemed like people liked what we did. I mean, as daughter June often exclaimed: "WTF?"

I considered that it might be time to end my suspension of visits with Jan Baumgardner. She was seven times smarter than me about matters like this. Or, I could broach the subject with a very appealing woman who would hopefully be serving me from behind the horseshoe bar in Grand Lake. That is, if I could present this conundrum without frightening her away.

The temp was twenty degrees and falling after I checked into the lodge and began wandering down the slope into town. I hadn't called Catherine ahead because I wanted to come even if she wasn't there. And, there was the possibility that she could say no to a visit over the phone easier than in person. Now *there* was another sign of insecurity on my part. If she wasn't working, I couldn't take it personally.

At five o'clock I parked at the bar. I was the only customer and Catherine was the only bartender. How's that for good fortune?

"You're back, Jake. What can I get you?"

"Hi. Why not whiskey, Makers, with rocks and a half lime that I'll squeeze in myself. Not that I don't trust you."

"You don't think I'm strong enough to squeeze a lime?"

"No. I need something to occupy my hands while I get used to seeing you. It's hard to look unassuming and stuff my hands in my pockets while sitting down and wanting to sip my drink."

"I see," she set all the components for my cocktail in front of me, stood back a step, tilted her head, hands on her hips and asked, "You're kind of an odd one, aren't you Jake?"

I froze.

"I don't mean that in a critical way. I've just never heard anyone answer a question quite like that."

I remained frozen, with my mouth open.

Catherine picked up a glass of water and sipped. I gulped from my glass, before I squeezed the lime. Then fumbled the lime as most of the juice squirted outside the rim of my glass. She handed me another half, as though daring me to toss a beanbag again at a target that I missed by three feet on my first toss.

This time I used both hands and was marginally successful for a man without palsied fingers. Another big gulp. I would very soon need a refill and I hadn't said a word.

"I didn't think I was, an odd one, that is. But this is more or less proof that I am. I don't know what to say. You hardly know me and you've seen right through me."

She laughed, hands covering her face, shaking her head, finally spurting, "No, no, no! I don't know what got into me. I just opened my mouth and that came out. You seem more than OK. Not even peculiar. It's . . . well, I just haven't run into someone like you while I've lived up here. Or, anywhere, actually." And she burst again into her special laugh with that appealing ticking sound in her throat. "I will make myself a drink, and maybe I'll come to my senses."

She made herself a vodka and tonic. I watched her squeeze her lime wedge efficiently and on target. She stirred it and toasted me, though I found my glass empty but for a quarter-ounce or so. She laughed and took my glass, refilled it and squeezed a lime effortlessly and perfectly aimed and returned it with a dry paper napkin. "This is on me. I really don't want you to run off just yet. I hardly know you."

And then her laugh, bending her over. And she coughed, then verged on choking, and gasping, "Oh no. I'm so sorry. I really am, Jake. This is just awful. You must think I'm a horrible person." More laughter though I could tell she was nearing exhaustion.

"I hold no grudges. And I'm glad you didn't throw up. Although I thought you actually might a moment ago."

"I'm so very sorry. I'm ashamed. I don't know what happened. I guess I'm glad we are alone. I'm so embarrassed. Whew!"

I caught my breath. It seemed like the danger was past. And I had one of those cathartic feelings inside. Even though I think it was Catherine that actually experienced some version of a real catharsis.

"I think what you did was somehow just what I needed. Go figure. What do I owe you?"

"Ohhhhh. Nothing at all. Absolutely nothing. This is all a surprise to me. What was pent up, I have no idea. Cheers!"

We clanked and drank. And she eventually dragged a stool from the wall of bottles and sat down nearer to the bar.

"I'm going to trust you because I can't imagine you have an evil bone in your body, Catherine." I took a breath and continued. "All the way driving up here, I was tossing around some personal stuff, contemplating that I would cancel my two month break with my shrink, and get her take on what I was struggling with. Don't worry, it's nothing gruesome, or evil. I don't have a police record, I haven't abused anyone, or cheated anyone. So, I'm just a guy who is trying to understand something about myself that I don't like very much. Can you take it?"

Noncommittally, she replied, "I don't know. I'm not a psychologist, Jake. Go ahead, I'll tell you to stop."

Right, I thought. Do I really want to do this? Do I want to be that guy that unloads on the bartender? I guess I did.

"It's really not a big deal. It's just that I've been a pretty successful guy much of my life. A reasonably good father to two daughters. And now I'm doing something that is really exciting and I'm doing it with a couple super people. Still, I find myself too easily falling into the dumps. Like I need a boost, from someone. I usually find that I'd like it from a woman, probably since I've been divorced for so long, and being retired, I no longer am lost or consumed in my career. There. That's it, I think."

Catherine sat, staring at me. I quickly regretted what I'd said. I felt like I was dumping my stuff on an almost stranger. Like sitting on a plane and spilling my guts to someone I'd never see again. Imposing on someone's good will.

"I told you I wasn't a psychologist, Jake, so I'm not sure what to say. Let me think a little. I do think you're being honest. I don't think you're telling me this to hustle me. I hope I'm right about that. I would like to hear your radio show sometime. It sounds really important to you."

I felt quite deflated. Not at her answers, but that my "problem" seemed so lame. The answer seemed so obvious: Buck up! "Now it's my turn to apologize. I didn't come up here to unload on you. And I'd be lying if I said I wasn't interested in you. There are several good reasons for that. My only excuse is that you seemed, last time and in our rather unusual interchange over a lime complication, just so damn unpretentious, and, well, there you have it."

Saved by the bell, she was. A couple entered, jangling

the sleigh bells on the front door. She greeted them, Hi, Welcome! Evidently she didn't know them. "You can sit anywhere, tables or the bar, I'll get you a menu if you're eating. And drinks. We have a full bar."

They looked around, and at each other, and the woman pointed to the other end of the bar where he hung her coat on the back of the barstool. They both seemed quite happy, and nodded at me, smiling. I gave a brief wave. I thought it would be easy to begin a conversation with them, but hesitated and pretty soon they were asking Catherine questions about drinks and the menu.

Another man arrived and walked quickly to the bar, rubbing his cold hands together, waving and saying, Hi, Catherine, my usual. He nodded at me and reached for a bar napkin to blow his nose.

"Hi, George. Right away. You look like you've been raked by the frost. Like you drove all the way in on your ATV."

"I did. I misjudged the bite. I should have come in with the truck."

Now it was my turn to think. Let the space between me and Catherine be. And suddenly I was struck by how few words it took to find out a whole lot about a few people, and how easily a couple of drinks among strangers can evolve into some kind of warmth and good will as the booze takes the edge off.

"We'll get back to your question, Jake," Catherine said as she passed me with a drink for George. "I've got a thought or two." I liked the sound of that. I hadn't been asked to leave.

Catherine returned from the kitchen with the cook's report that anything on the menu except the flank steak and the rainbow trout was available. I started thinking about food. As each of us had our drink, George raised his glass, "Well, I guess it's too early to say, Merry Christmas, but what the hell, it's sure cold enough." We responded with our glasses. I asked the couple how they found this place?

"We're from Dallas," she said, her drawl confirming. "We're returning after visiting our daughter for Thanksgiving and she said we should drive down through the Park on the way home. She also said there was a nice bar with food here. I think this is it."

One more customer entered, a lanky thirtyish man, attired as some kind of mechanic who had had a grueling day, judging by the grease on his overalls and various smudges on his face. He stomped his feet to the point where I wondered if his bones shattered in his work boots. "Whoa, it is damn cold. Or I'm getting soft. Hey, Catherine. Hi everyone." He sat at the bar with a beer soon in his hand. I ordered a burger and the couple placed their order. Then George rose, left a bill from his wallet and announced, "I got milk and eggs stashed in blankets for Josie and I don't want them all frozen. Enjoy your dinners. See you Catherine, Larry."

I listened as Larry chatted with Catherine about his father having a heart attack and not recovering very well. She nodded and brought him a second beer. The couple, the Wilsons, it turned out, were getting a kick out of being stuck in a cold mountain town for the night. "I hope the heat in the Lodge is turned up. I'm not sleeping in the car," she giggled.

Then the door slammed open and another foot stomper entered. "Hey, y'all! It's really coming down with an attitude." His baseball cap was topped with fresh white stuff and his cheeks were shining with melted, snow. "I don't know if it will last but driving is going to be lousy soon, or already is, actually."

With that warning he offered a wave and "Have a safe night!" as he turned, opened the door and walked out, allowing us to see the heavy snow falling in the street lights and to feel the burst of cold air snapping at our backs.

"OK, folks, Catherine announced, "let's give it a half hour so you can finish your dinners and maybe another drink. If it hasn't stopped, I have to close up. I have a bit of a drive, and you have to walk, somehow, up the hill to the Lodge."

She turned toward me, "Jake, how long are you up here. Will you be here tomorrow afternoon?"

"I will. I leave early Thursday morning for a run through."

"Good. I'm here at three. Maybe we can finish up our talk, Okay?"

"I'll be here." At thirty minutes the driving snow was obviously going to continue. We all bundled up, Catherine locking up behind us and crossing the street to her Jeep. I joined the Wilsons trudging up the slope to the Lodge. Inside it felt very cozy with a robust fire popping in the huge stone fireplace. My room was comfortably warm as well and I quickly hung my clothes and spread an extra quilt on the bed. With my magazine and a book in hand, I slid under the weight of warm goose down. I checked my phone as I plugged it in next to the lamp. There was a text from Elizabeth, *Hi, Jake. I'm just leaving Chicago, I had to change flights and stay an extra day. Linda came down very sick on Sunday. She's ok now. I'll call you tomorrow when I'm home.*

The text said 3:24 PM, about the time I slid down the hill for a drink. I felt a twinge of conflict. Thinking about two women. Liking them both, though I barely knew Catherine. But, there seemed a lot to like about her.

Wednesday, November 29, 2017

With the fire bristling and snapping, I had my coffee at a low wooden table directly in front of the blaze. I got up from my chair to say goodbye to the Wilsons, and returned to my laptop.

I was quite content to be the only lodge resident. My oatmeal and toast and jam would sustain me until lunch.

I proceeded to work on the show, first opening a doc for my "sensible" Christmas gift list: starting it with colorful socks, and a bottle of Gosling's Black Seal Rum.

A second doc was for a new phone interview. Perhaps a Christmas greeting to Sub Minister Camilla Thistlepink Birtwistle. Or, to Bingston, in the remote chance he was still employed as her assistant. Another possibility might be with the Journalist for Al Jazeera that Roxy met while covering The Mooch from up in Jackson Hole. I recalled she was based in Beirut, and, what with the tensions and instabilities increasing in the Middle East, she could be a good source. But, could we make that somehow funny? Could we ignore the political pawn that Lebanon is to the super powers including Washington. The more I thought about it, global politics, the quicker I moved to delete the blank document.

I also considered a phone interview with Santa. Let's get his take on drones delivering Christmas packages. That seemed promising. So I spent an hour jotting down questions and splinters of humor and discomfort. Grudgingly, in the next hour, it began to morph into a possible phone call.

ME: Hello, Santa. There's been talk down here about drones delivering the Christmas presents.

SANTA: Who's talking about it?

ME: Well, we've wondered. On our radio show. And certainly Amazon is considering drone delivery of items up to a certain size. I don't know who else. But definitely it's on the front burner.

SANTA: Well, I hope they choke on their drones. You know, we just don't need them. Why do things have to be delivered so goddamned quickly? If you need a new something. A shirt, shoe polish, a coffee pot, you can just go to the store. And if you can't drive, get an Uber. And if you don't want an Uber, order on line. Who can't wait for a few days? Really. We're trying to convince people they need everything this very instant. Can't wait. What'll I do? I mean, Cool your jets. Stop spiking your blood pressure. Stop having to have something immediately to make you feel good about yourself. Calm the fuck down! And if you need some medication or something else vital to your survival, hit the ER or have it sent next day air. Those are the absolute exceptions.

ME: Uh, so you're thinking the drone idea is pandering to business. To the growing compulsiveness of our society to have even more and have it instantly?

SANTA: Whatever. I mean, get a life, for God's sake. Trim your nails, wash your car. Geez, does anyone do that for himself anymore? Strip some furniture. Poach some eggs, shine your shoes. Blow your nose, clean your glasses, polish your smart-phone screen. Edit all your photos. Make a quilt. Get a third job. Chew your kids out for watching too much TV. Stop watching so much yourself and rake your leaves or iron your underwear. Or read . . . anything. Squeeze your nuts. What do I care? Or, perish the thought, talk to each other about something you haven't talked about for at least a month. Like what's your name again? Or where are we on the issue of divorce or getting counseling? Make an appointment for a colonoscopy.

By now I glance up at Roxy and Edgar only to see the color draining from their faces.

ME: Boy, now that's a lot to think about. So, Santa, you're quite OK with how Christmas presents are currently being delivered I take it?

SANTA: Gee, where did you get that idea? Yes, I'm extremely content. And if someone doesn't like the way we do it, they can shoot one of my Elves, or fuck a reindeer or set fire to my sleigh or poison my seal meat. And rather than one more fucking video game, (I had given up bleeping by now. It was moving way too fast) *and one more fucking (bleep) tie, or novelty that you get uncle so-and-so because uncle so-and-so always sends a check to you because he doesn't know what the fuck you really need. And if you'd both just send a card or make a short phone call, the world would be a far better place. And don't tell me you can't do that. It's impossible, you say! It's so fucking possible that you have to be an ignoramus to not see how possible it is. And it's really fucking stupid to buy something you or someone else might not really need and then insist that it be delivered in twenty-four hours by a fucking drone. YESSIREE! Santa is coming again . . . and he is going to be pissed!*

I glance at Roxy and Edgar, panicking, their worry lines lodging in formation. Santa definitely had a point to make. Would the world pay it any attention? Maybe that will be a poll question?

Obviously this needed more work. And many more Bleeps. But it felt so good to blast it into print. I must have some deep-seated guilt fueling my effort to stop people from buying things they don't really need. But, I don't need to force Santa to intercede against unnecessary purchasing. I should just pour gasoline on myself in our largest mall and light a fire to protest excessive consumerism. Ouch. Where have I been hiding this venom? I am such a grouch about this. I do need to see Jan. Before I hurt myself.

What else am I sitting on?

At three-thirty, with the road melted by unobstructed sunshine, I tromped down to the bar, my head cleared of purchase-bashing for the time being, and eager to talk with Catherine.

Again, I was the first man standing at the bar, and I

rubbed my hands together as Catherine approached with an apprehensive smile on her face. "You're back, Jake. Good to see you.

"Yes, I am. Good to see you, too. I suspect you've been dreading my reappearance."

"Not at all. What can I get you, a beer?"

"You can."

I watched the ease with which she moved with her duties. Graceful. I could watch her all day. "The snow seems to have disappeared pretty fast. Just like in Denver." *Come on, Jake, you can do so much better than the weather.*

"Yes. Amazing. Gee, Jake, talking about the weather doesn't sound much like you, somehow." She set the beer in front of me and smirked. (That's right, she smirked.)

She continued, watching my mouth drop. "I'm sorry that we couldn't continue yesterday, but that's how things go in this job. You never really know what'll come up. It provides a little drama, don't you think?"

"I do, Catherine. So you aren't dreading this conversation?"

"Far from it. I'm only concerned that I might not have much to offer. I'm not a psychologist, as I told you."

"Well, I've already got a shrink. A really good one. And I'm sure I'll get her take on this. But, if you're willing, I'd really like to know what you think."

She pulled the stool closer again and made her Vodka Tonic. "First of all, I don't think you have a serious problem. Like most of us you just have an issue that's challenging you right now. Not disabling or making you dysfunctional. How's that?"

"In the jargon of therapy, it's reassuring. I've regretted bringing it up. I almost put it in the class of whining."

"You shouldn't. It's real. So don't ignore it. And don't fall for what some men would say: Tough it out! I was glad you were open. Quite unexpected, really. As for my thoughts, they are very unprofessional. And please be ready to break out laughing."

"I will try, but don't count on it."

"I have a fabulous sister back home. One of the few of my family that understands me. She always seemed to go up and down more than I did, emotionally. It was noticeable to me, but maybe to no one else. And she struggled with it, for years, mostly when she was in a down mood. Finally she pressed her doctor during a physical. She took a test, a brief one, and in fifteen minutes her doctor said, yes, you have some symptoms of depression. Not heavy, but I see it is affecting you. The upshot was that she tried a mild anti-depressant, she still takes it after twenty-some years, and she thinks it helps a lot. It seems to level her out a little. I can tell the difference. So that's one thought."

"I like the notion. Thank you. It's easy to check out." I raised my beer to clank with her glass.

Catherine waited a moment, then resumed. "When I moved here, sixteen years ago, I left a lot behind. Some things I left were really unhealthy and good to dump. But there were also good things in my life that I walked away from. My professional life. Some of my family. Some of my friends. Big things. Big things to replace and some were irreplaceable. After the initial euphoria out here, I felt empty and lost and uncertain of what to do. Other than I had to get a job to support myself. This went on for at least a year, some days better than others. One day I was hiking above the lake and I sat down on a boulder and just stared out over what was in front of me. I was startled when I found myself asking, What or Who created all this? I mean, I've thought of that question before, you probably have too. But this time it was different. It was so strong that a few minutes later I thought I'd snapped out of a dream. I really tried to imagine who could even conceive of any of it. The lake, the sky, the animals, people, air. I'd never felt that wonder before. And all of a sudden, some things fell into place. One of them was that I wasn't alone in this world, or on the rock I was sitting on. It was exhilarating . . . breathtaking. I must have sat there for at least an hour before I hiked back into town. I still think of it. That moment. And I think it's part of the way I look at everything now. Me. You. The people who stop in here that I've never seen before. Familiar people. Friends. It's like I discovered all those things that were missing. And it's still with me. Does that make any sense, Jake?"

I was blown away. I was afraid I would say something inane, stupid. I drank from my beer bottle; it didn't taste as good as I anticipated. "I don't know how to respond. It's been a long time since I even asked myself those questions. Serious questions. Thank you. So you think that's made a big difference in your life."

"For me it has. You have left some things behind with your retirement, don't you think, Jake? The people you worked with. The praise you got for your work. Just the actual business and the way work determines how you spend most of your time. Your kids are gone. The pressure to earn a living, I would assume, doesn't preoccupy you anymore. You have some holes to fill."

"Thank God for the radio show. Really. I can see why it is so important. Thank you again, Catherine. I won't insult you by saying 'send me a bill.'"

"So it wasn't crazy, then?"

"It was brilliant. I'd like to know you better. You're easy to be around. And you're extraordinarily funny. Yesterday was unforgettable. I've never seen anyone laugh so hard. It was thrilling."

"Well, Jake, I'm not seeing anyone right now. And if you like to come up here, we could spend some more time together. Maybe I can show you that rock I was sitting on."

The clarity and honesty of our conversation seemed to clamp my mouth shut for fear of spoiling my sense of contentment. I was floating and I didn't want to land.

Promptly the door pushed in from outside and several folks began the foot stomping to deposit the slush in the entry floor-mats. Three women and two men who turned out to be locals, exchanged quips and greetings with Catherine. She introduced me, we all shook hands and I happily became an observer for the next hour until I ordered my dinner.

I found myself watching and listening and evidently searching for material for the Radio Guys. That felt somewhat uncomfortable, like a spy among friends. This hadn't happened before, and I concluded this was a new lens that I was viewing life through. I wanted to find things that were funny. Things that were funny but hopefully not hurtful to people. It was what Catherine had talked about, but on a secular plane. A new way of looking at the world for me. Maybe that was enough to know right now. As I had a couple more beers, and a great bowl of stew, I concluded that, yes, I was seeing differently. Very little politics, much more awareness of how funny we are. How, even in bad situations, there might be some humor that could lighten the load. Maybe Santa's rant would make people laugh who rarely laughed, at Santa or Christmas or Fruitcake.

Thursday, November 30, 2017

I drove back in the morning, planning to stop in Idaho Springs at Two Brothers, for a wrap of all wraps. I was still shaking my head at the resounding laughter that Catherine unleashed from wherever.

Unforgettable.

At ten o'clock we met at the AM1480 studios. I didn't mention one word of my encounters with Catherine and friends. I hurried to print up Santa's Rant for reaction and revision. Our session vibrated with fresh energy and I sensed Saturday would be full of surprises. I called Elizabeth and made a date for Friday at five. I didn't call Jan for an appointment. I felt I should wait a few more weeks. I also didn't schedule a colonoscopy.

Saturday, December 2, 2017

I was pretty confident that we'd pull off a good show. It just felt right. What I didn't expect was what happened after. As we were relaxing with beers and sandwiches.

It was Tina, one of the waitresses, who poked her head into the office. "Excuse me, uh, there's a man at my table that asked if he could see you for a minute. He's very insistent. I told him I would ask. Sorry. His name is Larry. He says it's important. He doesn't seem violent or weird. But you never know."

I added my shrug to all our shrugs. "Go ahead. Send him back."

Larry appeared instantly, as if he might always be in motion. He was forty-five or so, a narrow face and bushy hair, suggestive of a young Kramer. He quickly reached for handshakes, glanced around for a nonexistent chair, then stood back in the doorway and began.

"Give me five minutes. First, I liked your show. Some great stuff. And I'm in the business. Of Entertainment. I'm based in New York and I represent people who entertain, and I help them with their careers. My waitress told me you've been doing this show since last summer and she said the shows are all good. So I'd like to ask you a few quick questions.

He glanced at each of us as we sat dumbfounded and began before we could respond. "First, do you like doing this show, a lot?" We nodded. "Would you consider living in New York or LA?" More emphatically we each shook our heads. "Could you do more than one show a week?" We looked at each other and shrugged but without enthusiasm. "Who writes your stuff?" Edgar and I said, We do. Roxy pointed to us. And Edgar quickly clarified, "And Roxy does, and she does most of the voices of guests and other characters. She's a genius.

Larry nodded respectfully to Roxie. "So you were Dr. Nadine, eh?" Roxy giggled, "I am."

"Ok, then. That was pretty painless, right? I need to know those things as a start. I don't know what I might come up with but I'll leave you my card in exchange for yours. And when I have an idea, I will contact you. Which one of you should I call?"

Two fingers pointed at me. "Jake"

I quickly looked at his card. "Larry Fillmore."

"How did you know about the show?"

"My mother. I'm visiting her. She lives here and she's kind of a loose cannon. When I arrived, she was being released for disturbing the peace and trespassing at some big meeting or whatever. Later she told me about an outrageous radio show that was insulting, immoral and degenerate. She has some narrow and bizarre views. I thought I'd better check it out."

The three of us barely kept our chairs under us. "Oh my God," sputtered Roxy. Edgar and I clammed up, absolutely dumbfounded, remembering her stomping off out front after Edgar's devastating response undid her.

"You've got your hands full, Larry," I offered. "We couldn't figure what got her so livid about us. I hope she's OK."

"This goes in cycles," he said, gravely, "She's never hurt anyone or caused serious damage, unless making outrageous statements that interrupt and interfere with people and their events is serious. I guess some of it has been. I didn't know she'd targeted you all. I apologize."

"We just didn't know what to make of it," Edgar said.

Larry forced a smile, apologetically. "Well, I'm not much like her and I hope that doesn't squash the possibilities of us trying to work together. I still secretly imagine I'll find out there was a mix-up in the post-natal nursery, or Mildred kidnapped me from an adoption agency or a foster home. Meanwhile, she *is* my mother."

Edgar offered a knowing remark. "And none of us chose our mothers. And I guess our mothers didn't really choose us, did they?"

"Very true, Edgar. I do have to come out here and check on her, so that might be helpful if we did work together."

"Let's just see where this goes," I said, "I have no idea what kind of things you have in mind. We're pretty happy with the way things are going."

"I understand. Oh, do you have some of the shows recorded that you could send to me? Just a few."

Roxy looked at his card. "I will."

We stood and said goodbye and collapsed back in our chairs, simultaneously taking a gulp from our beers.

"Maybe he could persuade Mildred to be a guest on our show." Edgar had that innocent boyish look that confirmed he was making up shit.

I considered bringing up my date with Elizabeth the night before, but decided not to. Right now I had too much rolling around in my head, and I wasn't ready to call in the therapy troops to help me determine if I was on track or not. Or what track I was on.

But after we parted, I walked home and watched football, had a couple drinks and my thoughts switched back to Elizabeth. We did have a good time last evening.

Her daughter, Linda, had made a twenty-four hour recovery. And Elizabeth had finally received some good news on her divorce proceedings. It sounded like they were actually proceeding. "My attorney says they have agreed in principle, but there were details to agree upon in writing. Which all sounds to me like ka-ching, ka-ching."

But, she laughed about it, and squeezed me from behind while I was sautéing shrimp. We sat in front of the gas fireplace after dinner, listening to blues radio, and held hands on the sofa while sipping iced vodka and vermouth. She was full of energy, and asked me lots of questions about the show. Then she thought for awhile. "I really don't know what all I'm going to do. But, I'd like to do something that I'm as enthusiastic about as you are, Jake."

"I'm sure you'll find it. You have so many possibilities. I can see that now, after the news you've gotten. And hearing about your visit with your daughter."

"Well, I hope you're right." She twisted into me and we kissed, one of her long specialties that was unambiguous. "You've got a show in the morning, Jake. So I'm not going to ask you to show me your upstairs. But I will, soon."

I could feel all the conflictions seize up inside me. Here she was, basically offering herself. And I was tempted to say I really don't need to get any sleep before a show, and insist that she come upstairs to see my stamp collection. I liked how she looked tonight, what she said, and her new energy. What was there not to like? But for a micro-second, another image flashed in my mind: an image of me sitting next to Catherine on her big rock.

PART IV

"Pulling your leg" is not the same
as   "pulling a fast one".
Or is it?

Jacob Finnegan

December is usually a beautiful time in Denver downtown. Our shows were strong. They felt inspired at times. Our lists of "practical and needed" Christmas gifts were giving way to absurd and amusing ones. Edgar put a bike lock on his list. Then said he'd ask for a bike next year. Roxy asked for a Man blow-up doll. With no penis. I would demand an explanation a bit later. Ever the practical one, I asked for a 5/8 " wrench to replace one missing from my set of twelve. Open at one end, closed at the other. Should be easy to find? Hardly an inspiring item.

Saturday, December 9, 2017

Our call to Santa was the highlight of the show. Roxy, by now, had a rich pool of male actors to draw upon in the Denver area. The growly, indignant voice of Santa ginned up the rant to an apostolic level. He had drawn a line in the sand, or in the snow, and conveyed his pissedness in no uncertain terms. It would spark the most feedback on our website, a few unusable on air, but many with high, or at least, encouraging praise.

You just never know.

It was also the right time, the season of parties and events and entertainments and celebrations. All which begged for appropriate security considerations. For which we had the answer, of course.

ROXY: *Why don't you introduce our new sponsor, Edgar?*

EDGAR: *Will do. And that, good friends, would be:* **Betty's Bouncers.** *Betty's Bouncers for whatever level your security needs. Let's just say you're auctioning off a Van Gogh. Or hosting an interracial BBQ in your front yard. Maybe you're holding a Bingo party fundraiser in your basement, or an open house tour of your recently redecorated historical mansion.*

ME: *Or what if you're fencing stolen goods and you don't trust your cronies to keep their hands out of the till.*

EDGAR: That's right! Well, Betty's Bouncers come attired as you'd like them to be. Maybe as Hall Monitors stationed throughout your mansion, or Nazi camp guards, or overweight parking lot attendants, or cage fighters, or TSA team leaders. Even Secret Service Presidential Bodyguards. Whatever your need. And remember, Nobody, I mean nobody has Bouncers like Betty. Your kid's 16th Birthday? Or Confirmation day? Or a bash like St. Paddy's Day with armed Leprechauns from Betty.

ME: Impressive, Edgar.

EDGAR: It certainly is. And remember, no one, I mean no one, lays a hand on Betty's Bouncers.

ME: Whoa. That Betty must be some woman.

Tuesday, December 12, 2017

Our session this morning roared. We needed timely sponsors and novel new products for Christmas. And some jokes, of course. We were good, if not on fire.

In the afternoon I learned that Catherine was leaving for her annual two-week trip back to Atlanta, something she dreaded. We chatted easily for some time before she left. It seemed that we both were interested. I was definitely interested.

I think it's fair to say that Elizabeth and I were also both interested. I was also aware that her being married had provided me easy excuse for backing out, or backing away, should I have reservations.

And then, a phone call I don't think any of us anticipated. It was Larry Fillmore, talent agent and son of Mildred. He was coming to Denver and wanted to meet with us. He said he had a couple ideas.

Saturday, December 23, 2017

It doesn't get much closer to Christmas Eve than this. And our show was built around last-minute holiday panic. All the things you worry about not being done, or wrapped or delivered. Or the calls you were going to make and the parties you couldn't attend.

ME: *That's right, we are brought to you right now by, HBO, that's Holiday Bail Out. A highly specialized holiday team to do the last minute things you cannot do. Buy, wrap and deliver, for example. Call, cancel and return. In fact, if you want to cancel your Christmas dinner that you always hate, that has become your annual nightmare, the Holiday Bail Out Team will impersonate a friend, a doctor or even a police officer and call whoever is invited with a story that will make cancelation seem like the only possible option. Or, maybe you're panicked about the meal, the one you've never been successful with. The meal that your guests try to force down in an act of gastric tolerance. These folks at HBO, Holiday Bail Out, will bail you out with a complete dinner that will actually be prepared in your own kitchen and they will disappear right before your guests arrive, leaving you with clear and fail-safe directions for the gala dinner. And, if you like, they'll have someone come in the morning to clean up.*

Yes, that's just one of many bailouts they can perform for you. They're competent, super fast, and do what they say they will do. They're not cheap, as you would imagine, but you'll get your money's worth. Holiday Bail Out. Go to their website and call. Then take a tranquilizer or a stiff drink and relax. You are being bailed out. Merry Christmas, my friends.

EDGAR: *I wonder if they could tell me what to get a woman who has everything she could possibly want? Because I've already gotten it for her.*

ROXY: *Edgar, I hope, I really hope, you're not referring to Marge.*

EDGAR: (Meekly) *Well, she does have lots of things.*

ROXY: E---D---G---A---R . . .

EDGAR: Just kidding. Marge, I've bought you that set of shish kabob skewers that you always wish I had for the grill.

Dr. Nadine inquired if the Holiday Bail Out folks had an office in Hope, Arkansas. She needed books, *When Recoupling Sucks,* delivered to stores in the general area, later today. They didn't.

We also managed to squeeze in our first dual sponsor. In this case it was two brothers with adjacent businesses on East Colfax. In fact, they share the same parking lot.

EDGAR: Yes, we are happy to welcome two unique sponsors, owned by two unique brothers. One is named Paint Your Wagon: high velocity and high gloss painting for your truck or car. The other, of course, is called Paint The Town, a glam bar that will infuse their craft vodka with any edible ingredient of your choice. They are located right next to each other on East Colfax.

And, to anticipate your first question: Yes, they can paint your wagon while you're painting the town. So, welcome guys.

And with Edgar's melodious voice covering mine, the three of us sang, "We Wish You a Merry Christmas" and the bass rumble took us out. We went outside and sold a few last minute T-shirts, signing them, and thanking our fans for showing up. It was cold, and we were teeth-chattering shivering when we pulled away to go inside.

Where we met up with Larry Fillmore in the back office. He was busy with his mother most of the weekend and this was the easiest time for the four of us to meet.

We ordered the usual, Larry also. And he got right to the crux. "Thanks for sending the show recordings, Roxy. They were very helpful. I've asked several people to hear them. To confirm my enthusiasm and get suggestions. Since you're not moving anywhere soon, the ideas broke down into these: A remote visit with you, say with Stephen Colbert. Yes, I know one of the writers. Or a number of other shows. It could be a segment with one of your specialties, like your "special sponsors. It could be on Public Radio, like the old Click and Clack, the car guys. There might even be a more serious show that takes it on a different slant. Not Charlie Rose, I'm afraid."

I believe each of our jaws dropped.

"What I'd like is for you to tell me you'd be willing to try something when I have an interested client. If you are, and I find someone that is very interested, I will ask you to sign a contract to be represented by me. If, for example, someone offers you a show or show segment, or a guest appearance, that will pay you for your part in it. It's pretty standard stuff, but it protects me for my efforts. What do you think?"

Yes, what *did* we think?

"You first, Jake," said Edgar.

"Hmmm. I've got to say I had really put this out of my mind. We haven't even talked about it, Larry. I don't know how I feel. It *is* very flattering. Even if nothing comes of it. So you really think there's a possibility that someone might be interested?"

"I do. I think you've come up with some good material. And that's not easy to find."

Larry's a man of few words so it was back to me. I looked at my partners. Each had those kind of weird looks scrunched into their faces that read: I haven't a clue. Which was my reaction as well.

"Here's what I think we need to do. First, thank you, Larry, for your interest; it's really a shock to me. And your time. We need to hash this over. Probably come up with some questions. I think we should get back to you. Right after the New Year. Like you, I'm sure, we're jammed right now. Let's say by the tenth of January. Is that good?"

"Fine with me. You might check my website, here's another card. You'll see some of the things I've been associated with. Meantime, thanks much, and keep on having fun. It shows on your faces."

Saturday, December 30, 2017

Resolutions. That was the theme. Not very surprising, but our guests had some curious takes, to say the least. Beginning with our Denver Gadfly, still unique not only in yellow but in his year-end wisdom.

SAUL: I've made them. I've kept them. And I've broken them. Have any been crucial in my life? I guess not really. I do know that our actions speak louder than our words. So, I guess I say, unless they're for fun, let them go.

ME: So, Saul, in general you'd say don't bite.

SAUL: Probably. Although I remember one time, about twenty-five years ago, I made a major career change. And I think the fact that New Years Eve coincided with the fiscal year of the restaurant that I sold, the forth one in my life that I let go of, and the last one that I owned, it was a significant date to act on a major life decision.

ME: Tell us what that decision was based on, Saul. I'm sure our listeners are curious.

SAUL: OK. It's not so unusual. But, for me it was a shift. I changed from running businesses to offering advice on how to run businesses better. I thought I'd learned a lot and managing was no longer interesting to me. In fact I grew to strongly dislike it. It was something important to admit to myself.

ME: Well, we're sure glad you made the shift. For those out there who don't know, Saul was a key source of advice when we were thinking about starting a radio show. In fact, he was the one who connected us to Whiskey 'N Ribs, his PR client. We think that was a brilliant idea and key to our successful beginning. Thank you Saul.

ROXY: Yes, thank you, Saul, and also for your innovative segments on what's happening with Denver Culture and Dining. We look forward to this coming year. Now, I have another guest from this past year on the phone to comment on New Year's Resolutions. I'm talking about Lorraine X, Life Coach and Personal Trainer from Los Angeles. Jake?

ME: Welcome back, Lorraine X. I'm betting that you have a very distinctive point of view about resolutions.

LORRAINE X: Yes I do. I take a more West Coast view on New Year's resolutions. If they make you feel good, jot them down. If you can't keep them after jotting them down, forget about them. Most people do, anyway, and guilt is counterproductive. You've probably already got enough shit to feel guilty about. Having a couple major setbacks so quickly in the New Year, when you're in the middle of reconstructing a new image for yourself or choosing a new highway, could be disastrous.

ME: So you'd say dump the ritual of Resolutions.

LORRAINE X: Dump. Bury. Whatever. It's only a date, New Year's Eve. You didn't choose it. Somebody else did. It's too risky to work on someone else's timetable. Could I say on your show, Take this List and Shove it?

ME: Uh, I think you just did. So, that was our name changer, date changer, Lorraine X. I guess she's quite a free spirit out there in sunny California.

Of course Dr. Nadine had quite a different take.

DR. NADINE: If you can't keep one or two resolutions, you're threatening to sabotage your coming year. You don't have to make resolutions that are life changing, but, how about a couple that give you the feeling that you're controlling your destiny. For example, don't say you're completely changing the way you eat, like a fat free diet. How about giving up pie? Something you only have occasionally. Or, sugar-coated breakfast cereal? If you can't do that, you're kind of a loser, aren't you? See, that's the thing. I go into it further in my new book: When Recoupling Sucks. You've got to have some determination not to go back when it seems so enticing. Such an easy fix for your feelings of loneliness. Giving up pie or sugar-coated cereal will show you have some backbone. Give yourself a New Year's Gift.

ME: *Thank you Dr. Nadine, for your personal advice about resolutions for the coming year.*

Finally, Edgar, Roxy and I offered our quick takes:

EDGAR: *First, thank you all for making this show work. You who have come out, most especially. My resolution is simple: I will continue to set the fashion pace with new ties.*

ROXY: *And I will continue to take credit for keeping you two on script. If we ever get a script.*

ME: *And now that you all know the secrets of how we run things around here, I promise to shower and shave before every broadcast, just in case we happen to run into any of you after the show. And now, that familiar pulsing sound of the bass track tells me that, yes, we still have a pulse. And it's the end of another show, the last of this year. Happy New Year, everyone.*

Tuesday, January 2, 2018

We're in the New Year. We're in the old AM1480 studio. From what we know, the station is still up for sale. We've heard rumors that there are some ugly and drawn-out disagreements, legal, I would guess, within the family of the last living owner. So we're in limbo. Not only about using the studio to put our shows together but the use of their airwaves.

Details suck!

Roxy suggested we get our work done, and then listen to our very first recording from last July. We liked the idea. But first, the white board and as many ideas as we could conjure. The fact that we were beginning a new year did make a difference. I think we realized the need to continue to improve and not take anything for granted.

Edgar suggested we reconsider the concept of a séance where someone talks with famous deceased people. Questions such as what thing did you get away with in your lifetime that no one knows about? Or, who do you wish you had ratted out? A list quickly included Marilyn Monroe, J. Edgar Hoover, Richard Pryor, Phyllis Diller, Al Capone, Amy Winehouse, Fidel Castro, John Belushi, Gilda Radner and Joan Rivers.

With enough starters on the board, we each picked three that we'd work up for Thursday. Roxy urged us to develop ideas that required her impersonations.

Then, something that I think we were all dreading: What would we do about Larry Fillmore's upcoming call? The one about moving beyond our current show format in Denver.

"I still find it hard to believe that someone might want us on a national program, even for a short segment," Roxy began, "I've been trying to imagine what it would be like."

"I just don't know," Edgar said, "Marge thinks it would be cool, but would it interfere with our retirement plans? Travel? Exhausting sex every night?"

"More about that, Edgar." I said. "You've been holding out on us."

"That's because it's nothing new. We've always lived a no-holds-barred carnal marriage. We absolutely don't want to interfere with it."

"Well, I don't have that problem. But I do have a life.

And I started to recall some too familiar reminders from my career: Unreasonable due dates and having to please someone else when I knew I had a better idea. Not that I'm infallible. Just that it would be other people who would have to sign off on what we did."

Roxy jumped in, "I don't know about you guys, but I really enjoyed that Saturday when we had a rerun. With my web business, I'd like to have more of them. I'm not sure I want to stretch beyond what we're doing, and I know it would be more work if we got others involved."

"I've been thinking about why we did this in the first place," I said, "and one thing that wasn't on my list was becoming famous, in the sense of a national audience or big money or celebrity status. Not that I don't enjoy the kind of adulation we seem to have. It's absolutely great."

"It sounds like we're very tentative," Edgar said. "Should we just call it off?"

I concurred, "It sounds to me like we're happy with what we have. It suits each of us. And the idea of doing more is setting off alarm bells. I'm okay with that. Maybe we should look hard at how we might expand the listenership without altering the program. Getting back to Click and Clack. They broadcast from Boston but became a national show on Public Radio. Is that not a possibility for us?"

"Let's ask Larry." Roxy started pacing; the stress was getting to her. "Maybe there are other networks that would be interested. I mean, I go through the channels and so much is old, old reruns, or pretty lame shows that get syndicated somehow. And, I think with our unusual broadcast setting, it would televise pretty well. Of course we'd have to get Rocco and Sebastian on board. And competent make-up artists."

"So, we'd like to do the show just as it is. If someone wants to show segments on their show, fine. Just so it's simple.

And we'd like the entire show to go beyond Denver, right?" I felt my own nerves relaxing. I guess I was protective of our comfort zone for the time being. Maybe forever.

"It's a real effort to make each hour interesting and fresh," said Edgar, "I think we do pretty well. But, some weeks, I'm really digging hard for new stuff. And we're only into it for half a year. I still think that's a real achievement."

"So, do we just tell Larry that we're basically maxed out? That we love the freedom we have. And if he knows how to expand our audience with the show as it is, we'd be interested?"

"Yes," said Roxy.

"Yes," said Edgar.

"OK," I said.

That afternoon, I took a sober look at my life, what with no serious resolutions to contend with. Sober isn't quite the right spirit. I cracked a beer before I considered anything. I was relieved at our decisions about the show. And I was conflicted with where to go with Elizabeth and Catherine. Yes, it was a nice problem to have. Maybe that was the problem. That I thought it was a problem.

I worked out; Elizabeth wasn't there. I hadn't heard from her for a week. And, Catherine was arriving tomorrow from Atlanta, her foot in a cast, she had texted. She declined my offer to help her at the airport. It was her left foot, and she could manage getting her car from the car park. She said she'd call when she was comfortably back in her mountain house. So, there I was, with myself. Horrors!

Wednesday, January 3, 2018

Early in the morning I called Larry in New York and he called back an hour later. He was disappointed, I think, but also complimentary that we had drawn the line given our circumstances. He was interested in helping us expand our show audience and would stay in touch. I had absolutely no pang of regret. Or, very little pang.

I worked on content for the show: two new sponsors, and an attempt at an interview with the deceased Princess Diana. That did not go very well, so I switched to Margaret Thatcher, to still take advantage of Roxy's skill with a British accent, and the success we'd had interviewing Her Ladyship, the Sub Minister. It went far better. I also came up with a new product: A device to reduce the amount of time on cell phones and all the reacting we do to every message or notification we receive. I wondered, though, if I was just pouring cold water on what was vital to the younger generations. And quite a few older folks.

I quit at noon, and walked the mile to Whiskey 'n Ribs for lunch and a cold beer. I intended to look at our broadcast setup for inspiration and to see if our recent alterations still needed further upgrading. The cutout photos were in place, looking smart and relaxed. Maybe we should reshoot in more animated poses. One of the bartenders said they had an increase in questions from diners about the show. I think my real intention was to see what we had and to imagine what we'd do if we lost AM1480. We had an open-ended arrangement with no real guarantee. Maybe I should meet with one of the owner family and see if we could get something in writing. Caution prevailed, however. Why rock the boat? If I approached one of the family members, they might do something stupid (for us) and just try to eliminate a problem or distraction to their family squabble. I should ask Saul what he would suggest if we lost AM1480.

Elizabeth called mid-afternoon; she was ecstatic. "Jake, it's going to be done. My husband, soon to be ex-husband, is flying back Saturday to hopefully sign what we've agreed to. He says he's with it, but just wants to see it in front of him with his lawyer. I'm almost confident it'll happen."

"It will, Elizabeth. I'm happy for you."

"As soon as it's done, Jake, let's celebrate. I haven't been ignoring you. I just needed to hang with this on my own. With the help of my kids on the phone. They've been terrific."

"Let me know when you're ready," I said.

"Don't worry. We've got some real catching up to do."

I was relieved to hear those words. She was practically jubilant.

Catherine called about eight o'clock. "Hi, Jake, just wanted you to know I'm back safe in my mountain retreat. The cast is a bummer, but I can get around, and I think I can tend bar. Especially with such little business right now. How are you?"

"I'm terrific. Thanks for calling. It's really good to hear your voice."

"Well, I've been talking for most of two weeks. It went reasonably well. There are those who never fail to remind me that I've done something foolish, or wrong. I've learned how to respond or deflect or ignore most such comments. I've had a lot of practice."

"I'd like to hear more." I was thinking fast. "We've got work all morning, but what if I drove up in the afternoon. Will you be working?"

"Hmmm. Let me think. I will try to work. But I'm just thinking about making a transition from Georgia to paradise, including the several incidents that always leave a bad taste in my mouth from a family visit."

I didn't want to push. But, I wanted to see Catherine and Friday and Saturday were pretty much out.

"You know, Jake, if you can get a room at the lodge, I'm

sure you can, why don't you come up. While I was home, I thought about how much easier it has been talking to you than to my extended family. Horrible to say."

"I'll do it. I have to be back Friday afternoon for the Saturday show, but I like the idea of another conversation with you. I'm guessing we won't be hiking to your rock where you have your big thoughts.

"See you tomorrow. Just let me know if you're not coming."

Thursday, January 4, 2017

In the AM1480 studio again, we chopped and channeled and fine-tuned Saturday's material. I was on the road into the mountains by two, negotiating the wet and slick surfaces, finally checking into the Lodge at five minutes to four. Was I pumped about seeing Catherine? Absolutely.

She was alone, very nice, and favoring her left leg, leaning just a bit. A bit unsteady myself, I leaned the same way, then leaned over the bar and kissed her quickly and said, Hi, you look great. I guess you won't need me to care for you overnight.

She gave me a look. "I don't know about you, Jake, but it's good to see you. I think.

I sat down, and she brought me a beer.

"So, Catherine, how do you figure, breaking your foot on flat ground?"

"Not so difficult, Jake. I didn't see the bottom step. I have other bruises, but nothing else fractured. And I'm very glad to be back here. It's far less dangerous than being around my family. Very tense. I'm convinced I was adopted and no one has told me."

"I know someone else with that family tree question. I'll

explain sometime. If there is a sometime, of course. I'm assuming nothing."

"I don't believe you. Or did you come up here to say you won't be coming up here again?"

"Nothing of the sort. I'm just taking nothing for granted."

"Something tells me you're fishing, Jake. Am I right?"

"Absolutely. Obvious, huh?"

"Well, it's kind of sweet. As long as it doesn't become a pattern."

"OK. Busted. I was just looking forward to seeing you, a lot. And here you are."

Several other customers came and went, mostly locals. Then it was six o'clock. So we had time. We covered our holidays and volunteered modestly that we'd missed each other. By the time another woman came in, the wife of the guy I'd met on my last visit, Catherine and I had gotten comfortable with each other, maybe even inched ahead some. I ordered a huge burger, my fourth beer, and nursed it until close to eight.

She decided to close up early; nobody was on the streets. I walked her to her Jeep, careful not to trip over the crutches she was using. I was really hoping for an invitation to her home. As it didn't seem forthcoming, I lamely offered, "Just for your safety, maybe I should follow you home and help ready you . . . get ready . . . get you ready for bed." That look from her again. She started her engine, then leaned to the open window, "That's a little more direct, Jake, keep working on it. I'm almost persuaded. But it is quite a slow and awkward process for me to get around with or without these crutches. You don't want to watch." (Actually I did want to watch.)

Then she leaned out her window, slightly, inviting a very warm and tender kiss. "Good night, Jake. I'm glad you drove up."

I read off and on, and thought off and on about Catherine. I think I was hooked. Twice now. That was when I started thinking about what could get in the way of our relationship growing more serious. Like we didn't just live down the street from each other. Then I wrestled with various scenarios. What was I doing? I hadn't even watched her awkwardly trying to navigate her home with her cast. I hadn't even been invited to watch her.

Saturday, January 6, 2018

Overnight the temp had plummeted. Eighteen degrees at show time, and slightly more than flurries. Our expectations for our fans coming out were minimal. We were surprised when there were more than thirty by ten minutes to noon, and others were slowly arriving from their cars or some warm place nearby.

The New Year felt promising. We'd clarified our feelings about expanding the show in terms of the time we devoted to it. We weren't hungry for national fame, or big bucks. Although, I admit, I would have loved to hear that Colbert had heard about us, and had his producer contact us with an idea. That would be sweet. But, unlikely. And I never shared that fantasy with Roxy and Edgar. We really had clear sailing, given we remained healthy and none of us were charged with sexual harassment. Something I was confident wasn't in the offing.

Unless, of course, Mildred Fillmore decided to also make up shit and accuse one or all of us of some act against her person. We were living in a new era.

So, on with the show, the bass track was revving, the Jaws rumble without the fear of the great shark. After welcoming in the New Year with a message from one of our original sponsors, *Driver's Side Window Savers. Moist towelettes for when driving, and you cough up something, and have to spit it out your window, and, horrors, you can't tell your very clean window is not open, and the result is an unspeakable mass of guck sliding slowly downward into the inners of your door. You simply reach for the ready packet of moist Window Savers and swipe away the embarrassment. Great for this time of year, folks.*

We were off and running in 2018. First we cleaned up old business from our website.

ROXY: I can't believe all of you outside in front, in this bitter cold. Just know that we're very grateful that you've come out. You're our inspiration, I hope you know.

ME: That's for sure! So what we want to do now is go back through our website from last year, all the comments you've made and questions that were left kind of dangling. Edgar, start us off.

EDGAR: Let's begin with our question: What is the worst thing you can imagine happening to you? We did qualify this to not include medical diagnoses. And we had great responses. Here's the one we picked: Finding out that your wife is really your sister. Yes, that's a good one. Like one couple from the same Mama.

ME: And, of course, it could be finding out your husband is really your brother.

ROXY: And I believe this could be the case regardless of sexual orientation.

EDGAR: That's right. The obvious rationale would be that you were somehow separated at birth, or orphaned or some other kind of early separation where you completely lost touch.

ME: Remember we also considered you might live in Alabama or Arkansas. And never really separated . . . and I think I should not have mentioned this consideration, although I do see most of our audience laughing outside.

ROXY: But you promised, Jake.

ME: I know, I'm sorry, I couldn't help going for the joke.

EDGAR: And we decided we could mention cloning as a future consideration, right?

ME: Yes we did. What's next, Edgar?

EDGAR: The question came up about which vocations might become obsolete? Of course most guesses came from seeing already existing trends. Some likely examples: Tanning salons. Coal miners, and New Car Salesmen or women.

ME: So much of this centers around technological advances. Robots, for instance. Or classroom teachers being replaced by online classes and lectures. We did agree that, so far, there didn't seem to be a threat to the oldest profession in the world, right?

EDGAR: That's right. It's always thriving somewhere, I've heard. And then there are truck drivers, cab drivers and even pilots. Of course we just went through the threat of drones to Santa Claus. Anything that could be replaced by robots or the Internet or self-driving vehicles. Mail delivery?

ME: There are so many to consider, but we also don't know about what new professions might be created. So, we simply concluded that nothing stays the same, ever, and it stays the same for a shorter period of time today. Nothing brilliant. But, just look at the self-checkout counters in supermarkets. It's in a sea-change mode right now. Let's get to the question we like a lot. What's the most embarrassing question you've ever been asked? There were some great ones. Mine was echoed by many of our listeners. Are you the grandfather? In public, when I'm in the company of my two daughters. There were so many versions of this that reveal the changing patterns of age in relationships.

EDGAR: I was asked if I was the father of my sister? She's one year older than I. That was almost fifteen years ago.

Then we got a call from Dr. Nadine taking exception to my snide remark about interfamilial marriage in her home state of Arkansas. She took a slightly different take than what I expected. She pointed out that we prize pure breeding of various animals, dogs, horses, cattle, for example.

Dr. Nadine: Isn't that a form of inbreeding? I have an aunt and uncle who are sister and brother and are married to each other and they seem perfectly well adjusted. Not like some of these crazy cross bred racial marriages."

How do I answer the guest who says that, and who is also one of the favorite guests we have on a regular basis? And *who* brought the issue of Arkansas up in the first place? Yours truly, I regret.

We announced the results of our polls for the year also. Favorite guest interview: Her Ladyship, Sub Minister for Economic Withdrawal, Camilla Thistlepink Birtwistle of the UK. Second, you got it, Dr. Nadine.

Favorite sponsors: Out Damn Spot, Gluten Fix Supplements. And, Betty's Bouncers. Surprised?

Favorite show: Our very first broadcast, the partial disaster with traffic stopped in front because of Carly, and our general sense of chaos, including the foiled robbery attempt inside the restaurant. A close second was our coverage of the Eclipse, The Mooch, and all the fallout from it.

And finally, the best pie recipe for using the fabulous craft whiskey from our good friends and landlords at Whiskey 'n Ribs. There were dozens and the several best included lots of butter, pecans, molasses, various forms of chocolate and sugar and maple syrup. And, of course, their top shelf craft whiskey.

Saul arrived midway with his signature yellow derby and a stunning, politically incorrect sheepskin fur coat. "I thought it only right for me to interview some of your stalwart listeners who showed up on this very cold Saturday. So, I'm prepared."

He went outside and was spot on, bringing out great comments and stories about why people showed up on such a day. From, "I'm hard up with nothing else going on in my life", to, "I just never know what to expect, and I like that". I think he got almost fifteen different answers and kept the pace moving like a pro. Which he is.

ME: (As Saul nods to us that he's finished outside,) *"Thank you Saul and thank all of you for thoughtful comments. We expect nothing less from our esteemed listeners.*

ROXY: Edgar why don't you end our show with a timely message from one of our great sponsors.

EDGAR: Will do. So, friends, while you're beginning a fresh new year, I urge you to give a call to Adam & Eve Environmentally Conscious Mattress Repairs. There's no better way to begin the year. And don't you worry, Adam & Eve have seen it all. No matter how jiggy you've been this past year, they know how to repair and refurbish your mattress. They are the miracle workers. And, this new year they are offering free legal advice to any of you who have been arrested for removing your mattress tags. Now, that's quite an offer!

Monday, January 8, 2018

We had selected Tuesday for our first meeting. Which left Monday wide open. Which found me answering a call from Elizabeth at ten-thirty in the morning. She was in exceptionally high spirits.

"Jake, guess what? We just signed the papers. It's over! It's done. I can't believe it. Really. Oh my God. Can you believe it?"

"Fantastic, Elizabeth." I could and couldn't imagine exactly how she felt. But she sure as hell sounded relieved and fabulous. "You've done it. Congratulations!"

"I know. Thank you. Wow. You're the first one I've called. Except for my kids. They were pretty cool, too. And relieved, I could tell. Jake, we have to celebrate. What are you doing later?"

I was doing pretty much nothing and I said, "I'm sure I can fit celebrating in." Then I added, "I'd love to."

So I picked her up. She insisted on taking me to SUSHI! SUSHI!, the best Sushi spot in Denver, we both agreed, and we were both giddy when we arrived. She was pumped with relief. No wonder. So she went on and on while we drank Martinis, and added various exotic rolls as we finished one dish after the other. She admitted that she ended up with her mansion; her ex was comfortably settled into a penthouse loft with his new squeeze.

After our eating frenzy she begged to show me her home. And she did, at least all the way to her second floor bedroom where we flopped on her elegant four-poster and fumbled to undress each other and have great sex, twice, and fell asleep entwined.

And that's how Elizabeth and I really broke through. And I felt pretty damn good about it. Until Tuesday afternoon after the three of us had finished with our rehearsal session, and Catherine called me to say she was coming to Denver Thursday morning to have her foot checked and possibly have her cast removed. And maybe we could have lunch afterward.

OK, I thought, as the guilty feelings clutched at my nerves. It didn't help to tell myself that hey, I'd made no commitments to anyone, I was an adult, I liked Elizabeth, a lot, and, hell, I liked Catherine, too. So what's the big deal? I'm positive most guys wouldn't judge me for my circumstances.

But I felt my gut tighten. We left it that she would call me as soon as she was done and I would pick her up at the clinic.

Thursday, January 11, 1018

It was a short drive to the clinic. I did not have that relaxed, free and easy sense that was part of my last visit to Grand Lake. I kept trying to shake my conflicted feelings. I brought her to Whiskey "N Ribs, thinking that it might relax me more, and she would enjoy it. She had to get back by three to tend bar, so we didn't have a great deal of time.

Her cast was gone and she lifted her foot upon my lap at the bar so I could see her ankle, which was covered by a comfy warm gray sock, which I slid down so I could see and rub her beautiful foot and ankle. I was surprised at how intimate it felt, for me, at least, and maybe for her. She did give me a bit of a look, like what are you doing there, Jake? But maybe that was my interpretation, because she did say, "Nice hands, Jake."

I soon realized how much I liked looking into her eyes as well as at her feet, how unassuming she was and, well, that I was hooked. For the second time in a week. And all I could feel was a surging battle of emotions and loyalties and a bunch of other crap that was robbing me of the extraordinary pleasure of being with Catherine.

I don't know if she had any idea what was going on with me. I hoped not. I needed time for some serious sorting. She drove away from the clinic parking lot and headed west. We said we'd stay in touch and figure some time very soon to see each other. I called Edgar; I felt I needed to fess up to my good friend. Maybe he'd have some wise counsel.

Later that afternoon, Edgar and I met at a bar four blocks from his house. He walked; I drove. I'd been there before, maybe five years ago and nothing had changed except the older bartender was now older and the gal helping him couldn't be more than twenty-one. We sat in front of the window at a tall round table. I turned away from the late sun that was ferociously bright. I'd mentioned to Edgar that I needed his fatherly advice.

"I know you don't need fatherly advice, you never did in the past, even from your own father. But I know you need something, so bring me up to date."

I quickly told him my sob story.

"And you want sympathy, Jake? Men die for your situation. But you know that, don't you?"

"Yes. But I don't think it's that easy. I really like both of these women, and I'm feeling like a schmuck because neither of them know I'm seeing someone else."

"But this just happened, didn't it? Like Monday, right?"

"True, but I'm afraid I'll make the wrong choice. It's some time since I've had someone that I really cared about. And, Christ, now this."

"That's just luck, Jake. It has just turned out this way. You'll figure it out."

I didn't believe I'd be able to make a wise decision very quickly. And I felt under pressure to do so, why, I'm not exactly certain. Hey, maybe I do have a conscience? Where did that come from?

I admitted that to Edgar and he chuckled like maybe I was way too old to be bothered by this conflict. But that wasn't his reason. He told me that he was so panicked before his wedding to Marge, even though they'd been in love for a couple years. But, he'd seen a woman that really turned him on, and maybe he was rushing into this marriage thing.

"Jake, it's always something. There are always questions. In relationships, I'm talking about. I don't think anyone avoids them completely. At least guys don't. I can't speak for women. Like I said, you'll sort this out. You'll decide whether to listen to your conscience or have a wild time for a while. Two women. How exciting. Keep your heart pills handy."

I knew Edgar was giving me his best shot. He knew I

would have to decide what to do next. And I knew he would be OK with whatever I decided. That's pretty fantastic in a friend.

I admitted that I wanted to sleep with Catherine, and sleeping with Elizabeth had been spectacular. And I wanted to muzzle my conscience until I'd done that. As I shook my head, laughing at myself for my conundrum, and knowing I was headed for something that might be ugly, I also knew I needed to accept that I couldn't make a choice right now. At least that's how I saw it.

Saturday, January 13, 2017

After struggling with sleep for two nights, I put my struggle aside and walked into our broadcast Saturday pumped for a great show. It seemed like all three of us were primed.

The bass track growled a little louder, like it was on board with our attitudes. The temp outside was almost forty, and our crowd was psyched, greeting each other, waving to us, and generally in a super groove.

EDGAR: Welcome, Denver. All of you right here in front of Whiskey 'n Ribs, and all of you on your radios. If you're close by, head on over and join us for our second broadcast in 2018. I'm Edgar, and the guy with the lame blazer is Jake. And, the beautiful woman with us, the brains and looks and talent of the show, is Roxy. Thanks for tuning us in. We plan to entertain you for the next hour.

ME: That's right. Thank you, Edgar. We're happy it's so much warmer than last Saturday. You never know in Denver, this time of the year. Roxy, what's first up on our show?

ROXY: Well, first just a couple of cleanups from our New Year's show and the issue of Resolutions. You remember we had a couple of very different takes from Life Coach Lorraine X and Dr. Nadine. Lorraine X suggested that if the resolutions make you feel guilty or it's not the right time for you to make a very strong commitment, just let the whole idea go. And Dr. Nadine said something a bit more confrontational: She said if you can't make and commit to a resolution, how can you make any progress in the new year about anything important in your life? Very different approaches, to be sure. Well, we received several comments pro and con to each of their views, and one that tried to wrap them together. I'll read that one from Tim K: "I've tried it both ways. I've felt guilty for failing to keep my resolutions, and, on other years, I've felt guilt for kicking the whole idea of resolutions to the curb. And, here's the thing, I've felt guilty for both choices. So, in my opinion, we're trapped. There has to be a third option. And I see it as this: I'm going to make one resolution that I know I cannot keep. And I'm going to tell everyone I know exactly what I'm doing, and that I'm resolved to failure. I can't keep this resolution. And by failing to keep the resolution that I know I'm unable to keep, I've actually kept the resolution and fulfilled it. Bingo."

EDGAR: Hmmm . . . I'm not going to ask you to reread that, Roxy, but I'm wondering if I've missed something?

ME: It's slippery, but it might stand up in court. It's like two negatives make a positive. Or they don't. I'm not sure. I say that we put it on our radioguys.com listener poll. Does this listener have it figured out, or are we hearing a very clever weasel?

ROXY: Okay. And there's one more announcement. Evidently our interview with Sub Minister Camilla Birtwistle of the UK has been posted on Youtube. And we're getting some hits. I suppose this is owing to the clever, but subversive wife of Edgar. That's right, I'm pretty sure it was Marge who got it up there. If you're curious, you can go on YouTube, to Radio Guys Talk to Sub Minister.

ME: Thank you, Roxy. I can see you've given Edgar a sheet

with BREAKING NEWS. What is it, Edgar?

EDGAR: Here we go. Breaking News: THE BRONCOS WILL NOT BE IN THE SUPER BOWL THIS YEAR. That's right! (He repeats)

ME: Well, how is that news, Edgar? They finished the season last in their division and they've not drafted a franchise quarterback in three years.

EDGAR: I'm only reading what I've been given. It's true isn't it?

ME: Of course it's true. It's also true that it's January 13. Is that breaking news? The Broncos were eliminated two months ago.

EDGAR: Maybe if you've been in solitary confinement for a while it qualifies?

ME: We need to talk about this. After the show. Meanwhile let's get to our sponsor for this segment. It just happens to be . . .

ROXY: This is why we need to have a script, sometimes. Jake, it's time for you to tell our listeners about Veggie Sculptors.

ME: Veggie Sculptures it is. This is brand new, just out of test market, I've been told. Veggie Sculptures do what they say they will do. Turn your vegetables into shapes that entertain you while you're eating. And, while you're preparing. You can turn mushrooms into fireplugs, carrots into noses or toes and cucumbers into belly dancers. Easy as shucking corn. With your own hands and this kit of tools that make it more than easy. You can turn potatoes into pigs or porn-stars, radishes into elves or Santas, or bloody finger tips. And String Beans into, well, a string of beans. Imagine the excitement at your table when you've shaped Acorn Squash into wishing wells, or cauliflower into frozen corpses, or, better yet, chubby little sheep.

EDGAR: Frozen corpses? Are you sure?

ME: For med students, I suppose. Anyway, these are

moving fast into the culinary sections of stores everywhere. No longer will you have to force your kids to eat vegetables. Or your husband. And, here's the best part. Unlike Mr. Potato Head, which is made of plastic, when you're done forming your vegie creatures, just stir-fry them all, and make strange and eerie squealing sounds like they're being sautéed alive. Let your kids join in. And, at this moment, I notice Edgar has turned to the window and some kind of commotion developing out front. My immediate thought is that it is about time that Mildred Fillmore reappears, takes stage out front and accuses us of violence against vegetables or something more insidious.

I glance at Roxy who is alertly focused outside as well. Kind of a *what-to-my-wondering-eyes-should-appear* look. I try to get her attention, holding up my sheet with Veggie Sculptors copy. She nods and reaches for her next notes to contact Dr. Nadine. I can't see very clearly, but some kind of protest seems to be forming out front. Saul, who had just come into our booth, quickly grabs his remote and disappears into the crowd. I stand up for a better view. What is clear is that traffic is slowing irritably, all our listeners are faced away from the window and someone, not Mildred, is waving a sign and bouncing around like one of those kids flipping a sign around on a street corner, with an arrow pointing to new apartments opening or a new retail outlet for cannabis products.

I can see it is a woman now, her hair shining in the sun, partially covered by a white knit hat, both hands waving the sign. I sit back down, wanting to help Roxy. Edgar looks at us and turns back to the scene. And the scene is agitating as a female Moses parts the way with her elbows toward the window, fans resisting giving up their places. But she makes it, holding the sign in front of her face and waving it side to side.

I'm Sorry Jake. I was wrong. You made me laugh. You're

funny and kind.

Of course it was Carly. And she held her ringless left hand up to the window.

EDGAR: Is that who I think it is, Jake?

ME: (I nod, speechless. With a dropping jaw I mouth WTF!)

ROXY: (audible only to me and Edgar) I have Dr. Nadine on hold boys, remember our escape routines, for when something major happens, like someone streaking out front, or, worse, like this.

EDGAR: I can take Dr. Nadine. Hold for one more minute. Jake, you weren't completely open with me about what was going on with you.

ME: (Still no words. My thoughts are addled; is this a joke? Did she want media attention? She is backing away, but our growing crowd is expanding over the curb and into the street and horns are honking and some of the wait-staff is hanging over our curtain, straining to catch the spectacle.

ROXY: Dr. Nadine, could I call you back in five. Or Ten. We have a kind of demonstration happening in front of our broadcast booth, and I'm not sure where it's going.

DR. NADINE: Of course, darlin', but I don't mind staying on the line, I love a good ruckus now and then. I've been in quite a few in my day. I could write a book.

EDGAR: I can see Saul pushing toward the woman, and she is elbowing her way toward him. Let's see what Saul does.

SAUL: I'm out on the sidewalk in front of Whiskey 'n Ribs (Don't fail to get a mention for your client, Saul) *and I have with me a pretty woman, with a great smile and a sign that seems integral to this unexpected circus out here. Could I have your name?"*

CARLY: Carly.

SAUL: And this sign you have?

CARLY: It's for Jake. Here let me have that mic. (And quick as an egret spearing a fish, she held the mic and stepped forward a couple steps as Saul got bumped away by another of the crowd) *Hi Jake, it's me, Carly. I just wanted to tell you I made a huge mistake. You can see I don't have a ring anymore. You're the person who makes me laugh. Even if I don't always know what to make of you. And I miss you terribly.*

At this moment, Saul, like a ninja warrior, wrests the mic from Carly, holding it in the air for us to see. I also note that Carly is moving into the street, edging into the traffic, waving a greeting to the drivers and reaching the other side where she begins to lope down the sidewalk and out of sight. (WTF, I thought, again. What is happening?)

DR. Nadine: Whoa. I'm glad I didn't miss a second of this. I can tell this was unrehearsed, live from New York, as they say. Jakie, you might be a good interview for my next book, All the Wrong Things in All the Wrong Places. You must have quite a following of women, now that you're a radio personality.

ME: (Still speechless)

EDGAR: Our friend, Jake, seems quite overwhelmed by this turn of events. I'm sure there is a big story behind it. We will attempt to get every bit of it on the air, of course. If not today, for sure next Saturday. This is the stuff that gets you in The National Enquirer, or TMZ, maybe. And, it wasn't planned, as far as I know, and Jake seems too undone to be faking or able to explain.

I don't really know how we finished the show. My part was minimal, to the best of my recall. More than a week would pass until we heard from Marge that her friend's son had caught this incident on his phone, and, you guessed it, helped Marge launch it on YouTube.

Afterwards, back in the office, questions were flying. From Roxy and Edgar, from Rocco and Sebastian, and silent inquires as members of the staff passed the open door, leaning in and beseeching an explanation. I do remember that Roxy spent a good deal of the time laughing uncontrollably. Edgar obviously didn't believe me when I tried to explain that there was nothing going on between me and Carly and hadn't been for half a year. Honest, Edgar!

All of which brings up another matter: If you make up so much shit, can your friends still take you seriously?

I don't recall how I got home. I wasn't drunk. Just dizzy. For all I know I could have checked into and been released by a neurologist from the ER at Denver Health.

What I do know was that I had a voice mail on my phone from Jan Baumgardner, "Hi, Jake. Yes I have time for you Monday morning at nine."

As it turned out, the first thing I said Monday morning when Jan directed me to sit on her familiar sofa was, "You don't know the third of it."

Monday, January 15, 2018

"You don't know the third of it, Jan. Here I thought I was doing pretty well on my own. But, all of a sudden . . .

"Okay, Jake, I know about Carly, why don't you tell me about the other two thirds."

So I did. I told her how much I liked Elizabeth and Catherine. How lovely and exceptional each of them seemed. How I thought making a choice between them was impossible right now. How I had slept with Elizabeth. And wanted to do the same with Catherine. How guilty I felt about that. And when it came to Carly, I was stunned. I never saw it coming. I really didn't know what to make of it. And finally, I didn't trust myself to sort this evolving and bewildering conundrum.

Jan sat processing, I assume. I looked around wondering

if there were other folks listening in on my whacky story.

"Interesting, Jake. This might take some unwinding."

She asked questions about how was I feeling? How was I going to go about sorting this out? I refrained from being a smartass, I did not say "with a dartboard" for example. I really was grasping.

"Here's one thought, Jake. You seem to be most bothered by guilt. To the point of it precluding your ability to get a handle on this. Nothing wrong with feeling that guilt, but I'm going to suggest you act on it, and be honest. Tell each one of them the situation you find yourself in. It's all happened so fast there's no way you could have avoided it. You'll learn something about yourself and each one of them in the process. And you'll start to think more clearly. And rushing to a decision is not necessary. After all, you want to make the best decision that you can. Right?"

"I know you're right, Jan."

"And, Jake, I don't tell any of my clients who they should be with. And I won't tell you. But I know you, and I would suggest, as you work your way through this process, pay attention to who is the best laugher. That's my only suggestion."

She tipped her head with a knowing smile.

I left Jan and began to walk through the city for the next four hours. I thought about her comment about who the best laugher was. Very wise, but I wasn't sure it would be very helpful in my case. Each of these women displayed well-developed funny bones. In the end, my dogs were barking, my hips were growling and my mind was barely chirping. But, I was preparing myself for that next step. Being honest. It felt good to have that clearly in mind.

As I walked up the steps to my front door, my cautious calm was shattered. I wasn't prepared for what awaited me.

There was a voice mail from Elizabeth: "So, Jake, who is the woman you've been keeping secret from me?"

Then a text from Catherine: "You know, Jake, I think I'm well enough to invite you to my house. If you're still interested?"

And, an envelope wedged into my already stuffed mailbox containing a note that was signed by Carly: "I realize my way of communicating with you is a bit over-the-top. But, I really would like to see you. Maybe get another chance, Jake?"

I walked unconsciously to my kitchen and tossed some ice cubes into a cocktail glass. For a moment I thought of Celia, the mother from Guadalajara, who stood out front during our broadcast and asked if any of the content from our show was actually true? Good question.

If she were present right now I would say: "Celia, you can't possibly make up all this shit." Which brings up another matter: If you make up too much shit, can your friends still take you seriously?

Sipping from my cocktail on the back deck, I thought about what lies ahead. My confusion. Wanting to make the right choice for me. Not wanting to hurt anyone in the process. Knowing the outcome is not entirely in my hands. I have a lot of thinking to do. And I don't want to end up as a chapter in one of Dr. Nadine's upcoming books.

Meanwhile, a voice of conscience: *Attention, Jake! This is Monday and we've got a radio show to put together for Saturday morning.*

What a relief. Our radio show. At least that was something I thought I could pull off. With the extraordinary help from my friends.

ABOUT THE AUTHOR

Ray Stock has been CEO of a national fine-art business, Creative Director in advertising, counselor in an adolescent drug treatment center, political activist, and Democratic nominee for U.S. Congress.

He is the author of www.funnyornotfunny.com. He lives in Denver Colorado.

My special thanks to the wonderful folks at Steam Espresso Bar on South Pearl in Denver for providing such a superb cup of coffee and a great ambience for conversation and making stuff up.

R.S.

RAY STOCK